PRAISE FOR *The Medici Seal*

'A richly drawn and fascinating look at 16th-century Italy'
The Bookseller

'Not only is [*The Medici Seal*] a gripping historical thriller, it is an
exceptionally touching exploration of a relationship between a man
and a boy. [Leonardo's] fastidiousness, compassion, intellectual
curiosity, wit and boundless creativity are all described by Breslin
with deft scholarship and sympathy. . . This is an enchanting novel
about genius, and a gift to an inquiring mind' Amanda Craig,
The Times

'Carnegie Medal-winner Theresa Breslin can write. This is a
very substantial read. A gorgeously produced book [which] will
be treasured for its handsome form as well as its content'
Guardian

'Absolutely fantastic . . . brilliant descriptive passages which
drive the story forward . . . I was transported back to medieval
Italianate fiefdoms in a way that's never happened before . . . a
brilliant book for all readers, a great story, beautifully researched,
wonderfully written'
Paul Blezard, *One Word Radio*

'An action-packed historical novel that will entertain and
educate readers'
The Newmarket Journal

'The intriguing world of one of the world's greatest painters,
inventors and scientists has been brilliantly brought to life'
Kirkintilloch Herald

'This story has everything you could possibly want: murder, mystery,
secrets, action, drama, love, hate and all that lies in between . . .
If you love reading, you will love this book – trust me, *do* read it!'
CBUK website

Also by Theresa Breslin

REMEMBRANCE
An epic tale of young lives altered by World War One
'Immensely readable, passionately written' *Guardian*

SASKIA'S JOURNEY
A haunting tale of self-discovery
'Truly memorable' *The Bookseller*

DIVIDED CITY
Two boys are caught up in sectarian violence in Glasgow
'This is a book with far-reaching appeal and universal themes that
will encourage young readers to challenge bigotry' *Guardian*

For junior readers:

THE DREAM MASTER
'Pacy, clever and entertaining' *The Sunday Times*

DREAM MASTER NIGHTMARE!
'Excellent dialogue, a good deal of humour and evidence
of in-depth research' *The Scotsman*

DREAM MASTER GLADIATOR
'Funny, warm and clever . . . thought-provoking
entertainment' *Guardian*

DREAM MASTER ARABIAN NIGHTS
'A stretching and rewarding read' *Glasgow Sunday Herald*

www.theresabreslin.com

THE MEDICI SEAL

THERESA BRESLIN

CORGI BOOKS

THE MEDICI SEAL
A CORGI BOOK 978 0 552 55447 3

First published in Great Britain by Doubleday,
an imprint of Random House Children's Publishers UK

Doubleday edition published 2006
Corgi edition published 2007

3 5 7 9 10 8 6 4 2

Text copyright © Theresa Breslin, 2006
Map by Stephen Raw

The right of Theresa Breslin to be identified as the author of this work has been
asserted in accordance with the Copyright, Designs and Patents Act 1988.

All rights reserved. No part of this publication may be reproduced,
stored in a retrieval system, or transmitted in any form or by any means,
electronic, mechanical, photocopying, recording or otherwise, without
the prior permission of the publishers.

Set in Sabon by
Falcon Oast Graphic Art Ltd.

Corgi Books are published by Random House Children's Publishers UK
61–63 Uxbridge Road, London W5 5SA,
a division of The Random House Group Ltd,
in Australia by Random House Australia (Pty) Ltd,
20 Alfred Street, Milsons Point, Sydney, NSW 2061, Australia,
in New Zealand by Random House New Zealand Ltd,
18 Poland Road, Glenfield, Auckland 10, New Zealand,
in South Africa by Random House (Pty) Ltd,
Isle of Houghton, Corner Boundary Road & Carse O'Gowrie,
Houghton 2198, South Africa,
and in India by Random House India Pvt Ltd,
301 World Trade Tower, Hotel Intercontinental Grand Complex,
Barakhamba Lane, New Delhi 110001, India

THE RANDOM HOUSE GROUP Limited Reg. No. 954009
www.randomhousechildrens.co.uk

A CIP catalogue record for this book is available from the British Library.

The Random House Group Limited supports The Forest Stewardship
Council® (FSC®), the leading international forest-certification organisation.
Our books carrying the FSC label are printed on FSC®-certified paper.
FSC is the only forest-certification scheme supported by the leading
environmental organisations, including Greenpeace. Our
paper procurement policy can be found at
www.randomhouse.co.uk/environment

MIX
Paper from
responsible sources
FSC FSC® C016897
www.fsc.org

Printed and bound in Great Britain by Clays Ltd, St Ives PLC

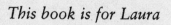

This book is for Laura

Author's Note

Renaissance Italy

Italy, at the time of the Renaissance, did not exist as a single distinct country. The peninsula was comprised of various city states in different regions, with the kingdom of Naples in the south. This kingdom of Naples was claimed by France and Spain, which meant that armies of both these countries occupied Italian territory. On the northern border the mighty republic of Venice also sought new conquests.

In addition to spiritual matters the Pope had temporal powers, with authority over a central area which included the Romagna.

Within the Italian city states wealthy and influential families held control, one of the foremost being the Medici of Florence. The Medici patronage, particularly that of Lorenzo the Magnificent, nourished a splendid epoch of art and culture. But when Lorenzo died, it was only a few years later, in 1494, that the Medici were banished from Florence.

SWITZERLAND

Milan● ●Kestra

●Pavia

FRANCE

River

Castel Be

Italy 1502

N

PART ONE
MURDER

*Italy, in the Romagna,
summer 1502*

PART ONE
MURDER

Italy, in the Romagna,
summer 1502

Chapter One

The first blow struck the side of my head.

I stagger, almost falling to the ground.

Sandino moves forward, stepping over the man lying dead at his feet. The man I saw him murder. Now he means to kill me.

I stumble back.

He thrusts out his cudgel, jabbing it hard into my gut.

Doubled up, I scrabble onto the rocks away from him.

He grunts in annoyance and follows.

I glance around desperately. Only the river, behind and below me, rushing in full flood.

Sandino grins. 'No escape for you, boy.'

He raises his arm. Swings his cudgel again.

I jerk my head away to avoid his next blow. My feet slip on the wet surface.

He shouts a curse.

I am falling.

The sudden shock of cold water.

And the river has me.

The current batters my body, grabbing at my clothes, dragging my legs. I swallow great lumps of water but I force my head to the surface and try to swim. My flailing is useless against the strength of the flow as it hurtles me onwards in its greedy grasp. I must try to reach one side of the riverbank. I must.

But I am weakening. Unable to keep my head up.

Then a sound fills me with terror. A waterfall!

The noise becomes louder, the water swifter. I am seconds from death. With a last effort I throw up my arms and scream for help. I am flung over the waterfall and slammed down into the foaming, broiling torrent.

A thundering mass of churning water pounds at me, driving me under. Caught in the whirlpool, I cannot break free of its deadly force. My face is upturned, mouth stretched wide, desperately sucking for air. The falling water distorts my vision. A shattered rainbow. Beyond it is light and life. My eyes roll back, blood roaring in my brain.

Now I seem to see myself from a great height. As though my mind views my body from another plane. Removed from this Earth to a different place, I look down and watch the frantic, dying struggles of a ten-year-old boy.

Clawing. Breath. None now.

Splintered light and utter darkness.

Chapter Two

Two hands grasp my head.

I see nothing. Hear no sound. No smell enters my nostrils. But touch, yes. Long fingers under my chin and, firmly, across my brow. A mouth, oh so gently, over mine. Covering my lips with his own. Completely. Breathing life into me with his kiss.

My lids open up. The face of a man looks down on me.

'I am Leonardo da Vinci,' the man says. 'My companions pulled you from the river.'

He tucks the folds of a cloak around me.

I blink. The colour of the sky sears my eyes, cold, and painfully blue.

'What is your name?' he asks me.

'Matteo,' I whisper.

'Matteo.' His voice curls round each syllable. 'That is a fine name.'

The features of his face blur. I cough, vomiting water and blood. 'I am going to die,' I say, and begin to cry.

He wipes my cheeks with his hand. 'No,' he replies. 'You are going to live, Matteo.'

Chapter Three

He calls me Matteo.

This is because, when he rescued me from under the waterfall, although half drowned, I had enough wit not to give my real name, and Matteo was the first one that came to hand.

Like the name, almost everything else I told him about me after that was a lie.

On the day of my rescue they made a little campfire there, he with his two companions, beside the waterfall, to try to dry me off. I would have liked to put as much distance as possible between myself and that place but I had no choice. My head was cracked from Sandino's blow and I could scarcely stand, let alone walk away. They wrapped me in the fur-lined cloak and laid me near the fire they had built. It was late summer. The weather was not very cold, but the days were growing shorter and the sun swung lower across the sky.

'*Zingaro?*'

The fatter of his two companions spoke their word for 'gypsy' as he put kindling on the fire.

I closed my eyes as the one called Leonardo glanced in my direction. 'He has the look of those people, and yet . . .'

The third man, whose cloak I was lying on, shook his head. 'It could be he's one of a group travelling south. The nomads have now been banned from entering Milan, accused of all sorts of theft and chicanery.'

'There is a gypsy encampment at Bologna,' said the fat man. 'That's not so far from here.'

I tensed as I heard them say this. Bologna was where my people would settle to pass this winter. If these men thought me Gypsy then they might decide to take me to them. If that happened, then I would be recognized, welcomed and brought in. But I did not want to go to Bologna. It would be one of the first places that the brigand Sandino would look for me if he thought there was a chance I was still alive. Indeed he might have already sent some- one ahead on the road to catch me in case I sought refuge there. He would surmise I had nowhere else to go, so some of his own vile men would be dispatched with instructions to bring me to him, their leader, if I appeared. I shivered as I recalled the blow Sandino's great cudgel had struck me, which had caused me to fall into the river and be swept away.

The man Leonardo, who had breathed on me to force the water from my lungs, said, 'The boy is small-formed, but then that might be due to malnutrition. It will become clear soon enough if he is one of those proscribed when we listen to what he says when he awakens.'

I knew then not to tell them my origins. They might be sym- pathetic to a drowning boy, but their minds were already set against my race.

Travelling people are known in many lands. We have a repu- tation as good farriers, skilled basket weavers and metal workers, and the gift of being able to foretell the future. This latter talent is suspect, but if requested, with payment, to tell a person's destiny, then a gypsy, like anyone else, can make a fair guess as to what that person's future might bring.

My grandmother was very good at it. She practised the art of conversation, so that anyone who spoke to her soon found that they had told her much more about themselves than they imagined. Then she would fit her advice to the situation, as a tailor cuts cloth to suit the customer. But my grandmother was a true healer. She understood sickness of the body, and of the spirit. Often it was the ache of humanity that troubled people – unrequited love, loneliness, the fear of growing old.

Many came to her for remedies. It was not mystical insight that allowed her to discern what ailed a person, but simple observation, as straightforward as studying the sky to predict the weather, or the trees to tell the seasons of the year. One only had to look with attention and interpret what one saw.

A person whose eye-whites were tinged with yellow had sickness of the liver or the kidneys and needed an infusion of parsley herb to purify the blood. For someone showing sleeplessness and anxiety, she recommended camomile for relaxation, and the milky juice extracted from lettuce as a sedative. She could tell if a woman was barren by the condition of her neck. Dry skin gathered there, or folded wrinkles, indicated an empty womb. The woman would be in awe of my grandmother, who knew her request without being told, and would go away with new hope, holding a purge made from rue and juniper berries to clear the pathways to the womb.

Young girls often wanted a means to tell the identity of their true love. They were given stalks of yarrow to place under their pillow and some words to recite before going to sleep:

By the feet of Venus thou dost grow,
O herb whose true name is Yarrow,
Let me dream of my true love,
Ere I wake tomorrow.

My grandmother knew all these things and many more secrets of country lore.

She also knew the time of her own dying.

This was not because she had second sight. More that she had knowledge of how the heart should beat, and became aware that hers was becoming weaker.

These divinations are not magical and do not require any special gift – that is, unless the absence of stupidity is deemed a gift. But such skill arouses jealousy in others and this was why we could never rest in one place for long. The town guilds and other businessmen did not like any kind of competition. And such is the prejudice against us that, without having been convicted or even accused of any wrong, being gypsy alone can mean death.

So I decided that I would lie. I began to prepare a story to tell my rescuers as I watched them from under half-closed lids.

They certainly weren't mercenaries for they carried no arms. Their horses were of fine stock, with sturdy haunches rather than for show, built for covering distances more than for speed. No hunting equipment was attached to their saddles; their food consisted of basic items: cheese, bread, fruit and wine. I deduced that they must travel each day and rest in accommodation of some kind by night.

I tried to puzzle the purpose of their journey. The saddlebags were bulky, but not with goods or cloth. It was books and papers they held. But these three men were neither merchants nor traders, and between them rank did not seem to matter much. They were at ease in each other's company, yet they deferred to the man Leonardo da Vinci, he who had pronounced my name so carefully.

From the beginning I called him Maestro. I was corrected later by one of his companions to use the term Messer, which, in some ways, is of greater status, but at that time he interrupted and said, 'If it pleases the boy to call me Maestro, then so be it. Let him call me Maestro if he wishes.'

In my mind he is always Maestro.

Chapter Four

It was past midday, and they warmed themselves by the fire and took out food to eat.

The fat one, who was called Graziano, saw that I was awake and offered me some. I shrank back. The Maestro stopped eating, held out his hand and told me to come nearer. I shook my head.

'Then we will wait until you do.' He set his food aside and took up a book. I watched to see what would happen. No one disturbed him.

His two friends talked quietly as he read. Their food lay on the grass. I was very hungry. The chill from the water had entered my bones. So I came to the fire and sat down.

The Maestro put down his book and handed me a piece of bread. 'We eat together in this household,' he said.

I looked around at his companions. They chatted with each other, passing food and drink to me as though I were an equal.

'We should move on,' Graziano said, 'if we're to reach our destination before nightfall.'

'Is your family home near here?' the Maestro asked me.

'I do not have a family. I am an orphan. I work as a stable boy when I can get work, or with the harvest.' I had the sentences ready to reply at once.

'Where's your place of work? Surely they'll be looking for you now that it's getting dark?'

I shook my head. 'No, they will think I have moved on. And

that is what I was doing,' I added quickly. 'They kicked and beat me and didn't give me enough food, so I will go and find another place to work now.'

'Yes,' said the thinner man, 'it's obvious that you've not eaten in a while.' He laughed and indicated the large amount of bread I had consumed.

I flushed and dropped the piece in my hand.

'Hush, Felipe,' his master chided him. 'The boy is hungry.' The Maestro picked it up and gave it back to me. 'Felipe is making a joke,' he said.

'A boy like that is always hungry,' said Felipe gloomily.

I was to find out later that Felipe was responsible for buying supplies and food, and it required all his accounting skills to ensure that the Maestro and the rest of his entourage could work and live with sufficiency.

'Do you want to travel with us to our next stop?' the Maestro asked me as they made ready to go.

'Where is that?'

'We cross at the bridge downstream and go back up country on the other side to a place called Perela.'

I tried to think of what Sandino might be doing at this moment. He would want to find me – not that he cared whether I drowned or not, but for another reason altogether. I had something he desired, a precious object that he'd deceived me into stealing for him.

Months ago he'd turned up at the gypsy camp where I was living after my grandmother's funeral. From my earliest memory my grandmother and I had travelled the roads together by ourselves, my mother having died when I was a baby and my father being unknown. Mostly we kept separate from any other band of gypsies, until my grandmother, realizing that she was very ill, took her wagon to a camp north of Bologna so that I would not be on my own when she died. Sandino claimed some kind of kinship with my grandmother. She, being dead, could not agree or disagree. I went with him, because he promised me the life of a pirate and I'd been enchanted with the idea of sailing across the ocean. To be a buccaneer, as he described, appealed to me. But taking me on a ship was not his true intention. Sandino had heard of my dexterity in opening locks, and he, in the pay of others, had a murderous plan which required my skills. I was the person he thought could help him, and in part I had. Except that I had not handed over the thing I had stolen on his behalf. I still carried it with me.

So I feared that Sandino would follow the river downstream to try to retrieve it from my body, dead or alive. I had no way of knowing how far I had come. The river had been swift moving, swollen and flooded with rain. I guessed it had taken me several miles. Sandino and his men did not have horses and would therefore have to walk. Also he would spend time searching for my body along the banks. Hopefully he'd think I had been swept into the sea, or was caught in reeds somewhere being eaten by eels. Even if he suspected I had survived, if I crossed over and went back upstream with these men to the village of Perela, Sandino would not think I'd gone that way, back in the direction I had come from. My rescuers had horses, which meant I would travel faster. I decided that I should go with them and then run off when it was safe to do so.

'We should be at Perela before dark,' said Graziano.

'We're lodging at the castle there.' Felipe addressed me. 'It's likely that they would feed a boy who could help in the stables.'

The Maestro reached out and put his hand on my forehead. His fingers were finely tapered, his touch gentle. 'You're still half stunned from knocking your head. I think we should carry you with us on one of our horses and take you there. Yes, Matteo?'

I nodded.

'Will the Borgia be there to speak to you?' Felipe asked him.

The Maestro shrugged. 'Who knows where Il Valentino is, or will be? Isn't that one of the features he has as a military commander? No one knows his exact location. He strikes like a snake, and then is gone, to reappear somewhere else when least expected.'

It was the first time I'd heard them mention Prince Cesare Borgia, known as Il Valentino, although I was familiar with the name. Who was not? The Borgia family was known throughout Europe. Rodrigo Borgia sat on the throne of St Peter and ruled the Church as Pope Alexander VI. This wicked man with his bastard children, the infamous Cesare and Lucrezia, meant to bring all Italy under their dominion.

His daughter Lucrezia, fair-haired and beautiful, was recently wed to the heir of the Duke of Ferrara. And I had seen this Borgia marriage celebrated in the spring of this year in Ferrara when I had been going about Sandino's business. Her wedding had provided an entertainment for the citizens and spectators. Although, not all of them were kindly disposed towards her, the bride being regarded by many of the Ferrarese as a deceitful woman whose father, the Pope, had paid their Duke Ercole a vast dowry to marry her to his eldest son, Alfonso, the future Duke of Ferrara. I'd heard murmurs and cat-calls on the day of her wedding as I moved through the crowd.

One woman commented on the shield given by the King of France to Alfonso as a wedding gift, saying, 'The duke's new shield portrays an image of Mary Magdalene. Was she not also a loose woman?'

Many people in the woman's vicinity laughed, though some looked nervously over their shoulders to see if anyone had noted that they mocked the house of Borgia. The revenge of the Borgia to those who offended their family was terrible. But the mood of the crowd was festive and the quips continued.

As the procession passed to the great cathedral for the marriage ceremony a loud whisper echoed in the piazza: 'Let the groom pray well, that he might live longer than her previous husband, strangled on the command of her own brother.'

So I discovered that these men who had rescued me, and with whom I had agreed to travel, had some connection to Cesare Borgia. But I reckoned that, at the moment, this might be more help than harm for me.

We crossed the river at a little stone bridge and turned towards Perela. It was a popular crossing place and many horses had trampled the path between river and road. The Maestro had placed me on his saddle in front of him. I was still bundled up in Felipe's cloak and I kept my face hidden as he showed the bridge keeper the pass he carried, signed by the hand of the Borgia himself.

By the time we reached the village of Perela I'd had time to think more of Sandino and what he might do. I thought now that I should not run away at the first opportunity. In addition to covering Bologna, Sandino would have spies on the main roads around this area. But he knew that I had discovered that the Borgia family paid him to do their evil work. If these men, my rescuers, were to be lodged in the castle at Perela then, for a short time at least, remaining with them was the safest thing for me to do. Perela, a Borgia stronghold, would be the last place Sandino would expect me to seek shelter. He would not look for me there.

That is what I truly believed.

Chapter Five

'Perhaps you will let us hear your own story, Matteo?'

We were a number of days in the keep of Perela before I was called upon to tell the tale of my life. One evening after supper the Maestro beckoned me to him as he sat by the fire. He put aside the lute he was strumming and spoke to me.

'You might wish to entertain us tonight, Matteo. I'm sure our hosts would like to hear how it came to pass that you nearly drowned under the waterfall.'

They had welcomed us warmly and fed us well, the commander of the keep, Captain Dario dell'Orte, and his family. And their hospitality seemed to me to stem more from the fact that they were plain and friendly people, than that my master carried a Borgia pass.

Perela was a very small village, no more than a great keep positioned on a hill, with a farm and one or two houses straggled about. The keep was a well-constructed building with solid high walls, and a stout castle door to protect it. On one side it over-looked a gorge, where the land fell away for several hundred feet to a ravine below. The kitchens were on the ground floor, with the hall on the first floor where meals were eaten and the family spent their daytime hours. Above that were bedrooms for the captain and his family, and two or three spare rooms. This was where they had lodged the Maestro and his two companions, giving them sleeping quarters and a workroom for him to set out his books and materials. The few castle servants there were slept in the kitchens, and a dozen or so men-at-arms in rooms above the stable block at the back. I was given a mattress in the attic under the roof.

Il Valentino, Cesare Borgia, being a cunning military commander, saw the position of the town as a key place between Bologna and Ferrara. In March 1500 Cesare had been made Gonfaloniere of the Church and Captain General of the Papal Armies, with instruction to conquer those parts of the Romagna that had slipped from the Pope's dominion. But his dream was not just to assert the authority of the Pope in the areas that belonged to the Vatican; he wanted everything he could take. Italy was studded with important and wealthy cities – Ferrara, Imola, Urbino, Ravenna and Bologna. By assault, siege or trickery, over the last two years town after town had fallen to the Borgia, so that now Il Valentino sat firmly astride the peninsula and had Italy by the throat. And as he wanted his towns made proof against attack, each one had to be inspected and its fortifications strengthened. Thus was his appointed engineer, Leonardo da Vinci, now in Perela.

Captain Dario dell'Orte had been injured in the service of the papal armies some years ago. Due to his damaged back he could no longer ride for long hours and had been installed as commander of this keep. He had come to the sleepy backwater of Perela in disgust, regarding himself as an old warhorse farmed out and, so he told us, prepared to be miserable and to end his days in dullness. But then the unexpected happened.

Despite being past his youth he had fallen in love with a young village girl, Fortunata, and to his astonishment she with him. He told us that the years he had been here were the happiest of his life. They found their joy in each other and their four children. His eldest son, Paolo – at twelve a year or so older than me – was a big lad with the same cheerful disposition as his father. After him came sisters closer to my age, both born on the same day, one more outgoing than the other, as is often the case with twins, and then another baby son, called Dario for his father. The whole family greeted visitors with enthusiasm and treated me as a guest rather than a servant. I was not set any task to do. The children saw me as a new playmate: Paolo, the older boy viewed me as a comrade, someone with whom he could practise jousting and fighting. He was delighted when I arrived. There was a lack of boys of his own age nearby and he made friends with me at once, ignored my withdrawn manner and coaxed me to come outside to join him in training for soldiering. Almost as soon as I was well enough to stand, the girls pulled on my arms for me to play with them. Paolo, their elder brother, batted them away firmly but good-naturedly. He was their leader and they heeded his word.

This night when I was asked to speak he made his younger siblings sit on the floor to listen while they urged me to tell them my story.

So I did.

But I lied.

Partly because I did not want to admit to my origins, but also my terror of Sandino made me want to lay as many false trails as possible. So I lied, instinctively and easily, flouring my tale with a little truth to bind it together. I meant only to give them some brief outline of my life. But as we gathered round the fire that evening and I related my history, it gained more in the telling, and grew, as a snowball rolling down a slope.

I told them that I was an orphan. I said that I had been brought up on a remote farm far away in the hills but I could not recall its name. When my parents died a wicked uncle had taken their land and made me work for him for nothing.

'Was your farm near the mountain that has snow on top in the winter?' the more talkative of the girl twins asked eagerly. Her name was Rossana and, like her sister, she was very pretty.

'I think so,' I said.

Rossana nodded. 'I can see that mountain from my window. It

is very high. Mama says it is so high because the angels live there to be near Heaven. But it looks very cold. Was it cold when you lived there, Matteo? Did you see any angels? Does that mean that Heaven is cold?'

Elisabetta, her twin sister, shivered. 'I don't like to be cold. When I go to Heaven I will take a blanket from the bed with me.'

'Hush, Elisabetta,' her mother said. She picked up the littlest child, Dario, who was falling asleep with his thumb in his mouth, and sat him on her lap. He cuddled in to her and she stroked his head. 'Hush, Rossana. Let Matteo continue.'

I didn't mind the girls chattering on. It gave me time to consider my next lie.

'The winters were very cold.' I took the strand that Rossana had given me and wove it into my tale. 'And I never had enough to eat. My clothes were thin and I was made to live in an outhouse and there was no wood for a fire. So a year or so ago I waited until it was spring time and then I ran away.'

'Did you have many adventures?' Paolo asked eagerly.

'Yes,' I said, 'but I will tell them another time.'

'I'd love to go out on the road,' said Paolo.

His father laughed. 'And sleep under a hedgerow? You, who cannot rise from your warm bed in the morning?'

I saw that their eyes were eager for a good story and I forgot about my need to be careful. Inhabitants in quieter places long for any diversion. Packmen and the hawkers who travel the country know that their customers live for news, any news. No matter how trivial the incident, no matter how insignificant the event, people thirst for a story. And those who add gossip to their goods make a bigger mark-up on their wares. A storyteller is often fed and accommodated for free in inns and castles. I've seen ladies buy more bundles of ribbons and hanks of embroidery yarn than they could ever use in order to keep the seller talking.

So, although omitting any mention of travellers or travellers' camps, I could not resist using some of my real experiences. My journeying took me to many places, I said. I had been in Venice, the city that has water in its streets, and we had watched the gondolas sail over the lagoon. I had wandered past shipping docks and seen boats disgorge cargoes of silks and spices from Cathay and Arabia, and others laden with unusual fruits and strange delicacies that had come all the way from the New World. I had stood in the public squares of famous cities and witnessed executions and carnivals. In Ferrara I had been in the houses of wealthy men and women. Such furniture and furnishings! Chests of golden oak and cedar wood, tables covered in damask with gold embroidery, colourful frescos and wall hangings, statues of bronze and marble, satin cushions in many colours. And how they dressed! It dazzled the eye to behold them!

The dell'Orte girls begged me to describe these clothes and jewellery and I knew why they were so interested. The keep where the dell'Orte family lived in Perela was not richly furnished. A single tapestry covered one wall of the great hall, but the rest of the inside was only roughly plastered. The girls' clothes were not made from expensive cloth, nor were they of the latest fashion. They and their mother were keen to hear any details I could supply about more up-to-date clothes, shoes and hairstyles.

I described to them the things I had seen earlier that year in Ferrara – at one of the celebrations on the occasion of the marriage of Lucrezia Borgia to Alfonso d'Este. Special platforms were erected in the street so that people could have views of the clergy and the nobles and their attendants as they passed by. Their dresses and doublets were of padded silk under velvet cloaks trimmed with miniver. They wore perfumed gloves with heavy rings upon their fingers. Musk-scented rosary beads trailed from the ladies' hands. Rubies, emeralds and pearls decorated their necks and hair.

Lucrezia Borgia had given a dress made of cloth of gold and adorned with a long train in the Spanish fashion to one of her jesters. He put it on, and minced through the streets after the procession, aping the gait of the nobles. In one hand he held a fan, in the other, a long staff, painted red and hung with little bells. In the piazza this buffoon shook his stick under the nose of Cardinal Ippolito, setting the bells jingling, and would not leave off until the cardinal took a coin from his purse and flung it at him. Then he capered about in front of the cathedral, flouncing his petticoats and preening himself, for the amusement of the crowd. And Lucrezia Borgia, who was renowned for her earthy sense of humour, had laughed and applauded his antics.

That night at Perela everyone gathered round me, listening intently to hear about the most scandalous woman in all Europe.

'Is she as fair as they say?' Donna Fortunata asked me.

'She is very fair,' I replied. 'Her hair is long and when she moves it shimmers like water when the sun is upon it. In an inn I heard a man whose wife worked as a servant in the palace telling everyone that it took Lucrezia's handmaids two days to wash and dress her hair. She uses a preparation containing saffron and myrrh, both very expensive, and this is why her hair shines like gold. And to keep her complexion fair, the whites of six fresh eggs, the bulbs of six white lilies and the hearts of six white doves are ground together and mixed to a paste with fresh white milk. She applies this to her skin each month.'

'Did she look wicked?' Rossana asked me.

'She looked . . .' I paused, to search for the truth in this matter, for it would not make any difference to my own history to tell my true impression of Lucrezia Borgia. 'She looked young, and – and—' I glanced down at Rossana gazing up at me, lips parted, eyes shining, her hair loose around her shoulders, and the next words I spoke were intended with no artifice at all. 'She is almost as beautiful as you.'

There was laughter, and I looked up, confused.

'If you wish to pay court to my daughter, Matteo, you must first speak to me,' Captain dell'Orte said in mock severity.

Rossana's face coloured pink.

'Elisabetta is also very beautiful,' I said quickly, thinking to cover any embarrassment, but also because it was true.

The adults roared with laughter.

'Now Matteo seeks to woo both girls with one compliment,' said Graziano.

More laughter followed his remark.

'Such economy Felipe would approve of,' the Maestro added.

My face flamed red. I did not know what to do. When I said that Rossana and Elisabetta were beautiful it was because I saw that they were. As the comments and the laughter continued through the company in the hall I realized too late that I had made an error in etiquette. I did not know how to proceed.

The girls clung to each other, giggling.

Paolo, who had more authority over them than either of their parents, quietened them down. 'Enough,' he commanded them. 'Allow Matteo to continue with his story.'

'They say that Lucrezia Borgia can speak many languages,' said Donna Fortunata, encouraging me to begin again. 'And that she has an agile mind, more clever than many men.'

'But that she uses her wits to scheme and plan the undoing of others,' murmured Felipe.

Suddenly the room went quiet.

We were in dangerous territory. I recalled the real reason that I had been in Ferrara and I knew I should find a way to move my story to a safer place.

Captain Dario dell'Orte must also have become uncomfortable at the direction the conversation had taken. He, being a captain under contract to Cesare Borgia, was aware of the consequences if any wrong words were related to his master. It was known that Cesare held a strange affection for his sister and it would not do well if anything untoward about her went back to the ears of Il Valentino. Not so long ago, in Rome, a man accused of speaking ill of the Borgia family had half his tongue cut away and nailed to the door of his house.

Captain dell'Orte shifted in his seat and spoke quietly to his wife. 'Perhaps we should let Matteo continue his own tale?'

'Of course!' Donna Fortunata was silent at once, but she smiled at her husband to show that no offence had been taken.

I said that I had nothing more to say about that part of my life anyway. Cities, although interesting, were crowded and unsanitary. I told them that the reason I had left Ferrara was because I preferred the fresh air of the countryside and could live by hiring myself out. At the last place I worked I spread the nets and knocked the olives from the trees with a pole, as people had been doing since ancient times.

'It is why I am so brown,' I added, recalling that my rescuers had noticed that my skin was light for a traveller but darker than theirs – by saying this I hoped to disperse any remaining speculation in their minds. The olive grower, I explained, was not a good master so I had decided to move on. On the day of my mishap I had gone to the river to fish and had fallen in and been swept away.

Paolo asked about the bruise on my head, if that had happened when I had fallen into the water.

I said I did not remember. I found that if ever I hesitated or stopped my story, then one of my listeners would offer a suggestion or even finish my sentence for me. Thus I could agree or disagree as it suited. I did not say that it was the blow from a cudgel that had caused me to fall in the river.

'Can't you swim?' asked Rossana. 'Paolo can swim.'

'Yes,' said Elisabetta. 'Paolo can swim very well. He will teach you and then you won't be in danger again.'

'I can swim,' I said. 'But the current was fierce and . . .'

'. . . at some point your head struck something hard.' Graziano supplied a solution for me.

'You must have hit it on a rock as you went over the waterfall!' declared Paolo, pleased with his own skills of deduction.

The girls nodded.

'Poor boy.' Their mother, Donna Fortunata, leaned over and stroked my head. 'And you are so thin too. We'll feed you up.'

I felt myself waver. I had no memory of the touch of a mother and it made me feel an emotion I had not experienced before. Sitting among this little family, having their attention and interest, had made me become vulnerable. I swallowed and went back to where I had been telling of striking my head. 'Yes,' I said, 'that was how it happened.'

I opened my mouth to continue when the Maestro spoke.

'Name the fish,' he said.

'What?'

'Tell me the kind of fish you were trying to catch in that river.'

I narrowed my eyes. Why did he want to know this information? Was he trying to trip me with his question?

'Many kinds of fish,' I answered him.

I thought of the fish that I'd taken from rivers and lakes when I'd travelled with my grandmother. We always stopped by a stream, for fresh running water holds special powers. It has healing properties, and one should bathe in it, drink it, and look and listen to it. My grandmother could detect the presence of water even in the drought of high summer by putting her ear to the ground. Then she would point to where she heard a stream in the belly of the earth and I would dig to find a spring.

I had enough knowledge of fish to name a few that we had eaten at one time or another. 'Perch, salmon, eel, trout,' I said. 'All of those.'

The Maestro was puzzled. 'That cannot be.'

'Why not?'

'Because of the waterfall downstream from where you were fishing – the one that caught you in its whirlpool. It's a natural barrier, and would prevent certain species from passing upriver.'

I shrugged, and replied as calmly as I could. 'I did not know exactly what I fished for. I only hoped to find something to eat.'

He took the small notebook that hung from his belt and

23

opened it up. 'I'm not familiar with this place.' He spoke to Captain dell'Orte. 'What kind of fish would you eat from your rivers here?'

At once Paolo and the girls rhymed off the names of several fish and the Maestro began to make swift marks in his notebook. Then he closed it up, fastening it by its little toggle and loop, and put it away. He leaned back and shut his eyes, but I knew that he did not sleep.

He must have guessed then that the history I claimed as my own was not all of a piece – my story, like a beggar's cloak, was full of holes. Perhaps, from the very beginning, he was aware that I was not what I appeared.

Chapter Six

My time in Perela I look upon as a small oasis in my turbulent life.

At first I did not know quite how to behave within the loving family of Captain dell'Orte, his wife and four children. My mind was not attuned to their ways.

My experience of the wider world was greater than that of Paolo, Rossana and Elisabetta, but this did not assist me in my dealings with them. I was physically different, lean where they were plump, with gawky arms and legs. Their mother gave me clothes to replace the ones I wore, but the sleeves of Paolo's cast-off tunic were too long and hung down over my wrists. It made me appear odd, and indeed I was odd. My manners were unsophisticated and coarse compared to theirs. The girls especially, although around my own age, were slightly taller and much more elegant in all things. They spoke politely and with deference to the adults, whereas it went against my nature not to speak plainly. To many people speaking plainly is the same as speaking rudely. Whereas to me, if one was direct, it saved time and misunderstanding.

At table they ate with skill and a deliberate slowness. I, who had known hunger, saw no reason to wait when food was placed before me. It was only when I noticed the stares of those watching me throwing meat into my mouth as fast as possible that I took note that their table manners followed a prescribed pattern.

25

It was Rossana who helped me, placing her soft hand over mine, asking me something about my time in Venice, and making me delay my next lunge at the serving dish to grab another piece of food. Nothing was said between us, but I knew she was guiding me. So I watched and listened, and learned their ways of addressing each other, and how they conducted themselves.

Paolo wanted more than anything to become a soldier like his father and had me practise swordsmanship and other military sports with him. In our jousting games he would beat me easily, using his wooden lance to give me a great whack on the chest. At first I took this badly and sulked and would not parry with him. But each time I fell down, the girls pleaded with me and Paolo coaxed me back, and I let myself be persuaded.

It was their favourite game. Rossana and Elisabetta would pretend to be high-born ladies bestowing their favours on the brave knight who must fight for them. Rossana, the more vivacious of the girls, always claimed me as her champion and tied her ribbons round my neck. But I soon became angry with my constant humiliation of being bested by Paolo. He had no thought in his head to shame me, only taking advantage of his greater weight and strength. But he was not superior in every way. What I lacked in bulk I made up for in cunning and speed. And in one thing I did have expertise that he lacked. He carried at his waist a poniard, a short dagger stuck in his belt for show.

In my upbringing knives were for use, not display.

One day, as he stood above me brandishing his sword and declaring himself the victor once again, I reacted by instinct. I stretched up swiftly, plucked the dagger from his belt, and had the point at his throat before he drew another breath. That silenced his crowing. It also silenced the cheering of the watching girls.

Paolo's eyes widened. And I saw something there that both thrilled and frightened me: fear.

He opened his mouth. I held his gaze with mine. What thought went through his head I do not know.

He said one word.

My name.

'Matteo?'

'*Matteo!*'

Another voice called on me. The Maestro looked down from the wall of the keep, where he was overseeing some repair work.

I stepped back and turned the handle of the dagger to Paolo. He took it from me. His hands were shaking. He replaced it in his belt. Then he recovered himself and bowed low before me in a great salutation.

The girls applauded. Rossana jumped down from her seat on the wall and ran towards us. She had in her hand the crown of berries and evergreen that she and her sister made each day for the victor.

'Kneel, Sir Knight. I will crown you victor of the tournament.'

I knelt down before her and she placed the crown upon my head. I looked up and saw her eyes brimming with tears. And at that moment I felt us tipping towards love.

It was a sign of Paolo's chivalry and good nature that he bore me no ill will for my threatening him with his own dagger. His lance and sword were made of wood, and though the clouts he gave me winded me and set my brain whirling, no real harm could be done. I, however, had held his life within my arm's reach. And he had seen on my face the intent, if only for a single second, to drive the blade home. But Paolo, being a true gentleman, apologized for his unfair jousting matches. He said he had been so taken up with having a companion that he had not thought of my feelings at being constantly defeated. Thereafter, before we went to combat, he made sure that he was handicapped in some way so that we were more suited in our sparring. It happened then that I won as often as he did.

Thus the days passed there in Perela, with me spending my time doing something I had never done in my life before.

I played.

Probably I had toys as a very young child, but I have only hazy recollections of myself as an infant toddling on the surface of a tiled floor, music playing in the background. Travelling from place to place left little opportunity for games. My role was to carry the basket that held our medicines and remedies for sale. I used to watch other children amusing themselves with balls and sticks as I stood with my grandmother exchanging the time of day with the women of a country farmhouse. But we had no money and no time for such trivialities. Three seasons of the year we had to sell, save and store in order to survive the fourth – winter.

If I was not helping my grandmother collect or prepare herbs I'd gather kindling for the fire or see to the horse. We were better off than many of our kind. We had a good little wagon where we could shelter if the nights were bad, and it meant that my grandmother could ride if she was tired. Usually, though, we walked the roads, the forest paths and mossy tracks until she became too breathless to do so.

But in Perela with Paolo, Rossana and Elisabetta and baby Dario I learned proper games. They had lessons in the morning but I said I did not need these. I had watched from the schoolroom door one day and saw that the girls could read very easily and form the letters to write without hesitation. Paolo, under the tutelage of the local priest, was progressing in his Latin and Greek. I knew that my lack of learning would show up very quickly if I sat down beside them. They would surely laugh at me when they found out that I did not know the words that they could chant so fluently.

Captain dell'Orte and his wife loved to see their children learn. The girls were well tutored, although very soon they would be betrothed. In truth they should have been long ago, but Donna Fortunata had persuaded their father to wait a little. She teased him, saying that if they held off maybe the girls would find a love match as she had. He only pretended to protest. He clearly doted on his daughters, and it would break his heart when the time came for them to leave and take up residence away from under his gaze. So the older children carried on with their lessons each forenoon, and I, who had no mastery of books, pretended that I was too advanced for their tutor. I said I had learned everything I needed to know from my parents, when they were alive, and I went off and amused myself in the kitchens or stables, or more often watched the Maestro at work.

He was overseeing the men-at-arms rebuilding one of the walls and I liked to look at his plans and see how they came to fruition in actual stone and cement. I kept myself inside the keep, so as not to be seen outside by the farm workers in case I became the subject of gossip. But as far as anyone knew I had arrived with the Maestro and was one of his household.

So it was by accident, one day, that I overheard him consulting with the captain on a secret project that Cesare Borgia wished him to undertake in as many of his castles as possible. I had been in the stables with the horses, for in addition to missing my grand-mother I also missed the companionship of the horse that had served us by pulling our wagon for many years. The day was hot and I hauled myself into the upper rafters to take a siesta among the hay baled there. I awoke to find Captain dell'Orte standing directly below me, with one of my master's drawings unrolled in his hand.

They were discussing the construction of a hidden room, a secret place, so that in the event of the castle being overcome, one or two persons might hide and be saved. They had come into the stables, away from the sight of any other, to be private. It was obvious to me that I should not be party to this conversation but there was nothing I could do. I remained silent as they decided upon the best location.

The Maestro told the captain that the two of them alone must build it and no one else in the keep was to know of its existence. Cesare Borgia himself had thus commanded it.

'I understand,' Captain dell'Orte replied.

'Not even your wife.'

'Certainly not.'

'But I have seen your wife,' the Maestro teased him. 'A man might not be able to keep a secret from such a woman. She is very pretty.'

'Exactly!' Captain dell'Orte laughed. 'So when I am with Fortunata we do not waste time speaking of buildings, bricks and mortar!'

One evening the children were asked by their mother to show their reading skills to their father. The evening meal had been cleared, and books and parchments were lying open on the table. As Rossana waited her turn she asked me, 'Can you read, Matteo?'

'Of course,' I said at once, and then, quickly, before I was called upon, I added, 'But I choose not to.'

'Oh, but you would find it most enjoyable,' said Rossana. 'It's not all dull learning. There are lots of interesting stories to read.'

'I already know many stories,' I boasted. 'I do not need books for that. In any case reading and writing is a job for artisans. When my parents were alive my father employed a scribe to write our letters for us so that we did not have to toil with a pen.'

'Your father?' The Maestro looked at me. 'When you told us your life history, Matteo, you did not tell us much about your father. What was his name?'

'Pietro,' I said quickly.

'A good name,' said the Maestro slowly. He did not look up as he spoke. He kept his gaze upon the manuscript before him. I followed his look. There was a scroll laid out in front of us.

The scribe had put his name at the foot of the page. A simple name that I had recognized.

Pietro.

The Maestro picked up the scroll and rolled it tightly. 'A very good name,' he said again. 'A person with a name such as that would certainly read and write most excellently.' He tied the cord around the scroll. Then he stood up and placed it among some others on a high shelf.

As soon as I could I excused myself and left the hall.

I went to the room I had been given at the top of the house. It was a small attic with a rough mattress that sat on a wooden platform. I bundled up my clothes and checked the pouch I kept secured on the belt around my waist.

Suddenly I knew I was not alone. I whirled round.

The Maestro was standing in the doorway. Had he seen me checking my belt pouch?

'What are you doing?' he asked.

'I will leave at once,' I said.

'Why?'

'To avoid a beating.'

'No one is going to beat you.'

I watched him. For a boy to be caught lying always merited punishment.

'Tell me why you lied.'

I shrugged. 'I do not know.'

'Think about it and tell me why.' He went over to the window and looked out. 'I'll wait until you do.'

I watched him. He did not act as though he was about to strike me. 'I am ashamed,' I said finally.

'Of not being able to read very well?' He smiled. 'You had sufficient skill to decode the scribe's name on his manuscript.'

I did not reply.

'Lying eats into the soul,' he said. 'If it becomes a habit it frays the edges of your spirit. Truth telling, although sometimes harder to do, strengthens your heart. It serves a person ill not to tell the truth.'

Not so, I thought privately. He had never gone hungry, never had to steal to eat. Lying had saved my skin on many occasions. But I did not speak this thought aloud.

'What is your truth, Matteo?'

I would never tell him all of it, but one thing at least he might know. 'It was not so much the shame of not being able to read fluently,' I said. 'It is the shame of not knowing my father.' I hung my head. 'I am a bastard child,' I whispered.

'Oh, that!' He gave a short laugh. 'Half the courts of Europe and most of mighty Rome itself are bastards. Our employer, my patron for the moment, Cesare Borgia, is a bastard.'

'That is no recommendation for bastardy.'

He laughed, and then laughed again. 'That joke is one we must not share with anyone else. To malign a Borgia is dangerous.'

'He is of noble birth. It is different for those of noble birth.'

'It can be harder for them. They have so much to prove, so much to fight for. So much to lose.'

I shook my head. 'It is shameful to be a bastard who does not have a father's name . . .'

'Your mother would have loved you, Matteo.'

'My grandmother would never speak of her so I cannot be sure that she did. It may be that the shame of my birth caused her to hate me.'

The Maestro took a moment to answer. In the silence I heard the wick of the lamp sputter, the clack of a shutter being closed elsewhere in the building. He gazed at his fingers. Then he spoke carefully. 'It is inherent for a mother to love her child whether the baby is illegitimate or not.'

'Not always,' I said stubbornly.

'You're impossible!' he cried. 'You refuse to be persuaded.'

I trembled. I had made him angry. 'I am sorry,' I began. 'I did not mean to annoy you.'

He shook his head. 'You did not annoy me. You make me sad.'

He rested on his elbows and looked through the narrow window. These were not glassed like the rooms in the lower part of the keep, but open to the elements, with a wooden shutter to be pulled over in bad weather.

A bird had flown down and alighted on the sill. The Maestro drew back so as not to disturb it. His hand strayed to the notebook at his belt, then he recalled my presence, glanced at me and said quickly, 'I am a bastard.'

I stared at him.

'I am a bastard.' He repeated the sentence again.

'But you have a second name,' I replied.

'Ah yes,' he said. 'Leonardo of Vinci. But Vinci is not my father's name. Vinci is a place.'

'I do not even have that,' I said. 'I am only Matteo.'

He turned from the window. 'Sit down upon your mattress and I will tell you a story' – he smiled – 'Only Matteo.'

He leaned against the window recess and began his tale.

'There was a good man who went about his business very honestly. One day another man reproached him, by calling to this honest man's attention the fact that he was not the true-born child of his father.

' "To be born out of wedlock means you are illegitimate," this man said.

'The honest man replied that illegitimate meant illegal, and there was no such thing as a child who was not legal. "How can a child, of itself, be illegal?" he asked. "A child is a child. Born of the union of a man and a woman. A child does not know, care, or indeed have any control over the circumstances of its conception."

'Therefore, according to natural law, the honest man declared, he was a legitimate child of the human species. It was the other man who was the bastard, because he behaved more like a beast than a man.'

I said nothing.

'Matteo, listen to me. Being legitimate is a . . . a . . . technicality. It does not mean that there is anything wrong with you. Men use "bastard" as a curse. But to use the term thus is to show that they themselves are less than a proper human being. My

33

grandfather brought me into his house and my beloved uncle cared for me, and I have benefited more from this upbringing than I could have from any other.'

He turned again to the window. The bird had flown off but he continued to gaze at the spot where it had rested. He fell into one of his reveries. Then he roused himself and surveyed the room. 'This will not do,' he said. 'It is becoming too cold at nights for you to stay here. You may sleep on the floor of my studio, if you wish. Although in a few days I must move on. I have to inspect the castle at Averno and it is much larger and must have more attention paid to it, so I will be there for a month at least. Have you given any thought as to what you want to do for the winter?'

I shook my head.

'Then you may come with us for the present. There will be tasks that you can perform to earn your way.'

I was sorry to leave the keep at Perela.

Until you experience love and friendship you do not realize how lacking your life has been without it. But I knew that I was safer away from that area. Perela was too close to where Sandino and I had parted company. Some spy of his might pick up my story, and if he heard of an extra boy appearing out of nowhere he would come to investigate.

My heart dipped as I looked back and saw them waving from the wall of the keep: Paolo, Rossana, Elisabetta, with baby Dario hoisted on Paolo's shoulders.

Their figures diminished as we rode away. Never before had I felt such regret at leaving a place. They had made such a fuss on our departure that I could see they held me in some affection, pressing many small gifts into our hands and making us promise to return when winter had passed.

The Maestro had said that I could go with him further on their journey. He could not at that time have anticipated Graziano's illness and Felipe's absence. But not long after we reached Averno his two companions became unavailable to help him in his work.

In return for food and accommodation I was engaged as a servant, and thus it was I that he turned to when he needed special assistance.

PART TWO
THE BORGIA

Italy, in the Romagna,
winter 1502

PART TWO
THE BORGIA

Italy, in the Romagna,
winter 1502

Chapter Seven

My heart.

Seeming too large for the space beneath my ribs. Thudding so noisily that I thought my master walking just behind me, following the light of the lantern I held up to show our way, must hear it.

'Halt here, boy.' He spoke softly, took the lantern from me and raised it to the street name painted on the wall. '*Street of Souls*,' he murmured. 'Yes, this is the place.'

He kept the lantern and went into the alleyway.

And I was left to hasten after him. Glancing around fearfully. Walking down the narrow street, he lifted the light high, and the darkness dispersed. But the shadows scrolled in once more as we passed, creeping at our heels, bringing the spectres who hover in the night to pounce on the unwary.

I made the gesture used by the gypsies to keep away evil, and then, as I caught the amused glance of the Maestro, I fumbled the sign of the cross on my forehead, breast and shoulders. He laughed out loud at me then, but not unkindly.

'Keep your magic signs to ward off the dangers of *this* world, Matteo. The harm that men do to each other in battle is more wicked than any the spirits can offer.'

We came to a door set in a wall. Unmarked but not unknown. The mortuary door of the hospital of the city of Averno.

'Hold the satchel, Matteo.' He handed me the large bag that contained his working tools, his papers, parchments and chalks.

I'd only been with his household a short time but I knew that this was an honour. I put the strap around my shoulder and clasped the heavy leather bag carefully in both hands.

He positioned the lamp so that it would shine on his own face. Then he knocked on the door. We waited. At this time of night the porter would be asleep or drunk at his post. After sunset no one came to collect their dead.

The Maestro raised his fist and pounded on the door. Minutes elapsed. Then the grille slid back. A bad-tempered face regarded us.

'I have permission from the magistrate to examine the bodies of the dead.' The Maestro took the order from the inner fold of his sleeve. He held it up.

'You are . . . ?' Through the grille the porter spoke in the superior way of men of little authority.

'Leonardo, engineer, and . . . painter. From the place known as Vinci.'

'Vinci? Never heard of it.'

'I also carry another pass' – the Maestro spoke quietly – 'which allows me free entry to wherever I choose. It has the personal seal of the Borgia on it.'

The man recoiled.

'Il Valentino,' the Maestro continued, without changing the expression on his face, 'Cesare Borgia – you may have heard of him?' He placed a caress rather than an emphasis on the last word of the sentence.

The mortuary attendant had the door open before the Maestro drew another breath. He bent so low that his brow almost touched the cobbles.

As we passed through the Maestro winked at me.

My heart lifted. For to begin with, in those first weeks of being his servant, I was not always sure of his mood. Was not familiar with his deep periods of reflection, when he hardly spoke or ate or slept. Had not yet become accustomed to his intensities and preoccupations.

Chapter Eight

We were now in a small courtyard.
I had never been in such a place. There was a rancid smell that soap, scented herbs and incense could not smother. It was the stench of death.

The burial customs of the travelling people are different to those of house-dwellers. If a gypsy leader or a respected man or woman dies their dwelling is burned.

Thus was my grandmother's wagon sent with her spirit into the next world. My grandmother, who had cared for me in the absence of any other, was laid to rest in the traditional clothes of her people, with herbs and flowers scattered over her. The tools of her trade – her infusion pot, her spoons and measuring scales and recipe book – were buried in a wooden box near the place where she died.

After my grandmother had gone, I rejected offers of shelter from the rest of the camp, preferring to roam free by day, and at night lie under the wheels of any cart with the dogs on either side to keep me warm. My memory is of being constantly hungry despite kindness and meals shared by the other families. My ever-empty belly soon forced my hands to take whatever was available to fill it. A kitchen door standing open, a market stall left un-attended, and I was as quick as a kingfisher by a lake. Nothing edible was safe from my hands. And if the food was not on display, no matter, I soon developed an aptitude for opening locked storerooms. Hunger was the spur to my learning the craft of thievery.

And it was my talent for stealing that attracted the attention of Sandino, who entered my life and took me to join his band of brigands. Which was how I became fatally entangled in his ways of intrigue and murder.

Now the Maestro and I waited just inside the door of the place of death while the hospital porter regarded us with a mixture of fear and curiosity.

My master set the lantern down and stared at the stars, murmuring their names under his breath: 'Castor and Pollux, and the great Venus beyond. Can those others be . . . ? Too late in the year surely for them to occupy that position for the winter solstice with the moon in that phase.' He pulled out the little notebook that he carried always at his belt and began to make marks in it.

His gazing at the moon and muttering made the porter uncomfortable. It had the sound of incantation, and the Maestro's great outer cloak, swept round his shoulders against the chill of the night, gave him the appearance of a sorcerer. The porter understood that we were not there to collect a relative or loved one, and we didn't wear the garb or carry the equipment of any of the medical profession. But the terror that the Borgia name invokes forestalled him from asking any questions.

The porter pulled the interior night bell. The hospital in Averno was conducted by the brothers of the Order of the Holy Compassion of Jesus, and after some moments a monk approached along the outside cloister.

He moved silently on sandalled feet, the grey of his cloth merging with the shades of night. The cowl of his habit was raised. The flaming pitch torches set at intervals along the wall flung dark shadows on his face.

This man introduced himself as Father Benedict, the monk in

charge of the mortuary. He regarded both my master and myself with interest. Then he took the Borgia pass and the magistrate's order and read them closely.

'This document, signed by Cesare Borgia . . . Il Valentino, the Honourable' – was there a hesitation upon that word? – 'Duke of Valentinois and Prince of Romagna, gives leave for you to access the castles and fortified houses in the Romagna and other parts under his domain.'

'That is so.' The Maestro inclined his head.

The monk held up the parchment. He read unhesitatingly:

'*This Order is to all our lieutenants, castellans, captains, condottieri, officers, soldiers and subjects, and to any others who read this document.*

'*NOTICE THIS:*

'*Our most beloved Architect and General Engineer, Leonardo da Vinci, who bears this pass, is charged with inspecting the palaces and fortresses of our states, so that we may maintain them according to their needs and on his advice.*

'*It is our order and command that all will allow the said Leonardo da Vinci free passage, without subjecting him to any tax or toll, or other hindrance, either on himself or his companions.*

'*All will welcome him with amity, and allow him to measure and examine any things he so chooses.*

'*To this effect, we desire that delivered unto him should be any provisions, materials and men that he might require, and that he be given any aid, assistance and favour he requests.*'

The monk raised his eyes. 'This is not a fortified building.'

'Yet it is under his rule now,' my master pointed out.

'We are very aware of this.' The monk spoke quietly.

There was a silence.

The brutality of Prince Cesare Borgia's regime and its enforcement by his governor in Romagna, General Remiro de Lorqua, was becoming known in all parts of Italy. This Remiro de

Lorqua, in effecting the prince's instruction to impose civil order locally, while the Borgia armies conquered and subdued the rest of the region, had caused widespread terror throughout the area. His methods of public torture and execution intensified the fear and hatred of the name of Borgia.

It would be a brave man who sought to oppose so ruthless an overlord. Brave monk, braver than I knew. The last sentence of the Borgia document, which he had not read out, said: *Let no man act contrary to this decree unless he wishes to incur our wrath.*

'It would please me to make a donation to your funds,' my master suggested.

But this mortuary monk was a brother of the Holy Compassion Order, whose reputation also spread wide. Established during the Crusades by a devout knight named Hugh, they were enjoined by their founder to care for anyone in need of medical care. This good knight, doctor, soldier and, latterly, saint would not allow any distinction between men and women, civilian and army, Infidel and Christian. Braving the arrows of both sides, and without payment from either, he tended the hurt and wounded where they fell on the battlefield. At home his monks nursed the poorest of the poor, the victims of plague and pestilence, the beggars and the penny whores. Unlike others they turned no one away, not even those for whom the road was home. Theirs was a true vocation, not like the secular clergy who joined the Church for personal profit. There was no bribe that could corrupt this monk, no threat that he feared. He walked with death many times every day.

He ignored my master's offer and said, 'If you are engaged in engineering studies, what interest do you have here?'

'Is not the human body the most perfect piece of engineering constructed?' my master asked him.

The man held the Maestro's gaze for a long moment, and finally replied, 'That is your purpose then? A study of the human body?'

'Yes. Most sincerely it is. I am an engineer, and a painter.'

'I am familiar with your name, Messer da Vinci,' the monk interrupted. 'And your famous works. I have seen your fresco of the Last Supper at the Dominican monastery in Milan, and your cartoon of the Virgin with the Christ Child and Saint Anne in the Church of the Annunciation in Florence. The images you have produced are masterpieces . . . with God's grace.'

'Ah!' My master regarded the monk, then asked thoughtfully, 'You are interested in how Scripture can be illustrated by man, through visual art?'

'Messer da Vinci,' the monk replied, 'it is said that your works have many codes and symbols contained within, and that we should seek to find their true meaning.'

My master said nothing so Father Benedict went on, 'The explanations of these works, as offered by the brothers of the monasteries, propose them as theological meditations. In the Last Supper the Apostles are struck in poses of astonishment and disbelief at the accusation that one of them is about to betray Our Blessed Lord. Yet it could be said that the force that emanates from Christ is also spiritual.'

The Maestro did not comment on this interpretation of his work, but tilted his head as if listening attentively.

'And in the Florence cartoon the depiction of Saint Anne, with the Virgin and the Christ Child, displays the concept of the Three in One. My attention was drawn to the fact that the whole is constructed as a kind of pyramid and, at the bottom of the piece, only three of the feet of the adult figures are shown; these factors indicating the Trinity. Also, we can see that the Virgin, fearful for the safety of her child, tries to draw Him back onto her lap away from the danger He is stretching towards. Yet Saint Anne's expression indicates that she knows the Child must fulfil His destiny to effect the Salvation of Mankind.'

'Then you would see the challenge to depict the interaction

between Christ and his Apostles in the fresco, and between the three figures in the cartoon.'

'I found the dynamic force of the movement within your drawing astounding.'

'I make studies of various aspects.' My master appeared to ponder and hesitate before replying. 'Many, many sketches of different poses. The hands of Christ in the Last Supper, as he reaches to the dish at the same moment as Judas. The Virgin's arm . . . Striving for the form of the limbs, considering most carefully all options . . .' He allowed his voice to fade on a questioning note.

'Yes. I understand that your work requires a great deal of reflection.'

The Maestro seemed to take these words to heart. He nodded slowly and waited.

'I would say,' the monk continued, 'much of the impact comes from how the figures are grouped, and within that, how they are portrayed in their various actions.'

'Therefore you appreciate that the depiction and composition of these holy figures is dependent on my study of anatomy. It is unachievable without it.'

The Maestro had brought the monk to where he wanted him. The monk acknowledged this with a slight inclination of his head.

My master advanced his case: 'Furthermore, this interest in anatomy that I pursue has more uses than true representation of figures, human and divine. Medically it is of great value to examine the bodies of those who have died. It is the way to discover what has caused death.'

'God causes death.' The monk spoke firmly.

'Indeed, Father Benedict. But death can be delayed. Surely your work in this hospital must show you that?'

'When the Divine Creator calls you to Him, then your time here is done. No mere mortal can change that.'

'Nevertheless,' my master persisted, 'it cannot but be a good thing to help prolong life.'

'You cannot cheat death. God has ordained the time and the place. The Bible says, *You know not the day, nor the hour when thy soul is required of thee.*'

'I do not strive to thwart the plans of the great Creator,' replied the Maestro. 'Research begets knowledge, and knowledge is beneficial to all.'

'One could say that we are not intended to know too much. Man ate from the Tree of Knowledge of Good and Evil and was banished from the Garden of Eden. Knowledge can be dangerous.'

Knowledge can be dangerous.

This was the first time I heard that phrase uttered. I was to think of it again when its truth was proved to me most barbarously.

My master gestured with his hands but did not reply.

The monk slowly folded the official documents and handed them back to the Maestro. He took one of the torches from its bracket on the wall and indicated for us to follow him.

Chapter Nine

We entered the mortuary.

Along the cloister. Down many steps.

The room we arrived in was subterranean, with a low arched ceiling and a flagged floor. It was desperately cold. Halfway up the wall was a counter which ran round the room. Under it were brooms, buckets, mops and cleaning materials. Upon it, tidily stacked, were jars of unguents, spice boxes and folded burial cloths. Rough trestles and boards were stacked to one side. Two tables had been made up in the middle of the room. Sheets covered whatever lay on top of these.

'Our recent dead have been collected by their relatives before sunset. Except one man and woman. We believe these two will not be claimed.'

The linen shroud sheets were newly laundered. Father Benedict was careful of his charges and treated each body with respect. It is clear that the hospitaller monks of the Holy Compassion did not measure out their mercy as some other religious did.

'Here is a female who died after giving birth yesterday.'

'Is it possible to see her?'

The monk led us to the first table. He uncovered the head. 'This young woman was a prostitute. She worked the streets by the river, mainly with the traffic passing through, bargemen, muleteers and such.' He paused. 'It is very likely she is infected.'

The Maestro looked at the young woman. Her hair had been

combed and now lay loose on each side of her head. But it was still damp, as if matted with the sweat of the labours of childbirth. Her face was thin with starvation.

'No.'

'Her babe, stillborn?' The monk indicated the little bundle tucked in at the girl's side.

My master glanced at me, hesitated, shook his head.

The monk gently re-covered the girl. He moved to another table.

'A vagrant? Found half dead in the mountains.'

This old man had been discovered collapsed at the side of the road by a hill shepherd bringing his flock to lower pastures for the winter. The shepherd felt life still flickering in the ancient body and, out of pity, had hoisted the man across his back and carried him six miles to the hospital. The old man had died in his sleep only this morning.

'What illness claimed his life?'

The monk shrugged. 'He complained of nothing specific, just a general weakness. His heartbeat was not strong. After a while it stopped altogether. He was very old. It may be that in itself was the cause.'

'Ah, yes,' said the Maestro at once. 'I would like to examine him. If I may?'

The monk nodded. He heard the quickening of interest in the Maestro's voice. There was faint displeasure on his face.

My master did not seem to notice. It was something I was discovering about him. He could quite quickly become detached from the nuances of common human emotion. Particularly if he was engaged in some aspect of a scientific problem or research. His work excluded any consideration for the feelings of those around him. And he rarely excused himself or justified his behaviour. It was as if he was compelled to focus all his energy on one subject and was unaware that others did not follow his obsession.

'May I begin my work, or is there anything more you have to do to this man?'

'They have all been shriven.'

'And washed?'

The monk regarded us coldly. 'In this hospital we do not wait until our patients die before we clean them. The brothers, and the good sisters who help us, wash all sick on arrival, no matter what the disease.'

'Forgive me, Father.' At last the Maestro caught the tone of the monk's voice. 'I did not mean a slur upon your hospital.'

He lifted the leather bag from my shoulder and rested it on the counter. He opened it up and took out a solid bundle wrapped in chamois leather. He unwrapped it.

I saw the monk frown.

As it was laid flat I could see that the length of chamois had been constructed with various-sized pockets stitched inside the roll. Each of these slots contained a knife. I know about knives. I am Gypsy. But knives like this I had never seen. Some were long bladed, some were short. Slender shafts curved away from the handle while others resembled daggers with wicked points. All were sharp, with the keenest cutting edge. The handles were shaped both for those who favoured right and left grip. Specially made for the Maestro's own fingers to hold. Particular for the purpose. Wrapped in a linen cloth was a small whetstone and beside it a wineskin which held some water.

The monk cleared his throat. 'I will have this body removed to another room where you may work undisturbed.'

'Of course.' The master rolled up the leather knife pouch and tucked it under his arm. 'Thank you, Father Benedict. May I also have a second table set up there, please?' He lifted the bag and turned to me. 'Matteo, bring the lantern and one of those slop pails from under the counter.'

The monk paused before he left us. 'The man's name. You might wish to know. It is Umberto.'

Two attendants came. They carried the table with the body of the old man, Umberto, still laid upon it, to a nearby smaller room. There they set up another trestle table, with a large candelabra, a basin, a jug of clean water and some cloths. My master gave them a few coins and they left.

We were alone with the cadaver.

I was shivering.

My master bent down. His face was on a level with my own. He put a hand on each of my shoulders.

'Listen to me, Matteo. There is nothing to fear from death. The spirit has departed. This man has been shriven by a holy priest. His soul has gone to meet its Maker. This' – he indicated the body on the table – 'is but the husk wherein the spirit dwelled. It is of no use to the man who once lived and breathed within it.'

My eyes slid sideways from his steady gaze. This did not sound like the true teaching of the Catholic Church. Even I, an ignorant traveller, knew that. The soul is entwined within the body, and though the spirit flees on death, do we not need the body for our resurrection?

'I will not take any human parts away from here,' the Master reassured me. 'Umberto will be buried whole, for the Second Coming of Christ.'

But I could see this man's hand protruding from under his shroud sheet. And it was not just the spirit world that sent fear shuddering through me. His nails were dirty and long, yellowed and gnarled, like the tusk of an old boar. They reminded me of another, Sandino, who grew his thumbnails long and sharpened them into great horny claws. Earlier this year, in Ferrara, I had seen him use them to gouge a man's eyes out.

The Maestro drew back the cover.

I saw the dead body. All of it.

The face.

The chest.

The torso.

The tufts of pubic hair. His penis flaccid between his legs.

The Maestro followed my gaze. 'Such an insignificant-looking organ. And yet the source of much misery.' He held his knife in his hand.

For a moment I thought . . .

He glanced at my face. 'Don't be so worried, Matteo.' He pulled the sheet back up to the waist. 'At the moment I am seeking the cause of death in old age. I want to look at the inner workings of his body, those parts close to his heart. I might be able to determine why it ceased to function.'

The Maestro put his leather satchel on the second table. From this bag he took out many things: another smaller lamp, measuring instruments, paper, chalk.

He unrolled the pouch of knives.

Chapter Ten

'**U**se the slop bucket and piss on this.'

In the mortuary my master handed me a pad of cloth. 'Soak it, then squeeze it a little so that it is not dripping wet.'

I stared at him. 'Why?'

He put his head on one side. 'You ask why, Matteo. That's good. I will tell you. It's for you to use as a breathing mask.'

A shock went through me. I managed to stammer, 'I will find the privy and do it there.'

He smiled. 'Very well. I'll explain more when you return.'

My hands were shaking as I held the cloth and tried to piss over it into the drain.

When the Maestro first took me in and fed me I considered him a kindly person. Now I began to think I had fallen in with a madman. To a true traveller it is grievously impure to touch any kind of human excrement. Body waste is to be disposed of away from the dwelling place, avoiding any contact that might lead you to ingest it, by touch or via the air. House-dwellers might wear expensive clothes but they were wont to use a piss pot, then, directly afterwards, without washing their hands, lift a piece of food to their mouth, eat, and go on to lick their fingers! It made my gorge rise to think about it. He expected me to breathe my own piss through my mouth! I could not do it. In any case my organ would not function properly to wet the pad he had given me.

I thought again of running away. But how could I manage this? Almost certainly the porter at the gate would not let me pass freely to the street outside the wall. He would question me as to why I was leaving alone, perhaps even alert my master. Then the Maestro would demand an explanation. What excuse could I give that would not make him view me with suspicion? He, with his great learning, might be aware of travellers' rules regarding body functions and deduce the reason I had acted so strangely.

In any case, if I did escape from this place I would have to move away from Averno and the surrounding region. And I felt safe here. It was some weeks since my master had plucked me from the waterfall and restored me to life. With each passing day I grew more confident that Sandino had moved out of this area, either thinking that I'd escaped his hand, or, more likely, that I had drowned on the day he had struck me and I had fallen into the river.

On considering all of this I also saw that I was safer with the household of the Maestro, despite his odd ways. At present he was in the employ of Cesare Borgia and carried his pass. And thus I too was under the protection of the Borgia and residing mainly within his estates. It was, I believed, the one place where Sandino, knowing that I knew he was in the pay of the Borgia, would not look for me. He would think that I would try to put as much distance as possible between myself and any Borgia connection. I was more secure now than if I were out in the hills or the woods, where the brigand leader might be hunting me with men and dogs to retrieve that which I had stolen from him.

My water splurged out from me in a golden stream onto the cloth. I closed my eyes as I wrung out the extra moisture. With great reluctance I brought the sodden pad back to the Maestro.

He had been busy while I was gone and had emptied his leather bag and arranged its contents in a methodical line upon the second trestle table. Notebooks, paper, pen, ink, pencil, charcoal, chalks, lengths of cord, bottles and flasks of liquid, powders and ointments. In addition to the knives there were technical instruments, strange-shaped scissors and a small saw.

I poured clean water from the jug into the bowl, plunged in my hands, then rubbed them furiously on a cloth. I emptied the bowl into the slop bucket. I saw the Maestro watch my actions while he encased the pad in a linen cloth and shaped it to the lower part of my face.

'Breathe in through your nose and then out via your mouth. Your nasal passages help filter impurities from the air.'

'I cannot breathe my own piss!'

'Your urine is clean. It's your own waste matter. It cannot harm you.' He laughed. 'I also find it helps overcome the smell of the dead.'

'Then why do you not wear such a thing?'

'I did in the past, but it hampered my vision. Anyway I find that as I work I forget about the smell. Curious, isn't it? That your mind can become so occupied with a subject that your senses fail to register its proper effect. But see!' He opened his mouth and breathed out a huge sigh. A puff of white mist immediately formed in front of his face. 'It's so cold in this room that the body will be slow in decomposing. We should not be troubled with rancid smells tonight.'

He secured the pad around my nose and mouth. I gagged as he did it but he tied it very tightly with cords wound round the back of my head.

'The acid in your urine will help protect you from any ill elements released into the air when I open up this body.' Then with a gleam of laughter he added, 'And the sting in your eyes means that you should not faint.'

I noticed that he had packed his satchel with several candles and had lit these and set them up around the table. They were not cheap tallow candles but ones made from good beeswax, which burned clearer and perfumed the air. The heavier outside lantern he had set down on the floor. The smaller lamp with a glass shield that he had brought with him he passed to me.

'You must hold this lamp near to my hands, Matteo. You're exactly the right height for this. It's important that I have light when I work. It's not an accident that I asked you to accompany me tonight. I chose you because I have seen that you are capable and strong minded. Hold it close and steady. I know you can do this.'

Thus with praise and trust he bound me to him, tightly, as the cords bound the pad around my face.

He pulled the stopper from a little bottle and dripped some sharp-smelling liquid onto a cloth. With this he swabbed down the man's chest.

Then he selected a knife.

With force he cut into the man's skin. First he made two cuts in a V-shape. He did this by inserting his blade into the front of each side of the man's shoulder and carving down and into the centre so that these two cuts met at the base of his neck.

The skin opened quite easily, which did not surprise me. As soon as he began I could tell that this was not the first time he had done this. There is an artistry to this type of work that is part technical, part intuitive. My grandmother could skin a rabbit in half a minute. And the skin of this man, Umberto, was old, with a consistency more like parchment than vellum. It split easily under the knife.

Next the Maestro made a long incision from the point of the V. He sliced right down to the man's navel. Then, selecting a different tool, he began to cut away the skin from the flesh to peel it back on each side.

Not so long ago I had been in the marketplace of a town near Imola when a man was brought there to be flayed. He'd been implicated in some resistance when Cesare Borgia had swept into Urbino and sent Duke Guidobaldo running for his life.

Il Valentino had captured Urbino, and anybody thought to be help-ing Duke Guidobaldo must be punished. As an example to others this prisoner was to be publicly executed. But in the way of the governor of the Romagna, Remiro de Lorqua, it was decided that he should be tortured first. The streets around the market were so crammed with people I had been unable to avoid the sight of the man's body being stripped back to reveal the living flesh beneath. His screams and cries for mercy penetrated above the noise of the crowds. In contrast the old man, Umberto, lay here on the table unprotesting, dignified in death.

I saw then, suddenly, that this was why Father Benedict, the mortuary monk, had told us the man's name. It was so that we would be respectful to the person of Umberto, who, although dead, occupied his own place in creation.

I watched my master work. He peeled back the skin on both sides, and the ribs with their coating of human tissues lay revealed. Again he used a swab, this time to wipe down these exposed parts. Then he took a little saw and attacked the ribcage. It might seem a paradox, for to dissect a man is indeed an act of butchery, but the Maestro did this with grace and consideration.

There was noise when he began to saw through the bones at each side. It was unlike any I had ever heard before. More cruel, it seemed, than when a dog tears at a hunk of meat, more visceral than the sound of a hungry man ripping the limbs from a chicken.

Blood.

My head swam. I gasped. The acrid smell of my own piss caught the back of my throat and I coughed and regained my senses.

My master smiled at me and looked directly into my eyes. 'The dizziness will pass,' he whispered. 'Be steady.'

I held fast.

He reached into the well of the body. Then he became quite

still. He was staring at something he held in his hand. A pulpy brownish organ, heavy and plump.

It was Umberto's heart. The flesh quivered. My own heart trembled in response.

'Look,' he said. 'Look, Matteo.'

I swayed, but he did not notice.

'This is the heart. Only hours ago it was pulsing as ours is now.'

I nodded to show I understood.

'It is not so great, is it?'

'But it is,' I said, voice muffled by the mask.

'And yet, without it a man cannot live.' He continued as if he had not heard my response.

I saw that he was not really talking to me, more musing aloud.

'Yes, it is vital, because injuring it means death, whereas losing a limb can be survived . . .'

I knew this. A man can exist without an arm or a leg. I saw a man once with neither arms nor legs. He made his living telling stories. Propped up in a chair and wrapped in an old blanket, he would tell tales at dusk beside the great fountain in the public gardens of Bologna.

'You want to find out why the heart stopped beating?' I asked.

'I would also like to know how it began beating.'

This I did not comprehend. Did he mean how a life began? Surely he must know how young are made. Even I, as a boy, knew this. I had seen it happen often enough with the horses at the gypsy camps. Each year in the season a stallion is brought to the mares for covering. Many gypsies would meet up for this event and pay for a special stallion to impregnate their mares. The male of the species has the organ for that function and that is why he has been given it. It is much the same between a man and a woman. My grandmother explained it to me. The seed comes from the man. Within the cavity of the woman's body is a chamber where the baby grows until it is time to be born. The man must plant his seed in the woman, and this happens when the man goes into the woman when they lie together. It gives great pleasure to do this. It can happen that they do it once only, in error, in lust, or in love, and a child can be formed. And once formed it cannot be unformed. But equally a man and a woman can do this thing many times and a child may not appear.

To bring forth sons to rule, and women to attend to them, requires more than copulation. Even though my grandmother sold medicine to women desperate to conceive, there were some she knew whose wombs would never bear fruit. And all the money and power in the world cannot guarantee that you will have a child just because you want one. The King of France had to petition the Pope to have his marriage annulled because his first wife could not produce an heir.

The Maestro spoke again. 'When we are not, at what point do we become?'

I could not reply. For I had grasped no shape of his thoughts. I understood neither what he said nor his intent behind it.

'Yes,' he went on. '*That* is what I would like to know. But for the moment I will content myself with discerning how this heart ceased to move.'

'Father Benedict told us,' I murmured. 'It was God's will.'

'These passages here' – my master pointed a bloodied finger – 'are the ones crucial to its function.'

'How do you know this?'

'I have dissected animal bodies, for my own interest . . . and previously done some work on human remains.'

By this time I had already guessed that he had experience of performing dissections on dead humans. I supposed it must have been on criminals executed for crimes and therefore, although useful for studying anatomy for painting or sculpture, it would not be of so much interest for investigating the cause of death, this being whatever method the executioner had employed.

'I think we can conclude that it was the man's great age that caused the heart to stop. The passageways are narrowed and the blood has been halted.'

'As rivers silt up and slow down the water flow?' I questioned him.

'Indeed!' He looked at me with approval. 'Exactly like that.'

I thought of my grandmother's heart, struggling inside the cage of her chest. Her body reducing as she entered old age. Her skin and bones like those of the vagrant, Umberto, lying dead before me, dry and thin.

This man whom I called Maestro, with his sharp knives and even keener mind, ventured into an unknown land. And he did it for more than passing curiosity. For I could see the truth, at least in part, of what he had said to the mortuary monk. If we discover a problem we can explore a way to solve it. For it was plain what had happened here to the heart of Umberto. With age the canals going in and out had narrowed and restricted the blood flow. But knowing did not help. There would have been no way to clear those pathways so that my grandmother could have lived longer. In the last months she was alive, her heart was staggering under the weight of her years.

I recalled my grandmother taking my hand and placing it upon her thin chest. Under the rickle of bones beneath her withered breasts I felt the flickering, unsteady rhythm. Within the cavity of her body her heart fluttered, shook, then steadied itself. My grandmother had known that her body was wearing out, but she did not know exactly what was happening.

'Perhaps this is how my grandmother died,' I said.

'What age was she?'

I could not answer that question. With us age was a thing not measured in years. The seasons are how we mark our passing through this life. She had lived many seasons on this earth. This was the second summer that had passed since I had buried her metal goods and papers and watched her wagon burn. I shrugged. 'Very old,' I replied.

My master looked at me curiously. 'I didn't know that you knew your grandmother, Matteo. You've never mentioned her before.'

My fingers gripped the lamp. I did not speak. When I'd related my life history in those first days that we'd spent in the keep of Perela I'd declared myself an abandoned orphan. I had not referred to my grandmother.

I had been caught out!

Chapter Eleven

'Your grandmother?'
  I blinked.
    My master paused in his examination. 'Matteo?' he prompted me. 'You said that your grandmother was old when she died.'

'I – I . . .' I cast my eyes down and mumbled a few non-committal words.

He returned to his work. While he was busy with this other part of the anatomy I would have time to contrive some fictitious stories about my grandmother. I relaxed a little.

'Were there more in your family than your grandmother?'

I wasn't ready to reply, but he didn't seem to notice my upset and went on smoothly, 'I noted that when you told your story in Perela at one point you said "we".'

My gaze flickered in alarm.

'It was when you were talking of the time you were in Venice.' He smiled encouragingly. 'You indicated that you were with others when you watched the boats in the lagoon. Was it your grandmother you were with then? And when you said "we", did you mean only your grandmother, or are there others in your family?'

My heart turned with fear.

'I – I don't remember saying "we",' I stammered. 'It is nothing. A way of speech . . . bad grammar. I am not educated.'

'No, no, it's not that. Your grammar's very good, though a little old fashioned. If it was from your grandmother that you learned speech and vocabulary, then she taught you well. You say you were originally from a hill farm in the Apennines, and yet in their speech some vowel sounds have an edge that you don't often hear anywhere else. It's because of how they position the tongue when forming the "u" and the "o". They place it more to the front part of the mouth. You don't do this, Matteo. But if you spent time with your grandmother, whose family roots are elsewhere, then you probably picked up some of her speech inflections. But where was she raised? Do you know? It would be interesting to find out. There are phrases you pronounce with an almost eastern flavour.'

I did not reply. I could not. Was he a magician that he knew these things? To discover so much about me in the few weeks that we had been together meant he must have been studying me closely, yet I had not been aware of his attention.

He gave me a quizzical glance. 'And your use of "we" contains more than linguistic meaning. It's as though you think of yourself as being different.' He looked at me carefully. 'At first I took you to be a gypsy, but now I'm not so sure. Your skin tone is lighter than most of those folk. Although that was not the only reason, because skin tone is not consistent in any race. The travelling people are supposed to have smaller hands and feet, and you appear to have this feature. But it's more than that. It's to do with your independent way. You hold yourself distinct . . . apart.'

I shook my head.

'You should not be ashamed of your origins, Matteo.'

At this I raised my head and looked at him fiercely. I had no shame of my grandmother or her people.

'Ah!' He recoiled. '*There*, I touched a nerve.'

He had stopped working and was looking at me curiously. I dipped my head to avoid his gaze.

'Now here is a mystery,' he said slowly. 'When we were at

Perela I learned from your own lips that you were a bastard child and that you were embarrassed by this. I know that you feel humbled at having been born out of wedlock because you told me so yourself. Yet' – he stretched forward and tipped up my chin so that he could see my face – 'yet when I mention your origins you glare at me in fury.'

He took a moment to study my face. But the pad of cloth he had given me concealed my mouth and nose, and I had recovered myself enough to veil the expression in my eyes.

'Well?'

I was not going to escape without replying.

'I am not angry,' I said. 'I take any slight to my grandmother as a personal insult. Yes, you are right, she did look after me . . . for a while.'

'And she was your first teacher.'

'Yes.'

'Your only teacher?'

I nodded my head. And then, feeling compelled to defend the one person who had ever shown me love in my early life, I said, 'She taught me many things. She was full of knowledge, but more with the wisdom of years and lore learned from nature than with any book learning.'

'But that's the best kind!' my master cried. 'I don't despise that at all. As a child I wasn't taught Latin so the texts of the great minds of the past were denied to me. I feel that loss deeply and have taken pains to try to remedy the situation. I've learned Latin so that I may study certain writings in the original. These have included treatises on the human body and I absorbed their teachings. But now, as I progress in my own study of animal life forms, and when I anatomize a human body, I am beginning to find that I shouldn't lean too heavily on received wisdom.'

He waited. He seemed to expect me to contribute to the conversation. And I was beginning to learn that not to speak when you were expected to could attract more attention than remaining silent.

'My grandmother made her own observations and deductions on illness and injury to the body,' I said. 'At times she was in conflict with the doctors.'

'She was a healer?'

I nodded.

'Then she was a wise woman to trust her own wisdom. There's only one way to truly know a subject, and that's to explore and examine it oneself. I am compiling my own treatise on each subject that interests me, using drawing and text to combine the fullest coverage than I am able to make.' He indicated the cavity of the body open before him. 'This is why it is important that I conduct my own dissections, that I examine every part in detail, and make drawings and notes of each aspect as I see it.' He pointed to the paper lying on the smaller table, on which he had paused to draw and write from time to time.

I glanced at the paper. And then again.

At first I did not realize what was written there, because at that time I did not know many words to read. My grandmother had instructed me in her folklore, so I knew most plants and herbs and how to make healing preparations from them. I could not spell the words for dog or cat, but I knew the Latin, Sicilian, Florentine, French, Catalan and Spanish for cold cures, stomach ache, pox, plague, gout and the cramps that women take when they have their monthly flux. I could recognize some words my grandmother had taught me, but those words were mainly names. Firstly my own name, Janek, and then others to memorize. This was so that I was able to deliver orders to our customers. I had to take care of this in every town we passed through.

The family Scutari in the Via Veneto require an ointment to help with an outbreak of boils.

Maria Dolmetto, who lives above the shop of the candle maker, needs a salve for her bunions.

A poultice for the child of Ser Antonio. You will find the father at the notary office just off the Piazza Angelo.

Deliver this flask to Alfredo, who keeps the inn at the Mereno gate. He has the falling sickness and needs an infusion.

And not only for people but for horses also. The horse trainers from the noble households sought out our remedies for their prize stallions, the brood mares, or sickly foals. We were cheaper than the apothecaries and our medicines sometimes more effective. My grandmother had a reputation for healing and easing pain.

So, though I could not read fully, I was familiar with the forms of the Florentine language that my master spoke and wrote. But the words that he marked on the paper this night were not in any script that I had seen before. At first I thought it the language of the Jews, or the letters used by the Turks and the Muslim men, yet as I looked more closely I saw that it was not either language.

And then I saw another thing. There was an oddity in how he placed the pen to his paper. When he drew he would use both hands, transferring the chalk or pen from one to the other, from right to left, seemingly without noticing. But when he wrote he used his left hand. Yet his act of writing was not awkward, as was the norm with left-handed people, the paper at an angle and the hand bent like a hook. The Maestro wrote seamlessly from right to left. I watched as he did it. This was a clever trick, so that his hand did not obscure the work.

But still I could not puzzle it out. How could he read it then? How could anyone read it? Were the words in the wrong order? Or did he think backwards inside his head, and write it that way upon the paper, to enable the reader to read in the correct order. I leaned closer. I peered at his writing, but I could make nothing of it.

Then I saw why, and my soul chilled like marble.

His writing was running left to right. Not the words in reverse order, but the letters themselves. All of it. It was mirror writing – to be read by the Devil.

He must have heard my intake of breath.

'You will find it difficult to read this writing, Matteo.'

'Why do you write thus?' I asked him. 'How is it that you can read what you yourself have written?'

'I've become accustomed to it.' And then, without pausing, he said, 'Tell me more of your grandmother.'

'There is nothing much to tell.' In my head I had constructed a story to satisfy him which I now related. 'I lived with her at different times of my life. But she was old and could not take care of me, so I found work here and there. Then she died and I was on my own.'

'How did she live? No, let me guess,' he added before I could reply. 'She was a healer and she sold her medicines to those who had need of them?'

I nodded warily.

'And she didn't charge much. Being poor herself and *simpatico*, she would not wish to make a profit from the pain of others.'

How could he do this? Assess so accurately the character of my grandmother, never having met her, and with the briefest of information from me?

His eyes gleamed as he saw from my expression that he was correct.

'My guess is that, as her reputation grew, people with money and title sought her out and preferred her remedies to those of the doctors and the established apothecaries.' He waited for my reaction. I was still too stunned to speak but gave a slight incline of my head. He went on in the manner of a man hunting, who sees his prey ready to be caught. 'So I think . . . I think then that these professionals and guildsmen would see her as a threat and she, not being wealthy and of little status, could easily be driven out of her business. She would probably have to move on from town to town. Did you meet up with her when this was happening? Yes, that would explain your complexion. You have lived outdoors for a great part of your life, Matteo.'

Now that he had made me disclose the existence of my grandmother, what else did he wish to know? Or already guess at?

Chapter Twelve

It was almost daylight when we returned from the mortuary. Cold dawn was beating back the winter dark. Thin fog drifted up from the river. This is when the dead who have walked abroad hurry back to their graves before daylight catches them and destroys their soul.

I stayed close to my master, almost running to keep up with his long stride. He was humming a catchy folk tune that country people sing at harvest time. He had worked through the night, cutting, exploring, dissecting; uncovering layer upon layer of once-living organs. I held the lamp while he measured and made notes, checking and rechecking dimensions, then sketching what he saw; sometimes swiftly and precisely in one smooth flow, at other times painstakingly, with tiny strokes, delineating the minute threads of blood vessels and veins.

The lamp was not heavy but my arm ached with the effort of keeping it held in one place. Once he reached behind him blindly with one hand while the other held some part of the body unknown to me. I realized that he required scissors and I picked them up and gave them to him. He gave a start, and I saw then that, far from appreciating my efforts at standing still for so long and keeping the light steady, he had forgotten I was there. He did not rest until we heard the chanting of the monks at their morning office and the stirrings of the hospital making ready for a new day.

Now I was exhausted, yet he strode towards the castle, energy thrumming through his whole being.

We had to wait until the night guards identified us properly before we were admitted. The gatekeepers gave him curious glances but did not ask what business he had been about. They knew the Maestro to be under the protection of their commander, Cesare Borgia, and that it would go ill with anyone who questioned or delayed him. But their security was tight, and we had to pass three checkpoints before we entered under the ramparts. These soldiers did not operate in the same relaxed fashion as the ones at Perela. Being closer to the Borgia head-quarters at Imola meant that the guards here were vigilant at all times.

The castle of Averno was much larger than the keep of Captain dell'Orte, and its fortifications more robust. In addition to the castle wall it had a moat and a drawbridge. My master was instructing the builders in raising the wall and making abutments to install more cannon. Every day he drew plans for strengthen-ing the defences, and constructed diagrams and models of complicated war machines. Copies of the drawings were dis-patched with messengers for inspection by Cesare Borgia, while the models were placed on shelves in his studio awaiting the day Il Valentino would arrive at the castle to approve them.

After we arrived in Averno, Felipe went to Florence to order and bring back more of the particular supplies that the Maestro required to do his work. He had hardly left when Graziano took to his bed, ill with a sickness in his stomach. That was when it fell to me to attend to a variety of things: the Maestro's clothes, meals, and keeping his workplace tidy, so that he was not troubled with the daily minutiae of living.

He was fastidious in his toilet, requiring a clean shirt and underclothes every morning, and I, following a practice of my grandmother, asked the castle laundry women to hang lavender beside his shirts as they dried.

He noticed at once and made a comment: 'Since you have taken over supervising my laundry, Matteo, my shirts smell of something better than washing soap.'

It could hardly be counted as great praise, but I was ridiculously pleased. I made sure that his clothes were in good repair and his boots and shoes well polished. In the studio I kept his drawing implements in order, and laid out fresh supplies of paper each day. (He used an enormous amount of paper.) And I fetched and carried for him as needed. Thus I observed the workings of the castle and all that happened within it.

The stable block was extended to make room for more horses. Storerooms were cleared out and fresh supplies of wheat, barley, bran, millet and chickpeas stacked away. Butts of wine, barrels of dried fruit, salted fish and preserved meat were rolled down into the cellars. Quantities of animal fodder, chaff, straw and hay piled high in the yards. Stone was transported from the quarries at Bisia, huge blocks trundling through the gate each day in bullock carts. Tiles, timber and other building materials were brought in on river barges and unloaded on the wharves below the town. The castle was being prepared for action – possibly to withstand a siege.

For now, in the Romagna and further afield, wild tales were beginning to circulate – stories of double dealing by the condottieri, the mercenary military captains who had promised Cesare Borgia their loyalty and had brought their own troops to fight for him. It was said that these captains had become disillusioned by Cesare and fearful of his ever-increasing power, and that they were alarmed at how easily he turned on a person who had pledged him friendship. And the name of the town Urbino was the example they used.

Earlier this year Duke Guidobaldo of Urbino had received and welcomed Cesare Borgia's sister, Lucrezia, as she travelled on her way from Rome to Ferrara for her wedding. To show Lucrezia due honour Duke Guidobaldo had given over his magnificent palace of Montefeltro to Lucrezia and her retinue. He had hosted a ball in her honour and lavished many gifts upon her. But his generosity had not protected him from the ambition of Lucrezia's brother, who later marched in and took his city.

Afterwards Cesare Borgia proclaimed loudly that his actions were necessary: he had received evidence that the duke was plotting against him. No proof of this was ever shown. But everyone knew that the mountain stronghold of Urbino commanded the passes through the Romagna and Tuscany. Cesare needed to be sure that his armies could move freely as he wanted them, and that was the real reason he took the dukedom of Urbino for himself.

This act shocked all Italy. The other lords and princelings believed that their positions were threatened, and that Cesare and his father, the Pope, had become tyrants who would not stop until they had brought the whole land under their own dominion.

In Averno, kitchen gossip had it that the nobles wanted to fight back. Rumours told of a secret league, a conspiracy to bring down Il Valentino, involving the condottieri captains. But I had seen the Borgia's swift justice so I did not take part in this careless talk. It was a time to be watchful and say little.

The Maestro put his hand on my shoulder as we walked to the suite of rooms set aside for him.

'Matteo, it is better that you do not discuss where this night visit has taken us.' It was in his nature that he did not make me promise to keep silent. Once he had admitted a person to his circle of friends he put faith in them. I believe that he thought if he trusted someone then that was enough to make that person trustworthy. He was careful about his most personal thoughts and his private affections, and he kept his work secret with mirror writing and symbols known only to him. Yet he freely welcomed people into his household, sharing meals, jokes and stories with them.

When we reached his rooms in the castle I set the lantern down and waited for permission to go and rest for a while. I slept in a little room just off his studio where he could call me if he needed me.

'You are disturbed by our visit to the mortuary tonight?' He set out pen and ink and fresh paper. Obviously he was going to continue working.

'What you do is . . . strange,' I said.

'It's not so uncommon a practice to do an anatomy of a body.'

This was true. I had heard of corpses being used in this way by universities. Usually it was the dead bodies of criminals, executed for some transgression against the state. Sometimes sculptors were allowed to observe or even take part in these dissections in order to help them portray their bronze and marble statues as real flesh.

'It will prove useful for many branches of science,' my master went on. 'But there are those who, through fear or ignorance, would make trouble about it.'

'The mortuary monk,' I replied, 'Father Benedict. He might speak of what you were doing.'

'A good point, Matteo. That order of hospitaller monks has no vow of silence in its ordinances.' He thought for a moment. 'But no. I do not think Father Benedict will tell anyone of our visit. My feeling is that he was very aware of how my work might be viewed by others of a more limited understanding.'

'He frightened me.'

My master looked at me with interest. 'Why?'

'He seemed to say that what you were doing was wrong.'

'He didn't go quite as far as to state that.'

'What if he reports you to the authorities?'

'I don't think he will.'

'He argued with you. Did you not think that he was very annoyed?'

'Not at all.'

'He threatened you.'

'Not so,' said my master. 'Father Benedict was enjoying a challenging discussion. Didn't you see how his eyes were enlivened as he deliberated on whether he should let me have access to those in his care?'

While he was speaking the Maestro took a piece of charcoal and with a few lines drew quickly on the paper in front of him.

I gasped.

He had captured Father Benedict's likeness in several little cartoons. His first sketch showed the monk standing at the head of the prostitute. The girl's hair cascaded down each side of her face like rivulets of rain. Father Benedict's hands offered his blessing as he leaned over her. Compassion showed in every line of the monk's figure, in every shadow that was shown, and not shown.

I looked at my master. I thought of when we first entered the mortuary room. How his mind must have been working: thinking on his scientific research, weighing up which body to choose, measuring his interest against the bodies available, and at the same time debating the ethics of the situation as the monk demurred. He'd led the monk in his evaluation of Art to the point where he had to concede that the Word of God was finely portrayed by an artist who utilized the study of anatomy to do it. My master had done all this, and argued lucidly with the monk, while memorizing every detail of his face.

The Maestro drew again, this time only half a face, a nose, a brow, an eye, the mouth.

'I know Father Benedict enjoyed the debate,' he said. 'You see, he had a habit of frowning when arguing. There was a little line that appeared at the bridge of his nose just at the point where it meets the brow.' The Maestro reached out and touched the bridge of my nose lightly with the tip of his finger. 'But it was not a bad-tempered scowl, more that his face showed the energy of his mind when he had to think to reply to me.' My master tapped the paper. 'It wasn't there when he was on safer ground quoting Scripture.'

'Because he has learned that by heart,' I said.

'Why yes, Matteo!' The Maestro glanced up at me for fleeting second. 'How perceptive of you to realize that.'

His hand began to sketch again as he spoke.

'What you say is true. And also the monk believes the verse, so maybe the mystery of the words is now lost to him, or—' The Maestro broke off and said, half to himself, 'No, perhaps better to say in this particular monk's case, at any rate, that he has absorbed the Word so thoroughly that he could repeat it fluently without having to ponder on it.'

I waited, not knowing if my master had finished, unable to comprehend completely the meaning of his speech.

'Do you understand what I am saying, Matteo? He believes the Word. Has given himself over to it, and therefore it is part of him. He lives Christ's Word, obeys the Lord's teaching to feed those who are ill and unfortunate.'

'Fortunate for those who are in need and have nowhere else to go,' I replied. 'Do you mean he no longer thinks of the meaning, that he just says the words?'

'Why do you ask that?'

'Because it does not have any true value if you do that. Anyone can recite a passage from Scripture.'

He looked at me keenly. 'Like what?' he asked.

My heart jumped. Was he testing me?

His hand was still drawing, but I knew he expected an answer. His brain, I now appreciated, could deal intently with more than two things at the same time. I would have to recite some passage to him. It would show if I were Christian or not. But I was confident I could pass this test. My grandmother had liked to read aloud psalms and passages from the Bible, and I had an accurate memory for rich language.

'Oh, any well-known piece,' I replied carelessly.

'Quote me now.'

My mind stumbled. Then I recalled the mortuary monk and his

reference to the Book of Genesis where Adam and Eve were banished from the Garden of Eden. I took this as a guide and said: '*And when they heard the voice of the Lord God, Adam and his wife hid themselves from the face of the Lord God, amidst the trees of Paradise.*

'*And the Lord God called Adam, and said to him, "Where art thou?"*

'*And Adam said, "I heard Thy voice in Paradise; and I was afraid because I was naked, and I hid myself."*'

'And you think nakedness is wrong?' The Maestro kept on sketching with light strokes but I knew his mind was on our discourse.

'I do not know,' I replied. '"*Naked we came into the world and naked we will go out of it.*"'

'You intrigue me, Matteo. A person who travels alone, yet thinks in the plural. A traveller who is not a traveller. A boy who is not a boy. Dressed like a peasant, you speak like a scholar.'

'If I displease you then I will leave.' I said this stiffly. I had no idea whether I had been insulted or not.

He stopped drawing but he did not raise his head. There was a long silence in the room.

'You do not displease me,' he said finally. 'Far from it. But it must be your decision whether you remain within my company.'

Chapter Thirteen

As the castle of Averno prepared for war my master had less time for his excursions to the mortuary. Yet on the occasions when he did venture out he still chose me to accompany him, even when Felipe came back from Florence and Graziano had recovered from his bellyache. In their absence I had become his constant companion on his daytime trips too. They saw that I knew how to prepare for these excursions and began to leave many of the details involved to me. Thus they came more and more to depend on my presence.

Felipe had returned with two pack mules bearing boxes and packages. In addition to paper, vellum and fresh brushes, he had brought a variety of materials, with some fur and leather skins for new clothes, hats and boots to be made for the da Vinci household members to see them through the winter.

It did not occur to me that I would be included in this outfitting. So it was a great surprise to be summoned by the Master of the Wardrobe in the castle and told that I was to be measured for a suit of clothes and some footwear. Graziano and Felipe were in the wardrobe quarters when I arrived.

In addition to being fond of food Graziano also liked to dress well and was holding an ermine fur draped around his neck.

'Do you think that this makes me look like a great lord?' he asked me as I came in.

The fur only served to emphasize the rolls of fat around

Graziano's neck, which meant that he did indeed look like some of the great lords and princes I had seen in Ferrara and Venice. I nodded, standing back at the door, but Graziano took me by the arm and led me into the room and presented me to Giulio, the Master of the Wardrobe.

This man, Giulio, was very fond of his own opinions and thought himself sophisticated above others. He looked me up and down as the tailor measured my arms and legs. 'I'd advise his hair to be cut,' he said.

'What is wrong with my hair?' I asked. My grandmother had always insisted I kept my hair long and I was used to having it that way.

Giulio wrinkled his nose in distaste. 'Apart from the fact that there's altogether too much of it?'

'In winter it is sensible to have longer hair.'

'What has *sense* got to do with fashion or style?'

Everyone laughed, including the Maestro, who had just entered the room.

Giulio took a comb and flicked my tangle of hair back from my face.

'Let me see what is actually under this horse's mane and what colours and style of clothes might enhance this boy's appearance.'

I stood, still fearful that if I irritated him any more he might suggest my head be shaved in the manner of the stable boys when they were deloused each year.

He bent close to me and said, 'I see you have the mark of the midwife's fingers on the back of your neck. Don't worry – we will trim your hair to hang below your ears.'

I felt my face burn red as I was prodded and inspected and tutted over.

When I tried to protest Felipe looked at me sternly and told me that the master had ordered this.

They talked as if I were not there, pondering the colour of my hose, the style of belt I should wear, and whether my boots must be fitted to above or below the knee. I felt like a doll such as a girl should play with, to dress and decide which clothes it would wear each day.

'They say the French style of sleeve is now the most fashionable in Europe.'

I looked up in surprise. It was my master's voice that had made this comment. He was rummaging among the half-unpacked boxes and parcels, taking out bolts of cloth, brocades and velvets, and setting one colour against another. 'I'd like Matteo to have a padded doublet. He must have clothes well enough for formal appearance. It may be that I want him to stand by my place while I'm at dinner.'

'Too much padding on his torso will serve to emphasize his thin legs,' Giulio demurred.

'I had thought this moss-green hose would suit him?'

'A dark colour certainly,' Giulio agreed, 'but if you put him in green, then, with those legs, he may be mistaken for a grasshopper.'

There was laughter, and I began to feel an edge of irritation to add to my discomfort. I shifted from foot to foot.

Graziano, seeing me standing there, said: 'Why not let Matteo decide?'

'I do not care what style is current,' I said. 'Clothes serve the purpose of cover and warmth.'

'Oh no, Matteo,' said the Maestro. 'Clothes have more purpose than function.'

I should not have been surprised that my master took an interest in these things. The effect of colour and cut was all part of the same attention he gave to everything.

He looked at me. 'Do you wonder, Matteo, if it's such an important issue whether a cloak should have fur stitched on the edge or not?'

'That is not so much a fashion consideration,' I replied. 'The fur of an animal, especially the stoat, is designed to deflect the wind.'

The Maestro was beside me at once. He held out an ermine skin. 'Show me, Matteo.'

I took the pelt and ran my fingers against the lie of the fur. 'See how it springs back into place. The hair grows like that for a purpose, as its coat changes in winter to white ermine to conceal itself in the snow.'

'Why?'

I looked at him as he spoke. He must know the reason for this. I felt again that I was being tested.

'Why?' I repeated. 'In order that it might live.'

'Wouldn't it live in any case?'

'The stoat is prey for birds like kite and hawk. In winter they would see it easily. The fur changes colour the better to conceal the animal as it goes about its own business among snowfall.'

'And how did this come about?'

'By God's hand of course,' said Giulio. 'The nature of things is by God's design.' He and the tailor exchanged looks.

My master did not notice. But Felipe did.

'What else for this boy?' he interrupted. 'Quickly now, Giulio, before Messer Leonardo decides to examine the detail in the knit of each sock.'

Giulio smiled. Felipe had diverted his attention and altered it from mild suspicion to lightheartedness.

'Let us look at the coloured cloth Felipe obtained from Florence,' said Graziano, 'and how these might suit the rest of the ensemble.'

I watched as they rummaged through the fabrics and noticed then that my master himself sought to look comely and innovative. He paired colours that others would not think of, like burgundy with pink or violet and blue, suggesting gold slashes in a tunic of deep green.

'And the boy's hair must be cut,' Giulio called out when we finally left.

So I reported to the castle barber and had my hair cut.

Then like a shorn sheep I went back to the Maestro's rooms.

'Why, Matteo, you do have eyes under that head of hair after all,' said Graziano when he saw me.

They were sitting on stools together as I entered the studio.

The Maestro called me over, and taking me by the chin he studied my face. 'His features do remind me of some painting or other,' he mused. 'Your brow has depth, and your lips full rounded out. The cheekbones are well set, which is good, as that will define your look as you mature. I think you could aspire to be haughty, Matteo, if you so wished.'

I lowered my head and tried to escape his grasp but he led me to a large mirror which he had placed against one wall of the room. He had set this mirror at an angle opposite the window so that no matter where he worked in the room he could see the outside view. This seemed to please him, but having this reflective glass indoors uncovered, and having to pass back in front of it, made me uneasy.

I was not comfortable in the sight of mirrors. It was something that my grandmother and I had disagreed upon. 'You have superstitious blood in your veins,' she chided me when I insisted that we kept any mirror we owned covered up.

But I had listened to the stories round the campfires of the other travellers and I knew that a person's soul could be lost within their reflection.

My grandmother laughed at this belief. 'A mirror is polished metal shaped for the purpose, or a piece of glass with liquid metal painted on behind it and left to dry. It is a simple thing: some elements have this property. Water, which is the source of all life, is one of them. On a still day if you look into a lake you will see yourself and the sky.'

'But,' I replied, 'see what happened to Narcissus who, looking into a pool of water, saw himself and mistook it for another person of great beauty. He fell in love with this reflection and would not leave the image and spent the rest of his days there waiting for this hopeless love. And being for ever unrequited, he pined and died and flowers grew up at that place.'

My grandmother shook her head. 'This is a tale invented by the ancients to explain why the flower called narcissus often grows beside water.'

But I was not convinced. There must be some truth in the tale, that the water acted as a mirror and pinned Narcissus beside the lake. Why else would such a story be conceived?

'Because we do not understand everything, Matteo,' my grandmother answered. 'And being human we always seek to try to do so.'

I remembered now that he, the Maestro, had said this too: *We strive to understand.*

'And when we cannot do so,' my grandmother continued, 'then we make up stories to explain what we think is unexplainable. In the olden days we thought of the sun in those terms. Men told the tale that light came to earth from the great god Ra, who was born each day as a child and died at night as an old man, and was carried in a golden chariot across the sky. We know now that this is not true. So also do we know that there is nothing to fear from a reflected image.'

In the case of a mirror, though, I was not convinced that there was not a charm therein. The story of Narcissus is one of many told about those who become trapped for ever behind a looking glass. So, as the master led me to look at myself, I only glanced in the mirror. That is, I only meant to glance briefly, but my attention was caught by the figure there.

I stared.

The boy in the mirror stared back.

I did not know him. His appearance was both strange and familiar, with ears sticking out, huge eyes and his face full of sharp angles.

The Master must have seen my look of alarm.

'Don't fret,' he said. 'You're in the awkward stage of being neither child nor fully grown. Your baby fat is gone, but you have yet to become adult. It is a difficult time. But I believe that when you fill out in manhood you will make ladies' hearts flutter.'

I pulled my brows together in what I hoped was an ugly frown.

He laughed at me and patted my head. 'If you are trying to be repulsive then you are failing in your ambition. It makes you more interesting when you are fierce, Matteo. When you glare so angrily you have a dangerous air of menace that women will find very attractive.'

I scowled even more and pushed myself away from him abruptly.

'Matteo,' said Graziano kindly, 'you must learn to accept a compliment.'

I had retreated to the furthest corner of the room from where I snapped a reply. 'I did not know that it was a compliment.'

'Even if it wasn't, you mustn't respond to something that displeases you by stamping off and coiling in on yourself,' Felipe pointed out.

'Or by striking out with your hand on a dagger,' said the Maestro.

My breath caught. Was he thinking of the time he saw me put the point of a knife to Paolo's throat?

'You must learn not to react in emotion.'

'Then that is not being true to one's self,' I said.

'One is living in society,' said Graziano mildly.

'There are rules of behaviour,' said Felipe. 'Manners help us get along together, even if one knows some of these courtesies to be a little foolish.'

'All the more reason to keep to one's own way of thinking,' I said stubbornly. 'What you feel here' – I placed my hand on my heart – 'is what is true, and you should act on that.'

'But wouldn't it be better,' said the Maestro, 'if you were in charge of your emotions, rather than them being in command of you?'

'Does that not mean then that they are no longer your emotions?' I asked him.

They laughed but he took my point seriously, as he frequently did.

'I agree that this is hard to determine, especially in youth, when being loyal to oneself is a matter of great importance. And indeed should remain so. But understand me, Matteo, it is not your feelings that we are denying, it is the application of action consequent upon your feelings that we question. Unrestrained action can be disastrous. For yourself and others. Can you appreciate that?'

I mumbled a yes.

'Better to think carefully and then act,' he added. 'It is much more impressive, and effective.'

'That could be a motto for the Borgia,' murmured Graziano.

Felipe glanced his way and at once he was quiet.

Chapter Fourteen

The one part of my old clothing that I did not discard was the thin belt with the pouch that I wore under my tunic. It was not on display, and with my heavier clothes it was well concealed. I had decided, if questioned, to say that it had been a special gift. Although the small weight I carried at my belt was a constant reminder of Sandino, I had not thought of him for some time. We were miles from Perela, south of Bologna and away from Sandino's territory.

My master was working on military things. And so, in addition to etiquette, I acquired information relevant to soldiering and conflict. I learned that one hand's span from the collarbone is a most vulnerable part of a man's body. Situated on the neck is a long blood-carrying column which is vital to life. If it is severed, the blood flows away very fast.

'A knife,' said the Maestro, 'a sharp knife, or sword, applied here' – he placed his hand at the side of my neck – 'would effect death in seconds. It's why I have changed the underclothes of the soldiers.'

He showed me his new design for the chain-mail necklets which hung down from their helmets. While the castle armourers were busy making these the Maestro watched the soldiers training, and stood discussing tactics with the bombardiers in charge of the cannon. He had plans for an immense cannon and was calculating the dimensions and weight of the barrel. It was a puzzle to me that he could love nature yet construct instruments of death. But his salary was not secure. He was not a legitimate son and therefore could not call on any rightful allowance from his father. His whole existence and that of his household relied on the patronage of others.

He still managed to go out into the countryside on occasion and he was interested in the plant lore that I could tell him. He sought to learn each intimate thing about the world we live in. He asked me more about my grandmother and her herbal skills and he wrote down the preparations I could recall. But I did not have all my grandmother's recipes inside my head. Her book had been buried with her goods when she had died.

One day when we were riding a good way beyond the castle wall of Averno, Graziano, who had been groaning and holding his stomach since morning, called on us to stop. He had seen a plant growing by the side of the road. We dismounted and he plucked a leaf and made to eat it. As Graziano had knelt to do so he was on a level with me as I stood beside him. Without thinking I snatched the leaf from his hand as you would from a child about to put some dangerous object in their mouth.

'You must not eat that,' I said.

'It is mint,' he protested. 'It will help my stomach ache.'

'It is not mint,' I replied.

'What have you found?' The Maestro's voice quickened in interest.

Graziano laughed and said, 'I am being given instruction by a boy. Matteo says if I eat this I will die.'

'You will not die,' I said. 'But you would have bellyache before sunset and for many days afterwards.'

'I've taken this mint for a long time because I have constant bellyache.'

'It is not mint,' I repeated. 'It looks like mint, but it is not.'

The Maestro took the plant in his hand and studied it.

'How do you know, Matteo?' He looked at me curiously. 'What makes you say this?'

This was a feature of our relationship. He asked me this not in any way sarcastically. He did not scoff that I, a boy, might know more than he knew.

'It is similar to mint but it grows in a different place,' I told him.

'There are many types of mint,' the Maestro said slowly, 'of different hues, from emerald to almost yellow, and a type called dittany with little flowers, which comes from Crete. Is this not just another variety?'

'No, because the underside of this leaf is patterned in a way that the true mint is not.' I searched around until I found a mint leaf. 'See?'

'I do see, Matteo.' He took the leaf from me. 'Variegated.' He said it again slowly so that I could absorb it. 'Variegated.'

I nodded to show that I had retained the new word.

'That means there is a difference of colour there within the leaf.' He turned it over in his hands. 'It must have mutated from the mint . . . or did mint evolve from it? This is most interesting.'

'Mint has been used in cooking since before Rome was ancient,' said Graziano stubbornly. 'Its properties to aid digestion are well known.'

'This one *unaids* digestion,' I said equally stubbornly. 'We would give it to animals to bring on vomiting if we thought they needed to relieve other sickness within them.'

'Graziano,' said the Maestro, 'remind me if you would. When did you first have bellyache?'

'Do we need reminding?' joked Felipe. 'The whole world knows when Graziano is unwell!'

'I was ill with the summer sickness from the plains around Milan more than two years ago,' said Graziano. 'The weather was humid. I was recommended to chew mint leaf, which helped me. Thereafter I take it as I find it.'

'You've been plagued with bellyache ever since then,' said the Maestro. 'Don't you see what's happened? You were ill and were prescribed mint, which does help, but then, as we have been travelling, you have picked up this false mint and, far from easing your stomach, it has made it worse.'

'Also you eat too much,' I added. Which was the truth. I had seen him do it late last night. 'If you overfill your stomach just before going to bed then in the mornings you will feel sick.'

'Speak plainly, Matteo!' Felipe roared with laughter.

The Maestro joined in. I looked from one to the other. I was not aware I had made a joke.

The Maestro clapped me on the shoulder. 'A child sees with the eyes of truth!'

Graziano hung his head in mock contrition. 'I cannot deny that I enjoy my food.'

'Enjoy less of a meal at night and you may enjoy breakfast more,' advised Felipe.

'Let me take a moment to sketch this,' said the Maestro. His friends exchanged indulgent glances as he sat down upon a rock. He looked up at them. 'It will only take a moment.'

'Like Graziano's meals,' quipped Felipe. But he said this softly so as not to disturb the Maestro, who had already begun to draw.

One of the items that Felipe brought when he returned from Florence was a supply of notebooks. These were made up by the bookbinders to the Maestro's precise dimensions so that he could carry one always at his belt. He could fill a notebook within one day, covering the pages with drawings and writings. So, although he never forgot a drawing or a note he had made, and all who worked in his studio knew that each sheet of even the roughest drawing must be kept carefully, it was tremendously difficult to keep any count or order to his manuscripts. His brain accumulated knowledge of every kind and he poured it back out in his sketches, stories, fables and many, many notations.

He quickly became absorbed – not just with this one plant but with others in the shady place where we had stopped. In the end we spent the day there. Felipe and Graziano kept loving and watchful eyes upon him. The Maestro laid out leaves or flowers or plants when he had finished drawing them and they would pick them up and press them carefully between special sheets of paper. They made sure that food was close by, some bread and a bottle containing wine mixed with water. I did what I could to help, grazing the horses, taking them to drink at the river, searching under the trees a little way off to seek out any unusual specimen that I could discover. Finally he raised his head. He called me over.

'Do you know this plant?'

'I know it. We call it—' I began. Then I stopped. I must learn not to say 'we' when referring to my people. 'In the countryside it is called the Star of Bethlehem.'

He showed me the page. It was a wonderment to me. He had very accurately drawn the leaf, the stalk and the tiny fibrous hairs that curled underneath.

There was something else lying beside him.

He saw my glance and asked, 'What do you make of that, Matteo?'

'It is a fossil, an animal that lived long ago.'

He turned the pages and showed me where he had drawn it too, and also drawings of rocks of differing shapes and sizes.

'Maestro,' I said, 'as an engineer, you are under a commission from Il Valentino, Cesare Borgia, to improve his castles to withstand attack. I know you are also a painter, but that is not the only reason you dissect and anatomize for you seek medical knowledge. Now you declare an interest in plants and rocks. What is your field of study?'

'All.'

'All what?'

He laughed. 'I seek to know about *everything*. I have an enquiring mind.' He placed his finger on my forehead. 'As I note that you have too.'

I recalled being at the dissecting table with him one time and leaning closer to watch what he was doing. He had paused, moved his hand to one side and said, 'Look then carefully, Matteo, and see what you can discover for yourself.'

He was examining the tongue under a magnifying glass. When we returned to his studio in the castle he had searched among his drawings for one of a lion and shown it to me. He then related how when he had worked for the Duke of Milan there was a lion kept in a pit in the castle there. One day he had sat and watched the beast, by using only its rough tongue, lick the skin off a lamb before eating it. He pointed to his drawing and said, 'The lion's tongue is particular to that purpose.'

Thus he educated me in many things and in return I gave him my knowledge of plants. I had no schooling but I knew what could cure and what could kill. I knew the herbs that healed and I knew the poisons.

I knew the poisons very well.

But that day, seeing then that the light was fading, the Maestro closed his notebook.

We packed up his botanical specimens and returned to Averno. Awaiting us at the castle was a summons from Cesare Borgia. Il Valentino had sent a message from his winter quarters at Imola. He wished Leonardo da Vinci and his household to join him there without delay.

Chapter Fifteen

B
y the evening of the next day we were in Imola.

The braziers burning on the castle walls lit up Cesare Borgia's black and yellow pennants fluttering from the towers. A swarthy man with a flaming torch came to meet us as our horses clattered across the bridge and under the flag with the emblem of the grazing bull.

'Messer Leonardo,' he said, 'I am Michelotto, personal henchman of Prince Cesare Borgia. His lordship, Il Valentino, wishes to speak to you immediately you arrive.'

'I am at his command.'

The Maestro glanced at Felipe, who nodded slightly and said, 'I will see to the accommodation and the unpacking of our things.'

'Let Matteo take my satchel and come with me and I can send him to you to fetch any further drawings or models the prince may require.'

We followed after the man called Michelotto as he conducted us through the corridors into the presence of the most feared man in Italy. When we entered the room on the first floor of the castle, Cesare Borgia rose from his seat behind a table and came to greet us. Not yet thirty, he was tall and walked with grace and determination. Despite his face being marked by what was called the French disease, he was darkly handsome with shrewd eyes. He wore a black tunic, finely stitched and corded, black breeches and long black leather boots. The only colour on his person was in the form of a ring upon the middle finger of his left hand. A heavy gold ring set with an enormous single ruby, red as blood.

'We have a crisis, Messer Leonardo.' He grasped the Maestro by his shoulder and led him to the table. 'My spies' – he inclined his head, and it was then that I noticed two men standing in the shadows of the room – 'have forewarned me to prepare for a siege.' He laughed, and somehow the sound of this laugh was more terrifying than a shout of anger. 'In this castle, here in Imola, I, Cesare Borgia, am to be attacked by my former captains. Therefore, with urgency, I need your advice on defence and military installations.'

He snapped his fingers and a servant leaped forward to take my master's cloak. We went to the table and I opened the satchel and took out the design papers for the new armour and war machines. Then I stood to one side as the Borgia and the Maestro laid these out and studied them, together with plans of the castle. For several hours my master made notes and sketches until they had agreed on the most immediate work to be done.

Then Cesare said, 'You must be hungry. Eat now and we will talk later.' He waved his hand in dismissal.

'Are all of his captains in this plot?'

We were in our quarters, a suite of rooms in another part of the castle.

Felipe replied to the Maestro's question in a voice barely above a whisper. 'It would appear so.'

'Even my friend, Vitellozzo?'

Felipe glanced towards the door and nodded.

The Master sighed heavily. 'Then his life is forfeit.'

'Drink some wine,' Felipe urged him.

Graziano had obtained food and drink from the kitchen and we sat down to eat while they discussed the situation in low voices.

The Borgia family wanted all Italy under their rule, but even with the papal armies in his command, Cesare had not enough men or arms to do this. He needed to make use of mercenaries and the armies of any who would back his ambition. With some support therefore he had taken much of the Romagna. But now his captains had become uneasy at his ambition and ruthlessness, and, fearing that he would turn on them, were conspiring with the deposed lords against him. Graziano had heard from the servants in the castle that it was common knowledge that the conspirators had met near Perugia to plot the downfall of the Borgias.

'Don't look so worried, Matteo.' Graziano smiled at me. 'Prince Cesare Borgia regards us with favour. But should the castle of Imola fall, one of the rebel captains, a man called Vitellozzo Vitelli, is a friend of the Maestro.'

Nevertheless I was uneasy. I had felt safe in a Borgia stronghold where Sandino might not look for me. It was a different matter to be in the place where Cesare Borgia himself resided. He had mentioned reports being brought to him by his spies. I had seen these men about the castle and I knew that Sandino acted as a Borgia spy. Sandino, who would still want to recover what I had taken from him. What would that vile brigand have been doing in the weeks when he had not found me? Some other murderous deed, no doubt, for whoever paid him most.

I did not sleep well that night. And neither did another, for Cesare Borgia was rarely seen during daylight and roamed the palace during the hours of darkness plotting revenge on those who had betrayed him.

Chapter Sixteen

We began at first light the next day.

There was a meeting with the commander of the castle and then, furnished with my master's drawings and details of the adjustments, the stonemasons and joiners were set to work. In the afternoon the Maestro summoned me to come with him and we went out into Imola.

Over the next days he paced out every street of the town, from the Franciscan church to the river, from the castle to the cathedral, with me by his side as he measured, calculated, noted and drew.

I, pretending to feel the cold, had the cowl of my cloak drawn close to keep my face hidden as I walked each alley with him carrying his materials. In the late afternoon he inspected the improvements being done to the fortress and made further changes as necessary. After his evening meal he set out his paper and worked on his plan of the town.

When the map of Imola was finally presented to him Cesare Borgia was amazed and delighted.

'Never have I seen such an image,' he declared. He put it on the table before him and walked round it to study it from every angle. 'With this I can see as if I were an eagle. Such power it gives me! Even if the town was taken, with this information we could devise a strategy for a counter attack.' His eyes glittered. 'Imagine if I had such a plan for every city and town in Italy!'

He was so pleased that he attended our apartments to dine with us that evening, and so it was he heard the fable my master told as entertainment after we had eaten.

It was the story of the nut and the campanile and went thus:

A nut was carried off by a crow to the top of a tall bell tower. Falling from the crow's beak, the nut became lodged in a crevice in the wall of the building. Saved from its fate of being eaten by the crow, the nut beseeched the bell tower for refuge.

But before it did this the nut first admired the beauty of the campanile, its greatness, height and strength.

'How wonderful you look, noble tower!' said the nut. 'You are so elegant and graceful. Your outline against the sky is beautiful for everyone to see.'

Next the nut praised the tone and appearance of the bells. 'The melodious chimes of your bells sound through the city and out to the far hills. Many stop from their work to listen and enjoy their music.'

Then the nut lamented how it had been prevented from falling from its parent tree upon the green earth.

'A cruel crow has carried me off to this place, but if you, most gracious and generous campanile, could suffer me to shelter within your wall then I will stay quietly and end my days peacefully here.'

And the campanile, moved to pity, agreed.

Time passed. Each day the bells tolled the Angelus from the campanile. The nut rested silently.

But then the nut cracked open, and, from within its shell, fine tendrils stretched out. It put roots among the cracks and crevices. Then it pushed shoots upwards which rose taller than the bell tower itself. Branches appeared, became strong. The roots grew thicker and thrust the stones of the building apart.

Too late the campanile realized that it was being destroyed from within.

Finally it was torn asunder and fell into a ruin.

*   *   *

This tale was not, of course, really about a bell tower. It was a fable to illustrate how a person might cleverly insinuate himself into the life of another, draw sustenance and favour from them, and then with ingratitude betray them.

Did Cesare Borgia take this story unto his own self, and allow his dark mind to reflect upon it as he pondered his situation? Messengers came and went at all times of the day and night, bringing him intelligence as to the whereabouts and the dealings of his former condottieri captains.

So in the last months of 1502 the other city states of Italy waited to see what would be the outcome of the captains' revolt. One in particular, whose territory bordered on that of the Romagna, was anxious to obtain information and dispatched a special emissary to Imola to find out the intentions of Prince Cesare. In previous years the affluent republic of Florence had driven out one powerful ruling family, the Medici, and did not wish them replaced with the another of equal but more sinister power, the Borgia. Thus the Florentine Council sent Messer Niccolò Machiavelli to Imola as their ambassador.

This Machiavelli was an intriguing and witty man and the mood in our apartments altered when he joined us. My master was able to talk of the classics with him, while he and Felipe cautiously discussed the political situation. They agreed as to the menacing demeanour of our host.

'His former captains have now taken for themselves some of the towns he captured,' Machiavelli told us. 'He will never forgive them for this. His manner bodes ill for anyone who has angered him.'

As Christmas approached Il Valentino seemed to be less tense and decided that he would celebrate the holiday season with a dinner. He invited one of his lieutenants, a man who had been known to disagree with him, to attend.

The weather had become intensely cold and we shivered as we

worked. Looking down from the castle wall on the morning of the dinner party, we saw the lieutenant ride in with his wife and retinue. There was to be a banquet that night in the great hall. Cesare himself came to greet them in the courtyard, helping this man's wife from her carriage and kissing them both warmly.

'Such a greeting,' said Graziano, 'should make the lieutenant happy.'

'Or,' murmured Niccolò Machiavelli, who was standing with my master, 'deeply suspicious.'

Chapter Seventeen

The eyes of Cesare Borgia flickered over his dinner guests. His gaze rested on me where I stood beside the Maestro's chair. 'Do we need this boy here?'

'He will fetch my sketches and plans should you require them, my lord,' said the Maestro. 'Matteo knows where everything is kept.'

The dinner began.

I reached out and lifted my master's wine cup. Before I handed it to him I drank from it.

The Maestro's eyes opened in surprise. 'You insult our host,' he said in a low voice.

We both looked to the top of the table. The Borgia had turned his head to listen to his dining companion. She was the wife of the lieutenant who had arrived that morning, and quite beautiful. She smiled at him coquettishly. He laughed.

His guests relaxed.

I did not.

Cesare Borgia ate heartily, but drank little. Frequently he glanced around the table. He had the countenance of a man who has just entered a brothel.

Dessert was announced with a trumpet fanfare. Cherries soaked in liqueur flavoured with *cocoa*, a delicacy brought from the New World. It struck me then that as few people would have tasted this plant it was the perfect opportunity to conceal poison.

I bent and wiped the Maestro's spoon with the napkin. I whispered, 'Do not eat this dish.'

'Tush, Matteo!'

This plate was to be served to every individual separately yet at once. Led by a drummer, a long procession of servants filed into the great hall. They each carried a single plate, and they positioned themselves, one behind each chair, preparatory to placing a dish before each guest.

Across the table from the Maestro sat the lieutenant. This man had displeased Cesare Borgia, and I remembered how, earlier in the afternoon, Il Valentino had made much show to welcome him, embracing the lieutenant in the courtyard as he arrived at the head of his column of soldiers.

But now the lieutenant's men were barracked some distance from this castle. And their commander sat alone at the table of the Borgia.

My eyes met those of the servant who now stood behind his chair. The breath in my chest thickened so that I could not breathe. This was no servant. It was Michelotto, personal henchman of Cesare Borgia.

The Borgia stood up and made a signal. Opposite me, like the other servants, the Borgia henchman, with both hands, placed the dish down on the table over the lieutenant's head. The servants kept their hands on either side of the plate and waited.

The guests at table made appropriate noises of delight at the unusual dish. Some of the ladies applauded. The lieutenant's wife scooped up a cherry and popped it into her mouth.

'Delicious!' she exclaimed. She tilted her head provocatively at Cesare Borgia. 'You must try one.'

He smiled at her but did not make any motion to eat. It was obvious that I was not the only one to have doubts about the strange dish, for although some people lifted their spoons, many hesitated.

As if he had not noticed any awkwardness Cesare Borgia sat

down then, picked up his own spoon and dipped it in the dessert. He put a mouthful to his lips. But it was not until he had eaten that the rest of the company followed suit.

The lieutenant took his spoon in his hand.

The Borgia nodded and waved to his servants in a gesture of dismissal. Everyone's attention was on the table in front of them. Everyone's except mine.

On the opposite side of the table I saw the Borgia executioner smile. He raised his hands to withdraw. Between his fingers, in the candlelight, gleamed the wire of a garrotte.

Chapter Eighteen

In a sudden violent gesture the lieutenant's hands clutched the table edge.

A choking, gurgling noise retched from his throat. His fingers grabbed wildly and his plate went spinning. It fell to the floor and shattered.

Michelotto tightened the torque.

Unperturbed, Cesare Borgia continued talking to the lady at his side. She glanced down the table to see what had caused the disturbance. The Borgia smiled and leaned towards her. He whispered in her ear.

She recoiled. Her hand went to her throat.

Then she stood up and gave out a long scream. But she was too late to warn her husband and it took several seconds for the rest of the guests to appreciate what was happening.

The lieutenant kicked out as he tried to twist away. His chair toppled back as his attacker hauled on the garrotte. The man's own weight now helped strangle him. He reached up desperately, hands clawing at the face of his murderer. Then his struggles lessened. Michelotto gave one last pull and flung the man away from him. The body twitched and jerked upon the floor, shuddered and lay still. The lieutenant's face was blue-black, with its swollen tongue protruding between his lips.

Some of the guests rose from the table. Cesare Borgia snapped his fingers and the soldiers of his personal guard ran into the room. Their swords were drawn. At once all the dinner guests became motionless in their chairs; those who had half risen sat down again.

The Maestro sank into his chair. He dropped his head into his hands. Felipe went to him and began to help him to his feet.

From the head of the table Cesare Borgia spoke. 'I gave no one permission to leave,' he said silkily. 'All will sit until I say otherwise.'

He stood up and approached the lieutenant's wife, who was crying hysterically. He slapped the woman on the cheek. She stumbled to her chair and sat down, still weeping.

Felipe faced the Borgia and spoke calmly. 'My master is unwell. I pray by your leave, my lord, that he may take his rest so that he may serve you to the best of his ability tomorrow.'

Cesare Borgia gazed at Felipe for several seconds.

Graziano had shoved his chair back from the table but he had not risen. His eyes were on Felipe. I tensed myself. By an effort of will I kept my hand away from the dinner knife lying on the table within my reach. I had already marked the soldiers by the door. Now I measured how many paces to the window. But I knew we had no chance of escape. If the Borgia chose to deem Felipe's request an insult then none of us would leave this room alive.

'Messer Leonardo' – Cesare spoke slowly – 'your work is valuable to me. Please go now and rest before your labours in the morning.' He looked at Graziano, then Felipe, then me, as if memorizing our faces and names, before he continued. 'You may take the members of your household with you.'

Within a second Graziano and Felipe were on either side of the Maestro to help him stand. I picked up his bag. We retreated from the room as swiftly and unobtrusively as possible.

As we left I heard Cesare Borgia call out to his musicians. 'Such gloom,' he cried, 'will not do during a holiday. Play us a merry tune, minstrels.' He took the sobbing lieutenant's wife by the arm. 'Perhaps now we will dance?'

Chapter Ninteen

That night no one slept in the castle of Imola.

My master did not eat or read or draw or undertake any of his studies. He sat by the open window with a heavy cloak about his shoulders and stared at the night sky.

Some time before dawn Niccolò Machiavelli came and spoke with Felipe for a while. He had written previously to the Council of Florence, saying that he was in danger and asking to be recalled, but to no avail.

'Perhaps now they will listen to me,' he said. 'I want to leave this place as soon as I am able.'

'And I must try to disengage the Maestro from the services of the Borgia,' Felipe replied. 'But how to do it safely?'

'Cesare Borgia's mind is locked on one purpose,' said Graziano. 'And he will destroy anyone that stands in his way.'

'Because he has deemed it a worthwhile cause,' said Machiavelli, 'he believes he has a right to employ any method to achieve his aim. It is an interesting concept.'

'Has there been any more word about what his captains are scheming?' Felipe asked him.

'I have my own men working for me,' said Machiavelli, 'and I have recently received coded messages. But I fear these have already passed through the hands of the Borgia so it may be that I only hear what he wishes I should hear.' He shrugged. 'For what it is worth, the French are sending troops to help him. I suspect that he will wait until they are close and then offer reconciliation to the condottieri captains. They will not know that he has gathered more troops independently of them and may believe him to be trying to make peace because they outnumber him. He is planning to arrange a meeting with them to parley.'

'Not here, surely!' said Felipe, aghast. 'They wouldn't be so stupid as to come into his den to be devoured.'

In the morning we had definite news. Cesare Borgia would meet with his former captains to discuss terms, but not at Imola. It would be on their territory, in a place they had just captured and where their forces were stationed. We had to make ready for a journey. Within the hour the Borgia, his men and retainers would leave for the coastal town of Senigallia on the Adriatic Sea.

'Has every one of his captains agreed to this meeting?' the Maestro asked Felipe as we set out. He was sitting beside me on a horse-drawn cart that carried his books and materials. Felipe and Graziano rode on their own horses beside us.

Felipe nodded. Unspoken between them was the name of Vitellozzo Vitelli, the captain who was the Maestro's friend.

Flanked by six hundred Swiss pikes, we rode in the train of the Borgia army down the Via Emilia. Snow was falling in the last days of that bitter December. The villages we passed through were deserted. I suspect the inhabitants flitted out at our approach and then returned after the army had gone. We stopped at Cesena, where they gave a ball in honour of Il Valentino, and he danced and flirted as if he had no other care in the world.

But secretly Machiavelli told us that the Borgia forces had been split up and were being sent ahead separately by different routes to converge on Senigallia.

In the days before Christmas Cesare Borgia feasted and listened to music. Yet still he exacted his revenge, for when his governor of the region, Remiro de Lorqua, came to join in the celebrations, he had him arrested. Under torture the man confessed to being part of the plot.

Thus on Christmas morning Remiro de Lorqua was beheaded in the main square and his body left for all to see. With this deed done, on the following day, the twenty-sixth of December, we set out for Senigallia.

Chapter Twenty

As a sign of good faith Cesare Borgia asked that his former captains withdraw their troops from the citadel of Senigallia itself.

They complied with his request.

So on the last day of the year we came to the river Misa where these rebel condottieri captains came out to meet him. Beside me, on the cart, the Maestro groaned when he saw them approach.

Graziano whispered to me, 'Vitellozzo is there! The master sees him!'

We watched anxiously as the two groups of horsemen met.

But Cesare Borgia was a man transformed. He rode forward joyfully and hailed the watchful and suspicious captains. His eyes flashed with pleasure at seeing their faces and he called their names individually. He leaned over in his saddle to embrace and hold each man to him as one would a friend not seen for many days.

For their part the captains seemed to relax. As far as they could discern Cesare had not brought troops with him in any great number. And they appeared mesmerized by his show of charm and attention.

The party prepared to go over the bridge into the borgo before the town. I clicked the reins but Felipe reached out and put his hand on my arm.

He said nothing to me but I pulled back and caused the animal to delay a little so that we lagged behind. I noted that Messer Machiavelli was doing the same.

On the other side of the cart, Graziano moved his horse closer to protect the Maestro.

Machiavelli told us later that Il Valentino had already sent his spies into the town in great numbers to lock all the gates except the one by which he would enter.

So now Cesare invited Vitellozzo and the rest of the captains to accompany him. As they crossed the river the Borgia cavalry swung in from their position and lined up guarding the bridge.

We saw the captains glance around and murmur to each other.

The procession entered Senigallia accompanied only by troops under Cesare's command: a division of Gascon infantry and his personal men-at-arms. Among these was Michelotto.

We were with the last of the retinue.

The gate shut behind us.

And now the captains' unease congealed into real fear. They hastened to say farewell to their prince and overlord and return to their own troops outside the walls. But Cesare entreated them to wait and speak more with him. His utmost friendliness and congenial manner served to confuse them. He told them he had a house already marked out where they might confer. He urged them to come and discuss what arrangements needed to be made for the future. He rode on. And they, like us, being pressed in by his escort, could not disagree.

When we reached the villa Cesare Borgia dismounted and the captains had no choice but to do the same.

Felipe and Graziano did not. Felipe gave me a significant look, and I, hoping I was reading his meaning correctly, began to manoeuvre our little cart back from the entrance. But the throng of soldiers was too great. We were stuck fast in the crowd.

Cesare strode on into the courtyard. His captains tried to catch up with him. There was an outside staircase leading to an upper level of the house, and Cesare went across and began to ascend the stairs.

The captains made to follow.

But immediately Michelotto and the Borgia men-at-arms seized them. There was barely a scuffle. So swiftly and firmly were these sorry men overcome that they did not even have time to draw their swords.

The trap was sprung.

'Wait!'

One of his young captains called out to the Borgia. 'I beg you,' this youth cried out piteously. 'My lord, allow us at least to speak with you!'

On the top step Cesare paused for a moment. He looked down upon his enemies. Then he turned away and went inside.

The soldiers behind us surged forwards. Graziano and Felipe took firm hold of the carthorse's bridle. The Maestro covered my hands with his own to tighten our grip on the reins, and we forced our way out of the mêlée and back towards the main gate. Ahead of us we saw Machiavelli, who cried out to us above the uproar.

'To me! To me!'

He led us round the inner wall of the town to another gate where he knew the men guarding it. His own spies, paid with Florentine money, no doubt. We went through without comment and came out by the riverside, where we found the place where the Borgia cavalry had made camp.

There we waited as the troops rampaged in the town, pulling citizens out of their beds and slaying any they thought had conspired against the Borgia. In the darkest watches of the night Machiavelli slipped away to learn what news he could. He did not return until it was almost dawn. His face was grave.

The condottieri captains had been bound and thrown into one of the lower rooms in the villa. In the early hours of the first day of the New Year 1503 Michelotto had strangled Vitellozzo and the young captain back to back upon a bench.

'Forgive me for bringing you this most dreadful news,' Machiavelli said. 'But you should know that Il Valentino intends to ride out this morning in full battle dress at the head of his army. He will go now to Perugia and also to the other towns who resist him. The rulers there are already fleeing before his wrath. The rest of these captured rebels he will bring with him as prisoners, but their fate will be the same.'

Felipe went to my master to tell him of the death of his friend. He did not return for an hour.

'The Maestro is ill,' he told us. 'He needs time to recover. We must try to make our way to Florence, where he can recuperate. I will send a message to Il Valentino telling him this, and hope that he is too concerned with his own vendetta to pursue us. Matteo' – he turned to me – 'can you make ready our horses?'

I went to where the horses were stabled in rough shelters against the cold. Hay had been put out for them but the sound of the screams and the sight of the fires in the town had made the beasts restless. They jostled and strained at their tether lines. I spoke to them and they quietened. I reached to unhitch the carthorse first and then stopped. Just beyond the trees two men moved under the moonlight. They had features I recognized. One had been in the room when I had first met the Borgia. The other was one of Sandino's men.

I sank down on my knees. Beside me the horse shifted and stamped and bent its head to nudge my shoulder. I laid my hand upon its long nose and blew softly into its nostrils. 'Do not betray me, my friend' – I spoke silently to the horse – 'my life depends on you.'

Their conversation came to me on the chill night air as they passed and I heard a name mentioned.

'. . . Perela . . .'

Perela!

'. . . there . . . the boy . . . Weeks ago.'

And then, quite distinctly, one man said, 'Already his men are riding to Perela. Sandino will go there as soon as he reports to the Borgia. He has vowed to burn the keep and all within it.'

My stomach knotted and I thought I might vomit.

Sandino intended to attack Perela.

Chapter Twenty-One

Felipe and Graziano came to meet me in the early light.

I had both Graziano's and Felipe's horses saddled and the shafts through the harness of the other one that pulled the little cart.

'Well done, Matteo,' said Graziano as he began to stack away our belongings.

Felipe put down the box he carried. 'I will go and fetch the Maestro,' he said. 'We must get away before the camp stirs.'

'I cannot go with you,' I said.

'What nonsense is this!' Felipe spoke sharply.

'Why ever would you wish to wait here, Matteo?' asked Graziano.

'I do not intend to wait here,' I said. 'I must go to Perela. I overheard two Borgia men talking and there is an attack planned upon our friends in their keep.'

Felipe put his lantern against my face. 'Is this true?'

'It is what I heard.'

'Why would the Borgia do such a thing?' said Graziano. 'Captain dell'Orte is a loyal soldier.'

'Yes,' said Felipe, 'but even loyal soldiers can be foully murdered.' He looked at me closely. 'How did you hear of this?'

'I was by the horses and heard some men who had just ridden in. Two of the Borgia spies in conversation.'

'It is good of you to want to go and warn them,' said Graziano, 'but—'

'Please do not try to stop me,' I said. I could not explain to them or even to myself why I would want to ride into danger when it would be more sensible to run away from it. My one thought was to reach Perela before Sandino and warn Captain dell'Orte. He had enough men and military experience to withstand an attack by Sandino and his brigands. But only if warned in time.

'You must use my horse,' said Graziano. 'I will travel on the cart with our master.'

Felipe took my hand. He gave me some coins. 'Take these,' he said. 'You may have need of money. I will tell the Maestro what has happened.'

Graziano also put something into my hand. It was a long dagger. 'This may also be of use to you.'

Before I left Felipe said, 'You will be welcome in the household if you decide to return. Do what you can.' He cuffed me gently on the head. 'I hope we meet again, Matteo.'

I led Graziano's horse quietly away. As soon as I was out of sight of any watcher I mounted and set a course for Perela.

Travelling as fast as I could, it took me until noon the next day to reach the place where the rivers met. I galloped across the bridge with the toll keeper shouting after me to pay my due. On up the hill to where the keep stood at the top.

It was then that I saw the smoke rising into the air.

I saw the great door smashed open.

I saw that I was too late.

PART THREE
SANDINO'S REVENGE

Chapter Twenty-Two

My first impulse was to kick the horse in its side and rush into the keep.

But I did not.

I reined her in and surveyed the building. There was no movement at the windows and no sound of battle. Yet whatever had happened here had happened only recently, else the fire would have burned out and the smoke would not be trailing into the sky.

There was a steading in a field close by. I dismounted and led the horse to it. Inside was some winter animal fodder. I left the animal to feed, then returned and made my way cautiously into the keep.

Captain dell'Orte's men-at-arms were dead. They lay skewered, hacked down where they stood. They had the appearance of soldiers taken by surprise, their resistance overcome in minutes by a force which had shown them no mercy. Inside and outside the buildings nothing moved. The utter quietness disturbed me. There was no sound of women crying or men groaning, only thick plumes of silent smoke.

Then I saw Captain dell'Orte.

He had been decapitated. His head was stuck on a pike near the stable block with his dismembered body crumpled grotesquely beside it. Two figures lay on the ground before him. Rossana and Elisabetta, one slumped against the other.

I stumbled towards them.

They were alive, but their clothes were in disarray and there was blood over them, whether theirs or their father's I did not know.

A great sucking of air from my lungs left me unable to speak. I had seen death in many forms. Had twice seen men murdered, defenceless men killed before me as I watched, unable to intervene. One I had seen garrotted on the other side of a dinner table; the first one, a priest, clubbed by Sandino until his head burst. But this was more. This was violent outrage.

A sprinkling of snow was beginning to fall.

'Rossana,' I whispered. 'Elisabetta.'

It is not right for a girl to be taken in violence. A man who would do that is lower than the beasts. And once a woman is violated it cannot be amended.

I fell to my knees before them. I stretched out my hand and touched their faces.

I looked at Rossana but she would not meet my gaze. She turned her face away from mine. And I too lowered my gaze for shame, but not for hers, for mine – to be a man when it was a man who had done this to her.

But Elisabetta, who had lived so long in her sister's shadow, did not take her eyes from mine. She met them boldly, but with scorn, as if to say, *Now I have seen what a man can do to a woman, and if that is where your strength is then I have withstood it. I despise you for it, and I will not be cowed by it or anything else ever again.*

My spirit was driven down before the intensity of her gaze.

Then, with wisdom, Elisabetta said, 'I am not ashamed to look at you for what happened to me here, Matteo.'

Only weeks ago I had left these girls in the innocence of their play; I returned to see them now, their childhood destroyed.

What had I done?

I brought some water for them to drink and Elisabetta told me what had happened.

'A man came to the door. He said that he was a journeyman on his way to Bologna and had become very ill with stomach pains, and that someone at a neighbouring farm had told him my mother had some healing salves. My parents, being kindly, admitted him. He lay on a pallet in the guardroom and while we were at dinner he stabbed one of our men and opened the gate. There were others waiting outside. Only two of our guards were armed and they fought to defend us as best they could, but they were overcome. When he heard the commotion my father looked down from the window and saw what was taking place. He placed Dario in my mother's arms and told her to run with us to our little chapel. He then took Paolo away with him. We went to the chapel and barricaded ourselves in. We heard fighting but could not see what was taking place because the chapel window overlooks the ravine and not the courtyard. After a while it was quiet. Then our attackers came and demanded that we open the door. My mother refused. They said if we gave them Paolo then we would be safe. But Paolo was not with us. They told us what they would do to us if they did not find him. My mother was very brave. She called out in a loud voice, claiming the sanctuary of a sacred place. But they began to break down the door. My mother led us to the window then and spoke to us quietly. She said that our father must be dead as this would not be happening otherwise. She said that she was going to jump into the ravine with baby Dario. She would do this because she knew they would murder Dario. He was a boy child and they would not allow him to live to avenge his family, and she could not bear to watch this happen. She said she was going to do this also to avoid the fate that awaited her when they burst through the door. She urged us to do the same, but said that it was our choice. Then my mother took baby Dario into her arms and stood up upon the windowsill, and – and' – Elisabetta faltered – 'she was gone. And we were left. And the door gave way, and – and—'

'Hush, hush.' I took her hand. 'Do not speak of it any

more.' I glanced around. 'Are any of these brigands still here?'

Elisabetta shook her head. 'They went away when they did not find what they were looking for.'

What they were looking for . . .

My hand went to my belt.

Elisabetta misunderstood my action. 'Matteo, a dagger would be no use against them.'

But it was not the dagger Graziano had given me that I reached for. It was the object in my belt pouch that my hand had strayed to touch instinctively. The object that Sandino wanted, and had sent his men here to retrieve. And by keeping it from him I had brought disaster to this place.

Snow was blowing with the wind and I knew I must get the girls to shelter. 'Can you rise?' I said. 'I will help you.'

'Rossana has not spoken a word since it happened.' Elisabetta stroked her sister's face. Rossana looked at her with uncomprehending gaze.

'It's as if she does not recognize me,' said Elisabetta. 'As if she does not know who I am. As if she does not know who she herself is.'

Elisabetta stood, and with both of us supporting Rossana, we went inside the house.

I found bread and dipped it in wine and brought it to them. Elisabetta took some but Rossana would not eat.

'Where is Paolo?' I said.

'We could not find him.' said Elisabetta. 'When we knew we were being attacked he went with my father. They were arguing.'

'About what?'

'I don't know.'

I left them and searched for their older brother. But he was not among the dead. He would never have run away. Not Paolo dell'Orte. Where could he be?

I came back and spoke again to Elisabetta. 'Can you recall anything your father or Paolo said before they left you?'

She shook her head, but then said, 'Only one thing but it made no sense.'

'What was it?'

'My father had given Paolo an instruction. That was when they began to argue. Paolo cried out, "No!" He did not want to do what my father told him. My father said, "You must obey me in this." And then my father said something more. He said, "Messer Leonardo will keep you safe." '

Elisabetta shook her head.

'That is what I did not understand.'

Chapter Twenty-Three

But I understood.

It took me a moment or two. But suddenly I knew what had been in the mind of Captain dell'Orte as he had run to defend his keep, buckling on his sword and taking Paolo by the arm.

The secret chamber.

He had thought to hide his eldest son in the place constructed by Leonardo da Vinci and known only to him. The brave captain believed his wife and younger children would be safe in the sanctuary of the chapel, but a boy of Paolo's age would have no such protection. He must have realized at once that the keep would be overwhelmed, so therefore he had forced his son to go there to save his life.

And I, who had been in the hay loft looking down when my master had shown Captain dell'Orte the plans for the construction of the secret chamber, knew where to find Paolo.

He lay curled up like a child in the hidden room. He told us the walls were so thick he had heard nothing. His small stub of a candle had burned out yet he remained there in the dark, as his father had commanded.

Elisabetta sat with him and told him what had happened in the keep.

The news of his father's death he bore bravely, but when he

heard what had befallen his sisters, and how his mother and baby brother had died, he became distraught.

'My father did not think they would harm a baby, or women,' he said. 'He knew he might die fighting, but not that this would happen.'

Paolo looked at me pleadingly from his tear-stained face, imploring me to agree that he had done the right thing. 'I told my father that I was prepared to die,' he said. 'He told me that I was the only man who could live. No one knew of the secret room. He said it was not big enough to hide everyone, and anyway, if he did, then they would wonder where his wife and girls had gone and tear the castle apart to find them.

'My father forced me to stay hidden. He made me swear on his sword. He told me his honour was in the sword, his life was in the sword, our family name and all he held dear – my mother, my sisters, my brother and myself – he would defend with his sword.

'My mother, my sisters, my brother.' Paolo began to sob. 'My mother, my sisters, my brother.'

Elisabetta and I watched him cry until he could cry no more. Then he stood up and wiped his face. He went to where his father's body lay and he picked up his sword. 'With this,' he declared, 'I will avenge them.'

Thus violence begets violence and no man can stop it. When war is made all are drawn in and consumed.

'Paolo,' said Elisabetta, 'I must tell you this and beg forgiveness. Had I known where you were hidden I would have told them.'

Paolo went at once and kissed his sister. He drew her by the hand to where Rossana stood. He gathered them both in his arms. 'I would have gladly given myself up to spare you.'

'But you would not have spared them,' I said brutally. 'These men would have found you, murdered you, then turned their attention to your sisters.'

'How do you know this, Matteo?' Elisabetta asked me.

'I have been living with men such as these for the last weeks. You will not yet have heard what happened at Senigallia, where Il Valentino murdered his captains in cold blood. The Borgia pretended to forgive them and asked them to parley. Then he had them strangled. Afterwards his soldiers rampaged through the town, committing unspeakable atrocities.'

Elisabetta shuddered. 'Yet these men seemed more like brigands than enlisted soldiers. And they themselves seemed frightened that they had not found what they sought. They said their leader would be angry when they met up with him and had to tell him they had been unsuccessful.'

At her words fear rose in my throat. I knew their leader, and he would have been more ruthless in his search. He would not have left the girls alive. When his men reported back to him he would not be satisfied that a thorough search had been made. He would come himself to look.

And he was only hours behind me on the road.

At that moment, from the top of the tower, came the sound of the corncrake. We ran to the battlements. From this point we could see far beyond the bridge crossing. In the distance a group of horsemen were approaching.

Out in front a lone rider travelled at speed. A sudden tremor seized my body.

It was Sandino.

Chapter Twenty-Four

Paolo would have rushed outside had I not barred his way. 'Wait,' I said. And when he protested I added, 'Think of your sisters.'

'Why have they returned?' asked Elisabetta.

'Because they did not find what they were looking for?' suggested Paolo.

'But we have nothing here, no plate nor silverware, no great jewels.'

Rossana had begun to tremble.

'We must leave now,' I said to Paolo, 'to take your sisters to safety.'

'Where can we go?' Elisabetta looked around wildly. 'There is but one road. They will catch us as we flee.'

'We will go by another route.' I already had Rossana by the arm and was hurrying outside the door, with them following me. 'We must climb down the ravine.'

'It's impossible,' said Paolo. 'I tried it as a boy and could only get so far.'

By now we were round the side of the keep. There was a narrow lip of land and then the rock fell away at our feet.

'There is no other way,' I said. 'Listen. They are at the door.'

We fell silent. In the clear winter air a voice I recognized:

'You killed the old man, their father, too quickly.' Sandino was berating his men loudly. 'He would have given up the boy to save his girls.'

'What about this secret room you spoke of?' one of his men asked him. 'You said he might be hiding there.'

'I only recently learned that the Borgia has secret rooms built in his fortresses, so that there will always be a place for him to hide if any of his castles fall to siege when he is in them. I don't know where this one is located. But, no matter, we'll make camp, and if he's still here, then hunger will drive him out in time. I can be patient. I've waited already. A few more days will make no difference.'

I leaned over and put my mouth to Paolo's ear. 'We must go down.'

He shook his head and mouthed the words back to me. 'We cannot.'

Then Elisabetta spoke in a very quiet but firm voice. 'There is no other alternative.'

I went first.

I scrambled over and, gripping tightly with my hands, I found holds for my feet. Elisabetta came next. I guided her feet into position while she in turn guided Rossana. Paolo, with his father's sword fastened to his back, came last.

A little way down we found a ledge to rest on. Elisabetta was shaking all over but Rossana seemed indifferent to her fate. It was the difference between one who wished to live and one who did not care.

'Let us go on,' I said.

Elisabetta glanced over the edge and swayed back. 'Can't we stay here a little longer?'

'No,' I replied, for I thought that if we did we might lose our nerve.

'This ledge is an overhang, Matteo,' said Paolo. 'It will be very difficult for my sisters to climb out and then under.'

'I know, Paolo. But if we manage it, then we will be out of sight of the keep all the way to the bottom of the ravine.'

I crawled out to the rim of the rock. 'When you come to me,' I said to Elisabetta, 'try not to look down. Just let me guide your step into the right place.'

I pitched myself into the void. The wind buffeted me. My cheek was close to the cliff face. Even in the depth of winter tiny flowers grew in the cracks. A pebble dislodged from above struck my forehead. Someone was standing on the castle wall looking down. I pressed close in. A trickle of water poured past me. It was a man relieving himself. I took new hope from this. They could not think that anyone had escaped this way, otherwise it would be hot pitch, not piss, cascading down on my head.

I waited. After a while I used my dagger to cut some more earth from between the rocks. I scratched with my fingernails. I had stood for so long that my legs juddered in spasm. The thought entered my head that if I fell, then all of them were lost. Having no option but one makes a choice more easy to make.

My hands were slick with sweat, but the sun's arc in the sky was declining and the light no longer shone into the furthest reaches of the gorge. Half my body was suspended over the drop as I searched for a foothold. I burrowed the toes of my boots until I got some purchase. Now it was the turn of Elisabetta.

I was able to dig out some hollows and expose a stone that protruded enough for her to grasp. She was lighter than me and her body more pliable. She swung herself over and under, and was beside me on the cliff face.

'Well done,' I breathed.

Her mouth curved in the semblance of a smile.

There was a sudden flurry of air and a bird flew out next to her head. Elisabetta lost her grip. And started to fall.

Her scream was a whisper, as if she had begun to yell and realized what would happen if she cried out.

'Mama!' I heard her moan.

I snatched out at her. And grasped empty air.

But not quite. The unbraided mass of her hair caught in my fingers. I closed on this and clenched my fist.

She ground her teeth in pain. We had only seconds before her body weight ripped her hair from her skull.

'Grab my waist, Elisabetta!'

'I cannot reach it,' she gasped.

'My legs then. My feet. Anything.'

'I'll pull you down with me, Matteo.' Her voice sounded as if she had given up.

'You won't. I am well anchored here. Do it. Now!' I barked at her as she hesitated.

Small hands round my ankles.

But I had lied. I was not well anchored.

One of the rocks I was holding began to move. Around it the earth crumbled. I heard the patter of small stones.

'Can you find any place to stand on?' I asked her.

I heard her feet scrabbling below me.

'I have a foothold.' At the same moment her dead weight on me lightened a little. 'There is a tiny outcrop here, enough for me to rest my feet.'

We stayed like that while I thought what to do.

I knew there was no room for her to put her fingers where my feet were. She must see that too.

Then Paolo's head appeared just above me. He held out his two hands to me. 'Give me your hand, Matteo.'

I shook my head. 'You are bigger and stronger than I am, Paolo. But there are two of us, and we will drag you over.'

'I have lodged my belt buckle in the cliff face and tied Rossana to it. She has placed her back to the rock behind me and she holds me by my ankles. She will not let go.'

'If you fail to pull me up then she dies too.'

There was a silence. Then Paolo said, 'So be it.'

'I am with Paolo.' Elisabetta's voice came from somewhere near my feet. 'If this fails then we die together, Matteo, as is God's will.'

I reached my free hand towards Paolo. He stretched as far as he could towards me, and I to him. For any chance of success he would need to grasp my wrists. There were two handspans of space between our fingertips. I heard his sob of disappointment.

'We must think again,' I said.

But as we had done this it came to me that there might be another way to beat this overhang. It depended on the courage of Elisabetta. 'Listen to me,' I whispered to her. 'Are your feet secure?'

'Yes. I'm standing on a tiny ledge.'

'Elisabetta, I am going to climb over you. When I do this I will move one foot to begin with, then you must put your hand in its place. Do you understand?'

'Yes, Matteo.'

'I will have to rest that foot upon your shoulder. Do you think you could bear my weight for the moment or two that it takes me to get down beside you onto the ledge?'

'Yes, Matteo.' She spoke again, this time more resolutely. I sensed her tensing herself in preparation.

I called softly to Paolo. 'Paolo, leave your belt lodged in the wall. When Elisabetta and I are on the ledge, Rossana and you can use it to lower yourselves down and we will guide you the rest of the way.'

We gained the valley floor as the sun was setting.

We were near to the part of the keep below the chapel.

Paolo took me to one side. 'I must go and make sure that my mother and Dario are indeed dead,' he said.

'I will come with you.'

Donna Fortunata's neck had been broken. Baby Dario must have been torn from her grasp as they fell. His body lay a little way off, his head cruelly dashed upon some rocks.

Paolo bent to pick him up.

'Leave him,' I said.

'I would put him with my mother.'

'If you move him,' I said, 'then you let the soldiers above us know that we passed this way.'

He began to weep. 'Is my mother to be denied any comfort even in death, that she cannot have her child in her arms?'

'It must be so.'

He bent and kissed his mother on her lips. 'I will have revenge on whoever caused this to happen to them.'

I drew him away lest he linger too long. I reckoned we had a day, maybe less, before Sandino picked up our trail again. Then he would track us, and he would find us.

Chapter Twenty-Five

I used the money Felipe had given me to bribe a bargeman who had moored his barge for the night a few miles south on the river.

These were violent times and fugitives were not an uncommon sight upon the roads and rivers. But this man could not help but notice the particular condition of the girls, especially Rossana. I knew even as I paid him that it was not enough money to guarantee his silence. As soon as Sandino and his men began to make enquiries in the vicinity he would talk, either for more money or in fear for his life.

Rossana was frozen. She did not complain, but more and more she looked distracted, as though her mind were disconnected from her body. Did this show as a physical sign within the skull? I wondered. In an examination, would my master discover some part of the brain which had visibly become traumatized?

There was only one place I could think of where I might take them.

So, once again, by night, I knocked on the outer door of the mortuary of the hospital in Averno.

The porter recognized me and admitted us to the courtyard. Word of the Borgia's most recent deeds ensured that he let me in.

The monk, Father Benedict, was slower to greet me. 'What is your business here tonight?' he asked me.

'Father, we need your help.'

The monk regarded Rossana, Elisabetta and Paolo. His eyes came back to rest upon Rossana.

'I see that ill has befallen your companions. Who are these people?'

'The dell'Orte family from Perela. Their parents, with their baby brother, have been most foully murdered.'

Father Benedict spoke to Paolo. 'I knew your father and mother. Each autumn they sent part of their harvest to the hospital. Your father was a generous patron and your mother a most gracious lady.'

I saw Elisabetta's lip tremble at the mention of her parents, but Rossana did not appear to understand his words. Father Benedict frowned as he looked at her.

'What harm has been done to this child?'

No one spoke. Then I said, 'The soldiers of the Borgia attacked and overcame their father's keep at Perela. The women sheltered in the chapel but it did not save them.'

'And now you have come here?'

'Father,' I said, 'I could think of nowhere else to go.'

Before the monk could reply there was a violent battering at the outside door.

'Open up in there! We are here on business for Il Valentino himself! Open in the name of Cesare Borgia!'

Chapter Twenty-Six

Paolo drew his father's sword.

'At last I'll face these murderers!' he cried.

'Silence!' Father Benedict said sharply. 'Put your weapon away. This is a place of God and forgiveness.'

'I will have my revenge for the wrong done to our family!'

'They will slaughter you where you stand and not think anything of it.'

'But I'll kill one of them before I die!'

'And what of your sisters?' demanded Father Benedict. 'What fate awaits them? And the monks? And the patients in my care? If the soldiers find you here they're likely to kill everyone inside the hospital.'

The priest beckoned to the porter to come to him. He spoke rapidly to the man, telling him to delay the soldiers' entry as long as possible and asking him to declare no one had passed through the door tonight. 'Those men-at-arms may display the insignia of the Borgia but you must divulge nothing to them.'

The porter's eyes rolled in his head like those of a terrified horse.

The monk put his hand upon his shoulder. 'Ercole, it is the right thing to do. I, Father Benedict, am instructing you to tell this lie. The men outside mean these children harm . . . have already done wicked things to them.' His voice took on a gentler tone. 'Remember your own life previous to the one you have now. You

131

know how terrible it is to suffer such abuse. We can't allow this to happen again. You must help me protect these children. It is not given to every man to do a noble thing, but you are being called upon to do one now.'

Father Benedict's words seemed to calm the porter. The monk held his gaze. Then he raised his hand and, with his thumb, made the sign of the cross on the man's forehead. '*Ego te absolvo*,' he said quietly. 'We all have to die sometime, Ercole. If this is our time, then you will go to meet your Maker with the pure soul of a martyr.'

The man's face suffused with a strange emotion. He bent his head.

I watched the porter as he shuffled towards the door. Was he prepared to give his own life that we might survive? By his Faith this was his passport to Paradise.

Greater love than this no man hath, that a man lay down his life for his friends. Would Ercole's belief in that single great ordinance overcome the immediate danger he was about to encounter? Perhaps better to have threatened him with the Church's other promise – of excommunication, hellfire and eternal damnation. To put in his mind a greater terror to out-weigh the fear of the Borgia.

Paolo must have been thinking similar thoughts to mine. 'Tell him I'll slit his throat if he says a word.'

'I will not,' said the monk. 'Ercole is a true friend of the hospital. I rescued him from a cruel and abusive master many years ago, when he was but a child himself. He will do as I've requested.'

'As soon as he sees the soldiers he'll give us away,' Paolo insisted.

'I have confidence in him.' Father Benedict smiled at us. 'There's love in his heart, and it's very strong.'

How could the monk smile in this situation? He too would die a most horrible death once it was known that he had sheltered fugitives from the Borgia. The noise on the outer door redoubled. It sounded as though the men in the street were using axes and spears upon the wood.

'Hold off! I'm coming! I'm coming!' we heard Ercole shout at them but he did not move any faster.

'They'll threaten to kill him and he will speak out.' Paolo was in despair. 'Fear is what makes people do what you say.'

'I would say that the force of love is stronger,' said Father Benedict. 'But we haven't time to indulge in that debate. I must find somewhere to hide all of you. Come with me.' He took Paolo roughly by the arm and pulled him away. 'Put away your sword. If you cannot forgive, then now is not the time for your revenge.'

We followed the monk into the hospital. 'They'll look in every part of the building. Search every cupboard and storeroom. I thought I might disguise you as patients, but there are four of you and' – he glanced at Rossana – 'I fear that you wouldn't stand much close scrutiny.'

'Take us to the chapel,' said Paolo. 'We'll go there. The sacred rules of sanctuary will stop them from desecrating holy ground.'

'It didn't stop them at Perela,' Elisabetta reminded him. 'They caused our mother's death and then violated us.'

The priest's eyes flickered over her face and then he looked at me.

'It is true.' I confirmed her words. 'The most vile deeds were done within sight of the tabernacle itself.'

The priest drew in his breath. 'What brand of mercenary is this? These are vile brigands who pursue children in such a brutal manner.'

'That's why I want to fight,' said Paolo. 'You should've let me try to kill at least one of them, Father.'

'Is there nowhere then that's safe for us?' Elisabetta's voice trembled.

'Hush now,' said the monk. 'It must be in some other way that by the Grace of God we live or die tonight.'

He lifted a torch from the wall and took us into the mortuary. Down past the place where he and the Sisters of Mercy laid out the corpses and prepared them for burial. Beyond the little room that he had given over to my master to carry out his dissections. At the end of the corridor we descended some stairs. Where the passage ended there was a door. It was shut and barred with an iron rod set in a bracket.

'Help me here,' he said.

He and Paolo grasped the iron bar and slid it to one side. Then the monk led us through.

The light from his torch made great shadows of our forms upon the walls and the low arched roof of this last windowless room. There were bodies contained inside, a dozen or so, cramped together on trestles. These corpses were shrouded in sheets, and there was a strong smell of ammonia.

'What is this place?' Elisabetta asked in horror.

'Another mortuary room.' The priest hesitated. 'It's an overflow from the main room that we use.'

'But why are these dead people kept behind a bolted door?'

'They are here because' – the monk hesitated – 'because they are special cases. We await permission to bury them.' He went on quickly as he saw that Paolo was also about to question him. 'Each of you conceal yourselves under a sheet, and lie sideways, close to the corpse that is already there. I think it's better if you position yourself feet to head. I'll cover you and then I'll leave and bolt the door behind me. Your pursuers will almost certainly demand that this door is opened, may even come inside, though I'll try to dissuade them. Try to lie quietly if they do. If you make any sound we are all doomed.'

A great shudder came from Rossana. She slumped against her sister.

'I know you can do this,' Father Benedict said encouragingly. He looked directly at Elisabetta. 'Tell your sister to be strong. Pray to the Blessed Virgin to protect you.'

I saw that I had to take the lead, else the others would not do as he said. Paolo was still bristling with frustrated anger, the girls were half swooning with fear and revulsion. I dragged a sheet from the corpse at the far wall. It was an older man dressed in the rough garb of the bargemen. 'Elisabetta,' I said, 'show Rossana how this can be done. Close your eyes and let me help you.'

She stared at me.

'I beg you,' I whispered. 'We have very little time.'

She shut her eyes. I scooped her up in my arms and laid her down beside the body of the old man. She made a tiny sound and then bit her lip.

'Lie on your side. Put your face near to his feet and meld your body against his. You are so lightly made you will make very little outline.'

She did as I said. As she did so she opened her eyes and gazed at me with such trust that I wanted to kiss her. Not as a love token between a man and a woman, more as a brother to reward a sister who had done something brave and good.

I covered her with the sheet. 'Father Benedict is right,' I said. 'No one would know that Elisabetta is there. If we do this we might escape.'

Paolo needed no more encouragement. He uncovered the body next in line and helped Rossana climb up beside the person lying there. She lay down without a murmur and allowed herself to be shrouded up.

'There's a child. Here in the corner.' The monk showed Paolo where a smaller body lay. 'Place yourself beside this infant. It will mean that there's less bulk under this sheet.' He helped Paolo, and then came to me.

I had already found myself a space and clambered onto the trestle. I did not look to see whether it was man, woman or child.

'There now.' Father Benedict adjusted my shroud. 'I must get back to busy myself with some work in the main mortuary. When these men enter the hospital I want it to look as though they have

135

disturbed me at my duties. Do not stir until I return on my own and tell you it's safe to do so.'

I could hear the *slap, slap* of the priest's sandals as he hurried away, then the grinding of hinges and his whisper: 'Courage, children. May God be with you.'

There was the sound of the heavy bar being dragged back across the door.

Silence and darkness.

We were shut in.

There was no light in the room. I knew that the feet of the dead person beside me were close to my face yet I could see nothing in the dark.

We waited many, many minutes. Then we heard a clamour in the distance, becoming louder. Booted feet on the flagstones in the passageway.

'Matteo, I am frightened.' Elisabetta's whisper croaked from her throat.

It was only later that I realized that she called my name as if I were an older brother.

'Do not be afraid.' I strove to keep my voice steady.

'I'm shaking so much. They will hear me. I will betray everyone.'

I could hear panic rising as fear fastened its hold on her.

'No, you will not.' I spoke firmly. 'Remember what the monk said. Pray to the Virgin. Say your Rosary.'

'I cannot. My brain won't work. The words are scattering in my head.'

How could I help her when now fear ran wild inside me too? My own thoughts were racing in disorder like rabbits scattering from a burrow when a ferret is sent in to fetch them out. If we had to defend ourselves, what weapons did we have, Paolo and I? One sword, in the hands of a boy not much older than me, and my dagger, which was of use only in close combat. But if they caught us here they would not bother to engage in any fighting. They would barricade us in and put burning straw at the door to smoke us out, or wait and let us starve. We were trapped.

Outside the door I could hear the monk's voice and then that of another, more insistent, demanding.

'Think of something else,' I told Elisabetta.

'I cannot.'

'You can.' I searched desperately in my head for some pleasant circumstance to take her attention from what was happening. 'Remember the time we went together, all of us, to gather the last of the berries on the bushes down at the river at Perela? You and Rossana had been left sewing to do. Paolo and I had the horse brasses to polish and a new saddle to wax. But it was very hot that afternoon, and while the adults rested in siesta we stole away and went to the riverbank. Do you remember?'

'I think so,' she whispered.

'It was one of the last warm days of autumn,' I went on, 'and we crept across the stable yard together, away from the keep and out into the fields. You must remember that, surely?'

'Yes,' she whispered.

'And we found the spot where you knew the berries grew plentifully, and you and Rossana collected them until your aprons were overflowing. And then we had to eat them, as we could not bring them home for fear of being discovered berrying when we should have been attending to our duties. Our mouths were stained purple and I took a cloth and dipped it in the river and we had to wipe each other's faces.'

'I remember.'

'Think of that now. Only that. Think of nothing else.'

We heard the bar being removed noisily from the door. The priest being deliberately clumsy to give us warning to be quiet.

I hoped that Rossana and Paolo had both been listening to the dialogue between Elisabetta and myself. Paolo especially, who I feared might leap up with his father's sword in his hand.

Thinking of that day in Perela might occupy them and keep them still.

In my own head a memory came to me of Rossana among the blazing berries. Her cloth kerchief had slipped from her head, and her hair, unbound beneath it, became tangled in the brambles. She'd struggled to free herself, only to become more enmeshed. She'd pleaded with me to help her.

I found myself reliving that time: Rossana's innocent coquetry as she'd laughed with me at her predicament, my confusion at standing so close to a girl, the dazzling brightness of the sun, the warmth in the little valley, the silken feel of her hair among my fingers. It had been just before a festive day, the Virgin's Birth.

That night I had told the family of the great festival that took place at that time in the cities, the feasting, the processions in the streets, the dancing and side-shows to watch and take part in. Their parents had decided to have their own little Carnival. They'd had a pig slaughtered and we had played games in the courtyard. The girls had dressed up in costume of the region and danced the traditional dances, we had told stories, my master had played the lute and sung, and—

The mortuary door crashed open.

Chapter Twenty-Seven

Under the shroud my hand gripped my dagger.

'What is this place, monk?'

I opened my eyes. Through the cotton sheeting I could see the outline of a man standing in the doorway.

From behind him came Father Benedict's voice, speaking coolly. 'As you see. It is a mortuary.'

'What foul practices do you perform that you keep these cadavers hidden behind a locked door?'

'You've listened to too many tales of witchcraft and necromancy. This is a monastery and a hospital where the brothers tend the sick. There are no foul acts performed within these walls.'

'Why are these bodies here then, and not with the others?'

'We await the special arrangements for their burial.'

'What special arrangements?'

The booted stamp of feet entered the room. My throat constricted. I opened my mouth to ease my breath. The priest coughed.

There was rustling. The man must have pulled the sheet from the corpse nearest the door. 'This woman has the dress of a peasant, not a noble,' he declared. 'There can be no "special arrangement" for her. Why are these people being kept apart? Bodies are supposed to buried within three days of death. That's the law.'

'By order of Cesare Borgia himself these bodies are here

awaiting burial by volunteer gravediggers.' Father Benedict's voice had changed in tone. 'I advise you to go no further in your examination of these poor unfortunates,' he said with authority.

'Why? What have you hidden here, priest?'

'The room is small. Your view under the tables and beyond is not restricted. This place contains bodies and nothing else.'

'Come and show me.'

'I never enter this room unless I have to. I see you are wearing gloves. That is fortunate, as you've already almost touched one corpse.'

Now there was a hesitation in the man's voice. 'What do you mean? Why do you stand at the door?'

'This is not a place to linger in.' The priest spoke very slowly. 'The last illness of these people was such that I do not wish to breathe the air they lie in any more than I have to.'

'Their illness? What was it? What did they die of?'

'They were taken by the scourge of mankind, poor souls,' said Father Benedict in a very even voice. 'A terrible death to endure. These are victims of the Plague.'

The man gave a great cry and leaped back. His next words were muffled, as though he had his hand over his mouth.

'There is Plague here?'

'Unfortunately, yes. We have been sent this affliction. But by prayers and atonement we can accept our suffering.'

'Stay back from me, you pestilent priest! You should have informed the authorities.'

'I did. The city magistrate was notified at once, as is required. But your own commander, Cesare Borgia, ordered that no one else should be told. By his direct order a public pronouncement was forbidden. He did not wish people fleeing the region while he is conducting his campaign. The roads would become full of refugees and he wants them kept clear so that his armies can move swiftly from place to place. We were instructed that any victims must be kept locked in a separate place and buried quietly, in the middle of the night, well outside the city walls. There must be no word of this outbreak to anyone. You would do well to heed his order.'

'Close over this door at once!'

'I will be glad to do so.'

The door ground shut. The bar was replaced. We heard the footsteps receding.

By my reckoning it was more than two hours before we again heard the bolt being slid back on the door.

'That was a good ruse, Father,' said Paolo appreciatively as the priest took us into the main part of the hospital. 'To pretend that those people had Plague and so frighten the soldiers away.'

The priest had brought us into a small empty storeroom and closed the door. He stood before us.

'Paolo,' he said solemnly, 'all of you. It was not a trick. I did not lie. The people that you lay with were victims of the Plague.'

Paolo's face was open-mouthed in horror. Elisabetta grabbed hold of Rossana and held her. 'Plague victims!' she said. 'We were lying with Plague victims!'

'It was the only place where I thought the soldiers would not search properly. They have rampaged throughout the hospital, emptying cupboards, pushing their spears up chimneys, turning patients from their beds to search underneath. By hiding you there your lives were saved . . . for the moment.'

Paolo put his hands over his face. 'We escape one death to find another.'

'Perhaps,' said the priest quietly. 'We don't know exactly how this disease is spread. It may be that the Angel of Death will pass over you and you will be saved, as has happened already. Meanwhile we cannot delay.' He handed Paolo and me each a small hessian sack. 'I've only a little bread to give you for your journey, because to find you more food would involve someone in the kitchen being aware of your presence. It's best that Ercole and I remain the only two here who know about you.'

'Our journey, Father?' said Elisabetta. 'You're sending us away?'

'You must go at once. When they do not find you in any part of the town they will come back to search everywhere again. This time they will be even more thorough. In any case it's almost midnight. That's when the fraternity of charitable men who dig the graves for those who succumb to the Plague arrive to collect the bodies to bury. It's better that you leave as soon as possible.'

'But we've nowhere to go!'

'I'm about to tell you where you may go.'

He knelt down, and with his finger he drew a rough map on the earthen floor. 'Ercole is going to take you away from the hospital by a tunnel that comes out at the river. When he and you part company, go upstream.'

'Upstream,' said Paolo. 'That is back the way we came!'

'Yes, and you will be all the safer for that. After a mile or so you will branch off. So you will not be retracing your way to Perela. Instead you'll head into the mountains. It's one full day's climb over rough ground to the hill town of Melte, where there is a small convent of cloistered nuns. There you'll find sanctuary.'

'Sanctuary?' Elisabetta repeated the word. 'If only I could believe that were true.'

'Do believe it,' said the priest. 'Now, pay attention. Ercole can only bring you as far as the river. He must get back here quickly so that everything seems as it should be in the hospital when the gravediggers come, or the soldiers return.' Father Benedict pointed to the map he had drawn on the floor. 'Do you know the countryside on the other side of Averno?'

Paolo shook his head.

'I do,' I said.

The monk studied me for a moment. I knew he recognized me as the servant of Messer da Vinci but he had not commented openly on this. 'Very well. I'll show Matteo the way to this convent. You must memorize my drawing, then I will rub it out. Better not to be carrying maps or letters of any kind. It's dangerous to carry documents. If they fell into the wrong hands then it would put the hospital at risk. But once you reach Melte you won't need a letter. The Mother Superior is my sister. Say to her that you come from me and beg shelter from her. She'll take you in.'

'Supposing she does not believe us?' I asked him.

'My sweet sister would not turn four children away.'

'I'm not a child,' said Paolo angrily.

'Indeed,' said the monk sadly. 'No more you are.'

'Two girls she might accept, Father, but if they're cloistered nuns then two boys who are almost men may give her cause to refuse us entry,' Elisabetta pointed out.

'Ah, yes. Let me think . . . I'll tell you of an incident from our childhood that only she and I know about and then she'll believe that you come from me.' He paused, then went on, 'Remind her that it was she who took the roses to make a garland for the statue of the Virgin, but that it was I who took the beating from our father's gardener.'

'We'll tell her,' said Elisabetta, 'but shouldn't we also tell her that we have been with Plague victims?'

'Yes, you must.' The priest nodded. 'Avoid contact with anyone until you speak to her, and be careful of your clothing. There's no sure way to know how the Plague is spread. The first person we had was a rag picker. That might be significant, as some say it can be carried in clothes. But then another two of those who were brought to us to be nursed were barge workers who transport materials and food. They claim the infection lies in the mouths of rats and is passed by them to us as the vermin gnaw through our grain sacks. We cannot be certain. In any case warn my sister that you may be unclean. She will be guided by God and her own mind as to how to treat you.'

'On behalf of my family I thank you, Father, for helping us.'
Paolo made a formal bow.

'I wish I could do more.' Father Benedict sighed. 'Your sister
Rossana needs medical attention but it would be too dangerous
to delay your departure. What cause do they have to hunt you so
viciously?'

'They spoke of treasure,' said Elisabetta. 'They were seeking
some great treasure.'

'It must be a mistake,' said Paolo. 'We have no treasure.'

'Are you sure that that's what they said?' asked the priest.

'Yes,' said Elisabetta.

'Did you take any family jewels with you when you fled?'

Paolo gave a harsh laugh. 'The dell'Orte family owned no
jewels, nor good plate, nor gold coin. My father was a soldier all
his life. He lived, and fed his family and servants, on the produce
of the land around us.'

'I can see why they wanted to kill you at the time,' the monk
went on. 'They would know a son would seek to avenge his
family and would prefer that you weren't left alive, but I don't
understand why they still pursue you so vigorously. Do they fear
you for some reason? Have you relatives you can call to arms?
Kinfolk who will fight for you?'

Paolo shook his head. 'My mother's older brother lives somewhere near Milan but I know very little about him. This uncle
exchanged letters with my mother from time to time. I don't think
he's very rich or has any men to call to arms.'

'There's more here to discover.' The priest spoke slowly.
He looked at Elisabetta. 'You say you heard them mention
treasure?'

Elisabetta nodded. 'Great treasure. I heard them use those very
words.'

Father Benedict frowned. I saw the expression on his face, the
line appearing between his eyes – the one so well illustrated by my
master when he sketched the monk the night after we first made

his acquaintance. The indent on his brow that showed the priest was thinking deeply about something.

I began to sweat. I hoped that Elisabetta and Paolo would not recall the exact words the brigands had spoken as they had relayed them to me.

'Not treasure exactly,' said Elisabetta. 'They did not say that Paolo had treasure. They said he had *the key* to great treasure.'

'And you know nothing of this, Paolo?' asked the priest. 'Did your father own a key that unlocked a particular chest?'

'There was no treasure within our household, else my father would have hidden it with me.'

'Your father didn't give you any instruction, leave any message, write anything down?'

Paolo shook his head. 'I've thought about it over and over. He did not.'

'Your father knew that he was almost certainly going to die.' To my agitation the monk began to mull over the bones of the information he had garnered. 'He places his wife and children in the chapel of the keep where he hopes the soldiers will not violate sanctuary. False hope against such barbarians! And he hides his elder son because he knows the boy is old enough that they would kill him.' Father Benedict fixed his wise eyes upon Paolo. 'If there was any treasure, Paolo, he would have told you about it, surely?'

'Sir,' replied Paolo, 'my father said nothing to me about treasure. Only that I should watch over my mother and brother' – Paolo's voice broke a little – 'and my sisters. And to uphold my honour where I could.'

The priest looked at Elisabetta. 'Tell me again what you heard them say.'

Elisabetta thought before replying. 'They said, "We must find the boy. He holds the key to the treasure." '

The furrow in the priest's brow deepened. 'Did he mention Paolo by name?'

My stomach cramped in fear. Now I would be betrayed. This

monk was too clever not to see the flaw in the fabric of the story.

Elisabetta began to speak. 'As I recall—'

The door opened and Ercole came in. He held a lantern in one hand, in the other a long metal rod. 'Father, the hospital is quiet again and the street outside is empty. We should go while we can.'

The monk stood aside to let us pass. 'Follow Ercole now and do as he says.'

As we filed out of the storeroom he touched my shoulder. 'Do you wish me to get a message to your master that you are in trouble and need his assistance?'

'No,' I replied. 'My arrangement is that I will meet him in Florence and that I still hope to do. Also, he works in part for the Borgia and it would seem that Captain dell'Orte offended Il Valentino in some way so he decided to destroy him and his family. Therefore it's best that my master is not concerned with this. I will take them to the convent at Melte and then make my own way to Florence.'

'Yes, I can see the wisdom in that,' the priest agreed. 'But how is it that you are bound up with this family, Matteo?'

'They gave us shelter on our travels last summer. I – I heard that they were under threat and – and left my road to warn them, but I arrived too late. I could do no more than stay and help them.' I had thought that the monk might ask me this and had my answer ready. But even though I had rehearsed what I would say I stumbled in my explanation. Yet he seemed to believe me.

'You will earn reward in Heaven for your true charity.'

He laid his hand on my head. I felt my face burn with shame.

When we reached the cloister he bade us farewell and blessed us in turn.

'Now I will go to the chapel and pray.'

'That will be of little use against swords,' muttered Paolo.

'If I am to die then I can think of no better place to be,' the monk said calmly. 'Don't forget to tell my sister that I forgive her the beating I took on her account.' He touched Paolo on his chest.

'Your heart is full of bitterness. Try to find a little space to let in God's good grace. Remember, "Vengeance is mine, saith the Lord." '

Paolo waited until Father Benedict had gone beyond his hearing before he hissed between his teeth, 'And as the Lord saith, then so say I. This I vow, on my sacred word, for the honour of my family. Death, with no quarter, to those who robbed them of their lives.'

Paolo drew his father's sword from its scabbard and, holding it up, he kissed the blade with his lips.

'Sworn on the blood of my father, my mother and my brother. I, Paolo dell'Orte, will have my vengeance.'

Chapter Twenty-Eight

Ercole led us through the hospital. As we passed the entrances to the long wards where the patients lay asleep he dropped the shutter of his lantern and we flitted across the openings in turn. A small votive lamp burned under these archways but it gave little light. Hopefully any restless person glancing at the door would only see shadows in the depth of the cloister.

We followed him through the corridors until we came to the workshops and outbuildings, low-roofed sheds abutting the main hospital block. The laundry rooms were situated here. These were fitted out with drying racks and great sinks with drains in the floor. Huge vats were set on stones under which fires could be lit for bedding and clothing to be boiled clean. Behind the last of these was a narrow spiral stairway. With Ercole holding the lantern high, we went down these stairs, on and on, until, half dizzy, we arrived at the end. We were in a small room which held nothing except a large grating in the stone floor. Ercole put his lantern down and shifted the metal rod he carried so that he held it in both hands.

'What mischief is this?' Paolo's hand was on his sword. 'Have you brought us here to assassinate us?'

Ercole didn't bother to reply. He crossed the room, and using the end of the metal rod he forced one end of it under the rim of the grating cover. With a grunt he levered the lid up a fraction and tried to push it aside.

'You. Help.' He glared at Paolo and myself.

We went to assist him, and between us we managed to swivel the heavy lid to one side. Below us we could hear the sound of rushing water.

'In.' Ercole pointed to the hole in the floor. 'All of you. In.'

'What's down there?' said Paolo.

'We are below the laundry rooms,' I said. 'The hospital would need a big sewer passage to empty the washing tubs and get rid of the waste of so many people.'

'You are taking us into the sewer?' Paolo asked Ercole. 'Is that what's below us?'

'Water. River,' Ercole answered him.

'We might drown,' Elisabetta said.

Ercole looked at her more kindly than he had at Paolo or myself. He shook his head. 'Not drown. Way out.' He pointed to Paolo. 'You first.' And as Paolo hesitated he said, 'Go. You help them.'

Paolo looked at me. I understood the meaning of his look very well. It said: *I leave you with my sisters, protect them against this ruffian.*

I inclined my head. Paolo went to the open grating and sat down with his legs dangling into the hole. Ercole brought the lantern to shine above his head. Bracing himself against the sides, Paolo lowered himself into the darkness.

'There is a tunnel,' Paolo called out to us. 'With enough space at the side for us to stand up. And it's dry, above the water level.'

'Come.' Ercole took Rossana by the hand and to my surprise she allowed him to lead her to the edge of the hole. 'Sit.'

Rossana sat down. Ercole knelt in front of her on the other side of the opening. He held out his hands. She put both of hers in his. Ercole grasped her wrists and Rossana slid herself off the edge. We heard Paolo's voice from below: 'I've got her.'

Elisabetta went without being asked and sat on the lip of the opening. Ercole helped her down.

And then it was my turn.

'You are coming too?' I asked Ercole. 'To show us the way?'

He nodded.

Now I had to do what the girls had so easily accomplished, but my legs would hardly obey my wishes. I forced myself to walk towards the opening in the ground, the nothingness of the pit. Ercole was watching me. I bent my head so that he would not see the fear on my face. He held out his hands. I managed to get myself to kneel down opposite him. The void began to pull me in. Greasy sweat was forming on my palms, my face. I began to shake.

'Close your eyes,' Ercole grunted. 'Give me your hands.'

I closed my eyes.

Elisabetta voice came from below, speaking quietly but still audible above the rushing sound of the water. 'There is room for all of us here, Matteo.'

Blindly I held my hands out in front of me.

I felt Ercole's calloused fingers close around my wrists. He pulled me from my position. For one sickening second I dangled above the emptiness. Then he let me drop slowly downwards. My mind wavered and my feet scraped desperately against the sides but he held my weight.

'I have you.' Paolo's strong arms wrapped themselves around me and I stopped kicking. He guided me to a safe position and put his mouth against my ear. 'If that man above us chooses, he could replace the grating and entomb us here.'

I shook my head, to rid myself of that idea before it had a chance to grow, but also because I did not believe it. Ercole would come down and help us to escape as the monk said he would. 'No,' I replied to Paolo. 'Look.'

We saw a small light wobble in front of us. Ercole, with the lantern hooked in his belt, had negotiated his own passage from the floor above to join us under the earth. The frail glow seemed to make the blackness around us more intense. The girls' faces gleamed white; their eyes showed as empty socket holes.

'This way.' Ercole squeezed past us. 'We go in line.'

We shuffled close to each other to let him pass in front of us. Rossana's teeth were chattering. I gritted my own together to stop them doing the same.

'You' – Ercole pointed to me – 'the cunning one, walk at my back. And you' – he pointed to Paolo – 'you, who want so much to fight, go last. If anyone follows, then we'll see what you can do with that great sword you carry.'

I saw Paolo flinch. Being set upon from behind in a filthy sewer was not how he wanted to fight his enemies.

We assembled as Ercole had instructed us and followed him into the sewer.

When I had known fear before, I had felt it as a raw, gut-wrenching thing, accompanied by violent death, spurting blood, screams of pain.

This was a more insidious type of terror. Crawling, silent, it stalked us as we scurried under the earth, pressed in by the slime-coated walls, the odour of excrement, of soiling and hospital waste matters. A plash in the water at my feet and the red eyes of a rat glittered.

As the tunnel left the hospital it passed under the streets of the town. Above our heads we heard the tread of feet, the sound of smashing wood, doors rent asunder, the clash of metal upon metal.

'Wait.' Ercole halted after a few minutes.

There was another grating in front of us. Gobbets of filth clogged the bars. Ercole put his hands upon it without hesitation and with a heave he wrenched it from its position.

'Softly now,' he whispered as we climbed out of the tunnel into the sweet fresh air. 'You, boy' – he put a dirty finger under my nose – 'go last now, and make the call of a night bird if you hear or see anything.'

Ahead of us was a path trodden by the town washerwomen when they went to do their laundry and spread their sheets to dry.

Ercole extinguished his lantern. 'Take hands,' he instructed us. 'We will go the rest of the way in darkness.'

I was linked to Rossana. I had never held a girl's hand before in my life. It lay in mine like a soft mitten. Her fingers were very slender, her skin cool. This was not the way that a first touch between a boy and girl who were attracted to each other should happen. There should have been a dalliance at some fair or festival, a walk under the moonlight, or sitting in a garden, when someone's hand reaches out for the other. What was *she* thinking? At one point when the moon was uncovered by cloud I saw that Rossana's face was wet with tears.

When we reached the river Ercole pointed in the direction we must take. 'That way,' he said. 'Walk as fast as you can without stopping.' He looked at Rossana, opened his mouth as if to speak, but then only nodded, and was gone.

Chapter Twenty-Nine

We left the river and took the path into the mountains. I had been abroad in the dark before and the shapes of trees and bushes did not alarm me. With the monk's map unfolding in my head, I found my way partly by instinct, my ears alert for the sound of any pursuit. The ground began to rise steeply. Paolo and I had to help the girls more. Elisabetta and Rossana's stockings were ripped, our fingers torn as we scrambled higher and higher. After an hour or more Paolo suggested we should stop.

'My sisters are exhausted.'

I agreed reluctantly. 'A few minutes only.'

We ate some bread standing up leaning against a tree. I would not let them sit down, being worried that if we did we might delay getting up again.

As we went higher the snow was fresh. I was aware that we were leaving tracks but there was nothing I could do. Dawn came, coldly beautiful. We looked back down the mountainside and saw the town and the river unveiling in the morning mist.

'We must go faster' – I spoke urgently – 'so that we are not visible from the valley floor when the sun is risen.'

The great majesty of the mountain with its mantle of snow loomed over us. Through a small forest, and then we were beyond the tree line. Here the snow was deep. I risked another glance down. I could see a group of moving dots near the river. The bargemen making ready to load their wares? Or men gathering together to begin a hunt?

We trudged on. As the snow became deeper and deeper our progress became slower and slower. Our view of the town was less distinct, with only the outline of the monastery hospital and the bell tower of the church now visible.

'If we cannot see them then surely they cannot see us,' Elisabetta gasped out.

I said nothing. I had hunted in snow. A man could pick out a hare, dark against the white background, from a mile or more away.

The girls were floundering, sometimes waist-deep. I was thinking that we could not go much further without resting when Paolo voiced the concern in my own mind. 'Matteo, are we on the right course for Melte?'

We halted. My feeling was that I had kept to the way indicated by Father Benedict but I could not be sure. I must tell them the truth.

'I think so,' I said. 'But by now I would have thought we should have been able to see the way over the mountain top.'

We looked up. There was no indent or fold in the ridge above us.

'But the heavy snow fall of the last day may have obscured it,' Elisabetta pointed out. 'The mountain passes are often closed in winter time.'

Which meant then that our escape route was blocked.

We could not go back the way we had come. And at the moment we had not the strength to set out in another direction. 'There is a darker patch along the bottom of the ridge there,' I said. 'Less than half a mile away. It looks like a cave. We could shelter there while we decide a course of action.'

We were only a hundred yards or so away from it when the air around us split asunder with a mighty crack.

Elisabetta cried out and looked back.

Paolo turned cumbersomely, trying in vain to unsheathe his sword, prevented from doing so by the snow around him.

But Rossana raised her head and looked up. I followed her gaze, realizing as I did so that the sound had come from in front rather than behind us.

And I saw the whole weight of the mountain top tremble.

'Avalanche!' I screamed the warning. 'Avalanche!'

Chapter Thirty

I grabbed Rossana by the hand and dragged her to the cave opening.

Hampered by her skirts, Elisabetta followed. Paolo was left in the path of the oncoming snow.

A suffocating, blinding whirlwind roared down the mountain. I turned and flung myself out and over Paolo, and held onto him as we were caught up, and pummelled, and driven down with it. We crashed into the trees and were forced apart.

I knew nothing for several hours.

The girls came down and managed to haul us up to the cave. Paolo's arm was broken, my body was bruised and numb, but we had escaped with our lives. Elisabetta ripped up her underskirts to bind Paolo's arm and we huddled together and ate the rest of our food, apart from Rossana, who refused all sustenance.

By now it was late afternoon and as the light left the sky it began to snow again. Paolo said, 'God has put a curse on the dell'Orte family.'

'Or He sent the avalanche to help us,' Elisabetta retorted. 'It will cover our tracks from the river to here and has cleared our way through the mountains. I have been outside and I can see the opening to the other side. Let's make haste while the snow still falls, and it will cover the last part of our journey too.'

I looked at Elisabetta as she said this to her brother. She had changed. Since Rossana had been brought so low, Elisabetta had taken the dominant role.

As we set out again Elisabetta asked me, 'Why did you take us to Averno?'

'I knew there was a hospital there.'

'How did you know this monk would hide us?'

'Everyone knows of the goodness of the monks of Saint Hugh. Their fame for caring for those who have nowhere else to go is widespread.'

'I thought perhaps you knew the monk at the hospital as a friend?'

I shook my head.

'But he knew you.'

'I do not think so.'

'Yes, he did,' said Elisabetta. 'He spoke your name, even though you had not told him it.'

He had. I remembered now. When drawing the map Father Benedict had said my name, Matteo.

'I have been there before' – I mumbled an excuse – 'with the Maestro. He had permission to do anatomies and I accompanied him. But it is something that he asked me not to speak of as people misunderstand his work.'

She nodded and I turned my head away. I saw then that Elisabetta was very observant. In the past I had not noticed this, as she had been content to occupy a lesser place beside her more vivacious sister. But now, with that bright star dimmed, it was possible to see Elisabetta shine. I wondered how long it would be before her sharp mind thought more about her and her brother's conversation with Father Benedict when he had been asking them about the treasure. Questioning the reason why they were being hunted down. How long would it be before she recalled that the soldiers had demanded information about 'the boy' and had not mentioned Paolo by name? Would she then recall that there was another boy who had arrived under strange circumstances into the household of the dell'Orte family, a boy with no proper name, whose background was incomplete, and that it might be him and not her brother that the soldiers sought?

How long would it be before Elisabetta, Rossana and Paolo found out that their mother and father and brother had been murdered, not by looting Borgia soldiers, but by a renegade band of Sandino's men sent to find me?

That it was I, Matteo, who had caused the downfall of the dell'Orte family.

Chapter Thirty-One

The evening Angelus bell was ringing as we came finally into the mountain village of Melte.

We saw the convent of Father Benedict's sister at once. It was a small building nestled close to the steep sides of the mountain pass. The walls were high, with no footholds, and there was only one door with a light burning above it. The lamp illuminated the sign, which told us that this was the Convent of the Christ Child and St Christopher.

'Saint Christopher' – Elisabetta made a wry face – 'the saint who watches over travellers. Let us hope he is mindful of us now.' She made to go forward.

'We must be cautious,' I said.

'I will go,' said Paolo. 'I'm not afraid.'

'Being cautious does not mean you are afraid,' Elisabetta scolded her brother. 'It will cause less alarm if I go.'

'A man has more authority to command them to open the door,' said Paolo, stung by his sister's rebuke.

'They are cloistered nuns,' Elisabetta explained. 'The only man they see will be the local priest to say mass for them and perhaps a male relative on feast days. If you ring the bell as a stranger at night, you may frighten them and they will not let us in. I will go and beg the sister portress who keeps the door if I may speak to the Mother Superior.'

'They will refuse you,' Paolo argued. 'You are a child.

They will tell you to go away and come back with an adult.'

'I will say I bring urgent word from her brother at Averno and I must speak with her alone.'

Paolo glanced at me. 'I think Elisabetta approaching alone is the best way,' I said to him. Then I turned to Elisabetta and began, 'The monk said to tell his sister—'

'I know what the monk said, Matteo. You think because I am a girl I won't remember, but I recall the message very clearly. I will say to her, "Your brother bears you no grudge for having taken a whipping from the gardener when you gathered your father's best roses to decorate the Virgin's statue."'

We stood back and watched as Elisabetta went forward and pulled the bell rope at the door. Some time elapsed before the shutter of the grille was drawn aside.

Elisabetta spoke to whoever was on the other side. The shutter closed and we waited several minutes before it slid open again. After a moment the door itself was opened up. A nun stood there but she did not step outside. Under monastery rules the cloistered nun is not permitted across the threshold of the convent. Once she takes her vows she remains there for life; upon her death she is buried within the walls.

This nun bent to speak to Elisabetta and then looked in the direction she was pointing.

I nudged Paolo. 'Stand up straight,' I said, 'so that she can see us and know we mean no harm.'

Paolo straightened up but Rossana could not. With his good arm Paolo pulled his sister against him as if to protect a young child.

The Mother Superior beckoned for us to come forward. She looked at each one of us and then said, 'And how is my good brother?'

'He was very well when we last spoke to him,' I replied. 'But he put himself in great danger by sheltering us.'

'Then I can do at least as well as he,' she said and made to usher us inside.

'There is something you should know.' Paolo spoke up. 'We have been in contact with the Plague.'

The sister portress stepped back, but the Mother Superior held her ground.

'Your need must be great if my brother sent you to me under such circumstances.'

And she opened the door wide to admit us.

The Mother Superior showed us into a cellar below the house. This room had been cut into the mountain and was far removed from the rest of the community.

'You must remove all of your clothing,' she told us, 'and I will burn it. Then you must scrub each other with a hard brush. And you must shave your hair.'

Elisabetta's hand went to her fair curls.

'I'm sorry' – she looked at Elisabetta – 'but if we are to prevent the spread of any infection this is the only way. I will see if I can find other clothes to replace your own. We sew vestments for all manner of clergy – bishops and even cardinals. I'll search among the hampers and see if there is anything suitable that you can have.'

'I hold the high officers of the Papacy responsible for our misfortune,' said Paolo. 'I could not bear to dress as any member of that organization.'

'Perhaps a minor friar then?' the Mother Superior replied seriously.

As she said this she concealed a smile and I saw that this woman had the same astute mind as her brother.

So for the duration of our stay in Melte, Paolo and I and Elisabetta donned the garb of the Franciscan greyfriars. And we kept these robes when we left to go through the mountains to the other side of Italy.

As for Rossana, she did not ever wear the habit of the followers of the holy man of Assisi. When the Mother Superior took our infected clothes away she studied Rossana carefully. Then the good nun returned with a warm blanket, and wrapping Rossana's little body in it she carried her to the convent infirmary.

And there, two days later, with Paolo and I on each side of the bed, and Elisabetta holding her hand, Rossana dell'Orte died.

Chapter Thirty-Two

The winter wind still cut across the mountain, but the long teardrops of icicles on the eaves of the monastery had begun to thaw when the Mother Superior decided it was time for us to move on.

'The snow is melting. In a day or two the way down will be clear enough for a man to walk through. If the Borgia soldiers chase you with such ferocity it may be that they are waiting in Averno, and as soon as the mountain passes are clear they will come this way to look for you.'

We went to Rossana's grave to say farewell. To conceal our presence here, Rossana had to be anonymous in death. Thus the plain wooden cross that marked her last resting place did not have her own name written upon it. Like the nuns of all convents, she had been given another. Elisabetta had chosen it for her.

'We could see the tops of your mountains from the bedroom window of our home in Perela,' Elisabetta told the Mother Superior. 'Rossana and I often talked of the angels who must live here, so close to God. Now she is with them. So mark the name on her grave as Sister Angela, and let the angels welcome her to Heaven as one of their own.'

The Mother Superior arranged for a hill shepherd to guide us through the mountains.

Paolo and Elisabetta told me that I was welcome to go with them to their uncle, who lived near Milan.

I shook my head. 'I will go to Florence and meet up with my master,' I said.

I had caused enough trouble to this family and thought it safer for them if we parted.

'We will seek out my uncle,' said Paolo. He indicated the dress that he and Elisabetta wore. 'Two mendicant brothers should not attract too much attention on the roads.'

'I wish you well in your lives,' I said, 'should we never meet again.'

'We *will* meet again,' said Paolo fiercely, 'though it may be many years before we do. There is unfinished business that we have to attend to, Matteo. I need time to become stronger, to gather arms and train myself to be proficient in fighting. But when I am ready, I will find you so that we can hunt these men down. Matteo, swear an oath with me now to join me in this venture.'

What should I have done when Paolo said these words? Given the circumstances, I could only agree.

He gripped my arm. 'In the meantime, then, I would ask that you keep watch for me. Florence is so much closer to the happenings of the day, and you move in such grand company, Matteo. Use your eyes and ears on my behalf. I will write to you care of the studio of Messer Leonardo da Vinci.'

And so we parted.

They to Milan and I to Florence. They carrying grief and vengeance. Myself with the added burden of guilt.

And also, hung around my neck, the source of all the trouble.

When we had to burn our clothes the Mother Superior had noticed that I still held onto my belt with the pouch attached, and she had asked me if it contained some holy relic.

I saw this to be good explanation of my attachment to this

object. Many people carried relics about their person, or the badge of a favourite saint pinned to their hat or cloak. I nodded.

'We must make sure it carries no infection. I will make you a new pouch, Matteo. Give that to me and I'll wash whatever saint's bone it contains thoroughly with ammonia salts.'

'I will deal with it myself,' I said.

'Cleaning it will not make the potency of the relic any the less,' said the nun, misunderstanding my reluctance to hand it over into her care. 'The belief is not in the object. Faith is in your heart, and feeds the soul.'

'I understand,' I said. 'Nevertheless, I will do it on my own.'

She brought a dish with some salts of ammonia and a bottle of water. Then she gifted me a small leather bag with a cord, similar to those that pilgrims wear around their neck. I went to the furthest corner of the convent yard and set fire to my belt and the little pouch, and took the thing that it contained, and transferred it to its new hiding place.

But before I did that I looked at the object that had started a trail of death and violence since it had come into my possession.

Fashioned from solid gold, with lettering around the edge, it showed the coat of arms of one of the most powerful families in Italy. A shield with the design of six balls sat proud of the surface, the emblem of the merchant bankers whose influence reached into the furthest corners of the known world. The family who funded Italy and the Vatican, supported France, Germany, England and Spain in their constant struggles for power and conquest.

What Sandino had me steal. What Cesare Borgia must have promised him a fortune to obtain.

The Great Seal of the Medici.

PART FOUR
THE SINISTRO SCRIBE

Florence, 1505 – two years later

Chapter Thirty-Three

No one took note of the fact that the work was scheduled to begin on a Friday at the thirteenth hour.

No one, that is, except myself and the alchemist, Zoroastro.

'This isn't a good day to be starting a major project,' he said to me under his breath as we stood with the others awaiting the arrival of Maestro Leonardo.

I knew the day of the week. It was Friday. The fish sellers were in the street as they were every Friday because it was a Church day of abstinence. This was the day when Christians were supposed to forgo the pleasure of eating meat in order to recall to their mind the sacrifice made by their Redeemer, as it had been a Friday when Jesus Christ was crucified. It was a day considered by many, even those outwith the Christian religion, to be a day with a curse upon it.

'Because it is Friday?' I asked him.

'Because it is Friday,' Zoroastro repeated in answer. 'It is Friday, and also Messer Leonardo proposes to begin applying paint to the first part of the fresco at the thirteenth hour.'

I drew in my breath.

Zoroastro nodded gravely at me. 'Not the day nor the hour I'd choose to undertake such an important piece of work.'

'Did you mention this to the Maestro?' I asked him.

'I told him last night. He wouldn't agree to wait. Said we must make a start because he can't afford to pay the workers a day's wages for doing nothing. And he's been warned that the city councillors are becoming impatient. They want to see more progress. They've complained that too much time has gone by since he finished the cartoons for this fresco. One of the clerks told him that if he didn't begin putting on the paint today then the Council would count it to be yet another week's delay, and might try to penalize him.'

Zoroastro and I both knew the mood of the Council of Florence, and in particular their leader, Pier Soderini, with regard to this fresco. They had little respect for my master's talent, and had been carping and snapping at his heels since giving him the commission almost two years ago.

'When he arrives, Matteo, you speak to him,' Zoroastro went on. 'Tell him it would attract bad fortune to proceed at this hour.'

'He holds you in high regard,' I replied. 'I will not be able to change his mind if you could not.'

'Ah yes. He holds me in high regard for the things I do which are of a practical nature. My metalwork, my knowledge of the elements, their power and their properties, my skill in the preparation of coloured paints ... but my other claims, to interpret mystical portents? *Pfff!* He dismisses them as not worthy of an intelligent being's attention. Last night, when I begged him to put this off because I sensed unfavourable omens, he laughed. He actually laughed.' Zoroastro scowled at me from under his thick black eyebrows. 'It's not a good thing to laugh at forces that we don't understand.'

We lowered our voices and moved closer together as we spoke, united by this bond of respect for the unknown. The rest of the workers stood about chatting amongst themselves. By consent unsaid Zoroastro and I did not speak of our fears to them. I sensed that had we done so we would have been mocked. The people gathered here in the Council Chambers of the Palazzo Vecchio in Florence awaiting instructions from the Maestro were mostly skilled craftsmen. A mixture of journeymen, pupils and painters. Some were very learned men who studied religion, art and the writings of the ancients. One of them, the highly talented Flavio Volci – at fifteen only a few years older than me, but very well educated – had the ability to read Latin and Greek. They would have scoffed at the instinct that made Zoroastro and me wary. The ones among them, like Felipe, who adhered to the ways of the Church would have questioned such superstition, believing in the power of prayer to overcome any evil. And those who placed Man at the centre of the universe would equally have dismissed any belief in magical forces. But I had much in common with this stocky little man, Zoroastro, whom I had come to know well in the years I had been living in Florence. We had a deep empathy for the natural and supernatural forces that existed within our world.

'We'll try to hold him back for as long as possible,' said Zoroastro. 'At least until the thirteenth hour has passed. We must protect him as best we can.'

I saw that Zoroastro had tied red thread to the struts of the wine press he had adapted to crush the pigment blocks to make the Maestro's special paint mixtures. This red thread was an old folk custom to ward off evil spirits. It came from the legend that long, long ago, at the beginning of the world, Man, growing tired of living in darkness and cold, had obtained fire from heaven. So having the colour red about your home and your workplace reminds any wicked spirits that you have the power to make flames to burn them, and so they leave you alone.

In addition to Zoroastro's equipment in the Council Hall there were the tables and scaffolding taken from our workshop in the Santa Maria Novella monastery and re-erected here. There were wax and clay models of men and horses, and the cartoon itself, most of it still attached to frames made of wooden struts. Earlier this year a consignment of sponges, pitch and plaster had been brought in to prepare the surface, and over the last month the central part of the cartoon had been transferred to its position on the wall. A scribe and a storyteller employed by Niccolò Machiavelli, Secretary to the Council, had written out an account of the battle of Anghiari, a famous Florentine victory, for the Maestro to depict. From these notes my master had contrived the main scene, the Struggle for the Standard. This was seen as encompassing the spirit of the Florentine Republic upholding ideals of freedom and liberty against the despotic power of tyrants. It was the keystone of the fresco, and all those who looked upon it believed that when it was finally unveiled it would stun the world.

It had stunned me when I first beheld it.

The image drew you in – horses and soldiers strained against each other, contorted in the effort of their struggle. The horses rearing up with terrified shuddering flanks, nostrils dilated, men grimacing, their torsos twisted among the animals' flailing hooves – a whirling vortex of movement.

To one side a rider had been dragged down from his horse, his skull split open. Above him and the other fallen men, the hooves of the horses plunged, trampling the wounded crawling underneath. In the mêlée and carnage faces were shown screaming in spasms of terror, grinding teeth in the rictus of death. Soldiers hacked and grappled in close combat to win the battle standard. Yes, the moment was glorious, but within it I saw the brutality of men, fighting and killing each other to achieve their purpose.

On the evening the outline had been completed upon the wall of the Council Hall, Felipe, the most practical of men, stood before it. Then he asked the Maestro, 'Was it your intention that the men and women who visit this place should view so much horror?'

'Is that the thought your mind turns to when you look at this fresco, Felipe?'

There was a silence. It was known that the Maestro never discussed his private intentions. It was also known that he abhorred war, but in order to live he needed patronage, and those who paid him frequently demanded from him designs for implements of war. Was he using these drawings to show the awful truth of combat?

'If you can see the painting,' the Maestro said finally, 'then see it.'

As I looked at it now, inside my head flickered the scene at Perela: the smell of spilled blood, the hideous sight of the mutilated body of Captain dell'Orte. I felt the slipperiness of the leather between my fingers as I tethered my horse, saw again the blood puddled in the hoof marks on the earth at my feet. Yes, this fresco would indeed amaze those who beheld it. But each person would read it according to his own experience.

'Ho now, Master Zoroastro!'

We turned round. Maestro da Vinci had come up the stairs from the ground floor without us noticing.

'Good day to you.' The Maestro addressed us cheerfully. 'Good day to all. Everyone is ready to start work?'

His staff and workers greeted him warmly.

'And you too, Matteo. You are well?'

'Yes, sir.'.

'Then let us begin.'

Zoroastro glanced at me.

'It is very dull outside,' I said at once, hoping, as Zoroastro had suggested, that if we could hold him up, delay until the thirteenth hour had passed, then any harm would be less potent. 'The light is not good.'

'I know. There were clouds gathering over the hills at Fiesole, and as I came along past the Arno I saw the river was running very fast.'

'Then perhaps we should wait?' I suggested.

'Better not to,' he said. He took off his hat and placed it on a bench. 'If the storm blows in then the light will become worse, not better.'

It was June and should have been bright at that time of day.

But it was not sunny, although already very hot, almost oppressively so.

'But in this poor light we will have difficulty seeing if the colour is true.'

'I am anxious to begin,' he said abruptly.

'But—'

'No more, Matteo. Please.'

I exchanged a hopeless glance with Zoroastro.

Everyone gathered together. For this momentous occasion he had chosen a patch of earth at the foot of the central piece. Flavio Volci poured some wine and we raised our cups to the Maestro.

Outside it grew darker. Artists and pupils looked at each other. 'We *do* need more light,' one of them ventured to say.

'Bring lamps and candles then,' said the Maestro.

Zoroastro pressed his lips together.

He wanted to cry out, as I longed to: 'Leave off! Take heed when warnings are as clear as this.' But loyalty forbade him to say anything openly which might seem critical of his friend. He would not challenge the Maestro in front of these others.

I immediately went to bring the lanterns and some of the candles that were stacked to one side of the room. I lit a few and set them about. Then, holding the brightest lantern, I went to stand beside my master.

He took a brush in his hand and dipped it in a bowl of paint prepared to his own recipe. His intention was to make the first stroke upon the wall, then we would finish our draught of wine together. The brush was loaded with a heavy grey. The colour of mud, the colour of death.

'So.' He lifted his wine cup in one hand and the brush in the other. 'You have all worked very hard over the last year or so, helping me complete the cartoons and transferring this central scene. And still we have many months of work before us. But for now, let us enjoy the moment.'

He stepped forward.

At that moment a wind got up. It seemed to come from the direction of the river. We heard it quite distinctly, sweeping into the Palazzo della Signoria and rattling the window catches, buffeting the glass like some dervish trying to gain admittance.

My master hesitated. Zoroastro brought his eyebrows down and set his chin, so that his short beard jutted out in front of him. He folded his hands across his chest but remained silent.

There was a clatter at the higher level of the room, as if a tree branch or a tile had come loose and been flung against the windowpane. Everyone glanced up. The wind was louder now. More like a winter gale than a summer breeze. We could hear it howling outside.

Then, so abruptly that we had not time to prepare or shade the candles that were already lit, a window catch came loose, and suddenly the wind had gained entry to the hall. The flames flickered wildly. Then they snuffed out as if by an unseen hand.

The bell of the city began to toll.

'We should desist,' Zoroastro hissed under his breath.

The Maestro affected not to hear him.

The bell pealed out its sombre warning, telling the people to take shelter. Already we could hear a gaggle of voices as people gathered under archways and overhangs of the buildings outside. Down at the riverside the washerwomen would be collecting their bundles. Round the area of the Santa Croce the fullers would cease their work and the young boys would be scurrying to haul the covers across the big vats of boiling dyestuffs. The women in the tumbledown shacks of the poorest workers near the river-bank would gather their children and clamber to higher ground. All citizens of Florence knew that the force of the Arno in a flash flood could tear a baby from its mother's arms.

The wind increased in force. The loose window catch gave way completely and the window smashed against the outside wall.

'Saints preserve us!' exclaimed Flavio Volci.

Fierce, like a living creature, the wind circled outside and in. It sent a flurry of ash from the chimney and wrenched a door open. An enormous gust of air came roaring down the huge hall.

The cartoon itself began to unbuckle. The Maestro gave a great cry and ran towards it. He dropped the paintbrush and his wine cup fell from his hand. I went to pick it up. As I did so I tipped the edge of the wooden bench and the jug holding the water slid from the bench where it rested. Zoroastro leaped to save it. His fingers brushed against the jug as it fell and broke upon the floor.

Zoroastro gave a small moan. He whispered to himself,

'If vessel crack
And water wasted,
Bring some back
Lest bad luck be tasted.'

I had heard my grandmother say that rhyme many times. There was a ritual that should be done at once to show that you did not throw back any gift that Nature had so generously given to you, water being the prime one. Without it no life can exist. Zoroastro and I both went quickly to take some of the water into our hands to drink it. But before we were able to do so, one of the apprentices had found a cloth and mopped it up.

Zoroastro threw up his hands.

I dropped to my knees. Perhaps I could catch some remnant smeared across the floor? But it had all disappeared, soaked up or leaked away. I could find none of it to bring to my lips to show that we respected spilled water. There was not even a drop that I could lick to prevent it going to waste. I got up and backed away from the area.

The Maestro had recovered himself. Someone had climbed the scaffolding and boarded up the window, someone else had secured the door. He and Flavio had pinned the cartoon back in place.

'It's water that has spilled.' The Maestro looked at us irritably. 'Not gold that we've lost.'

'Water is more precious than gold.' Zoroastro spoke quietly.

'It went from a cracked jug,' I said urgently. 'And it leaked to earth without us catching any of it.'

'And this means?'

'I will not work in this place today,' Zoroastro declared.

He was so strange, this little man, Tomaso Masini, who went by the name of Zoroastro, and the pupils and artists who worked with my master were used to his unusual ways so that mostly they ignored him. But not today. I saw one nudge the other to pay attention.

'I'm going to my forge. Come, Matteo, you can assist me.'

I made to obey, and then halted. My master looked angry.

The pupils were now whispering amongst themselves. So these learned people *did* become uneasy when they saw the evidence before them. Outside the rain had begun, a downpour, hammering noisily on the rooftops.

But now the master was in one of his rare tempers and he would not be moved.

'You will remain here, Matteo,' he said coldly. 'You, Zoroastro, are a free agent and can do as you wish, but the boy is my servant and must do as I bid him.'

Zoroastro became flustered. 'I will stay,' he said. 'Though I can't persuade you to leave, yet I will not abandon you. I would not leave you to suffer alone. It's too late now to undo what has been done. Our lives . . . our deaths – are tied together.' He composed his face in resignation. 'The fates are decided.' And as he spoke his next words apprehension trembled in his voice. 'Our destinies are now meshed in such a way that no power of this world or any other can untangle them.'

Chapter Thirty-Four

'**M**atteo, I would speak with you.'

It was some weeks later. After the initial unfortunate beginning, work on the fresco had gone ahead and the paints were applying beautifully. Zoroastro and myself had worried unnecessarily, or so it seemed. Each day, under the Maestro's guidance, the fresco evolved before us like a living pageant. Horses and riders emerged from their shaded outlines, pulsating colours that beat a rhythm inside my head. When I looked at it I fancied I saw sweat on their bodies and heard the groans and cries of battle. In one area my master had achieved the appearance of smoke, a thing unheard of in a fresco, which can be a limited form of painting because of the difficulty in showing perspective. But he had contrived to make it look as if a cannon-burst had exploded just out of vision and the smoke from the discharge was drifting across the lower part of the wall.

All through this clammy summer, as soon as we arrived in the Council Hall we went straight to work. Some of the tasks I did were repetitive, but I did not mind. I had no aptitude with a brush and could not colour in the simplest outline. Despite being past twelve now I was still quite small and light. Therefore I was able to climb rapidly up and down the scaffolding and fetch the craftsmen their work tools as they called for them: the small pointed rod that the painters used to prick out the drawing, the silk bags which puffed on the dust to show the outlines. I refilled these bags a dozen times a day to apply the powder through the holes. At the end of the day after working in the heat I, like the rest, was exhausted, yet I did not tire of the fresco itself. It fascinated me. I would always find time to go and stand before it and discover a new aspect to intrigue me. Like now, when most of the others had cleared up and departed, I hung back and stared at the latest detail the Maestro had painted in.

What was that man's name? The one there, who was dying so piteously, unnoticed by his comrades. Did he have a wife and children at home? And the other, the younger one, why had he come? Had he been looking for excitement? Or, like Paolo dell'Orte, was he seeking revenge for some atrocity committed on his family? They, and the others, would have listened to the words of their orators calling them to arms. Which piece of prose had awakened in them the desire to fight? Was it the prospect of reward, or truly the idea of supporting a noble cause? Leaders went to war for many reasons, to gain land or wealth, for personal greed or fame. But why had these soldiers taken part?

'Matteo!'

I jumped. So lost was I in the construction of a life for each character that made up the fresco I had not heard the Maestro approach.

He stretched out his hand in a gesture of affection and ruffled my hair. 'What thoughts are inside that head of yours?'

I shrugged. It was a sign of how much easier I had become in company over the last two years that I allowed anyone to do that to me without moving away. 'I was thinking of the men in your painting. Who are they?'

'Soldiers of Florence.'

'What are their names?'

'Their names?'

'That one there,' I went on in a rush before he could continue. 'The man who is lying on the ground. Will he live?'

The Maestro stepped nearer to the wall to examine the body of

179

the fallen soldier. 'I doubt it. He's too grievously harmed. Likely he'll die later, as most men who are wounded do in battle.'

'It seems to me that his face has a resignation in it,' I said. 'He does not want to live.'

'Why not?' My master regarded me with humour.

'Perhaps he has no home. I think that might be the case. There is no one to grieve for him if he does not return.'

'That would be sad,' said my master. 'If no one cared whether you lived or died.'

'Whereas' – I pointed at one of the central figures whose sword arm was upraised to slash at his adversary – 'he seeks glory and does not care if he dies. Indeed perhaps he would rather die so that his name will live on in people's minds.'

'Men like that do exist.'

'They say that Achilles, the handsomest and bravest of all the ancient Greeks, was such a man. It was foretold to him that if he went to the Trojan War he would surely die, but his deeds would be told in song and story for ever. Should he stay at home he would survive to old age, unknown. He chose to go with Ulysses and fight to rescue Helen. He slew brave Hector before the walls of Troy, but he in turn was slain by Paris at the Scaean Gate. And it is true, the name of Achilles is not forgotten. Perhaps that is what that man thinks. That if he wins the standard his name too will live for evermore.'

'A painting has as many interpretations as there are people who view it. Many think of it as a captured moment in time.'

'I suppose I am interested in what happened *before* and *after* the moment depicted.'

'Ah, you mean the story. There is an account of the battle of Anghiari. In fact there are several accounts of this particular engagement, where the Florentines clashed with the Milanese. But you will find that it depends very much on the individual story-teller as to what actually took place. It's seen as a great victory for the Florentines, accompanied by the slaughter of their enemy. But my friend Niccolò Machiavelli tells me that the only casualty was a soldier whose horse was startled by a snake, whereupon the beast reared up, its owner fell to the ground, struck his head upon a stone and was killed. But he has a biting wit, Messer Machiavelli, and that might be his own way of reading the battle reports.'

'I'd like to know what happened to the individuals afterwards,' I said.

'You have a keen mind, Matteo. And, indeed, that's the very thing I want to talk to you about. Before you leave, come over here where we can speak privately. There is something I want to discuss.'

He led me to the centre of the room.

'It was the autumn of the first year you arrived in Florence when you came to live in my household again. Do you remember?'

I did remember.

It had been almost summer 1503 when I arrived in the city after weeks travelling through the mountains from the convent at Melte. It hadn't taken me long to find out the whereabouts of such a famous person as Leonardo da Vinci. I discovered that he was away and not expected back in Florence until October, when he was to set up a new workshop to begin the fresco commissioned by Pier Soderini and the City Council.

The weather was warm enough for sleeping outdoors so I found a sheltered hole in the embankment of the Arno and there made a den for myself.

Towards the end of August I heard news from Rome. The Borgia Pope Alexander had died. He had become gravely ill after eating dinner and had not recovered. Italy had been experiencing the hottest of weather and Rome was running with fever brought in by the insects from the surrounding marshes. But most believe he had been poisoned, either by others or in mistake by his own hand. He suffered a most horrible death. It seemed a fitting end to one who had lived his life in the manner he had.

For a while the Church and its leaders were in turmoil, but eventually a new pope, Julius, was elected. This Pope Julius, being a warrior in his own right, did not want a rival in Cesare Borgia and removed Il Valentino as commander of the papal armies in order to lead them himself. He also refused to recognize the Borgia's title of Duke of Romagna and demanded that the cities Cesare had conquered in the Romagna be returned to papal control. Cesare Borgia, in fear of his very life, took refuge in Spain. I immediately felt safer at this downturn in the Borgia fortunes for it was to Cesare Borgia that Sandino intended to sell the Medici Seal.

I had not known this when Sandino first instructed me to meet a priest called Father Albieri in Ferrara. At that time I was only told that a certain priest attending the wedding celebrations of Lucrezia Borgia in Ferrara knew the location of a locked box which held an object that Sandino was anxious to own. I was to find the priest and he would lead me to the box. My task was to pick the lock, remove the object and relock the box in such a way that no one knew it had been opened. When Father Albieri took me to where the box was kept within a certain house in Ferrara I accomplished my mission very easily. It was the priest who told me what the object was, and insisted that I should carry it. He put the seal in a leather belt pouch and tied the belt around my waist. He must have felt guilty at encouraging a child to commit an act of theft for he insisted on giving me absolution for my sin and blessing me before we set out together for our rendezvous with Sandino.

Foolish priest! He should have made his own confession for he was soon to meet his Maker. But neither he nor I had any suspicion that Sandino was going to betray us when we met up with him.

The priest spoke first after Sandino greeted us. 'I have brought what you sought,' he said, 'great treasure'.

Sandino grinned in triumph. He turned to one of his men and said, 'Now we will have gold aplenty! Cesare Borgia will pay us well for the Medici Seal.'

'The Borgia!' Father Albieri recoiled. 'You told me that you were working for the Medici. That was the only reason I agreed to help you.'

'I know,' hissed Sandino. 'If I had told you all of the truth then I would not have such a treasure now in my hands.'

And saying this, the brigand swing his cudgel and clubbed the priest to death, and would have done the same to me had I not managed to escape from him.

To begin with I could not reason out why Sandino would want to kill us. At first I thought it might be that he did not want to share the reward but then I came to think it was also because he could not trust us to be silent. For it was only when I grew older that I appreciated that the value of the Medici Seal was more than the gold of which it was made. The seal could be used like a signature to authenticate documents of any kind, and people would believe they had come from the hand of the Medici. So the Borgia, in his quest for power, could have procured loans, falsified papers and promoted any number of conspiracies – and laid blame on the house of Medici. But now, with Cesare Borgia gone from Italy and a whole year having elapsed since I stole the seal, surely Sandino would no longer pursue me to recover it?

Therefore, on hearing that the new Pope Julius would not tolerate Cesare Borgia's return to any part of Italy, I was much more at ease at being in public. I found some jobs in the shops around the marketplace in Florence. In return for a penny or two and scraps of food I helped with deliveries. I was good at memorizing names and addresses, having had practice in the past at doing so.

One day while I loitered in the street waiting for work a hand gripped my shoulder. It was Felipe. Leonardo da Vinci had returned to the city and Felipe was out ordering goods to provide for the new household. Felipe told me that the Maestro had recovered his spirits after they had left the employ of the Borgia and had resumed painting. He brought me back to the monastery of Santa Maria Novella, where they had set up a workshop and accommodation.

'I thank you for taking me in again,' I said now to the Maestro.

He sat down upon a stool beside Zoroastro's workbench, far enough away in the Council Hall so that the others could not hear us. 'I'm not asking you to recall the circumstances of your return to my service so that you can thank me, Matteo. Can you cast your mind back to our time in Santa Maria Novella during the autumn of 1503?'

'Very easily,' I said. It had been interesting for me to see the establishment of an artist's working studio. There was great excitement among the members of his household at him having being awarded the commission. It meant regular income for a few years and a chance to be involved in a magnificent enterprise. That was when I'd met Zoroastro. He had come and set up his forge in the yard at the side of the monastery and through those cold months we had all worked together to get the project under-way. 'Why do you want me to remember that autumn?'

'Because it was then, almost two years ago from now, that the merchant's wife, Donna Lisa, was delivered of her baby stillborn. I would like you to recall the nurse. The one called Zita, who had been Donna Lisa's own childhood nurse, and whom she kept on in the house.'

Zita was an elderly woman who had charge of Donna Lisa's children and the stepchild from her husband's previous marriage. We had first met her when she brought two little boys with her when visiting her brother, who was a friar in the monastery of Santa Maria Novella. These boys loved to watch Zoroastro working at his forge.

'I remember her,' I told the Maestro.

'This nurse told us that the reason Donna Lisa's baby was born dead was because a fat toad had hopped in her path on her way to church on All Saints' Day. Yes?'

'I remember she said that.'

'As it had sat there, unmoving, Donna Lisa had been obliged to step over it. And, she said, this was why the baby that Donna Lisa was carrying within her had ceased to live.'

I nodded. 'It is what the nurse told us when she spoke to us the evening we went to their house.'

'So,' my master went on, 'the nurse would have us believe that the toad caused the baby to stop breathing in the womb. Which was why, when it was time for Donna Lisa to give birth, the child was born dead.'

I nodded.

'Do you believe that, Matteo? That because the lady, Donna Lisa, stepped over a toad, in some way this caused the child within her to die?' I hesitated.

'Do you?' he insisted.

'It would not seem so,' I said reluctantly.

'Yes or no, Matteo.'

'No, but—'

'Yes or no?'

I shook my head, refusing to answer in the manner he wished.

'It is a matter of reasoning, Matteo. Think about it. A toad sitting in the path of a pregnant woman. How can that possibly cause the death of the child she is carrying?'

'My grandmother said that the old beliefs come from the seed of truth,' I replied.

'And I could not agree more. It may be that if a pregnant woman eats a frog or toad it could be harmful to her or the child. It's known that there are certain foods that we should not eat, and that can be especially harmful to women. You yourself are most aware of this. You're the person who told Graziano about the false mint and so saved him from perpetual stomach ache. And it may be that eating a toad or even touching one can spread some infection that's harmful to an unborn babe and that is the source of the story.'

'Well then,' I said. 'You have confounded yourself!'

He raised his eyebrows. 'I have?'

'Indeed. There it is. You have just said that it is almost certain that a toad can be the cause of such a mishap.'

'You irrepressible, troublesome boy!' he exclaimed.

I looked at him anxiously, but he was laughing.

'You see,' I went on, 'it is better for the woman who is pregnant to avoid such a thing altogether and be safe. So what the nurse said has truth in it.'

'Matteo, listen to me.' He put his hands on either side of my face. 'Something caused the child to die. But it can be useful for men or women to place the blame elsewhere. It means no guilt can be attached to them. Not the father who sired the child, nor the mother carrying it, nor the servants in the house preparing her food, nor her good nurse charged with looking after her, nor the midwife attending her, nor the doctor who was called to her bedside. They are all exonerated because it is the fault of the toad. You understand how convenient this is?'

'I understand.'

'But by blaming the toad,' the Maestro continued, 'it means that we do not need to seek out the real cause.'

He waited.

I did not say anything.

'What could you deduce from all of this, Matteo?'

'I do not know.'

'Let me help you,' he said. 'It will happen again. Somewhere a child will be born dead. Yet another mother will suffer this grief, with or without a toad being present. Though that will not matter, because in the absence of a toad some different portent will be adjudged to have caused the catastrophe. And so . . .' He looked at me expectantly.

'It will keep on happening,' I said slowly, 'and the real cause will not be discovered.'

'And what is the advantage of finding the real cause?' he pressed me further.

'We might be able to prevent it happening again.'

'Well reasoned, Matteo.' He regarded me with approval. 'Now consider this.' He indicated something for me to look at. As in many other instances when his actions had more than one purpose, it was not an accident that he had led me to Zoroastro's workbench. He touched the red thread that hung from various parts of the wine press. 'What are these for? To ward off toads?'

I felt my face blush.

'Is this a reasonable thing to do?' he asked. 'Why is it, do you think, that Zoroastro has these pieces of red wool and such like hanging here?'

'It is an old folk belief. Older than our forefathers' forefathers. It is a very potent symbol.'

'A symbol?'

'Yes.'

'Of what?'

'It is connected with fire,' I said. 'Hence it is red. With fire, man can protect himself. Even the Church teaches the power of fire to drive out demons.'

'Indeed' – he laughed – 'and if fire is effective against a demon such as Pier Soderini' – he mentioned the name of the head of the City Council, who was hounding him to finish the fresco – 'then a burning brand would be most useful. But red thread? I don't think that would keep him away, or make the wind blow less, or the rain cease to fall. Surely you see that?'

I bent my head.

'Matteo, you must think about this.'

'I do,' I said truculently.

'Your belief is based on fear. Fear comes from ignorance, and ignorance exists due to lack of education.'

'My grandmother educated me.'

'She taught you what you needed to know to be able to live the life you did. You have a different life now. There are matters to which your mind is closed, and should be opened before it is too late.'

'There are matters that men will never discern. There are things that cannot be explained.'

'All things can be explained.'

'Not everything.'

'*All* things can be explained.'

Heresy.

'The monk at Averno said there are things that are not given to men to understand.'

My master stood up. 'I say there are things that men do not understand because we have not yet developed the tools to do so. In past years we were unable to look closely at the moon. Therefore men made up legends to explain what they saw but could not understand. But now with mirrors and ground glass we can see the surface of the moon more clearly, and therefore we know that it is not a goddess, or the soul of a beautiful woman, or any of these things. So when the monk says that there are things not given to men to understand, I say there are things that men do not understand *yet*.'

He saw that I was unhappy. 'No matter,' he went on gently. 'I wanted to talk with you because I know that you cannot read. Every day I see you looking at the fresco. It shows men fighting so that they can live in freedom. I tell you, freedom is worthless if you do not also set your mind free. A person who cannot read is prey to superstition and can be led into error by the ignorant opinion of others.'

'Yet you have also said to me that you have found mistakes in the writings that you have studied. And these are books that are held in respect. You told me that when doing your dissections in particular you have noted with your own eyes things that are in conflict with the texts you have read.'

'Tchh!' He made a sound of exasperation, and for one moment I thought he would cuff my head. 'What I am saying to you is this. If you do not learn to read very soon then you never will. It's a mystery to me that your grandmother did not teach you, she who taught you so much. She must have seen that you have an excellent memory and are extremely quick-witted.'

'Perhaps she was unable to.'

'I doubt that. You said that she had her own recipes. She must have had some skill in reading them.'

'I know she valued her recipes. She made me promise that they would not be burned, although she could not read them very well herself.'

'I believe she could. Why did she not teach you to read them?'

'She taught me enough,' I said defensively.

'Only as much as she had to. You told me that she showed you the names of her customers and the streets or squares where they lived. She taught you only this. Just enough, and no more. I wonder why she did not want you to learn to read when she educated you in the stories of *The Iliad*, *The Fables of Aesop*, and the other myths and legends?'

I had no reply for this.

'We must arrange for you to learn to read.'

'No!' I knew a servant should not speak so impudently to his master but I would not allow him to sway me in this. 'I will not do it. The others would find out and the humiliation would be too great for me to bear.'

'I know it's embarrassing, but I think you have urgent need to attend to this.' He drew something from inside his tunic and handed it to me. 'Some packages arrived after everyone had left the workshop at the monastery this morning. Felipe had gone so I sorted through them myself. This letter was among them. It is addressed to you. I know that you have received other letters in the past. What do you do with these letters? How do you read them?'

I did not answer him.

'Do you ask one of the other pupils – Flavio perhaps?'

'I do not.'

'It must be very frustrating for you not to know what is in your letters.'

But I did know what they contained.

Because, although I could not do it myself, I had found someone to read them for me.

The Sinistro Scribe.

Chapter Thirty-Five

The first time I received a letter I endured many catcalls and whistles from the other younger apprentices. This was to be expected in the ordinary banter of the workshop, but one of the older pupils, Salai, possessed a malicious turn of mind. He snatched the package from my fingers and sniffed it.

'I do believe I smell perfume,' he declared.

'Give it to me.' I could feel my temper rise. I realized that it was a mistake to show Salai that he had annoyed me. It served only to make him torment me the more.

'He's the grey wolf who hunts in the dark watches of the night, is our Matteo,' declared Salai. 'The one who slinks against the wall, and we cannot make out which is wolf and which is shadow.'

'I *have* noticed that you are abroad in the night,' Flavio chimed in. 'Where is it that you go, Matteo?'

It was true that I went out at night from time to time, to accompany my master to the nearby hospital mortuary where a sympathetic doctor allowed him to undertake dissections. But he preferred to keep this as secret as possible. A magistrate could give an artist permission to undertake an anatomical study of a corpse if the artist could provide good reason for his interest, such as Michelangelo had done when sculpting his great statue of the boy David. But my master feared that it would become known that his interest in the study of the dead was more than merely to ascertain the position of certain tissues and muscles to perfect his art. If people saw his more detailed drawings of internal organs they might whisper to others, wondering what their purpose could be. It would make him vulnerable to gossip and bad feeling. Without the protection of a powerful patron, it was vital that my master kept this work unknown.

Salai knew about these night visits. At one time he had accompanied my master on his nocturnal excursions. But enduring long hours with nothing much happening had bored him, and also he was inclined to prattle to others in the wine shops whereas I did not, so my master now took me with him. Salai was aware of all this. Therefore he kept teasing me, knowing that I would not reveal the truth. He waved my letter in the air. 'Jump up and let's see if you can catch it,' he taunted me.

I went forward, pretending to comply. As Salai stretched his arms higher to keep me out of reach I kicked him hard in the groin. He crumpled, yelling in pain, hands clutching between his legs. I grabbed the letter from him and raced from the workshop.

I had made an enemy but I had my letter safe.

That was the first letter.

Of course I could not read it.

But I did recognize the name beneath the last line of the writing.

Elisabetta.

I kept it close on my person all the time. Salai had taken to watching me and I knew that he would steal it from me if he could. It was January and near the time of the festival of the Epiphany, when gifts are given by the master of a household. I asked if I might have a purse, one that I could attach to my belt to hold what little money and any precious possessions I had. I carried the letter there for a month or so before finding the person who could read it to me.

The man known as the Sinistro Scribe.

This was the name he gave himself, partly because he wrote

using his left hand. And it was that which drew him to my attention. One day, almost a year after I had come to Florence, I had occasion to be on the other side of the river. I was walking from the direction of the Santo Spirito, making my way towards the Ponte Vecchio, when I caught sight of him tucked in at the foot of a tower just before the bridge. There was a little niche there and he was in a good position to catch passing trade. He had enough space to sit with the box containing his materials resting on his knees, giving him a surface upon which to lean to write. I noticed that his pen was in his left hand. But he did not write backwards as my master did, with the words flowing easily so that he could see his work and read it as he wrote. This scribe wrote with his hand curved like a hook and he placed the paper sideways as he did so.

I barely paused to look at him. He was just an old man with white hair and, like many others in the crowded streets near the river, set up to sell something. I walked on, but then I remembered Elisabetta's letter tucked in my belt bag and a thought came to me. I turned back and stood a little distance away. He kept his head bent as he penned his letters. I watched him for a minute before addressing him.

'Ho there, scribe. I see that you write well enough. Can you also read?'

'Obviously you cannot, boy,' he replied. 'For if you were able to read, you would see that my sign' – he pointed to a piece of paper pinned to the wall above his head – 'says: *Reading and Writing – Careful and Discreet – the Sinistro Scribe.*'

'The Sinistro Scribe,' I repeated. 'How came you with that name? I see that you are left-handed, but although the Florentine for left is *sinistro*, the word for left-handed is *mancino*.'

He looked at me with interest. 'A boy who cannot read yet appreciates the subtleties of language,' he said. 'What is your name?'

'Matteo.'

'If you were more observant, Matteo, you would notice that I sit on the left side of this tower, which is situated on the left side of the river.'

I looked around and noted that what he said was true.

'It humours me to do so,' he went on. 'And when one has a service to sell, it's good to have a name that marks you out from others.'

'I see,' I replied.

'And what do *I* see?' He examined me more closely. 'A boy. And a servant boy, I'll wager, for your sandals, such as they are, are worn with running errands. And a boy who carries a quality leather pouch at his belt. Most likely a gift from his master as it's not so long since Epiphany. And I also saw that this boy's hand came to rest upon his pouch as he was speaking with me. Hmmm . . .' He stroked his beard theatrically. 'I'll warrant there's more than money in that pouch. I believe it's a letter that you have there, Master Matteo.'

I hurriedly folded my arms.

'Aha!' he declared in triumph. 'I've made a hit! The eyes of the Sinistro Scribe miss nothing.'

The old man was so pleased with himself that I could not help but smile with him.

'What's more,' he added, 'I will further warrant that the letter is from a girl and you don't want to admit to your friends that you're unable to understand what it says.' He held out his hand. 'Give me a florin and I will read it for you.'

'A florin!' I exclaimed in genuine horror. 'I have never owned a florin in my life.'

'Well, half a florin, then,' he said grudgingly. 'But I am astounded that you would cheat an old man in this way.'

'Half a florin is a week's wages for an artisan,' I retorted. And then, finding the rhythm of the barter, added, 'Brunelleschi, who built the dome of Santa Maria del Fiore, was not paid at such a rate.'

'Am I not as good a craftsman as any?' the scribe demanded. 'I, who was trained in the monastery of Saint Bernard by the venerable Brother Anselm? The same Brother Anselm whose scriptorium is renowned throughout Christendom for the elegance of its manuscripts. My penmanship is second only to his.'

'It is not your skills in script writing that I am interested in, scribe. It is your talent for reading that I wish to employ. That must be a lesser charge, surely?'

'Am I not deserving of the rate of any artist in this city?'

'Half a florin? For two minutes' work? Even my master is not paid that amount.'

'And who is your master that he sells his work so cheaply?'

'Leonardo da Vinci.'

'You bragging liar. I hardly think that the Divine Leonardo would have an illiterate youth in his service.'

I flushed and made to turn away.

The scribe reached out a bony finger to detain me. 'Tush, boy. Don't take offence. It's not given to all of us to read and write. Else how would I make my living? Let me see your letter. If it's not very long I may offer a special price to read it to you.'

I hesitated, then I pulled Elisabetta's letter from my pouch.

'It's scarcely a page. Why didn't you say so?' He made to peer into my purse. 'How much money have you in total?'

I took out a penny and held it out to him with my other hand. 'That's all there is.'

'I thought I heard it clink against another coin in there.'

'Take it or leave it.' I made as if to put the letter and the penny back into my purse.

'All right, all right,' he conceded. 'Though I will starve tonight while you will no doubt go back to your master's household for an evening meal consisting of nine courses,' he grumbled as he read my letter.

And so our friendship was born.

In his position by the bridge he saw and heard the happenings of the city so he was a ready source of gossip, with many amusing anecdotes regarding prominent people. His mind was sharp and he possessed a shrewd grasp of politics. From my conversations with him I became more aware of current affairs. I did not need his services again for some time as it was near the end of the year before I received another letter from Elisabetta.

Nevertheless I usually stopped and exchanged words with the scribe several times each month. If there was any errand to do for the workshop, generally I was the one requested to undertake it as my memory was such that I knew most streets of the city. Also my master regularly visited the Brancacci Chapel on the other side of the river to study the frescos there. I would accompany him and afterwards bring his satchel with any drawings in it back home while he would go and eat a meal with friends who lived close by. He rated these frescos very highly, but the howling faces of Adam and Eve being expelled from the Garden of Eden disturbed my dreams. On these occasions, after crossing the river I would loiter at the Ponte Vecchio to speak to the scribe, then run to collect the satchel from my master as he was leaving the Church of the Carmelites.

The scribe did not get much employment in letter writing. The kind of persons who had need of his services were superstitious, and as soon as they saw he was left-handed they would cross themselves and move away. But on saints' days, of which there were many, he managed to sell lots of little squares of paper on which he'd drawn the appropriate saint and written out a prayer.

This evening, after the Maestro had spoken to me, I went to the scribe for him to read to me the fourth letter I had received from Elisabetta. It was near the end of June, the eve of the feast of St Peter. He is the saint considered to be the founder of the Christian Church and claimed as the first Pope. This is because the Bible states that Christ changed the name of Simon, who was the leader of his disciples, to Peter, which means rock, by saying, 'Thou art

Peter, and upon this rock I will build my Church.' And Christ also said, 'I will give to thee the Keys of the Kingdom of Heaven.' Therefore, in preparation for the feast day tomorrow, the scribe had been busy and had already made up some prayer cards. He'd drawn a crude representation of St Peter with some large keys in his hand, and beneath this he had penned a line or two of text. Half a dozen of these were stuck on the wall around him.

As I came over the bridge I saw him bent over his box, raising his head now and then to call out, 'A prayer from the lips of Saint Peter himself. See! He holds the Keys of the Kingdom of Heaven. Pin this tract above the bed of the dying, and Saint Peter will unlock the Gates of Heaven and let the soul of your loved one enter Paradise. Only a quarter of a penny each!'

As he saw me approaching he left off his writing.

'And how is the great fresco proceeding?' he asked in greeting, as he wiped the end of his quill on his sleeve.

All members of the workshop were under instruction not to discuss details of the fresco, but it was hard to resist boasting, especially when I was so besotted with it myself.

'It is a work of such magnificence,' I told the scribe, 'that everyone will flock to see it.'

I was quoting Felipe. Felipe, despite having witnessed the creation of great Art over many years, had been overcome with the painting.

'From the cities of the civilized world artists will come to the Council Hall of Florence to study and learn,' I declared proudly.

'Especially as the drawings of the honourable Michelangelo have been so finely received, and his fresco will be completed on the facing wall.' The scribe spoke with an innocent expression on his face.

This was to test my reaction, but I knew him better now and only laughed at this baiting. It was the talk of all Italy how the Council of Florence had tried to arrange that the two greatest artists of the day, Leonardo da Vinci and Michelangelo, would be working in the Council Hall at the same time. Leonardo was to paint the battle of Anghiari on one side of the room, while Michelangelo painted the battle of Cascina on the other. But if this is what Pier Soderini and his fellow councillors had hoped for, then they had failed. My master had gone away while the sculptor had been working on his drawings. And now that Michelangelo had finished his cartoon, the new Pope, Julius, demanded that the sculptor come to Rome to undertake a project for him.

'My master does not trouble himself with petty jealousy,' I said, 'and in any case the sculptor Michelangelo has gone to Rome.'

'I'm not surprised the sculptor has gone to Rome,' said the scribe. 'Were I younger and fitter that's where I would be. It would be safer than staying here. The days of Florence as a republic will be counted off as a nun counts the paternosters on her beads, now that this Pope has been elected.'

'The last Pope plotted to bring Florence under his control,' I said. 'But despite his efforts, even making his barbaric son Cesare head of the papal armies, he failed to do it.'

'But this Pope is himself a warrior.' The Sinistro Scribe enjoyed an argument. He put his pen away in his box and went on, 'They say that when Michelangelo was casting the Pope's statue for Bologna he intended putting a book in his hand and Julius told him to replace it with a sword.'

'The Florentine Republic is strong,' I replied.

'The republic is as strong as the money it has and the soldiers it can pay to fight for it.'

'There is more affluence in Florence than anywhere else.' I knew this to be true. I had been in Ferrara and seen the lavish balls and celebrations held there at the time of Lucrezia Borgia's wedding to the son of the duke. The Ferrarese had made a great show of their wealth, but it was nothing compared to the commerce that I encountered daily within Florence. 'This town prospers as no other. And soon we will no longer be hostage to the best condottieri captains with men to protect us. We will have an army of our own.'

The Sinistro Scribe laughed out loud. 'You've been listening to the proclamations of Machiavelli and his talk of creating a town militia, and training men to defend themselves and their property.'

'Messer Machiavelli's idea is very clever,' I said. I had heard my master telling Felipe about it one night. 'He is forming a citizen army, a Florentine militia which will fight for their own land and homes. They will be more loyal than a band of mercenaries who can be bought and sold and change sides as they please.'

'And who would you wager your money on, Matteo? A citizen army of farmers and guildsmen? Or troops under an experienced condottieri captain? Eh? Peasants with pitchforks, or seasoned soldiers who know that when they triumph they will be let off the leash and allowed to pillage as they please?'

'A strong republic is a noble thing.'

'And a cannonball does not distinguish between a noble and a knave,' retorted the scribe.

'We have the protection of the French. They are the most powerful nation in Europe. And their army is not so far away in Milan.'

'This Pope will seek out anyone who can help him unite Italy under his domain. He will do exactly as the Borgia tried to do. He might not be as ruthless as Cesare Borgia or his father was, but no matter. He will do it more directly and probably with more success.'

'He cannot overcome the French.'

'I tell you that, with help, he can. He is making pacts and leagues with various rulers to isolate his enemies, then re-forming and changing these as it's expedient to do so. In the face of his intent this republic will crumble. When that happens, what need will there be of a fresco proclaiming man's own democratic spirit?'

I had no reply for this. Like any other citizen I could chat with the young men at the barbers' shops and on the street corners, but the twisted coils of politics entwined my mind so that I could not think straight.

'Do you really not see how dangerous it is, Matteo?' the old scribe asked me. 'Florence had a mind to be the republic that would last for ever, and she hoped others would follow. But the princes and dictators of their city states don't want ideas like that to spread.'

'But I thought the King of France and the Pope were allies?' I did not say this with any great conviction because I had begun to understand how often the great powers manipulated others to achieve their own ends, but I felt as though sand was running under me and I needed some stability to cling to.

'Only for as long as it suits them to be. Once this Pope has made enough gains to stand alone he will turn on the French and drive them out of Italy. Who will support Florence then? This brave republic will be on her own with the jackals circling to eat her up.'

'Florence helped the Pope. It was Florentine soldiers who captured Cesare Borgia's henchman Michelotto and sent him to the Vatican to be tried for murdering Vitellozzo and the other captains. Pope Julius is well disposed towards the republic of Florence.'

'He will be better disposed towards a single ruler who can be bribed and kept quiet than towards a group of free men intent on democracy. When the time comes to disperse the Great Council your fresco will not be permitted to remain.'

'Why not?'

'Do you think when they come back to take power that they will want a reminder of the ideals of the republic trumpeted across the largest space in Florence?'

'No one would dare destroy it!' The Sinistro Scribe was mad to think that. Or more likely only saying these things to make me dance like a fish at the end of a hook. 'Maestro da Vinci's fresco is a stupendous work of art.'

'But don't you see, Matteo? It's because it is such a stupendous work of art that it cannot stay there. From all quarters intelligent and cultured people may come and make discourse on it. It will serve to inflame imagination, and stimulate thought on an alternative way to achieve a life of harmony. The beauty and the power of this Art is precisely why they will not allow it to survive.'

'Who?' I demanded. 'Who are these *they* that you talk about so knowledgeably who will come and take our freedom away from us.'

He looked at me in surprise. 'Why, the family that ruled Florence once, and may do so again.

'The Medici.'

Chapter Thirty-Six

Within the da Vinci household we did not have a nine-course meal every night, as the scribe had once suggested. But after sunset each workday evening Felipe saw to it that large dishes of food were available so that everyone could eat as much as they wanted. Often my master did not eat with us. He used the time to work on other projects or to have dinner with the very many people, within and outside the city, who invited him to their homes. Sometimes he liked me to accompany him but I was glad that this evening was not one of those occasions. I gobbled my food and went straight to my own place within the house. I wanted to be alone to look over my new letter that the scribe had read to me before I'd left him.

The sleeping space that Felipe had found for me was underground: a former storeroom within the network of cellars below the floor of the monastery. By the time I came back into the service of the Maestro he had established his studio within the monastery of Santa Maria Novella, and the available rooms had all been taken. I knew it pleased Salai, the pupil who was jealous of the attention the Maestro paid me, to see that I had been allocated such a lowly place to sleep. But it suited me well. I preferred being away from the others and it meant that my master could call me to go out with him to his night-time dissections without anyone else being aware of it. I placed my mattress at the far side of the room, where there was a door set high up in the wall. It had been used at one time as a hatch to deliver goods into the monastery directly from the street. When the evenings were warm I opened it up. I could listen to the noises of the city, and on the wall outside was positioned one of the iron brackets where the night watch came and placed burning brands to illuminate the street during the hours of darkness. This gave me enough light to look at my letters.

Including the one that had arrived this week there were four in all. I had been in Florence two years now and Elisabetta was writing to me round about the half-year, at the time of the tax accounting of the farm where she now lived. I took her letters from my pouch and held them tilted to the open hatch to look at them. Whenever I brought him my letters I made the scribe read them to me several times (for which he'd tried to charge me extra) so that I could hoard the sentences inside my head. Later I would recite them to myself at leisure. And by dint of doing this I fancied that I recognized some of the words and knew their meanings.

Elisabetta's first letter had been very short, no more than few lines, written in haste.

From the farm of Taddeo da Gradella, near Milan

My dear Matteo, brother and friend,

We have arrived safely at the house of my uncle Taddeo. His welcome is restrained, but he has given Paolo and myself the use of two small rooms in his house and I am pleased enough with this as we are as safe as anyone can be in these times.

I hope you also are safe and well,

Your sister and friend,

Elisabetta

When I heard those words my heart had filled with gladness that she and Paolo were out of the way of future harm. This feeling took me by surprise. For years I had schooled myself not to display emotion. This sweetness running through me caused such a lift of my mood that even Felipe had commented on it.

'You're in fine spirits since that letter arrived,' he had observed dryly. 'The apprentice boys must have guessed correctly then. It was from a girl, wasn't it?'

I mumbled some reply and resolved not to have this situation repeat itself. From that day I tried to keep watch when the carriers were about so that I would be first to take charge of any letters or parcels. This took more time than I would have liked as very many packages and letters were delivered to our household. Most of them were for my master and were mainly letters asking him to undertake work, in particular painting commissions, for which he had a high reputation everywhere. These requests came from different parts of Europe, most persistently from Isabella d'Este, Marchioness of Mantua, asking him to finish a portrait of her that he had begun some years previously, but also increasingly from representatives of the French court in Milan. It was not hard for me to distinguish between the written form of my master's name and my own. Thus I managed to catch Elisabetta's next letter before anyone saw it. I immediately took it to the scribe and he read it to me, again for a penny, although he complained that this one was longer and I should pay him more.

Dear Matteo, brother and friend,

I wonder if my first letter ever reached you? Paolo and I are still in the farm of our mother's brother. Paolo has not taken well to the tasks he has been set to do here and there is friction between him and our uncle. Uncle Taddeo expects us to work hard to earn our keep but this is not unfair as he works very hard himself. I cook and do other household tasks, but recently, since my uncle discovered that I am able to count and write serviceably well, I am allowed to do his accounts. He is a dour man, given to prayer and fasting, with no fripperies or feasting allowed. There is little laughter here and my brother has become morose. I have thought of entering a convent and wondered if I would be happier there. I would not like to be shut away, although I know that the nuns at Melte were happy with their lot. But I could not bear never to wear a pretty dress again, or show my hair, although there are no fine clothes here in this house. I do wish I knew how you were, Matteo. I fear that some ill has befallen you.

   Elisabetta

I held the paper close to my face and studied the curl of the letters that made up her name. She was unhappy. I could sense it. This letter had cast me down as much as the first had made me glad for a while.

Her third letter, which I now unfolded, had engendered another emotion altogether within me. When reading it aloud, the Sinistro Scribe had paused in his speech and glanced up at me for a moment before continuing.

   My dear Matteo,
   The messenger I entrust this letter to assures me that it will reach you but I have no way of knowing this. So I have decided to put my letter in the care of Rossana. As I do not know which saint, if any, whose special duty it is to look after letters I will ask my dear sister, who I am sure is in Heaven with the angels, to ensure that this one arrives into your hands. I think of her often, and of you too, Matteo. There is a little river here where I sometimes go to be quiet, and sit in the shade of a willow tree. Sometimes I fancy she is near me and so I whisper secrets to her as I used to do when we were small. There is no reply, but perhaps it is her voice I hear in the rustle of the leaves, and I believe her spirit is close by. I think of the days of our youth at Perela and now know

them to have been the happiest of my life on this earth.
I pray for you,
Your sister and friend,
Elisabetta

I put this letter down to pick up the fourth and last. The one that I had not managed to intercept and that my master had given to me earlier this evening. The one I had taken to the Sinistro Scribe barely one hour ago and with the last of my money had paid him to read to me.

To Matteo, a servant boy, in the care of the household of
Leonardo da Vinci, sometimes of the city of Florence

Dear Matteo,
I am writing to you again, although having had no reply from you to my previous letters I do not know if the time and expense in my doing this is wasted, and whether I should continue to do so. If you receive this, and if there is any way that you can send me word to say that you are well, it would make me happy.
I will not squander my uncle's money and paper to send any more letters in this fashion unless I hear from you. I fear that you are not receiving my letters, or that you do not wish me to write to you. I will know then, if I receive no reply, not to write to you again. Nevertheless I hope this reaches you and finds you well.
Elisabetta dell'Orte, at the house of Taddeo da Gradella,
June 1505

Within my chest a stone slid across my heart. Unless I could send a letter in reply I would receive no more from her. And she would think that I was dead or did not wish to hear from her and Paolo. I looked again at the letter. Starting at the beginning I mouthed out the sentences I had memorized. I counted off the words until I reached 'Rossana'. I spoke it aloud and traced the outline of the letters of her name with my finger. *Rossana*. My memory was twinned with Elisabetta's sister, as they had been twinned at conception. Their whispers and their laughter like the river bubbling in the ravine below their father's keep. I brushed my hand across my eyes and flung myself back onto my mattress.

I wanted to reply to Elisabetta. But I had no money to pay the scribe to do this for me. There was no salary in my work. Felipe had set up accounts at various shops and services, and I was allowed to take advantage of these. If I needed a haircut or a tooth pulled I went to the barber's and he sent his bill for this to the da Vinci household. Similarly if I needed new hose or shoes I could go to the tailor and the shoemaker. If I had an ailment I visited the apothecary. My food and accommodation were supplied. No actual money was given to me but I fared much better than many other servants. The families of some of the pupils in the house paid Felipe an amount to be in the school of Leonardo da Vinci. The few pennies that I had earned some time ago were due to the kindness of a silk merchant. These were now gone. How therefore could I pay the scribe to pen a reply to Elisabetta?

I traced some of the letters again with my fingers. I found the E of Elisabetta, the M of Matteo. To draw and write was a talent I did not have. I had often watched my master make a drawing with a few deft strokes. Once I had picked up a piece of charcoal and tried to copy him, but the results were such that I had thrown the paper into the fire so that no one would see them. I could not draw. And I would not try again for fear of failure. I liked the work I did. I was good at it. It was interesting and I was favoured and well fed. I had no need to attempt to be skilful with a pen. But now I began to see the advantage if I could but do these things for myself.

Was it really so difficult to learn to read and write?

Chapter Thirty-Seven

'What are you going to make of yourself, Matteo?'
I stopped brushing the floor and looked over at Felipe, who was sitting at our dining table counting out piles of coins. He was settling the quarterly bills for our suppliers, who would call in today to collect their money.

'I am happy as I am,' I replied. I began to sweep more industriously so that I could finish and be off to do some other task. I did not want to linger in the room as I feared another lecture coming. About a month after my master had spoken to me about my lack of learning, Graziano had drawn me aside to have a quiet word about the possibility of me taking up some kind of book study. I thought of the humiliation when it became widely known that I was illiterate and the public mocking this would provoke from Salai and the other apprentices. I refused to discuss it so Graziano had shrugged and left off lecturing me. An interview with Felipe, I guessed, would not be so pleasant.

Felipe got up from the table and, taking the broom from my hand, stood in front of me. 'The master has said that your appearance must be attended to, Matteo. Look at you. Your tunic is quite tattered and you will need a pair of shoes for the colder weather approaching. And your hair.' Felipe lifted a strand of my hair and surveyed it with distaste. 'You never visit the barber as often as you should.'

I could not tell him that, since my conversation with the

Sinistro Scribe about the impending power struggle within Italy, I preferred my hair long. It hid my face and, although I did not truly believe that the Medici would ever be welcome again in this city, I deemed it better not to have my features in plain view. 'In the worst of the winter,' I replied, 'having more hair will keep me warm.'

'It isn't only your appearance that is causing him disquiet. There is the matter of your education.'

'I know enough for what I do within the house,' I replied. 'And, as you say, winter is coming. There is always more to do in that season, therefore no time to spare me from my duties in the household. I would not be able to undertake any studies.'

'Indeed the festival of Christmas is approaching,' said Felipe with an edge to his voice. 'Therefore why don't you take the decision to co-operate with those who wish to help you to improve your mind? Then we could have two festivals this year. One to celebrate the birth of Christ, and the other the birth of the new Matteo.'

'I do not want—' I began.

'Pay attention to me.' Felipe held my arm firmly. 'You are being given an opportunity that many other boys in your circumstances would never encounter. Messer da Vinci has offered to have you instructed at his own expense. You would receive an education such as others might only dream of having. Even you must recognize that you cannot remain a boy for ever. As one becomes a young man there are requirements in dress and proper conduct to be learned. To grow up into manhood requires more from a fellow than allowing the years to pass.' He gave me a rough shake. 'Accept what has been offered to you and be done with this obdurance.'

I hung my head but said nothing.

Felipe made an exclamation of annoyance and went back to doing the accounts.

So as summer faded and autumn burned out the colours of the

year through umber, copper and ochre to winter grey, I did not listen to their entreaties to better myself. The only thing that nagged at my mind was how to reply to Elisabetta's letter. One time I ventured to ask the Sinistro Scribe how much the cost would be to write out a letter of a few words.

'Aha, Messer Matteo!' he exclaimed in satisfaction. 'I wondered when you'd broach that subject.'

'What subject?' I asked, feigning innocence.

'Come now, I'm too skilled in wordplay to be fooled by a stripling like yourself. You want to reply to the lady Elisabetta and have need of me to write the letter for you.'

'There are many talented men within the da Vinci household,' I replied haughtily, 'and I am well regarded there. I might find another who would be eager to do this task free to oblige me.'

'But even say they did,' countered the scribe, 'there is still the expense of the ink and the paper, and then the carrier to pay. How much is it to have a letter transported from Florence to Milan? More than you can afford, I'll warrant.'

And there he had me. For of course I could not pay for that service. My master was in constant communication with Milan. He had many friends there, artists, academics and philosophers. Felipe would probably not mind if I included a letter in one of the packets to go. But it would be an extra cost to have it taken to the outlying farm where Elisabetta and Paolo now lived and I had no means of financing this.

'What is the thing that you carry so closely around your neck?'

The scribe's unexpected question startled me. So accustomed was I to carrying the seal that at times I forgot its existence. I was never parted from the little bag that held it, even when washing my body. The leather had become blackened with sweat but the cord held fast and now I hardly noticed the soft weight of it against my skin.

'I note how you react to my question, Matteo.' The old man's eyes narrowed. 'If it's a precious thing that you have there then you could sell it and pay me with the profit you make.' He reached his skinny fingers towards my neck.

I leaped back and clasped my own fingers round the cord and the leather purse the nun at Melte had made for me. 'It's of no value,' I stammered. 'There's nothing in it.'

'There must be something in it,' said the scribe. 'I see how closely you clutch it to you.'

'It is a relic,' I said. 'A holy relic.'

'What kind of relic?' the scribe asked me. 'If it's a primary one then it would be worth more.'

'A saint's bones.'

'Which saint?'

'Saint Drusillus,' I said, thinking of a statue I had seen in the convent at Melte.

'That's curious,' said the scribe. 'The relics of Saint Drusillus are very hard to come by.'

'My grandmother gave it to me,' I replied. 'She told me it was very old.'

He laughed. 'That's not the reason your relic is so rare. Saint Drusillus was a martyr, burned at the stake. There was nothing left of her but ashes.'

'I – I . . .'

'Your grandmother was duped by some pedlar.' He glanced at me keenly. 'Yet now that I know you better, I would have said that if your grandmother was like you then she would not have been so easily fooled.'

I parted from him rapidly that day. Our conversation had brought back memories I did not welcome: of Sandino and his intrigue with the Borgia. Italy was now feeling the absence of Cesare Borgia. Without his rule, the Borgia domains in the Romagna were falling into the hands of whoever had the power to take them. Some of the previous lords had returned to their cities, like the Baglioni to Perugia, but another mighty predator had cast its eye upon these profitable little kingdoms. The

211

Venetians had seen their opportunity and seized Rimini with some other smaller towns. As these places were part of the traditional fiefdom of the Church, Pope Julius was furious and was now massing armies and allies to help him bring these territories back under papal control. If the Vatican intended to take on the might of Venice, which side should Florence choose to ally herself with? The city had begun to hum with rumour. Was the Council, even with the advice of the wily Machiavelli, cunning enough to manoeuvre itself safely between these sharp rocks?

As I walked home that night via the Ponte Trinità I fingered the bag at my neck. I could not obtain money by selling the seal. There were no shops in Florence, even those of the more dishonest traders, who would buy such a thing without questioning me. The most innocent explanation I could give for having it would be that I had found it. That it must have been lost when the Medici Palace on the Via Larga was raided and the family driven out of the city a number of years ago, and that I had discovered it lying on the banks of the Arno. More than likely, the person I tried to sell it to would take me for a spy of some party or other and report me to the Council in the hope of a reward.

I looked over the bridge into the Arno. The river was swollen with rainfall and the water had changed from the sluggish, dry mud-brown of summer to the swift, treacherous, choppy grey of early winter. I could throw the bag with the seal inside into the river. Why not? It was a source of danger to me. But I hesitated. If I ever came across Sandino again it might be the thing that would save my life. And also . . . I touched the worn leather. It was a link to my past, to the dell'Orte family. If not the seal itself, then certainly the bag made me think of the time spent in the convent with Elisabetta and Paolo. I could not part with it.

But I needed to communicate with Elisabetta, else I would be cut off completely. I saw then that I would have to come to some agreement with Felipe. I took the opportunity to make my request when he was alone working at his ledgers.

He looked at me severely. 'And in return for this extra favour granted from this household, what will you do, Matteo?'

'I will set my mind to begin to learn, as you wish,' I answered humbly.

He did a strange thing then, something unexpected. He gripped my shoulder with both hands. It was almost a hug.

'I am glad for you,' he said.

As soon as I could I returned to the scribe and told him that I wanted my letter written.

'I don't work for nothing,' he said brusquely. 'You have money?'

'I have something here that is better than money. I have brought goods that you will be happy to trade your service for.'

'Bread? Wine?'

'Something of more value to you.' I unrolled the piece of paper that Felipe had generously given me to barter with the scribe.

The old man touched it with respect. 'This is excellent quality – Venetian, I'd say, or perhaps from Amalfi?' Then, as a thought occurred to him, he asked me quickly, 'You didn't steal it, boy, did you?'

I was offended and stepped back from him. 'I did not.'

'Don't be insulted by my question. I had to ask. There are so many people in this city eager to denounce each other through jealousy. It means that if anyone asks how I came by such paper I can assure them it was honestly.' He took the sheet from my hand. 'With this I can write your letter, Matteo, and still have plenty left over to make two dozen prayer tracts to sell.'

So the scribe wrote out my letter as I dictated, and Felipe undertook to have it despatched for me on my promise that I would apply myself to studies as soon as he could find someone suitable to teach me.

But before anything could be arranged we had a situation of a more desperate kind to deal with.

There was a problem with the fresco.

Chapter Thirty-Eight

The weather was now much colder.

In the great hall of the Palazzo Vecchio we worked with our caps pulled down over our ears, scarves wrapped tightly round our necks, and wearing gloves with the fingers cut off. Freezing draughts of icy wind found their way in through the chinks in the windows and the outside doors. Florence is a city nestling in a basin of the Arno valley, and the land around it is lush and fertile, due in part to the temperate Tuscan climate. It is protected by the hills and even during the worst weather has little snow, but that winter an intense chill seeped into the streets and buildings of the city.

The paint turned sluggish and difficult to manage. The recipe as laid down by my master was complicated to implement, and even his most experienced pupil struggled to follow his instructions. After my master's first application of paint in June the central section was almost completed and the figures rose, splendid in their terribleness. But as the rest of the cartoon was transferred the paint became turgid. On consultation with the Maestro a brazier with burning wood was placed near the wall and the construction of the scaffolding was altered to accommodate tapers and small torches to help the fresco to dry on the upper reaches.

On this morning when we arrived our tools were rimed with frost and we had to wait until the fire was alight before we could

214

begin. Felipe was pricking out another section of the cartoon and I was assisting Zoroastro to grind more powder for the paints when there was a commotion with the pupils and apprentices at the top of the scaffolding.

'Master Felipe!' Flavio called out, his voice high with fear. 'We have need of you here. At once!'

Zoroastro and I exchanged glances as Felipe clambered up the scaffolding. Within seconds he was scrambling back down again.

'Zoroastro, if you would, take a look at that section of the wall.'

Zoroastro too returned to the floor within a minute. 'Help me,' he cried and he grabbed hold of the brazier. 'The paint is coagulating on the surface,' he explained as we manhandled the fire basket closer to the wall. 'If we cannot dry it at once then the colours that have just been laid will trickle down the wall and run into the central part.'

'This has the makings of a disaster,' said Felipe.

'And they scoffed at us when we tried to warn them,' Zoroastro muttered under his breath. He pulled out the small axe he carried in his belt and began frenetically chopping some wood to make more fuel for the fire.

'We must find the Maestro and tell him right away,' said Felipe.

'He rose and went out very early this morning,' grunted Zoroastro, chips of kindling flying round his head, 'but I don't think he intended to visit Fiesole today.'

Having many other interests to sustain him, my master did not come to the Council Hall for the whole of each day. He took time to pursue his botanical or anatomical studies. Occasionally he would make a painting on canvas or board. But these were rare, and only in a particular case would he agree to undertake to do this, as when he was prevailed upon recently by the French king to paint a beautiful Madonna holding the Christ Child playing with a yarn winder.

'Matteo!' Felipe called me sharply. 'Do you know where your master is just now?'

'I left him this morning at the house of Donna Lisa.'

'Then go and fetch him. And,' he shouted after me as I went quickly from the hall, 'run, boy. Run!'

The Donna Lisa's house was by the Church of San Lorenzo. So now I, fitted out by Felipe in a winter tunic, new hose and good shoes, raced out of the Palazzo Vecchio, veering past the great colossus of the David, across the Piazza della Signoria in the direction of the baptistry.

The Donna Lisa lived with her husband, the silk merchant Francesco del Giocondo, in the Via della Stufa. He was the man who, two years ago, had given me the few pennies I had ever earned as actual money. I knew the way very well, as I had been to their house many times over the last years.

We had made their acquaintance through their children's nurse, Zita. The two boys she brought with her to Santa Maria Novella were attracted to Zoroastro's forge in the courtyard and would stare in fascination as the little man hammered furiously, with sparks showering around him. One day their mother, the Donna Lisa, came looking for them. She had become anxious as the children had been out for the most part of the day, and the nurse, Zita, who had been her nurse as a child, was becoming forgetful in her old age. It was just before the feast of All Saints, at the beginning of November of the year 1503, and the Donna Lisa was with child. I could see this clearly by her shape and the cut of her dress, yet she walked with a fluid grace that resembled St Elizabeth, carrying John the Baptist within her, in the paintings where she meets with Mary, the Mother of God.

'I am seeking my children, two boys,' she greeted me as she came into the courtyard, accompanied by a servant. 'They are with their nurse, who visits this monastery from time to time.'

'They are over there,' I said, 'watching Zoroastro making metal pins to hold our pulleys together.'

The boys were in their favourite spot next to the forge. My

master was standing close by, overseeing Zoroastro to ensure the correct dimensions of the metal pieces they were constructing.

'Oh,' Donna Lisa said as she approached. 'I didn't realize it was the workshop of Messer Leonardo da Vinci that the boys had chosen to frequent.'

'If one is choosing a workshop to visit,' said my master, 'then why not choose the best? Your children have obviously inherited good taste.'

'Indeed.' She laughed in amusement. She beckoned to the nurse, Zita, who was sitting on a bench by the wall. 'We must go,' she said. 'My time is near and I tire easily.'

It was a week or so before Zita brought the boys again. She told us that Donna Lisa was unwell and this was when I heard the story of the toad crossing her mistress's path.

A few days later Donna Lisa came into the courtyard alone. A black veil shrouded her face.

'I would speak with your master,' she said to me.

At this time the Maestro was totally absorbed with the cartoon for the fresco. He was making numerous models and sketches of horses in various positions, and drawing a vast amount of sketches of men's faces, arms and bodies. I glanced at Zoroastro.

'He cannot be disturbed when he is working,' Zoroastro told her.

'I will wait,' she said.

'He can work for many hours,' Zoroastro told her kindly. 'He is capable of going without food or drink or sleep.'

'I will wait.'

In the later part of the day Donna Lisa's husband arrived. He sat beside her and stroked her hand. He was older than she was, but that is the way of our times. A man lives longer and therefore often has more than one wife, and I believe Donna Lisa was Francesco del Giocondo's second or third. He whispered in her ear but she would not be persuaded to leave and go away with him. Why did he not command her to obey him? He would be within his rights as a husband to bring servants to seize her and force her to return to his house with him. But I saw how it was between them. He put his hand under her elbow and tried to coax her to her feet but she shook her head and would not rise.

Eventually he stood up. 'You, boy.' He spoke to me and gave me a few pennies. 'If your master can spare you I would be obliged if you would attend to this lady and bring word to me when she is decided to come home this evening.'

But evening came and still she did not move. It was cold. Zoroastro piled more wood upon his fire and placed a stool for her closer to the flames. I served her a plate of our food, which she refused, and some wine, of which she sipped a little. The night grew very dark.

Then the Maestro came from the workshop. He came into our common room via the internal door that had been made on his request so that he could pass from his own accommodation directly to the studio at whatever time he chose. His tunic was streaked with plaster and he had clay stuck to his fingers.

I pointed out of the window to where Donna Lisa sat patiently. 'This lady has waited all day to speak with you,' I said.

'A commission? I cannot take on any more work just now.'

'I told her this, but she said she must speak with you.'

He sighed. 'It would seem that every rich lady wants her portrait done but I am unable to satisfy the whims of these women.'

'I do not think this woman would come here on a whim, or to gratify her vanity.' It was Graziano, the best assessor of women, who made this observation.

I had brought a basin of warm water so that my master could dislodge the particles of clay from his fingers.

'Very well.' He immersed his hands in the water. 'Ask her what she wants, Matteo.'

I went to where Donna Lisa was sitting by the fire. I opened my mouth to speak but she spoke first. 'Tell your master that I require a death mask made most urgently. Tell him also that this is a task so particular that he is the only person to whom I would entrust it.'

I knew that this work would have to be done at once as, even in cold weather, a body could decay very quickly. It was a very popular custom and there were little workshops that specialized in it. Mainly it was given to apprentices, as by doing it they learned basic bone structure and the contouring of the human face.

I returned and informed my master what she wanted.

'Tell her that any jobbing craftsman can do this for her.'

'She says that in her case it is a task most particular.'

'There is a place in the next street where they do it as a speciality,' he observed.

The thought came to me that she must have walked past that shop to come here.

She did not bow her head in submission when I gave her my master's reply. 'I will wait to speak to him,' she said.

I returned to the inside of the house and told him of her intention. He made a small gesture of irritation. The dinner was set out on the table. The smell of hot food flavoured the night air. My master made to go away from the window but then he turned back and looked again to where she sat, the veil across her face, her hands folded in her lap.

'Do we know her? She is familiar to me in some way.'

'She is the mother or stepmother of the boys who come to watch Zoroastro work at his forge,' Felipe informed him. 'The wife of the silk merchant Francesco del Giocondo, who lives in the Via della Stufa.'

'Giocondo . . .' The detail in the name caught his attention. 'Jocund.' His tongue played on the syllables. 'A name with more than one meaning.'

'The merchant, her husband, came by earlier but he could not persuade her to go home with him.' Felipe paused. 'When we saw her last she was pregnant with child.'

'Ah, that is why I did not recognize her at first.' My master went to the doorway and looked at her.

She became aware of his gaze and raised her eyes. She did not drop her glance. Neither did she smile. Only looked at him steadily.

'Graziano,' he began, 'tell her – very gently, mind – that I cannot—'

He broke off, and then abruptly went out into the yard. He spoke with Donna Lisa for a few minutes and then came into the house.

'Matteo, I would like you to accompany me.'

'Now?'

'Now.'

We had not eaten since mid morning. My master went into his private rooms and came out carrying his leather satchel. He opened the door of our store cupboards and selected some materials. 'Save us a plate from dinner,' he said to Felipe, 'and do not wait up.' Throwing a cloak over his work clothes, he went out with me at his side.

Donna Lisa shivered as we left the warmth of the courtyard. Away from Zoroastro's forge we felt the bitter wind that swept up from the river to the city centre. My master took off his cloak and placed it around her shoulders. She looked up at him and her mouth curved a little, a half-smile, barely distinguishable by the light of the street torches.

I saw then the glimmer of the girl she had been. Earlier her face had the cast of a lady who would never smile again.

We had no need to pull the bell to gain entrance to her house. A servant had been stationed to watch for her and the door to the street opened as we approached. The house was shuttered and the inside doors were closed. The place was airless, with a sense of doom and foreboding.

We went upstairs and into a darkened room. The nurse, Zita, sat in a chair by the hearth but no fire burned there. The mirrors were covered. On a chest was a crucifix showing the broken body of the Christ with a candle on either side. Under the window stood a small table with something on it covered with a white linen cloth.

There was a smell in the room. It was one I recognized. The smell of death.

'I lost the child I was carrying,' said Donna Lisa. Her voice faded on the next words. 'A girl.'

She led us to the table. 'She died within my womb. I knew almost at once when it happened because she ceased to move and that was unusual, for in the latter months I felt her dance within me every night. By day she was quiet, but in the evening she became lively. She loved music, this little one. In the last weeks, when her restlessness kept me from my sleep, I would get up and play my lyre and the sound would calm her.'

She put her hand to her face as she struggled to continue. My master did not speak. He did not move, only remained still until she had the strength to go on.

'As she was born dead she cannot be buried in consecrated ground. They will not even let me name her. That is why I want you to do a death mask, lest I forget her.' Her voice trembled. 'I do not want to forget her. How can a mother forget her child? The doctors say I cannot have another child. So there is no comfort for me there. And according to the laws there will be no record of this child, no mark of her life, her death, her passing. But she did live! I felt her live within me.'

Her resolve weakened and her voice shook.

He reached out his hand. This man, who always kept his emotions in check, who rarely showed grief or anger. But she did not take it. She recovered herself. 'I will not embarrass you with my frailty, Messer Leonardo. I have cried all the tears in the world over the daughter I have lost. There are no more in me left to shed.'

My master waited and then said, 'Your husband is agreeable to this?'

'My husband is a good man.'

I remembered how tenderly Francesco del Giocondo had stroked her head when he was with her in the courtyard.

'I will leave you to your work,' she said, 'and go and speak with him now.'

It was not so long after this that Francesco del Giocondo came to see my master to ask him to paint the portrait of his wife. 'My wife has a melancholy upon her that makes me fear for her life,' I heard him tell the Maestro. 'She will not leave the house. She barely speaks or eats. She never plays her lyre, nor sings, nor reads. You are the single person she spoke to when this tragedy befell us.' He glanced at me. 'You, and the boy. I beg you, Messer da Vinci. If you would agree to come to my house, I would pay you what you wished. If only for an hour or so each week. She has gone so far inside herself that I can think of nothing else that might save her.'

And so it was that I knew where my master would be this morning as I ran through the streets of Florence to find him and bring him to the Council Hall.

I found them where they always were, in the little room which opened out into the inner courtyard of the house. Here he had made a painting studio for himself and had been working on Donna Lisa's portrait for nearly two years now.

On hearing my garbled message he excused himself at once. We left the merchant's house to hasten back through the streets to the Palazzo Vecchio, me running beside him, having to make two steps to each one of his.

Chapter Thirty-Nine

Inside the hall was chaos.

Pupils and painters were swarming over the scaffolding with lit tapers and cloths and brushes. Felipe, the coolly efficient Master of the Household, paced the floor, wringing his hands over and over. Graziano was distraught, calling out instructions to the apprentices then rushing to do the task himself. Salai was, for once, shocked into silence while Flavio sat huddled in a corner as though he expected a beating. Zoroastro, tears streaming down his face, ran shouting like a wild man to my master as we entered.

'What are we to do? The mixture will not dry! What are we to do?'

Among the tumult my master tried to assess the situation. The paint on the upper reaches was oozing down the wall and had already run in parts onto the completed section of the fresco. It appeared that the heat from the brazier had slowed what might have been a flood, but the colours still slid insidiously downwards.

'Build the fire higher,' my master ordered.

'But—' began Zoroastro.

The Maestro swept past him.

'We will have to send out for wood,' said Felipe. 'Our store is exhausted.'

'There's wood aplenty around us,' my master said grimly. He threw off his cloak and, grasping the axe, which Zoroastro had

223

discarded upon the floor, he made with firm steps towards the scaffolding.

'Assist me here, Matteo,' he said, and began attacking the supports of one side.

I glanced from his face to that of Felipe and Zoroastro. Such a look of horror appeared on Felipe's as he took in his master's purpose. The Maestro pulled a short plank from its position and ordered me to add to the fire.

'This will have to be paid for,' Felipe protested. 'The City Council was very clear in the terms of the contract. The wood and all other parts of the scaffolding must be returned to them or we would owe them the cost.'

'Let them come and take it back then. They can roast their penny-pinching fingers in the fire as they root about among the embers.' The Maestro made a mighty chop at one of the struts.

Felipe stepped back in fright.

My master loosened a spar. He wrested it from its socket and hurled it into the brazier.

Zoroastro leaped forward. 'The fire basket stands too close to the wall for safety.'

'Leave it be.'

'It will singe the work already done!'

'Leave it be, I say again,' the Maestro cried. 'Don't you know the Florentines love bonfires? It's not so long ago that under the encouragement of their great prophet Savonarola they rushed to burn their glorious art in the piazza outside. Then in the space of a year or so in the same place they burned the very man who ordered that bonfire of the vanities. Let them have another one!' He lifted a piece of wood and split it with his axe. 'Fitting that it should be within their Council Chamber this time. Open the windows and doors! When they smell the fire and hear the crackle of the flames they will run to witness this conflagration just as they did the others.'

We watched helplessly as he piled wood into the brazier. The fire surged higher with great licking crimson tongues. Viewed through the flames the figures and horses appeared to be struggling in some hellish damnation. The colour on the upper reaches curled at the approach of the enemy that threatened to consume it. Was it working? Was the intense heat drying the paint and plaster? But then Flavio cried out, the piercing wail of a lost soul.

'Eeee! Look!'

Through the wavering light we saw the lower part of the fresco begin to blister. Zoroastro rushed to the wall but Graziano pulled him back. All of us there within the hall were forced to watch. There was nothing anyone could do, for this was beyond redemption. The crackling, spitting fire gave no quarter. And we moaned and clustered together in our anxiety, the noise and the fierce heat adding to our terror of the ravenous monster that was devouring the masterpiece. The expressions on the faces of the doomed soldiers in the battle were reflected in the anguish on the faces of the craftsmen watching their creation destroyed.

When the fire basket could hold no more my master faltered. At once Felipe took his arm and coaxed him to walk with him to the furthest end of the hall. Zoroastro, paying no attention to the safety of his own person, went close in and, hooking one of his blacksmith's tools into the grid of the brazier, dragged it away from the wall. The others, moving like monks in a funeral procession, began to pick up the objects lying scattered around. No one spoke. I went to the table where we kept our food and found the drinking goblets and poured a large draught of wine into one. I added some cinnamon, then I put a long poker into the heart of the fire and after a minute I took it out and plunged it into the liquid. I lifted a stool and carried it, and the hot wine, to my master. When I placed the stool before him he looked at me as though he did not recognize me, but he sat down readily enough. I held the wine cup in front of him where he would smell the hot spice. He passed his hand over his eyes. Then he grasped the goblet and began to sip from it. I knelt down at his feet.

He put his hand on my head. 'Leave me,' he said. He glanced up at Felipe, who stood beside him. 'Leave me. I would be alone.'

The two of us went back to the centre of the room, where I prepared hot spiced wine for everyone who was there. There was no conversation. The only sound in the room was Flavio's teeth chattering. I made myself drink some of the wine. Only then did I dare to look at the wall.

The fresco was ruined.

The upper part was a confusion of colour and few clear outlines could now be seen. The hours spent meticulously forming models of men and horses, the months and months of careful drawing, the weeks of preparing the wall, transferring the cartoon, the careful application of the paint, all gone in minutes. The lower wall was scorched and blackened, and although the figures in the central part prevailed, as if their energy could not be extinguished, even there the heat and smoke had blown across to mar their definition.

After a while my master came from the back of the hall and went to where the tables and workbenches were grouped together. It was as if he was looking for something. Eventually he scooped up some of the prepared paint in his fingers and sniffed it. Then he rubbed it between his palms.

'Why did you change the mixture?'

Everyone looked at each other.

'Maestro,' stammered Flavio, 'we have not altered it in any way.'

'The proportions are the same,' agreed Felipe. 'I check these most carefully.'

Zoroastro said, 'You know the craftsmen you employ. No one here works sloppily.'

My master acknowledged this, but said, 'Yet there is something amiss.'

Everyone stood around miserably as he prowled among the

tables and workbenches, pausing now and then to turn and stare at the fresco.

'I don't understand,' he said. 'It worked when we tested it in Santa Maria Novella.'

'It was only done on a small section of wall,' Felipe pointed out. 'Perhaps over a larger area . . .' His voice trailed away.

Zoroastro had gone to the stone slabs, where the ground paint lay ready for mixing. He stirred one of them with his finger, put some powder on his tongue, closed his eyes and chewed it. Then he went to the jar of oil, newly opened when we began work today. He dipped his fingers in the jar and smeared some over the back of his hand. He walked to where Felipe stood. 'This oil,' he said in a low voice; 'who sold it to you?'

Felipe looked at him in concern. 'Why do you ask?'

'The consistency . . .' Zoroastro held his hand up for inspection. 'See for yourself. The quality is not the same as we have been using previously.'

'We use different suppliers.' Felipe went to the jar and examined the tag tied to the stopper. 'This one is from the riverside warehouse but the order was the same as the others.'

'It is not the same,' Zoroastro insisted.

'The Pope has begun so many new projects,' said Graziano, 'in his determination to have Rome outdo Florence as the centre for art and culture in Europe. The traders know they can get higher prices there. I've heard that they keep the best materials to send to the artists working for him.'

'That may be true,' said Felipe. He sat down very heavily upon a stool. 'In any case, if this oil is inferior, as Zoroastro says, it is my fault. I only tested the first batch to make sure it was all right. I didn't think to check each individual jar as it was delivered.' His face was grey and he looked as if he had aged a year in one morning. 'I must go and inform the master of my error.'

'My error too,' said Graziano, loyally flinging an arm around Felipe's shoulder. 'I didn't listen to Flavio earlier, when he tried to tell me that the paint was not settling and that we should leave off. I suspected that he wanted to go and warm himself by the fire and wait until the room was less cold. I told him to keep working.'

Zoroastro stuck his chin out. 'I also bear some blame. In my panic I placed the fire basket too close to the wall. When the fire was built up then the fresco could not withstand the heat.'

'I could have run faster through the streets to fetch him.' I added my voice to theirs. 'If he had got here sooner then he might have dealt with things differently.' This was not completely true. I had run so fast that I still had a stitch in my side, but I did not want to be left out of their confraternity of guilt.

Graziano stretched out his arm and gathered me in so that the four of us were linked together. 'Let us go and beg pardon from him now.'

'You see!' Zoroastro took the opportunity to hiss at me as we approached my master. 'This is what happens when humans ignore warnings they are meant to heed. This project was cursed by its start on that Friday at the thirteenth hour.'

The Maestro listened to us. And immediately declared that there was nothing to forgive. He had dismissed the others, telling them to treat it as a holiday, assuring them that they would be paid for the day's work. He suggested that we did the same. 'I will stay here a while,' he said, 'and I would prefer to be on my own.'

When leaving I looked back and saw him standing there, staring up at the wall, his tall figure silhouetted by the light of the fire.

Before we left he took pains to reassure us in order to raise our spirits.

'Don't be downcast,' he told us. 'I will restore it to the original state.'

Felipe turned away. I heard him say distinctly to Graziano, 'He will never restore it.'

Chapter Forty

His pupils and apprentices began to drift away.

Like many others, they travelled to Rome. Raphael, the painter, was working there and Michelangelo, the sculptor, was making a fresco within the Vatican, on the ceiling of the Sistine Chapel. It was said it would take years to complete. With that project ongoing and the many other commissions available, the Romans boasted that there was work in their city for all the artists in Italy. Our Maestro did not seem too concerned about losing his craftsmen. His restless, enquiring mind ranged over a great number of other subjects which kept him busy and he left it to Graziano to try to rectify the fire damage to his painting. Felipe's job was to placate the members of the City Council, who were beginning to enquire when the Maestro would finish their fresco in the hall of the Palazzo Vecchio.

Outside forces were pressing in on him, in addition to the many requests for paintings that he received. The French, having established a court in Milan, had become more insistent that they would like him to attend there. They had made representations to him, and now intended to petition the Council of Florence directly to release my master from his contract. There was also a long-standing argument over a piece of work for the Confraternity of the Immaculate Conception in Milan. The fathers considered it unfinished and were withholding payment. But I think that it was being used as an excuse to encourage the Maestro to go to Milan to deal with this himself. And although there were matters in Florence that required his attention, he was more inclined now to quit the city. He talked of returning to the place where he had spent earlier years working on projects that used all his skills – as an engineer, an architect and a designer – and where it seemed the French might be more appreciative of his talents. I knew that Felipe would be glad to have done fending off Pier Soderini and his Council, who were now, as he had predicted, demanding the return of their scaffolding.

'If we took it apart into the smallest pieces, then parcelled it up and delivered it separately, I wonder if they'd discover that there are spars missing?' Felipe asked us.

'They'd never notice,' laughed Graziano. 'Those men are so ignorant they could not find their own backside to wipe it.'

Graziano was very keen to be in Milan, where he deemed the French held a civilized court, full of style and wit and enough ladies to please him.

And Salai? He would go where the Maestro went, for although he had a devious mind I believe he did truly love him. He was loyal. Salai did not desert as the other pupils did, but then that might have been to do with his own self-interest. He had some talent in drawing and painting and, taking advantage of the reputation of the da Vinci workshop, would accept private orders to fill his own purse. Sometimes he would have my master do the outline drawing for him and then complete the portrait using the materials from our storerooms. Felipe was wise enough not to comment openly on this but it created a certain tension within the household.

My master either did not notice or did not care. He spent more and more time at the place where I had found him on the day of the disaster: the house of Donna Lisa.

It became his refuge. She now sustained him in his troubles, where once he had helped her out of her grief. He had few female friends, but she was one of them. She had educated herself and was slowly building a small library of both ancient and modern texts, and they spoke together on the books they had read. He respected her for this; also for her resilience – indeed, he admired the fortitude of all women.

'Women who marry and have children only live until they are worn out with childbirth,' he told me, walking back from her house one day. 'Some years ago I did an anatomy on the body of a woman who had borne thirteen children. I saw where the pelvis had been cracked many times with the labours of childbirth. And of these sons and daughters only one survived her. She'd had to suffer the bodily pain of giving birth, and also, in her mind, the torment of losing her children.'

I thought of Rossana and Elisabetta. What would have become of them if they had been left to grow up at Perela? By sixteen years of age they would have been married and ready to bear children for their husbands. Now Elisabetta was with her brother on some remote farm, and Rossana, her sister believed, dwelled among the angels. But I tried to turn my mind from this. When I remembered Rossana, it was as though someone struck a blow across my chest.

'Men do not think of these trials that women undergo as much as they should,' my master went on. Then he added, 'With the exception, perhaps, of one man that we know.'

He was referring to Donna Lisa's husband, Francesco del Giocondo. It was because he valued his wife and empathized with the desolation of her soul at the loss of their child that he had come and asked my master to paint her portrait.

'Donna Lisa is not his first wife,' my master said. 'He has one son already by a previous marriage to a woman who died. But I think he holds this wife close to his heart. My own father was married four times, each wife, save the last, dying before him.'

My master rarely spoke of his father, a respected notary of Florence, who had died about eighteen months previously. He

231

seldom displayed his emotions in any case, but in this instance it was more than the loss of a parent that he'd had to suffer. I'd heard Felipe say that while the law did not acknowledge a bastard child my master had been grieved when it became apparent that he was not to be given any share of his father's estate. Was he ashamed to have it so plainly marked that he was left un-recognized as a son? Like me, unacknowledged by both mother and father? This may have been the bond of kinship that connected us. Although as a child my master had had the care and attention of one woman who was as near to a mother as possible. His natural mother being considered unsuitable, after his birth his father had married another woman and had taken Leonardo, his bastard son, with him when he set up his household. His new wife had treated my master very kindly and he had been sad to leave when he came of age to do so. Though she was now dead he kept in touch with her brother, who was a good friend to my master. This step-uncle was a canon in the church at Fiesole, just outside Florence, and this was where my master went to rest after the destruction of the fresco.

My master stayed at Fiesole through Christmas and into the next year for the feast of the Epiphany, and then past the end of January. The leader of the Florentine Council, Pier Soderini, was deeply unhappy at this prolonged absence, and came to the work-shop at Santa Maria Novella to complain. Felipe had to seek any way he could to deflect his pursuit of my master. He would bring out his accounts and ledgers and pore over them in front of him. Then he would calculate and recalculate the payments already authorized by the Council, and mark off in his almanac how many days had been worked and how many were still required for completion. Meanwhile Graziano would press liberal draughts of our best wine upon this conscientious but dull man, and flatter him subtly by urging him to tell us his opinions on the political situation.

'He would do well to spend less time worrying about things

not done,' said Graziano one day as he watched Pier Soderini depart, a little unsteadily, 'and pay closer attention to what is actually happening within his own city.'

Felipe agreed. 'If he were such a shrewd observer of the political situation as he thinks he is, he would see what is cooking up under his very nose.'

I had begun to clear away the wine jug and goblets. 'What is that?' I stopped to ask them.

They glanced at each other.

'Better that you remain ignorant, Matteo,' said Felipe. 'That way you cannot be accused of being with one faction or another.'

'What factions are those?' I asked.

'The Pope has an army ready now to march into the Romagna. He is intent on taking more cities there than even Cesare Borgia conquered. There are those in Florence who see this as an opportunity to . . . make changes . . . here.' Graziano was choosing his words carefully.

'And there are spies who report conversations such as this,' Felipe said brusquely. He gave Graziano a warning glance.

I picked up the wine cups and went to rinse the dishes. This talk chimed with what the Sinistro Scribe had told me. But still I could not believe it possible. Florence teemed with commerce and life. It was obviously prosperous; why would anyone want to change it? The Council was part of the existence of the city. Pier Soderini had been appointed leader for life. He was so fixed there, backed by the matchless Machiavelli and his citizen army, that I could not see him toppled from his place.

Despite having a contract with the city of Florence to work on the fresco, my master spent little time now in the Palazzo Vecchio and became more occupied with his study of birds and their flight. His drawings on this subject numbered in the hundreds, and he pored over these with Zoroastro, making models of wire and cane and stretched linen. As these models became larger he sent Zoroastro to work in a different monastery, where he had friends who would give him space that could be private, for he wished this project kept secret.

Along with this he continued with his botanical excursions, his work in the mortuary and his visits to the house of Donna Lisa.

There he continued with her portrait. Her husband did not mind that this had been ongoing for so long, and that my master appeared sporadically, to paint or not, on his own personal whim. Francesco del Giocondo was happy that the company of such an intelligent and knowledgeable man as my master had pulled his wife back from the abyss of her grief.

The painting was kept at her house, for a few days after the death of her child she became so prostrate with grief that she was not well enough to walk any distance. Her husband had told us this when he had begged my master to come to her.

'I fear for her life. And if she dies, I think I may die too.'

'In the presence of such love, how could I refuse?' my master said to me.

The merchant agreed that he would make a small studio for my master within his house and that my master would work on the portrait as and when he pleased. To begin with he went quite reluctantly, though Donna Lisa won him over with her intellect and demeanour. And in the end, with his great fresco work spoiled, he found as much solace there as he gave.

From the first he treated her with respect and did not press her to sit too long or to chat. But one day, when he thought she had grown a little stronger, he asked me to wait and then commanded me to tell them a story.

'Matteo's stories are very diverting,' he told her. 'He has a fund of them in his mind.' He indicated for me to begin.

'What tale shall I tell?' I asked him.

'One of your own choosing,' he replied. 'Perhaps one of the myths as given to you by your grandmother?'

I looked around the room in which I stood. This had been

carefully prepared as a painting studio by his own hand and the lady was placed by the open casement to the courtyard with the light falling exactly as he wished. He had also chosen what she was to wear. In addition to a selection of magnificent dresses, her servants had brought glittering necklaces and other expensive jewellery, but he had rejected these, settling on a plain dress to which he would add his own design round the neckline. I think Donna Lisa's husband would have liked her to be attired in a more ornate fashion to show that he was successful and wealthy, but my master had persuaded him by saying, 'It is sufficient. Such grace needs no added gilt.'

The clothes and jewellery had been removed but a box of other decorations remained in the far reaches of the room. The lid was open and I could see, among the scarves and ribbons, one or two feathers – ostrich, partridge and peacock.

I placed myself out of her vision so that she would not be distracted and affect the Maestro's composition.

'So now,' I began, 'I will relate to you the story of the being whom the gods called Panoptes, which means all-seeing, but who is also known to us as Argus, the giant with one hundred eyes.

'One day, Jupiter, supreme of all the gods, was visiting the king of a certain island and he espied the daughter of this king walking in the garden. Her name was Io.

'Jupiter saw that she was very beautiful and he fell in love with the princess Io. And he stayed with her for a long time.

'In the kingdom of the gods his absence was noted. And when he returned the goddess Juno, to whom he had contracted to be faithful, asked him what had delayed him in the world of men. Jupiter told her that he had much business to attend to, but she did not believe him. She too went to the island of the king and discovered why Jupiter had dallied there.

'Juno became very angry. She was jealous of Io and thought of what she might do to harm the princess. Jupiter discovered Juno's intentions and he hastened to think of some way to protect the princess Io. He decided to turn Io into a beautiful heifer and appointed the mighty giant Argus with his one hundred eyes to watch over Io as she grazed quietly in the fields.

'But Juno was clever and she found out what Jupiter had done. Juno summoned Mercury, the messenger of the gods, and gave him instructions as to what she wanted him to do. Mercury sped swiftly to where Io gambolled in the fields. He waited through the heat of the day until evening came and Io stopped playing and lay down to rest. The giant Argus then also sat down to watch over her.

'Mercury put his flute to his lips and began to play. At the sound of this music Argus started to fall asleep. One by one each of his hundred eyelids drooped, until finally only one eye was left open. But then it too slipped down. The great giant slept. When he was sure that Argus was in a deep sleep Mercury put aside his flute. He drew out his sword, and made to cut off the head of Argus. But then Argus woke up with a terrifying roar. Each one of his eyes opened and he struggled to rise up. But he was too late. Mercury struck hard and the giant fell dead.

Io was forced to flee and to roam the earth through many lands without rest.

'Mercury went to tell Juno that her task had been accomplished and Juno hurried to the place. Argus lay there dead upon the earth, with all his eyes staring up at the sky.

'Then Juno plucked each of the hundred eyes from the head of Argus and, carrying them with her, placed them in the feathers of her favourite bird.

'And that is how' – I picked up the peacock feather and flourished it in the air – 'the peacock has a tail with an eye in each feather, for the wonderment of all the world.'

Donna Lisa clapped her hands.

I glanced from her to my master. He nodded at me. And I, in delight at their approval of my performance, grinned at both of them.

* * *

After that the Maestro would frequently ask me to wait and relate a story to them: an adventure of Ulysses during his wanderings after the siege of Troy, or some legend I knew, or a fable or folk-tale of my own choosing.

We kept to this custom when he recommenced her portrait in the spring. She still did not speak very much and he, concentrating intensely on his work, sometimes spent his time staring at the painting in front of him without lifting his brush. The silence in the room was never oppressive. But, if it needed to be filled, then I would root about in my head until I found one of the story seeds my grandmother had planted there and, nourishing it with my own hyperbole and metaphor, I let it flow out of me as water cascades from a fountain.

One day, near Easter, before she settled in her chair she handed me a small object. 'This is a little pamphlet from one of the new presses that print books in our Tuscan language. It has a story in it that my mother used to tell me when I was a child. I'd love to hear it again. Would you care to read to us from it this morning, Matteo?' she asked me.

I dropped my head in confusion.

My master interrupted smoothly. 'Matteo prefers to tell his stories from memory.'

Having rescued me from embarrassment, he sent a severe look in my direction, as if to say, 'See! Now you have disappointed the lady. She would have loved to hear you read.'

I told my own story that day, and when it was time for me to leave I made to return her book to her.

'Why, Matteo, I gave it to you to keep,' she said. 'I would like you to have it. I hope you find as much pleasure in the pages as I did.'

I stumbled back still holding the book in my hand. I looked at my master for permission to accept the gift. He inclined his head. Then he raised one eyebrow. 'Thank the lady,' he said quietly.

'I thank you,' I said. As I made a bow to her I felt tears start up behind my eyes.

She may have noticed for she turned her head away and made some talk with my master. She was a great lady, this Donna Lisa. Not high born, like princesses or queens who reign over subjects, but with her own innate nobility and the natural refinements of a woman who is good.

That night as I lay on my mattress I took the book out to examine it in more detail. I could make out some words: 'the', 'and', 'of'.

I held my finger under each one I could recognize and said them hesitantly out loud. Suddenly they blurred before my eyes. I realized I was crying.

And I wept. I wept for the mother I could not remember, the father I never had, and my grandmother who was dead. I wept for the loss of Rossana, my first love. Rossana, her parents and her baby brother. I wept for being separated from Elisabetta and Paolo. And I wept for what had been mine and had been taken from me, and I wept for those things I'd never had. I wept for all my miseries.

The next day I took the little pamphlet book to the Sinistro Scribe. He examined it. 'From where did you obtain this?' he asked me.

'I was given it as a gift by a lady.'

'What lady would give a boy such a gift?'

'I will not say who gave it to me,' I told him. 'But I did not steal it.'

'I believe you,' he replied, 'and thus its origin is more intriguing.'

'Show me what it says.'

He began to read aloud.

'No,' I said, 'not like that. *Show* me what it says, and where it says it.'

He pointed with his finger and read: ' "In a land far away there lived a dragon—" '

'Are you certain those are the words on the page as they are written?'

'Of course I am.' He spoke indignantly. 'I was trained by Brother Anselm at—'

'– the renowned monastery of Saint Bernard at Monte Cassino,' I finished for him. 'I recall your fine pedigree. So' – I leaned over his shoulder – 'how is it that you know the sound each word makes?'

'Because of the letters contained therein,' he said. 'Each letter has its own sound. Placed together in variable orders they come together to make a word.'

'Is that all it is?' I laughed. 'Then it cannot be such a difficult thing to do.'

'Oh really?' he said softly.

'Yes,' I said. 'Now go on please.'

'There is a charge for this,' he said.

'I will pay you.' I took out one of the pennies that my master had gifted me at Epiphany. 'Here is the fee you charged when I brought you the letters I received.'

'Oh no,' he replied. 'In this case it is not a matter of my reading out some lines. That's not what you're asking here at all.'

'What *am* I asking?'

'You are asking me to teach you to read. For that tuition the charge will be one penny per half-hour.'

I withdrew a little to count my money. 'How long will it take for me to know all the words there are to know?' I asked him.

The scribe smiled at me, and then said: 'Matteo, how long is your life?'

Chapter Forty-One

The secret project began to take shape.

Hidden from public view and under the Maestro's specific instructions there arose a magnificent, elegant construction of wooden rods and sheeting. My spare moments I spent with the Sinistro Scribe receiving reading tuition, but most of the rest of my time I was helping Zoroastro put together this most amazing conception of my master's mind. We worked together from first light, and as spring fastened a firmer hold upon the earth and the days stretched out longer, we worked late into the evenings.

It was decided that I would bring my mattress and the rest of my things to this new location. And it was while I was doing this that Felipe noticed the tiny scraps of paper covered with the letters and simple words that the Sinistro Scribe had written out for me to memorize.

'What are these, Matteo?' he asked me, taking several into his hands and examining them.

I glanced around. Salai had gone with Graziano to the Palazzo Vecchio to do some work there and my master and Zoroastro were conferring at the other end of the room.

'Those are my letters to learn,' I told Felipe in a quiet voice. 'You may remember me telling you about the Sinistro Scribe? The person who wrote the reply to my friend at the beginning of winter? I am paying him to teach me to read so that when you

240

have time to arrange a tutor for me I will already have some skill in this.'

Felipe regarded me solemnly. 'I am very pleased that you are doing this, Matteo.'

That was all he said, but the next day I found, lying on my mattress, some sheets of paper and a letter board of the type used to teach students their alphabet.

The Sinistro Scribe was not the most patient of tutors and I found this learning to be tedious and dull and not open to explanation. How had it come about that these particular designs were chosen as our letters? Who decreed what sound would accompany each shape? And how was it decided the manner they would come together to form a word?

'Why is this so?' I demanded to know.

Whereupon the scribe would rap his knuckles hard upon my head. 'Do not seek to distract me with unanswerable questions,' he growled. 'Only let the learning penetrate that thick skull. Go on with it, before I throw you in the Arno.'

But I think he may perhaps have enjoyed a little the struggle to educate me. And, as the weather became warmer, I did manage to distract him on occasions, and he would leave off from our studies and relate to me parts of his life story, and we grew closer. Thus I was lulled into becoming less watchful and more careless in my talk, revealing things from my own past. So that when the scribe casually asked the origin of the letters I received I chatted to him about Elisabetta and who she was and how I had met her.

It did not occur to me that it might be more than idle conversation on his part, that he garnered information as a squirrel hoards nuts against the winter famine. I did not think that the Sinistro Scribe might also be a spy.

The old man's gentle prying was concerned mainly with my master's business, but I was wise enough not to mention any of the things my master would not have wished discussed outwith his household.

From time to time the Maestro carried out dissections at the hospital, and his notes and drawings now contained a vast amount of work on all aspects of the human body. Working with him on these did not fill me with the terror and revulsion I had first experienced at the mortuary in Averno, and I began to take more interest in what he was doing. But I said nothing of this to the scribe, nor anything about the mysterious machine we were making, nor where it was kept.

Zoroastro was delighted to be working at a job that taxed his skills as an engineer. He was much happier doing this than grinding and preparing the mixtures for the fresco. But as the summer approached he became more and more impatient to test it out, and I came upon him one day in late spring, pleading with the Maestro.

'It will fly. This bird *will* fly! I tell you!'

'But not yet, Zoroastro,' said my master.

Although these two men had been friends for more than twenty-five years it did not stop them arguing. Zoroastro's face flushed with blood when excited and took on a curious blotched appearance. This was due in part to the many accidents he had when mixing his chemicals, and also his carelessness at his forge, when sparks would fly and land, still hot, about his person. His dark, wizened face showed powder burns and one of his hands had the tips of two fingers missing. Yet his eyes were quick and bright and his manner often nervous and impulsive, like now, as he tried to persuade my master it was time to test his flying machine.

'Look at it!' said Zoroastro. He stretched out his hand to where it hung like a great bird suspended from the ceiling by an iron hook. Under his touch the framework stirred and the sheeting trembled. 'It is restless. It wants to leave its nest and take to the air.'

'It's not ready, Zoroastro,' my master replied. He was standing underneath, studying the part of the internal framework where a man would sit. 'We must ensure that the person who is in command of the wings is positioned so as to be upright. It needs more work.'

'You are so stubborn!' exclaimed Zoroastro.

'I'm not being stubborn, Zoroastro. I'm being cautious.' The Maestro laid his hand on Zoroastro's shoulder and said: 'Remember that Giovan Battista Danti, attempting this same experiment last year, fell from his bell tower onto the church roof.'

'Then we should make our experiment from a hilltop,' said Zoroastro, adding slyly, 'Monte Ceceri is close to Fiesole.'

We knew that Fiesole was a place where the Maestro liked go to keep the company of his step-uncle, the canon. As my master hesitated Zoroastro pressed his case:

'You have always said that with the right equipment man *can* fly. And we have made the best flying machine imaginable.'

'I believe this too, but the engineering on the wings of birds is much more intricate than I can emulate.'

'Birds' wings are made of many feathers,' I said. 'Individual, and yet pieced together they make the unit that enables them to stay up.'

'Matteo's mind moves towards understanding the concept of air resistance,' said my master.

Encouraged by this I continued. 'I watch the birds and see that it is by the beating of their wings that they travel through the sky . . .' I hesitated. 'I see that they use the upward draughts of the wind to glide. But I do not truly understand how it is they fly when they are heavier than air and they have nothing underneath to support them.'

'The force of the air lifts them up,' said my master. 'It resists against them, inasmuch as they push against it. See how an eagle carrying a rabbit or a young lamb can still stay aloft and fly high enough to return to its eyrie clutching its prey in its talons.'

I looked at the machine. Could it really fly? It didn't seem possible that air could bear that amount of weight.

I had a sudden recollection of Perela, where a tall sycamore tree grew inside the wall of the keep. The autumn winds were stripping the trees of their greenery as we were playing in the courtyard. Paolo and I had been appointed by Rossana and Elisabetta to toss handfuls of leaves and seeds into the air and send them spinning for them to catch. Baby Dario was toddling around on his sturdy legs screaming in delight at the rain of leaves upon his head. My master, coming across us in our play, had stood and watched the corkscrewing sycamore seeds. He had picked one up and, gathering us about him, had explained how it was that the shape of the wings on the seed made it spin in such a manner. He had gone inside and then returned and called us to him. Under his guidance we made little stick men from twigs bound together with wool. Then he had attached each of these to a square of cloth by fine thread tied at the four corners. We had climbed to the window in the tallest part of the tower. And we had stood there and taken turns to throw down our twig figures and watch them float in the air for the longest time before coming to rest far below. But we had only laughed when he said that a man might also do that and fall from a higher height with no bones broken. I recalled that when it was Dario's turn to throw out his stick man he was so excited that Paolo had to hold fast to his wriggling little body lest he fall into the gorge.

'With this we will soar, and wheel, and turn, and look down on everyone from on high.' Zoroastro was now skipping about the workshop with his arms extended, pretending to be a bird. 'We will take turns and see who can fly the highest. Wouldn't you like to try it out, Matteo?'

I blinked away my memory of Perela. 'Yes, I would.'

'For it would have to be someone small' – Zoroastro winked at me – 'and not as heavy and large as a normal man.'

'No,' said my master at once. 'Not the boy.'

Zoroastro laughed. 'I would not endanger the life of anyone dear to you.'

'*You* are dear to me too, my friend,' said the Maestro.

'It would need someone stronger than Matteo,' said Zoroastro. 'Someone powerful enough to move the pulley cords.' He doffed his cap before us. 'I present myself as candidate to be the world's first flying man.'

'It's not ready,' said my master, but this time his voice had less conviction.

'Supposing you decide to go to Milan?' Zoroastro argued. 'There will be no opportunity there to do the experiment in private.'

'Perhaps you are right. And we must also consider the weather. If we wait until after May then the summer may be too hot.'

'Matteo knows country lore,' said Zoroastro. 'How say you? Will we have a hot summer this year?'

'The trees are already past budding,' I answered him. 'And the birds have built their nests high in the branches. I observe that as a sign of hot weather to follow, with little wind.'

'You have studied climate,' Zoroastro said to my master. 'You know about the currents in the air. Make your decision. But I say the time is now!'

As I gazed up at the flying machine I was uneasy. My master had studied the currents of the wind, but I knew the story of Icarus.

Icarus was the son of Daedalus and they lived in ancient times. This Daedalus was a very clever man and thus was asked by the King of Crete, who was called Minos, to undertake some work of special importance. This work that King Minos required to be done was the building of a labyrinth to contain the Minotaur, a terrible monster with the head of a bull and the body of a man. But once Daedalus had finished, King Minos became fearful that he might reveal to others the true path through the maze. So, in order to prevent Daedalus leaving Crete with his son Icarus, King Minos seized all the ships.

Daedalus had to think of another way to escape across the sea.

Being very inventive, he fashioned wings for himself and his son, so that they could fly above the water. Early one morning Daedalus and Icarus launched themselves from the top of a cliff. Daedalus flew low over the sea and landed safely in Italy. But Icarus wanted to fly higher.

The sun rose in the sky. Still higher did Icarus fly. Then the heat from the rays of the sun fell upon Icarus. It melted the wax that held the wings onto his shoulders. And Icarus fell into the sea and was drowned.

But some people say it was not the sun that caused his wings to melt. It was that the gods were angry with Icarus, as they would be angry with any man who dared to fly.

I thought about this as I lay on my mattress that night. Above me the great winged bird creaked quietly in the draughts that blew in between the gaps in the windows and under the door. I recalled the bad omen on Friday the sixth of June last year when, despite the warning from Zoroastro, my master had begun to paint his fresco at the thirteenth hour. Zoroastro had been proved right. It was not wise to ignore such portents. My master had not paid attention and now his magnificent fresco was all but ruined. Humans had not been born with wings to fly. Many people believe that anyone who dares to thwart the will of the Creator is doomed. Thus, if man attempts to fly, God might reach out His hand from Heaven, and the presumptuous man will be cast down to earth and destroyed.

Chapter Forty-Two

He readjusted her veil.

It was the sixth or seventh time he had done so. As he went back to his easel I looked more carefully at how the veil hung around her face. Why was he so unhappy with it today? The Donna Lisa was usually able to arrange herself almost exactly as he required.

On the days the Maestro decided he would paint her I was sent ahead to ensure that she was available and had time to prepare. She would dress in the agreed costume and go to the studio room. With the help of her nurse she would arrange herself in her chair, her clothes draped, her body posed, exactly as she had been doing for the previous months. When he arrived he made the minor adjustments necessary and then the session would begin. I would either leave or stay as he commanded.

Sometimes he barely waited half an hour in the house, other times he spent half a day or more. When painting her he might stand for very many minutes staring at her or at the portrait. This did not discomfit her. She was a woman who could sit in silence and with her own thoughts. He would come out of his reverie and say a word or two, and she would continue the conversation seamlessly as though an hour had not elapsed. She had her own time and occupied her space in it and was not uncomfortable with his long silences. However, if he felt that her mood was heavy he would ask me to tell a story aloud and I would oblige.

What was wrong with the veil today? Had she set it further back from her face?

He continued but only worked for a matter of minutes before putting down his paintbrush.

'You must tell me what is amiss.'

'There is nothing amiss, Messer Leonardo.'

'There is something troubling you.'

'Not at all.'

'The lady I have painted on this board is not the one sitting before me.'

He was teasing her. And she responded.

'I am my own best companion. I assure you it is I.'

He sighed and lifted his brush again.

But there *was* something altered in her. I studied her carefully and tried to see what he could see. Her dress was the same. Her hair, her veil, her expression . . .

She glanced at the nurse who always sat in a chair by the door. 'Zita,' she said, 'if you wish to go and rest for a little while I will be all right. I am well chaperoned here within the house. I will send Matteo for you when I need you to attend to me again.'

The nurse got to her feet gratefully. She went from the room across the courtyard to the servants' quarters.

My master looked at me. 'Matteo' – he spoke slowly – 'I see that I am in need of some Alexandrian white. Would you be good enough to go back to the workshop to fetch it for me?'

I stared at him. It was my responsibility to attend to his brushes and paints and I took these duties very seriously. He knew that there was a plentiful supply of Alexandrian white to hand. From where I stood I could see it clearly. I opened my mouth to say this.

Before I could speak my master continued, 'I would need some freshly prepared. Do not hurry with this. I will not expect you back within the hour.'

I bowed my head and left.

So I had an hour of free time to myself. As I went into the city by way of San Lorenzo I considered my choices of what to do. I could go directly to the secret workshop in the monastery. Even if Zoroastro did not require my help I enjoyed watching him work. But the day was balmy and I liked being outside.

Beside which, I felt a tug at my mind. What had begun as a chore had slipped, without my being aware of the change, into something else. With the alphabet and a multitude of basic words ensconced as part of the rhythm of my life, I was beginning to take pleasure in the action of reading. My stumbling phrases were becoming more assured, and as I went down the Corso towards the Arno I looked at the posters and handbills on the walls and picked out words I knew. Every day I did this, the number I recognized increased.

The scribe was in his usual place by the Ponte Vecchio. When he'd learned that Felipe would give me quality paper to bargain with, he'd agreed to tutor me for as long as I could spare away from my duties. Felipe, whose time was so taken up with trying to restore the fresco and placate the Florentine Council, had agreed to this arrangement. With the very first sheet I'd brought the scribe had made good money last Christmas and Epiphany. His drawings of the Magi and his script looked so elegant on the superior paper that he'd attracted customers who were prepared to pay a higher price. He was now eating better and could purchase firewood for the stove in the room that he rented.

'Ho, Matteo,' he said without lifting his head as I drew near to him.

For an old man he had the most acute hearing, and he was such a fixture in his place at the corner of the tower that people forgot he was there. Thus he gleaned snippets of information by over-hearing careless talk and passed it on to others for a free drink and a piece of bread. Now that I think on it, when times were hard with him it was probably the only way he could live without going hungry.

I knew what it was to go hungry. It had not been so long ago that, faced with a winter of starvation, I had agreed to steal something. And this act of mine had led directly to the death of at least one man: the priest that Sandino had bludgeoned to death.

I sat down to wait until the scribe had finished the text he was writing. And while he was doing this I took out the little book that had been my gift from Donna Lisa.

'How far have you got with that now?' the scribe asked me.

'I am on the fourth page and there are six words I do not know.'

'From the beginning then.' The scribe set down his paper to dry. 'Let me hear you.'

' "In a faraway land there lived a dragon," ' I read slowly. ' "This dragon was a fierce beast with a long, long tail. It had great red wings and a body covered in scales. When it opened up its mouth it breathed out fire with a mighty roar. On its feet were sharp claws and it killed everything that stood in its path." '

The book that Donna Lisa had given me was the story of St George and the Dragon. It was the first story that I had ever seen written and understood the words.

' "This dragon lived in a swamp on the edge of a city. Each day the people of the city sent out two sheep to feed to the dragon. And this way they kept it from destroying their city and killing everyone in it. But one day there were no sheep left. There was nothing they could do but to send out their children each day one by one." '

I stopped to draw in my breath.

'Do not hurry the story, Matteo.'

'But I want to find out what happened to the children.'

The scribe laughed. 'Indeed you shall. Go on.'

I continued, stumbling along, with him helping me sound out the more difficult words.

' "The day came when there were no more children in the city. No more, save one. She was the Princess Cleodolinda, daughter of the king and queen. They wept bitter tears as their daughter was led out to her doom. Then, just as the dragon came from the swamp to eat the princess, a knight, with armour shining like the sun, appeared on his horse. This knight was a holy man by name of George and he had the strength of ten men. From their castle the king and the queen looked down in terror as the dragon approached their child." '

I paused to look at the illustration in the text which showed the distraught king and queen standing on the castle wall. How did it feel to have a mother and father to care about what fate you suffered?

' "Saint George galloped fast on his horse. He dismounted and untied the Princess Cleodolinda. He placed himself between the princess and the dragon. Then he drew his sword and he smote the dragon. Not once but many times. But the scales of the dragon res— res . . ." '

'Resisted,' prompted the scribe.

'. . . resisted,' I repeated.

With the scribe's help, I continued with the rest of the story.

' "But the scales of the dragon resisted. Then Saint George mounted his horse once again. He took his lance in his hand and, seeking the place under the dragon's wing where there were no scales, he drove his lance deep into the flesh of the beast. And the dragon fell dead at his feet. Thus the princess and the city were saved." '

I finished with a gasp.

The scribe took the book from my hand.

I had expected praise. Instead he said, 'There is little point in reading if you do not also learn to write.'

'Many do not write.'

'They are fools.'

'How so?'

'Think on it. Your reading may serve you well enough, but if you want some business done, a contract or some other kind of accounting, then better to have the skill to write. If you ask a dishonest scribe to write your letter rather than doing it for yourself, he can write it in such a way that your true meaning is obscured. And what if your mind turns to story, poetry or song? How can another person write your thoughts and dreams upon the paper?'

At first he would not trust me with his precious ink and paper.

'I will look on the riverbank and find you a piece of tree bark,' he said. 'You can practise with a stick dipped in soot and water.'

This I did, halting and unsure. And at night by candlelight I practised with some chalk and the letter board that Felipe had purchased for me. The scribe was a strict teacher and he did not accept anything less than perfect. I would make a letter three dozen times or more before he was happy with it. But the day arrived when he had prepared the ink and the pen, and he set me down and gave it into my hand and told me that now I would write my first word.

And something happened within me. Like a mother sensing the baby quickening within her, suddenly, to me, the letters were no longer hostile and unwieldy. I had command of them, with my head and with my hand.

I wrote as he instructed me.

The long curve of the initial descenders with their feather of distinction at the top, the full bellies of the vowels, the twin letters in the middle to create the crispness of the sound.

Together. There. As if it was always meant to be thus.

I looked at the page.

The word struck, as clear and as pure as a bell peal on a winter morning.

Matteo

Chapter Forty-Three

Donna Lisa was with child.

The thing which her doctors said could not happen had come to pass. On the occasion of her loss over two years ago she had believed that she would have no more children. She had whispered these words to my master as we stood in the cold room beside the table on which lay her dead baby.

That night I had taken the small firebox from his bag and, using a flint, set some charcoal alight to melt the block of wax he had brought. He laid small pieces of linen across the slightly parted eyelids and lips, then, with a spatula, smeared the warm wax over the face of the little girl. When it had hardened he removed the mask and, cushioning it in straw, placed it inside his cloak. Whereupon he asked the nurse, Zita, to summon her mistress.

It was only then that Donna Lisa allowed grief to overcome her. We could hear her sobs echoing behind us as we hurried out of the house into the winter darkness.

So now she did not want to speak of her new pregnancy to anyone else until the baby within her grew stronger.

I thought it would deter my master from his painting, but on the contrary, it now became his favourite occupation. He went to her house more often, in the early morning when the light did not have the harshness of midday, and again when evening began its slow footfall across her courtyard. Often he did not lift his brush, only stared at the painting or spent the time in study of her face. On paper he made countless drawings of her mouth and her eyes.

It was so subtle that to begin with I hardly noticed. But being with her in the room, I slowly became aware of an illumination in her demeanour that had not been present before. And, as she changed, within the portrait on the board my master sought to capture her transformation. Until the day arrived, as the three of us knew it would, when she said, 'It is time to tell my husband.'

'Yes,' the Maestro sighed.

There was a silence.

'He would indulge me, I know. If I wanted to continue.'

'He is a good man,' my master replied.

'But—' she stopped.

'I understand.'

The sittings were not the same after that.

The main focus of her world had altered and perhaps she did not wish to be reminded of her former sad despair. It was time for her to move on. She showed us the preparations she was making for the birth of a new life in her house. She led us to where her marriage cassone stood, and opened it, and let us see the baby robes and the linen bands that would be wound around the child when it was born.

One day the Maestro went to the Via della Stufa by himself and took the painting away. He brought it back to the monastery swaddled in fine cloth that she must have given him. Still wrapped up, he carried it with him when we went to live at Fiesole. There were occasions when he would uncover it, sometimes to work on it, other times to stand and regard it thoughtfully for an hour or more. It went with him on all his future journeys.

To the end of his life he was never parted from it again.

Chapter Forty-Four

We waited until the middle of the night.

Felipe had arranged for a large cart and two heavy horses. By the light of the moon and shaded lanterns we carefully loaded the flying machine, and before dawn we were trundling out of the city, past the sleepy watchmen at the gate, onto the winding road to Fiesole.

Felipe, worried about the household income, was in favour of the move. The City Council had stopped payments and was now suggesting that money already paid to us should be returned to them. Having been made aware of this by Zoroastro, my master's step-uncle insisted that we spend some time with him. As canon of a church he had space enough for all of us.

The horses' breath plumed from their nostrils as they began the climb on the hillside. I stood in the cart with Zoroastro, each of us holding onto the frame of the great bird so that no harm would come to it as we jolted along the track. As the sun's light started to edge up along the lip of the hills to the east Zoroastro began to sing.

'Hush,' Felipe said at once from his place at the front of the wagon. 'The purpose of leaving in the dark was not to attract attention. Your caterwauling can be heard miles away.'

'You are jealous of my prowess in singing.' I could see Zoroastro's teeth gleam white as he laughed. But he fell silent at Felipe's order and the only sound that accompanied us that night was the noise of the horses' laboured breathing and the clop of their hooves on the road.

My master's step-uncle was called Canon Don Alessandro Amadori. He was the sort of uncle that every child should have. Generous, good-natured and kindly, he made us welcome and had prepared rooms for us as well as a special place for the flying machine. It was placed in a barn a little distance from the house, out of sight of any visitors or servants. This was where I set down my mattress and where I would stay to watch over it.

That evening we sat down to eat together. As I helped set out the plates and wine cups I saw the canon looking at me. What is it about priests that they can fix you with their eye and you feel your soul shake? As we ate I was aware of him glancing in my direction.

'Isabella d'Este.'

I had just taken a piece of bread from the common plate when he mentioned the name of the Marchioness of Mantua, Isabella d'Este. The same Isabella who was the sister of Alfonso of Ferrara, the man who had married Lucrezia Borgia.

'The woman is so persistent in her supplications,' the canon said to my master. 'She knows that I have a connection to you and has asked me to beg you to complete a painting for her.' He laughed. 'Any painting will do, it seems. She will not leave off pestering me. I'm beginning to think that it was my misfortune to make her acquaintance in Ferrara at the time of her brother's wedding.'

'Matteo was in Ferrara at that time too,' observed my master.

The bread was in my mouth. It saved me from the obligation of a reply. I made a small nod of my head.

'Why, yes,' said Felipe. 'Matteo told us a great story of how, during her triumphal entrance to the city, the fair Lucrezia tumbled from her horse. He even described her dress of cloth of gold edged in purple satin.'

Salai leaned forward and whispered in my ear, 'Now we will discover what a liar you are.'

'You have marvellous recall of mind, Matteo,' said the canon. 'That is exactly how she was dressed. And indeed her horse did rear up when the cannon went off, just as you said. And she recovered herself and climbed back on and the people cheered her for it.'

Salai glowered at me.

'How came you to be in Ferrara at that time?' The canon addressed the question to me. I felt the bread lodge itself in my windpipe. 'Who were you with?'

I swallowed. 'My grandmother,' I managed to say.

My master's gaze rested on my face.

Too late I remembered that I had told him that my grandmother had died before I'd reached Ferrara.

'So I might have seen you there in the crowd,' the canon went on. 'Perhaps that is why I thought I recognized you, for I do find your face familiar.'

My heart gulped. He *had* been looking at me earlier. How much did he know? It was from the hands of a priest that I had received the Medici Seal. It was not this canon, but perhaps he had been somewhere near when I had first met Father Albieri and I had not seen him. I concentrated hard to avoid touching the bag around my neck.

But the canon seemed to lose interest in me as the conversation moved on.

'Ferrara has opted to defy the Pope. It will go hard with them if he conquers their state,' said Felipe.

'Except that Francesco Gonzaga of Mantua, gonfaloniere of the pope's armies, is supposed to be enamoured of Lucrezia. Perhaps she hopes she can manipulate him to her advantage,' said my master.

'A more pleasant way to operate than the methods employed by her brother.'

'Cesare Borgia was an effective ruler,' stated Felipe.

His remark startled me.

'These petty princelings with their feuds allow their avarice to divide us so that Italy is open to any conqueror,' Felipe went on. 'Their main concern is filling their castles with gold while having no care to how their estates are managed. When Il Valentino established his rule he appointed magistrates and lawmakers, and businessmen could expect fair dealings.'

As I walked to the barn that night the sun was setting on the valley below me. The ochre walls and red roofs of Fiesole vied with Nature's palette of colours. From the terrace I could see the river, the fields and trees, and the distant towers and steeples of Florence, and above the city the dome of all the world. Like copper fire the ball atop the lantern glowed in the last rays of the sun.

The beauty of the view began to dispel my agitation.

But one last blow was to strike me that night.

Graziano, who had waited behind to attend to matters at the monastery, arrived late in Fiesole carrying packages. One of these was a letter for me.

He sought me out in the barn and said, 'Matteo, I am the bearer of bad news. A grave misfortune has befallen the old scribe who sat at the Ponte Vecchio.'

'What misfortune?' I asked. 'What has happened?'

'I am sorry to tell you this, Matteo, for I know he was a friend to you. He is dead.'

Ahh. I felt pain again, like the pain I had felt when my grandmother died.

'He was old and frail,' I said.

'They found him floating in the Arno,' Graziano said gently.

'He liked to drink more wine than was good for him.'

'Yes, but—'

'And the river is running fast,' I went on, not allowing Graziano to speak, 'with spring storms bringing the water down from the mountains. He would have fallen in because, although it is light in the evenings now, it is gloomy where he has to walk to reach his home. There are few torches on that stretch of bank. In the dark he would have slipped and fallen in the water.'

'He may not have died by drowning.'

I did not see the pit opening before me. 'He must have drowned,' I said.

'Matteo, the night police believe he became involved in a vendetta. They think he refused to pass on information and was killed for this. Whatever happened to him, it was most strange. When they recovered his body his eyes had been gouged out.'

Chapter Forty-Five

His eyes gouged out.

A monstrous way to die.

And all because the scribe would not give up information. What information? At his pitch, he saw everything, heard everything. He had shown me one day as he sat in his corner of the tower: how the sound made a natural acoustic circle around him just where people had to walk closer to each other as they left the street and entered the narrower passage onto the bridge.

Knowledge can be dangerous.

This is what Father Benedict, the mortuary monk in Averno, had said many years ago.

Who had pursued and murdered the Sinistro Scribe? And why?

I still held the letter that Graziano had given me. It must be from Elisabetta. No one else wrote to me. But it did not have her writing on the outside, yet it was a script I recognized. And then I saw whose hand it was.

It was a message from beyond the grave, written in the hand of the Sinistro Scribe.

Matteo, if that is indeed your name, I write to warn you that you are in grave danger.

You must leave Florence at once, and go as far from here as you possibly can. Do not tell me where, or try to communicate with me again. I myself intend to go away too. A man has recently come to Florence asking about a boy who bears your description. In the past when I had need of food I passed any information I garnered in the street to a spy who paid me to do this for him. This spy has told me that a certain man wishes to question me about you. I am to meet the man by the river this evening. But I will not go. For I saw the man standing by the bridge yesterday and he has a wicked appearance, a man who has his thumbnails grown like two curved claws.

Best that we do not know or speak to each other again. I wish you well. You have an astute mind, Matteo, and should not waste it.

Be careful.

The Sinistro Scribe

A spasm of terror went through me.

A man who has his thumbnails grown like two curved claws.

Sandino!

It could only be he.

I thought of Elisabetta's letters. Their contents were in the mind of the scribe. I struck my fist against my forehead. And the reason the scribe knew what they contained was due to my pride and obstinacy in refusing to learn to read when first asked by the Maestro. The scribe was – had been – an intelligent man. He would have remembered the names, the places she'd written of, the things that would enable Sandino to track me. I took Elisabetta's letters from my belt pouch and looked at them. She had mentioned Melte and Perela. My hands shook. Had the scribe told him where I was employed. How much had he revealed before being assassinated?

It was dawn and I had not slept. But I did not have time to think about what I would do. There was a commotion outside. Zoroastro burst into the barn.

'He has agreed! He has agreed!' He swung me up by my arms

and lifted me off my feet. 'Today we will do it! The bird will rise into the sky! We will fly, Matteo. We will fly!'

Between us we carried the flying machine to a spot above the woods and the stone quarries.

'You must run to launch yourself,' said my master.

Zoroastro nodded as he buckled himself into the frame harness. With his brawny blacksmith's arms he took hold of the supports, his veins corded with tension.

Zoroastro readied himself, and then began to run.

We ran with him.

For such a short man he made good speed. The edge of the cliff appeared.

Suddenly I realized I could not stop.

I would be carried over. A hand grasped my tunic. Felipe. I heard the cloth rip as I lost my footing. But another hand – hands – gripped my belt and my master dragged me back to safety.

With a rush and a swoop Zoroastro and the machine disappeared. We flung ourselves on the grass and crawled forward to see. He soared on the winds below us. We heard him cry out in wonder and delight.

He did fly.

It should be recorded that Zoroastro did fly.

But the wind that had lifted him high brought scowling clouds scudding from the mountains. Lightning flickered in their depth. The sky itself shuddered. A freakish gust buffeted the hillside.

And we could do nothing.

Only watch as the white flying bird was caught in the air currents and tossed like the frail plaything of an immense superior force.

Zoroastro crashed to earth.

* * *

It took him five days to die.

Five long days of utmost agony.

My master strode through the barn scattering everything in his path. 'Destroy these things! Hide them away from my face! I never want to see anything of this again!'

He must have wept.

He would have wept for the loss of his friend. For him to know so much about the human body, to have made so many drawings, to understand engineering, yet to watch, helpless, and witness his friend's broken bones and be unable to repair them must have caused the most profound grief. But we did not see him do this.

The canon administered the last rites and spent hours upon his knees in the church begging God to bestow the peace of death.

We gave Zoroastro a leather strap. He bit down upon it, his face running in sweat, stark against the white of the pillow on which he lay.

We had to put him in an outbuilding. The servants were so terrified at his screams of agony.

'Get me a dagger that I may slit my wrists!' he cried out. 'Bring me my axe! I implore you!' He called us by our names individually.

'Matteo,' said Graziano, 'is there nothing that you know of, some herb or potion that might ease his suffering?'

'If you can find me poppies . . .' I did not finish the sentence.

'This would help him?'

'I can make an infusion,' I said. 'But . . .'

'But?' The Maestro regarded me seriously.

'It is very dangerous.'

He waited. Then he said, 'You mean it could kill him?'

'Yes.'

'We will find these ingredients that you need.' And he went from the room.

It is not given to us to take away life.

This is what I believed. My conviction – a mixture of those of the Church and an older kind of belief – was that Nature bestowed life, and Nature decided when to call it back.

I said this.

'Make the potion, Matteo,' my master told me. 'We seek only to give relief of pain. Make it and I will administer it.'

As I prepared the mixture I wished that I could have my grandmother's recipe book beside me. Now that I could read I would be able to follow the instructions. Although this poison I did not forget.

And suddenly a recollection came to me of my grandmother making this same brew. One evening not long before she died a stranger had come to our fireside.

At the sound of the horse's hooves she had got to her feet and told me to hide inside the wagon. There was a murmur of conversation and I, having the curiosity of any child, peeked out of the canvas opening. I heard her say, 'I want no trouble.'

'Then give me what I have requested.'

He had a knife. She was calm, but then they both caught sight of me.

'Child,' she said, her voice sharp with anxiety, 'go back to sleep.'

'Who is that?' he asked.

'One of my own.'

'You are too old to have borne a child of that age.'

'A foundling boy.'

'Named?'

'Carlo.'

'A gypsy brat?'

She nodded. But Carlo was not my name. My name was Janek, so why had my grandmother lied to this man? She came quickly to the wagon, bundled me inside and gave me a sweetmeat to stop my mouth. 'In the name of all that's holy,' she whispered, 'do not speak another word. I beg you.'

The man had taken the mixture and left.

He had barely gone out of sight when my grandmother made preparations to move on. And while she was packing up I heard her muttering to herself.

'It's time anyway. We must go back.'

She had set off on a trail leading high into the mountains, a track where no one would have thought that a wagon might go. We were upon stony ground where the horse did not leave hoof prints. Yet she bound the horse's hooves with thick wads of cloth and chose the rockiest paths. We did not stop to eat or wash and carried our waste with us. Through the night I slept, awakening now and then to hear the horse scrambling as she urged it on, never stopping. By day she hid the wagon in a forest. Even though the weather was cold she did not light a fire until we were safely on the other side of the pass, near a place called Castel Barta. And it was there that she became unwell with her last illness.

Such a distinct memory, yet it was only now as I watched the poppy juice bubble that I recalled it. It was poppy juice that the stranger had demanded that she make for him.

Poppy juice, which brought relief from pain. And sleep. And silent death.

After we had buried Zoroastro my master spoke to Felipe. 'I am decided. The fresco is lost. Donna Lisa no longer requires me. I will ask the French to persuade the Florentine Council to release me from my contract and I will go to Milan.'

Salai was to be sent ahead with letters of introduction and to secure accommodation.

'What about you, Matteo?' Salai enquired of me innocently as he was making preparations to leave. 'What will you do?'

'I do not know what you mean.' It had not occurred to me that I would not accompany them to Milan.

'I don't think that our master will need an untutored servant to accompany him.'

'I am not so untutored as once I was,' I retorted hotly.

'You can neither read nor write,' mocked Salai. 'You think it such a big secret but everyone knows about your ignorance. We have been laughing at you as you pretend to read those letters and write replies to them.'

'Then laugh now at some other stupid joke,' I said, 'for I *can* read.' I snatched out my book from my purse. 'See now, here is the story of Saint George and the Dragon. It begins thus: "In a faraway land there lived a dragon" . . . .'

Salai laughed scornfully. 'We know how clever you are that you can memorize even the longest passage with the most difficult words. I heard the Maestro tell Felipe this one day when he thought no one was listening. The stories that you can recount without hesitation having heard them only once. He marvelled at your memory. I marvel at your stupidity.'

'I do not need to prove what I say to you,' I cried.

'But I would like you to prove it to me,' said a quiet voice from the door.

Salai whirled round. How long had the Maestro been standing there? How much had he heard?

The Maestro ignored Salai and went to the desk. He picked up a pen. 'Now, Matteo, let me see what you can write.'

I took the pen in trembling hands. I wrote out my name, *Matteo*.

Next he brought a book from the shelf and opened it at a random page. 'Now read.'

I stumbled over the text but I managed a line or two.

He did not smile. 'It is good,' he said. 'But not good enough. If you wish to come as part of my household to Milan you must give me your solemn word to undertake to be educated as I decree.'

I thought of the letter I had in my tunic, the warning from the scribe. I nodded.

'Say it.'

'I promise.'

'Then it will be so.' He left the room abruptly.

Salai departed the next day. Within the week the boxes were collected by carriers, and at the beginning of June 1506 we set out for Milan.

PART FIVE
WAR

Milan, 1509 – three years later

Chapter Forty-Six

'**S**tep – one – two.

'Now, forward – three – four. And—'

'Stop!

'Matteo, you are like a great ox plodding through the Piazza San Marco pulling a load of bricks.'

I let my hands drop to my sides and hunched my shoulders.

'*La Poursuite* is a dance of elegance, of style and wit,' Felipe went on. 'If you are to attend any of the French balls next week then you must be graceful. Try not to look as though you are trampling grapes at harvest time.'

'You must take smaller steps, Matteo.' Graziano spoke encouragingly. 'Imagine yourself approaching a lady. A lady, you understand. And you are a gentleman.'

'We aspire to make you one, at any rate,' commented Felipe dryly.

Graziano ignored him. 'So, Matteo, extend your hand. Thus . . .' He fluttered his fingers at me. 'And be mindful, you are not a bear offering a paw.'

Graziano, for all his great size, was surprisingly light on his feet. Acting the part of the woman, he danced towards me with tiny steps and delicately offered me his outstretched fingertips.

I tried to imitate his movements as best I could, walking on tiptoes and thrusting my fist at him.

He began to laugh at me. Felipe joined in.

I waited a moment then I laughed too. Despite years in their company I was still unsure of their Tuscan sense of humour. I heard my own laughter as strained and artificial. Even though I'd grown, and at sixteen considered myself a man, I was still young enough to take offence easily.

I tried again.

'That's better,' said Graziano. He allowed my fingers to brush against his. 'Now you go back and come forward to me once more. But this time the man moves in closer to the woman.'

Concentrating fiercely, I ensured that I adopted the right positions for my feet, held my body the correct way and paced out the specific movements of the dance. Guided by Felipe clapping time, I stepped up to Graziano and proffered my upraised hand. I managed to do this all together. I was quite pleased with my effort.

'No, no, no!' cried Felipe in despair. 'If you stride about the floor like that, the dance will be finished before it's begun.'

'For me it would be better to be over quickly,' I muttered.

Of all the new arts and graces my master had decided that I must learn while living in Milan this was my least favourite. I could see the purpose in being able to write and read, or developing a skill with a musical instrument, but dance, to me, was a foolish waste of time. To my mind the sooner the dance was completed the better, and I told my two instructors this.

'The intention of dancing is not for the event to be completed quickly,' responded Felipe. 'The purpose of a dance is more than to pass the time. You must enjoy the movement, let your body respond to the music.'

'And to respond also to the ladies or men with whom you are dancing,' Graziano chuckled.

'I am interested neither in ladies nor in men in that way.'

Felipe made a clicking noise with his teeth. 'Matteo, no matter what affairs of the heart you choose or choose not to undertake, you must learn to dance. Unless of course you intend to take Holy Orders?'

'With some clergy ordination is no deterrent,' said Graziano. He turned to me. 'To learn to dance is a great accomplishment. This dance is especially important, as it is a dance of intrigue. The steps are a pattern of approach and retreat. It's a lesson for life.'

'How can a dance be a lesson for life?'

'One could look on it as an apprenticeship in how to court a woman.'

'I do not wish to court a woman.'

'Ah, you say that now, but in time your heart will direct you differently.'

'If I did wish to court a woman, I would declare myself and be done with it.'

'That would be folly.' Graziano shook his head. 'It does not do to let a woman know directly that you have been smitten by her looks or charm.'

'Why not?'

'It would give her even more power over you.'

'But women have no power, or very little at any rate.'

Both men smiled.

'And I thought you said you had contact with Lucrezia Borgia at one time in your life,' Felipe pretended to muse aloud.

That name was like a past I hardly knew. My life had altered so much since I'd arrived in Milan three years ago. The circumstances in which I lived were more sophisticated than I had ever known. In this city Leonardo da Vinci was treated with high honour by the French, who ruled the duchy. The governor, Charles d'Amboise, admired and respected my master greatly, as did his own master in turn, King Louis of France. Our Maestro was housed and fed, and awarded honours and income, with the members of his household included in the hospitality.

And, as promised, my education began.

Felipe found me good tutors. Despite my late start and my initial inattention my teachers managed to build on the foundations of the Sinistro Scribe. Now I could write well, and read

273

fluently. And they were attempting to instil into me Greek, Latin, mathematics, history and philosophy.

I knew that I must attend to my studies. So, while the other members of the studio were working on artistic commissions I was with my tutors or at my books. If I fell behind in my lessons or received bad reports I saw that it would be difficult for me to keep a place within the da Vinci household. The Maestro's workshop did not exist here in the same manner as it had done in Florence. From the beginning, when we were lodged at the castle, within this offshoot of the French court, my duties were reduced. There were more than enough pages, cooks, cleaners and sundry other servants to see to anything Felipe or my master wanted. And then later, when my master had set up his own studio near San Babila, Charles d'Amboise ensured that the Maestro lacked for nothing. He took care of his personal comfort by sending him staff on a regular basis – washerwomen, tailors, cooks and his own barber to attend to him.

Salai had been right when he had warned me that the Maestro would have little use for an uneducated boy in Milan. Also, any professional personal assistance my master needed was now mostly undertaken by his new pupil, Francesco Melzi. This Francesco was a handsome, talented young man of about my own age whose father was a friend of the Maestro. Francesco was intelligent and courteous. He painted and wrote well, and he began gathering and sorting my master's vast collection of papers, treatises and books. He arranged his appointments and scribed his letters and saw to other tasks that I could never have done. From time to time I would be asked to set out my master's drawing materials or accompany him on an excursion, but even I now saw that I would benefit from a full formal education.

What I had not realized was that the lessons which I had avoided for so long would engage and draw me in. That enduring the struggles with grammar and comprehension and the arduous hours of recitation and learning and committing facts to memory would stimulate as well as exhaust me. To know the histories meant that I was able to take part in discussions that perplexed yet beguiled me. And all of this triggered by the ownership of that first little book, the story of Saint George and the Dragon given to me by Donna Lisa in Florence.

Sometimes when he went to dinner the Maestro still sent for me to carry his satchel if he had drawings to show the company. And it was there that I heard the conversations of the mathematician Luca Pacioli. No longer did I stand by my master's side, dull and staring, my mind half adrift from the babble of voices. Now I attended the discourse on subjects as vast and as interesting as the unexplored New World was rumoured to be. The Maestro debated with poets like Gian Giorgio Trissino, and Bernardino Zenale the painter. I began to empathize with the urge within the mind of my master – his need to know. Like him, I now wanted to know all things.

All things, that is, with the exception of the tortures of the dancing lesson. I did not like this social aspect of my education. With my natural reticence and a lingering fear of the discovery of my origins I did not foresee a time when I would ever wish to dance in public.

'Listen,' said Graziano, cocking his head. He went to the window and opened the shutter.

The steady beat of a side drum sounded from the street below. Another party of French soldiers were returning from their recent great victory over the Venetians.

'There will be a Carnival when King Louis arrives in the city,' Graziano went on, 'and I know that you enjoy Carnival, Matteo. This time I insist that you accompany me out in the later part of the night to join in the celebrations, and for that you must be able to dance at least a little.'

Chapter Forty-Seven

King Louis of France arrived in Milan the next day, the twenty-fourth of July. We watched from our rooftop. My master had designed some of the pageants and spectacles to celebrate the French king's triumphal entry into Milan at the head of his troops. King Louis was returning from his glorious victory at Agnadello, a small village north-east of Milan. The might of Venice had been trampled in the mud and the victorious French soldiers were laden with a variety of goods looted from the routed Venetian armies. Cannon fired from the battlements as, flanked by the marshals with the lily of France emblazoned on their surcoats, the royal procession made its way to the castle, scattering coins and comfits as it went.

And that night for Carnival I went out with Graziano, more as an adult than a child, to join in the merrymaking. Rather than going about the streets in the evening playing japes like the other young boys, I donned a long cloak and put a mask over my face.

It was the first time that I had worn a full Carnival mask and the effect of seeing my face gilded and sporting the long hooked nose was both disturbing and exhilarating. I paused in front of the great mirror that hung in our hallway. Mature enough now to look at my reflection without fear of any spirit trapping my soul, I looked at the figure before me. Sufficiently tall to be judged a few years older than I actually was, with my boyish features hidden under the false face and the cloak giving my stature length and elegance, I fancied I might be taken for eighteen at least.

A surge of excitement coursed through me as Graziano and I stepped out of our doorway. In my disguise I was unknown, unrecognizable to anyone, even myself. Immediately the current of the street engulfed us and we were at once part of the merriment and laughter. Carnival is the time when respectable men and women can dress up to conceal their identity and go forth among the crowds; when wine flows and people allow themselves abandonment.

A bunch of partygoers surged past us blowing trumpets and trailing streamers. The music increased in strength as we came into the streets leading to the main square. In the Piazza del Duomo jugglers spun plates and coloured balls in the air as their assistants canvassed the onlookers, begging and bullying coins from them. Huge stilt walkers clumped about above a fury of colours: purples, yellows, bright greens and reds. Boisterous clowns and jesters capered among the crowds. The smell of the burning bonfires and the wine, the heat of bodies close together with their mixture of acrid sweat and sweet perfume excited me.

A line of dancers swung past us. At the tail end, a woman, wearing a silk mask across the upper part of her face. Her mouth vibrant red. Through the slits of her mask her eyes surveyed me boldly. She stepped away, then stopped and beckoned to me.

Graziano pushed me in the back. 'Go on with you,' he said.

'I do not know the steps of this dance,' I protest.

'Matteo, Matteo' – he laughed – 'every man and woman born upon this earth knows the steps of *that* dance. It is the one you learn by taking part in it.'

The woman took my hand and pulled me along. Her grasp was firm, and when we paused now and then she gave me wine to drink from a leather wineskin she had in a pocket of her cape.

In the centre of the square she carried me off into a huge circle and someone else found my other hand. In the swirling frenzy I did not know with whom I was dancing. Was the woman deliberately pressing her body against mine? I sensed the trace of her fingers on my neck as we turned, and as she leaned towards me, bringing her hands together to applaud the music, her neckline gaped. The swelling of her breasts was evident. She moved, and the shadow between them deepened.

We were thrown out of the circle together, but almost immediately another group formed about us. Hands pulled at my tunic and dragged me into their line. The wine I'd drunk, the dancing, the woman's presence, all had made me dizzy. Suddenly the woman was in front of me again. She laughed up into my face, pinched my cheek and whirled away. I ran to catch up.

I *can* dance! I dance very well. I danced with everyone who let me, men, women, girls, boys, until the early hours of daybreak, until my vision blurred and I felt faint.

Somewhere amidst it all I lost Graziano.

Eventually I stumbled against a wall and tried to steady myself. I fought my way to the edge of the square and plunged into an alleyway. It was quieter here, almost empty. An open courtyard faced me. There was a fountain playing. I pulled off my mask and bent my face to the water to drink.

There was a woman beside me.

'Are you all right, young sir?'

Her voice was husky.

'I needed some air.' My head swam as I straightened up, but my mind was clear enough to know that this was the woman who had dragged me into the dance earlier. She must have followed me here. What was her interest in me? We did not know each other, and tonight I carried no purse.

She must have seen my hand reach for my belt to where my purse normally hung, for she laughed and said, 'I'm not interested in what you carry on your belt.'

She pronounced the word 'on' with a faint inflection, and as she saw me pick up on the significance of that she laughed again, deep in her throat. She reached her hand to put it to my cheek. I felt her warmth. She took off her own eye mask and looked at me.

Then she kissed me, full on the mouth.

I was so taken aback that I did nothing.

My mouth stayed open. I had never been kissed before. Not like that. My grandmother's benediction on my forehead or my cheek was a brief one, performed with closed lips.

This woman's lips had some kind of colouring on them. I tasted this. I tasted something else. Mixed with her breath was the fertile pulp aroma of some fruit she had eaten. And, underneath all of that, yet throbbing through it, something else, insistent and dangerous.

'Close your mouth.' She nudged me under my chin with her fingers. 'You look like a codfish gaping on a slab at the market.'

I clamped my lips together but opened them again as she handed me her wineskin. I drank some wine.

Not taking her eyes from mine, she took it back and wiped the neck and drank some herself. Then she put it down beside the fountain and turned to face me. She placed her two hands on my chest. Her nails were long and painted.

Into the courtyard with a burst of sound and energy came some dancers: twirling, frenetic. They called on her, and then two of them prevailed upon her to go with them, she protesting. She shrugged and blew a kiss at me as they danced away.

My legs were weak and my head hot. I went back out into the alley. The wall was cooler than the air about me and I pressed my face against it. Holding to its firmness I groped my way along until I reached one of the main streets, where I turned in the direction of the studio.

I found my bed but I did not find sleep until dawn came to the city and the last of the revellers were quiet.

Chapter Forty-Eight

'I saw you with that courtesan last night, Matteo.'

My face flushed crimson.

'Oh, what a gorgeous colour on Matteo's cheeks!' Graziano continued to tease me. He lifted an apple from the plate on the breakfast table and held its rosy skin next to my face. 'See? The fruit is dull by comparison. If only I could capture Matteo's blush in my palette then my sunsets would be glorious.'

'A courtesan?' I managed to reply.

'Don't tell me you didn't know!' said Graziano in mock surprise. 'What other kind of woman would kiss a man in the street in such a manner?'

'The question is, did she kiss *you*, Graziano?' Salvestro, one of the other pupils, rallied to support me.

'Of course!' Graziano replied. 'And before the night was over I'd had more than one kiss, I can tell you.' He winked broadly.

I was aghast. My woman of the Carnival who had so disturbed my dreams last night had also kissed Graziano. Graziano! It was not that he was not a nice person. He was very likeable. But he was much older than me and very fat.

'Oh now! Look at Matteo's face. He is devastated. Did you think she had kept her mouth only for you, little one?'

This was from Salai. And, as always, he took teasing to the point of hurtfulness.

He leaned over the table and flicked my ear. I pushed his

hand away. But it did not stop him from pursuing me further. 'I'll wager she'd kissed a dozen other men before Carnival was done?'

Other men.

How stupid of me.

I did not think. Of course she would have kissed others.

'Matteo' – Felipe, entering the studio, interrupted the banter – 'the Maestro intends to make a trip sometime very soon and he has informed me that you are to go with him.' He looked at me, taking in my clenched face, and raised an eyebrow. 'It will be good for you to get out of Milan for a little while perhaps?'

'Yes,' I responded eagerly. 'I will prepare at once.'

'With women pursuing him on all sides you'd think he'd be keen to stay,' said Salai. 'Unless of course our Matteo is afraid of females.'

Like the taunts of many bullies Salai's words had a stratum of truth within their seam. Although I seldom met girls, when I did so I was more awkward with them than other young men of my age.

'Take your schoolbooks with you and enough clothes for several months,' Felipe went on. 'The Maestro is planning to spend some time in Pavia.'

Although I had never been there with my grandmother I knew approximately where Pavia was. A town much smaller than Milan, it sat on a main road more than twenty miles away to the south.

'Is there a particular reason for choosing Pavia?' I asked.

Felipe nodded. 'A friend of the Maestro teaches at the University of Pavia. Messer Marcantonio della Torre is a doctor who conducts a school for medical students there. I expect that the Maestro will take the opportunity to catch up with his own anatomies.'

My interest quickened. It had been many months since I had accompanied my master to a dissection. For the last years he had been concentrating his studies on the terrain of the surrounding countryside, and how the geology of the area could lend itself to land irrigation and the construction of canals for transport and providing clean water. The idea of once again being party to his observations on the workings of the human body appealed to me. But if I was to leave Milan for some months then there was something I wanted to do first.

'By your leave then,' I said to Felipe, 'if I am to be away for so long I would ask permission to visit my friends at their farm in the countryside to say farewell.'

Felipe nodded. 'You may take tomorrow off to do so. But after that make yourself available to me. In addition to seeing to your own luggage I will need you to help pack particular things the Maestro might want to bring with him.'

I glanced at Francesco Melzi, who still sat at the breakfast table. It had become the custom for him to look after the Maestro's materials and so I did not want to intrude on duties he considered his own.

But Francesco Melzi was not like Salai, who was always watchful and jealous. He had a pleasant and graceful manner.

'It would be good to have you take care of that, Matteo,' he said readily. 'Now that you devote more time to your studies I think the Maestro misses your assistance when he is working. He complains to me when I have left something out of place and scolds me, saying that Matteo would not have done so. He told me that you devised an order for laying out his drawing equipment and he holds to it as the most efficient method.'

I took childish satisfaction from these words. If Francesco had made up the compliment then it was pleasant thing for him to do. If he hadn't, and it was true, then it was gracious of him to acknowledge me in such a way.

The next day I went to the stables in the castle of Milan to beg the loan of a horse so that I might ride out to Kestra, where the dell'Orte's uncle had a small farm.

Since we arrived in Milan I had renewed my friendship with Paolo and Elisabetta. Their uncle's farm was situated to the south-east of the city and I was able to go and see them from time to time. Their uncle was old and cantankerous and kept both his niece and nephew under strict control. It had been months since I had seen them but I knew they would welcome my visit as a respite from the hard work and austerity of their present life.

At the stables I met the head groom, with whom I had formed an acquaintance as I had prepared a physick for a favourite horse of his when it had been suffering from colic. Whenever I wanted to visit the farm at Kestra he would lend me this horse for the day. As I led the chestnut mare from the stable the groom told me that one of the young French officers, a Charles d'Enville, recently recovering from battle wounds, wanted to exercise his own horse this morning and was looking for company. This groom also appointed a stable lad to ride with us.

So the three of us left Milan in the early morning of a clear summer's day. We rode across the castle parade ground and under the arch of the Filarete Tower. Although damaged by the French soldiers shooting at it, the curved snake of the Sforza family coat of arms was still evident on the wall under the cupola. Duke Ludovico Sforza had ruled the duchy until driven out by the French almost ten years ago. The French king claimed this part of northern Italy but Ludovico's son, Massimiliano, in exile, plotted to regain Milan just as the Medici plotted their return to Florence.

Milan had the same excitement and bustle as the streets of Florence. The King of France extended patronage to the artists here, and the ateliers and studios thronged with young men seeking apprenticeships. Soldiers and their ladies strolled and gossiped, servant boys ran errands, traders did business around the bulk of the *duomo*, as their stalls were flooded with booty from the returning troops.

But I'd rather be in the countryside than in the city. When out under the sky my head cleared and my spirits lifted. The farm where Paolo and Elisabetta dell'Orte were now living was a little distance from Milan so we set our horses to gallop and enjoyed our ride.

Riding was one skill in which I needed no instruction. We sped along together, hooves thundering, horses' manes flying. We would be at the farm before noon – in good time for the midday meal.

An hour passed. We turned off the main road bearing east. The landscape around us changed. Lush fields and vineyards gave way to rocky outcrops and clumps of rough vegetation. We were now a few miles from the crossroads where we would go onto a lesser road that would eventually lead us to the farm track. The land was lightly forested and our pace slowed to accommodate the change of road surface. We chatted as we went, the stable lad and myself mainly listening to Charles, the cheerful French captain, telling us of his exploits at the battle of Agnadello, where France had trounced the Venetian army and its huge contingent of Swiss mercenaries. We were trotting along when, on a turn in the road, we came suddenly upon a Romany camp. A kettle was hanging over burning embers near their shelter beneath some trees in the lee of a little hill.

'What have we here?' The French captain reined in his horse.

'Gypsies,' the stable lad said at once. And he spat on the ground.

I felt my heart unsteady.

'They have no right to make camp next to the public highway,' the lad declared. 'There is an edict. They must ask permission from a landowner and that can only be granted under certain conditions.'

'I would hardly call it a camp as such,' said the French captain.

To make a rough shelter they had bent over some poplar saplings and thrown a covering over the stooped branches.

'They are not allowed to build a dwelling place,' the stable lad insisted.

The captain shook his head. I think he would have ridden on, except that now the stable lad had called attention to the situation he could not be seen to be lacking in authority by not dealing with it. He walked his horse forward and called out. A man came from the tent, followed swiftly by two ragged waifs. I hung back. I did not recognize this man from any campsite or gypsy gathering I had attended, but that was not to say that, even after all these years, he would not recognize me.

Since I had left Florence I had lived in peace in Milan. For the first year or so I had been with the da Vinci household, ensconced within the castle of the governor of Milan. So disturbed had I been at the fate of the Sinistro Scribe that in all that time I had not ventured beyond the castle grounds. Felipe found me a tutor among the castle staff to begin my lessons, so there was no need for me to go abroad. Then I heard news of the fate of Cesare Borgia. Over the last years Il Valentino had tried to raise his own army to fight to regain his dominions in the Romagna. But while doing this, the Borgia had become involved in a dispute and had died in an ambush while fighting in Navarre. His attackers left him lying naked in a ravine with twenty-five stab wounds in his body, a violent death for a man who had himself shown no mercy to others. Thus, when the Maestro eventually set up his studio in another district in the city, I felt safe enough there. I was sure that Sandino had not followed my trail to Milan, else I would have known it by then. I guessed also that Sandino would have work enough to keep him busy now. There was a plenitude of spying and intrigue between the factions of this war, enemy on enemy, ally upon ally. So, during this year, as the Pope secured most of the Romagna and allied himself with the French against Venice, my mind had rested more easily. The leather pouch around my neck had weathered until it was part of me. I never took it off. Neither did I think much of it, or what it held.

Until now.

'They are a sorry-looking bunch of gypsies,' the French captain said in an aside to me.

A young girl drew back the curtain and stood at the opening of their shelter.

'Not so sorry,' commented the stable lad, eyeing her figure.

She noted his look and stepped back into the shadow. I felt her humiliation at being appraised in such a way.

Her father made a very slight move towards the fire.

He had sensed danger and was seeking a weapon. I saw the long metal rod that held the kettle suspended over the embers. And then I saw something else.

A red scarf tied outside their shelter.

I urged my horse a few steps closer to the captain and spoke quietly. 'He has been forced to camp here,' I said. 'His wife is in childbirth.'

The gypsy's eyes flickered to my face.

From the tent came the piercing cry of the new born.

'My wife . . .' The Romany spoke haltingly in French. 'She has just been delivered of a child.'

The French captain smiled. 'A son, I hope?'

'A girl.'

'You have named her?'

'Dalida.'

Dalida. A gypsy name. It meant woodland, a group of young trees by water. I looked around me. A small brook ran near the roadside. This child was well named for the place she had been born.

Suddenly I realized that the Romany was watching me. He saw that I understood the meaning of his baby's name, in addition to the significance of the red scarf at the door of the tent. I ducked my head from his glance.

'A girl can be as much of a blessing as a boy.' The captain, who was not an unkind young man, took a coin from his purse and threw it down at the man's feet. 'Use this for her dowry.' He glanced at the stable lad and then, conscious of his rank, he added sternly, 'Now be gone from here. Do not be at this place when I pass this way again.'

I could hardly bear to look to see the gypsy grovel down to retrieve the money.

But he didn't.

His two little boys ran to where the silver gleamed in the mud. 'Leave it,' I heard him say in his own language. He gave me a steady look. Then he raised his hand to the captain and spoke again in Romany.

The captain tipped his hat to acknowledge what he thought was the man's thanks.

But I, who understood the man's words, knew that he had not thanked the captain. He had laid a curse on the Frenchman for the discomfort his wife must suffer at having to move on. I turned my horse's head away at once.

'Thieving rabble,' said the stable lad as we rode on. 'They should be exterminated like the vermin they are.'

And to my own dishonour I did not disagree.

I glanced back and saw the man gather his children and go inside his tent. Within the hour they would be gone but I knew this Romany would have taken in everything about us, including the age and the markings of our horses.

He would also not forget the face of the young man who had understood his tongue and customs.

Chapter Forty-Nine

We arrived at the farm in Kestra in the late forenoon.

Elisabetta was coming from the house carrying a basket of wet washing to hang on the drying lines. She put down her load and ran to greet me, kissing me on both cheeks as I dismounted.

I introduced her to Charles d'Enville as the stable lad took our horses to water. The French captain doffed his feathered officer's hat and bowed with a great flourish. Then he took Elisabetta's hand in his own and, bending his head, kissed her fingertips.

'For shame, Matteo!' he exclaimed. 'To keep such a beautiful flower as this growing in the countryside when her radiance should be blooming at court in Milan.'

I looked with his eyes at the girl I had always considered as a sister and saw that with the passing years Elisabetta had grown in her beauty. Her golden hair gathered loosely at the back of her neck revealed the contours of her face, and her figure was maturing into full womanhood. Her eyes, though shadowed still, were bright beneath strong eyebrows.

At the Frenchman's words two spots of colour came into Elisabetta cheeks. I wondered how long it had been since any man had paid her a compliment. She took us to where her uncle was talking with the owner of the neighbouring farm, a man called Baldassare. They shared an irrigation system to bring water onto their land from the river. They had their sleeves rolled up and were trying to find a break in one of the water supply pipes. Baldassare was of middle age, thick set, with a kindly open face and pleasant manner. Elisabetta's uncle was much older, stooped and worn with hard work. They both stopped digging with their shovels as we approached.

'Uncle' – Elisabetta raised herself on tiptoe and placed a kiss on his leathery cheek – 'Matteo is here to visit us and he has brought a friend who rode out with him. I would like to invite them to share our midday meal.'

Her uncle growled his agreement.

'He does not mean to sound surly.' Elisabetta apologized for her uncle's lack of manners as we walked back towards the farmhouse. 'He's lived alone for most of his life and is awkward with visitors.'

As we sat down to eat I thought how different this would be for Charles, accustomed to the formal and ornate manners of the French court.

'You were with the French army at Agnadello?' Paolo had come in for his dinner. As soon as he knew the history of the stranger at the table he began to quiz him eagerly. 'Did you see action?'

'One does not *see* action,' Charles replied seriously. 'When one is in battle it is a more visceral experience.'

They waited for him to go on.

His gaze encountered that of Elisabetta and he hesitated.

'You may proceed with your tale, monsieur.' She returned his look with courage. 'I have had some experience of such things. My father's keep was attacked, my parents and baby brother killed. My sister, who later died, and myself suffered grievously at the hands of the attackers.'

She had set out her life experience quite plainly for him, and waited to see how he would respond.

The chivalrous French captain did not disappoint.

'During war men can behave like beasts,' he said. 'On behalf of my sex I apologize to you most sincerely. There is no need for that kind of behaviour. One can defeat, and even kill, an opponent with chivalry.'

'Yes,' said Paolo. 'A knight fights for a true cause with honour.'

My friend Paolo's mind still hankered after his boyhood ideals of the glory of combat.

Charles d'Enville sighed. 'Alas,' he said, 'my experience is that true causes are rare. Men fight for greed, not glory, and fighting with honour is still a messy and bloody business.'

I thought of my master's fresco of the battle of Anghiari. His central scene depicting the Struggle for the Standard and the men therein. The figures straining. The warriors' faces twisted in their death throes.

'In a proper war men fight nobly,' said Paolo.

'But it is quite horrific,' Charles replied. 'Although we won at Agnadello, we were lucky. I was with the cavalry under our Seigneur de Chaumont, Charles d'Amboise, and we knew the enemy army had split into two divisions as they marched to engage us. The first Venetian commander took up position on a ridge above the village. We were ordered to attack uphill and we could not breach their lines. It was raining heavily and our horses were hampered by the mud. Then our king arrived with the remainder of the French army and we fought a bloody battle, killing over four thousand of their troops and routing their cavalry. When news of this reached the other Venetian commander his mercenaries deserted.' Charles looked at Paolo seriously. 'If these two men had managed to combine their forces against us, we might not have prevailed.'

'But a great victory then,' said Paolo. 'To defeat so many at once.'

'Each man died a singular death,' Charles replied gently.

'You have brought a rarity to our table, Elisabetta,' her uncle commented. 'A Frenchman who talks some sense.'

Charles inclined his head. 'I will take that as a compliment, sir.'

'You may take it how you like,' Elisabetta's uncle replied shortly. He rose up from the table. 'Now I must go and do some work.'

Elisabetta hung her head in embarrassment but Charles affected not to notice and said to Paolo, 'I do not wish to cast gloom upon you, but I feel it only fair to warn you that a soldiering life is hard. The casualty rate is very high.'

But Paolo was not deterred by the sobriety of Charles's comments on war. 'You yourself were wounded and survived,' he said. 'Was it a most terrible wound?'

Charles stood up. 'I see that there is nothing for it but to show you my battle honours.' His eyes were full of mischief. He pulled open his shirt. A great ragged scar ran across his abdomen. Against his tanned flesh the scar blazed white.

Elisabetta put her hand to her mouth.

'My battle wound never fails to impress the ladies.' Charles winked at me.

I saw that he had done this deliberately to distract Elisabetta from her upset at her uncle's manners.

'A Swiss mercenary tried to disembowel me with his pike,' he said cheerfully. 'My innards were hanging out. I had to clutch them to me and hold myself together while I screamed for help. If I hadn't been heard by my cousin, the Comte de Céline, who brought his own surgeon to stitch me up, I would have perished there on the battlefield.'

'Was it very painful?' Elisabetta asked him.

'Horribly so,' Charles admitted. 'All the while I was being stitched I bawled like a baby.'

I shuddered as I imagined how that must have been for him. I recalled one night in the mortuary of Santa Maria Nuova in Florence: the Maestro had removed for examination the great coils of glistening intestine looped inside a man's belly. I thought about this. Charles's attacker must have pierced the stomach wall but perhaps not the intestine itself. Else he would not have been able to eat so heartily at dinner just now. Though one of the anatomies my master had done showed a man with a damaged intestine and my master said he believed it had been that way for years yet the man had lived with it. In any case the Comte de Céline's surgeon must have been very skilful to repair Charles's wound.

Baldassare, who had joined us at dinner, coughed discreetly. Charles hurriedly closed over his shirt and sat down.

'Forgive me,' he said. 'I can become quite carried away at my own exploits.'

I helped Elisabetta clear the table and we talked for a little while in the kitchen. The conversation and the company had brought a light into her eyes and she chatted and told me of the progress of the herb garden that she had been planting when I had last visited the farm at Easter.

From outside we could hear the clatter of swordplay. Despite the heat of the afternoon Paolo had persuaded Charles to teach him a few sword thrusts and the use of the short dagger in close combat.

'Do you remember, Matteo,' Elisabetta asked me, 'the time when you drew the dagger on Paolo?'

'I do.'

She was looking at me now with eyes that were older and wiser than they had been at the time of that incident. 'You were used to handling such a thing, were you not, Matteo?'

Her question was more of a statement.

I managed to shrug and nod at the same time.

'Travelling on the road,' I replied, 'I had to learn to take care of myself.'

'You travelled on the roads?'

My blood chilled. What had I just said? I tried to gather my thoughts for an explanation to make a ragged patch over the things I had told her of my personal history when at Perela.

'Why yes,' I continued. 'When I first ran away from my uncle

I walked for many miles before I found employment.' My mind cast about for some way to change the course of the conversation. 'But you,' I went on, 'you are not too unhappy with this uncle of yours here?'

'No, it's not so bad,' Elisabetta agreed. 'He is very ill humoured but I find I can win him round with soft words. Paolo is too proud to do that. Also Paolo hates the farm work. He still dreams of taking arms to avenge our family.'

'But where would he seek revenge?' I asked her. 'These men are long since scattered, possibly dead.'

'Paolo thinks now that they worked for someone else and not just Cesare Borgia. There may be a link to the Medici. You remember the monk at Averno who gave us shelter when we were being hunted?'

I nodded. My stomach cramped. That night sheltering with the Plague victims. How could I forget?

'The monk wrote to his sister at the convent in Melte and she wrote to me here with some information. He found out that the men who were searching for us were led by a ruffian called Sandino.'

Sandino.

My gorge rose. His name said out loud in Elisabetta's sweet voice on a hot summer's day drove a chill of fear into my soul.

'This man Sandino is a spy and an assassin,' she went on. 'The monk wrote to tell me that he is a brigand who sells his favours to the highest bidder and he is a treacherous double agent.'

'Then how can we know for whom he was working when he attacked Perela?' I asked her.

'You know the good monk of Averno, Father Benedict, better than I,' Elisabetta replied. 'His reputation is such that I would take his word. He said that he believed that when Perela was attacked Sandino was in the pay of the Borgia.'

'Although that does not make sense,' I said, hoping to confuse her thoughts. 'Perela was a Borgia stronghold. My master had been instructed to go there to check the fortifications. Cesare Borgia wanted it strengthened, not destroyed.'

'Something must have changed his mind.' Elisabetta considered my statement. 'And in fact,' she went on, 'they did not destroy our keep. It was something else within it that they sought.'

My throat was now constricted so that I could not speak.

'But who could know the mind of Cesare Borgia?' said Elisabetta.

'Who indeed?' I managed to reply. 'And now Cesare Borgia is dead. He was killed over a year ago in Navarre. So there is an end to Paolo's quest for retribution.'

Elisabetta turned to look at me. 'But surely you know, Matteo, that Paolo lays the blame for all our troubles with the Papacy. The thought of harming the Vatican in any way is what occupies my brother's mind. He will not rest until he has exacted some revenge.'

Chapter Fifty

Charles needed to return to his barracks to report to his commanding officer but Elisabetta begged me to remain a while longer.

In the yard I watched Charles prepare to ride back to Milan with the stable lad.

The Frenchman bent his head again over Elisabetta's hand. 'It is very difficult for a soldier on active service to conduct any kind of correspondence with a lady,' he said. 'But I would ask permission to write to you, if I may?'

'Sir, I will look forward to your letters,' Elisabetta replied.

'And I would be honoured if you deigned to reply.' Charles smiled at her.

As he mounted his horse she said, 'Please try not to encounter any more Swiss mercenaries on your travels.'

She smiled up at him. And it occurred to me that I had not seen Elisabetta smile or speak in such a light-hearted way for a very long time.

After they left, Elisabetta and I walked quietly in the garden. She led me through her herbarium and we exchanged information about the drying of plants and the best way to make various preparations. I took from inside my shirt some seeds I had bought for her in the market in Milan. 'You must wait until the spring,' I said, 'but these will grow if given a shady place.'

'I have made this place my retreat,' she said. 'My uncle does not mind me spending so much time here as there is income to be gained from the plants. I take the dried herbs and sell them in the village, and one of the apothecaries in the next town has asked me to supply him with particular products.'

She seemed pleased with her project, and I promised to ask in Milan if any of the apothecaries there needed supplies.

I also spoke to Paolo before I left. His manner too was less heavy and more excited than was usual on my visits. But it was not my company that had affected him in this way, more his conversation and sparring session with the French captain.

'Charles says there are plenty of opportunities for fighting men,' he told me.

We had paused to talk before I led my horse out from their barn.

'You would not join the French army?' I asked him.

'I would not side with the Pope in any fight. But there are many independent condottieri looking for an able-bodied man with some experience in swordsmanship.' Paolo kicked the stable door in frustration. 'If only I had enough money to buy a set of arms and a horse!'

It was dusk as I made my own way back to Milan.

I approached the turn in the road where we had met the Romany with caution. But, as I expected, they had disappeared. There was no sign of their passing. They had untied the trees, collected their belongings and buried the embers of their fire. It was if they'd never been there.

Apart from one thing.

The coin.

I saw it shining on the earth.

I knew why the man, poor though he was, did not stoop to pick it up. We are not dogs, to be thrown a bone and scrabble for it in the dirt. Had Charles allowed the Romany some dignified leeway to accept his money, then the man would have taken it and gladly. The French captain should have made a semblance of trade, asked the man some information about the land, or even undergone the pretence of fortune telling. Or, if it was meant as a gift, he should have dismounted from his horse and offered the coin for the Romany to accept. But to throw it at a man's feet is demeaning. Romany pride prevented him from lifting it.

I left the coin lying on the earth.

A mistake.

I should have picked it up. They used it later as a marker.

It served to indicate a place I had passed, and was therefore worth watching, as I might pass that way again.

It showed the best spot on the road to effect an ambush.

Chapter Fifty-One

Before the end of the year I was in Pavia with the Maestro. His friend, Professor Marcantonio della Torre, lectured at the university there and conducted his anatomies in a theatre set aside for the purpose. When we attended these sessions the Maestro occupied a place of honour. He had a special chair near the anatomy table in front of the student benches and I stood beside him. On dissection days we had to push our way through the crowds of students and the few members of the public who had paid a high price for a ticket to attend. Throngs of pedlars stood at the university gates chaffering with these people over pieces of perfumed paper, scarves, and little silk sachets filled with *chypre*, all designed to overcome foul odours.

The first anatomy I attended was performed on a young man who had died of an internal abscess. His stomach was grossly distended and full of bile, and the smell when the barber surgeon pierced it was so disgusting that I wished I'd had a coin to buy one of the scented sachets on sale outside. My master did not seem to be aware of the stench. He rose to his feet to see the contents of the stomach as the doctor in attendance poured the green fluid into a glass container. Professor della Torre presided upon a raised platform, a naked live man on one side of him and a skeleton on the other. With a long pointer he indicated on both these figures where the barber was making his incisions, and discoursed on the organs held up by the doctor. As the abscess burst open, a woman in the public gallery fainted and had to be carried out. Her place was taken up at once by someone from the crowd of people in the corridor anxious to get in.

My master nudged me and indicated the attendants sprinkling quantities of vinegar about, and the braziers burning rosemary.

'More pleasant than using one's own urine to deaden the smell,' he said. 'But I'll warrant less effective once the surgeon fully exposes the internal organs.'

As the anatomy progressed many of the audience began to cough and gag. I heard the people crammed on the benches behind me whisper that the body was part decomposed, and must therefore have been taken from a grave.

That night at dinner my master asked Professor della Torre about this. Grave robbing is a crime punished by execution, but the professor told us that sometimes students would travel far outside the town to steal a body to anatomize for their own information.

'Not without hazard,' he said. 'Country folk now guard their burial places zealously, and attack anyone approaching their cemeteries by night.'

'Let your students but follow the various armies in Italy,' my master said heavily. 'There will be bodies aplenty in the wake of their progress.'

'You think this war has not ended with the French chasing the Venetians back into their northern state?'

'By allying themselves with the Pope the French think that they have consolidated their position in Italy,' said Graziano. 'But they have lain down with a fox. A cunning old fox. He will turn on them.'

'The Holy Father seeks unity,' Felipe, who was pious and traditional in his beliefs, argued, 'and to do this he needs to drive out foreign occupiers, bring down republics like Florence and install rulers in the city states that are sympathetic to the Papacy.'

'He would bring the Sforza back to Milan?' asked Professor della Torre.

'I believe he would,' said Felipe, 'and give Florence once again to the Medici.'

In addition to his dissections the Maestro at this time compiled notebooks of his studies on water and optics. And he worked on the painting of Donna Lisa.

He had visited her when he had to return to Florence to settle a dispute with his brothers regarding the inheritance from an uncle. He did not speak directly of this haggle over a piece of land, but I had heard Felipe mention to Graziano that the Maestro was forced to be plaintiff. Such a thing would not have happened to a true-born child. Thus the stigma of bastardy followed him into old age.

But when he had been in Florence he discovered that, in the Via della Stufa, the Donna Lisa had been safely delivered of a live baby boy.

The child was named Giocondo.

So we passed the winter in Pavia. And I discovered that it was not only for his own studies that the Maestro had come to the university; it was for my benefit also. The library held magnificent books and, with his guidance, I began to extend my reading.

One day as I set out pen and ink for him to draw the details of the sinews of the man's arm he said to me, 'Look at that, and marvel.'

He did not mean his own exquisite draughtsmanship. He was not so boastful. He meant the intricate and effective construction of the human body.

'Man is a machine,' he said, 'a most beautiful piece of engineering.'

I recalled the time of the chicken legs at Perela. He had taken the legs chopped from a newly slaughtered capon, and to the tendons within he had attached lengths of thin cord. Paolo and I had hidden these in our sleeves and crept silently upon Elisabetta and Rossana. We had touched the girls' necks with these leg stumps, pulling on the cords to make the claws open and close. They had screamed in fright and we had chased them until they ran shrieking to their mother to complain about us.

I had not seen that this childish game could be a practical lesson in anatomy. I held out my hand in front of me then I held it up so that it was between my eyes and the sun. Through the skin I could discern the darker shadow of the bone. If there could be made a light bright enough to shine through it then we might not need to dissect to observe the internal workings of the body in action. I curled my fingers into my palm and then straightened them again.

'What are you thinking, Matteo?'

He was watching me.

'I was wondering how it is that I can make a fist without thinking of it.' I told my master of seeing baby Dario at Perela sleeping in his crib. When the girls went to wake him they extended their little finger and placed it in his palm. In his sleep his fingers curled automatically around theirs. 'Why did he do that?'

'I believe it to be an instinctive reaction. One that serves some purpose in the development of a child, and necessary for its survival. But' – he paused – 'a theologian might say that God made it thus.'

'Why did God make it thus?'

He regarded me in amusement. 'There was a time, Matteo, when you would have thought that to phrase such a question constituted heresy.'

'I do not see that to discover the true meaning of things is wrong.'

'There are those who would disagree. They have a fear of finding out.'

'But God cannot be afraid of His own Creation,' I argued.

My master nodded his head in agreement. 'Not if He is the Truth, as the Church claims Him to be.'

'There is a legend from ancient times that says that it was Prometheus that fashioned man from clay. But he was punished for this.'

'Yes. He was considered a skilled metal worker and alchemist.'

'Like Zoroastro,' I said.

'Yes.' My master sighed. 'Like Zoroastro.' And his face drooped and the lines of his brow and mouth hollowed his features in sadness.

I never thought of him as old. His face, his eyes especially, were always alive with interest or intent as his mind pursued some question. As he worked – painted or modelled or wrote – the concentration brought a refinement to his features as though the genius that pulsated through him energized his being. But, at the mention of his friend who had perished so cruelly at Fiesole, I saw how he was ageing.

'Do you think we could ever know how to repair even such grievous injuries?'

'Perhaps,' he said. 'But now I am tired, Matteo. Leave me to rest.'

The next morning I rose early to be at my books. The sky darkened at evening now and I needed to make use of as many hours of daylight as I could. I was sitting in an inner courtyard, wrapped up against the chill morning air, when Graziano found me.

'The carrier has just been with some parcels. There is post here for you.'

As I reached out my hand to take it from him I saw on the outside of the paper writing that I recognized. It was a letter from Elisabetta dell'Orte.

Chapter Fifty-Two

My dear Matteo,

I write to tell you that my uncle is very ill. He fell down in the field one day where he was working. Paolo was away to the market in Milan and I was busy about the house. My uncle could not move or cry for help so he may have lain there for some time. I only found out what had happened when he did not return for the midday meal and I went to look for him and discovered him lying upon the ground. I knew that I could not lift him by myself so I ran then to the farmhouse of Baldassare. He brought a blanket and between us we managed to roll my uncle onto it and thus we dragged him to the house.

My uncle has lost the use of his limbs on one side and can barely speak to be understood, but must make signs to indicate what he wants. Baldassare has been very good to us and he paid for a doctor to come. The doctor bled my uncle twice from his arm. This has not helped and I believe has only made him weaker. I am administering hot compresses and feeding him barley broth and milk possets with preparations of camomile and valerian. I do not know what else to do to aid my uncle's recovery or give him relief from his discomfort.

Matteo, I believe you to be skilled in the art of herbs and medicines and I seek your advice on the best method of helping him.

> *I know that you will be occupied with your studies and have little time to spare from your activities, therefore I understand that you may be unable to reply to me at once.*
>
> *Your loving sister and friend,*
> *Elisabetta*

I took the letter to my master and waited while he read it.

'By your leave,' I said when he had finished, 'I would ask Messer della Torre if he has any advice on this matter.'

He did not reply but went to a shelf and pulled down a set of papers. He riffled through the pages until he found some drawings. 'Here, Matteo. Study this sketch.'

I looked at the page he indicated.

'Were you with me when I made that dissection? It was an old man of a hundred years or more, who died at the hospital of Santa Maria Nuova in Florence.' The Maestro opened up a little notebook that was tied in with the papers. 'I've written some of my observations here. His arteries had become thin and withered. It is evident that, like canals silting up, this must obstruct the flow.'

'Like Umberto, the old man you dissected in the mortuary at Averno?'

'Yes.' He nodded. 'And this seizure of Elisabetta's uncle is an affliction that men suffer as they age,' my master went on, 'and if the blood flow is impeded then it must be that some of the functions of the body can also be impaired.'

The drawing he showed me was not a dissection I had been present at. It must have been performed when he had returned to Florence from Milan to settle the question of his inheritance. I noticed that his method of illustrating his dissections had progressed. There was more than one aspect of an organ, so that it could be viewed as if from all sides. Unconsciously I put my hand on my own arms. I could feel the tendons, the sinews, and even deeper than that. Under my skin were the layers he had drawn.

His sketch was the result of many, many hours of anatomizing and the direct result of doing the dissections himself, rather than the usual custom of allowing a barber to make the incisions and have a doctor remove the organs.

'You must look and see for yourself, Matteo,' he explained. 'Some of my examinations refute the text of perceived wisdom. If you do not question, then one mistake is carried forward unquestioned to the next scholar.'

'Your observations can help us understand more fully why this happens.'

'You always seek the "why", don't you, Matteo?'

My eyes caught his glance as he spoke and I fancied he looked at me with pride. But the moment was fleeting so I was not sure.

'And yet why is this man afflicted on one side only?' he murmured to himself. 'Why is that the case?'

He made some notes on the margin of the paper, an instruction to himself: *Ask about this.*

'What else could it be?' he mused. 'What else would give the symptoms Elisabetta has described in her letter. A seizure? We know other illnesses or conditions to present in this way. From antiquity there are examples: Julius Caesar had the falling sickness. But' – he turned to me – 'you have met this uncle of Elisabetta dell'Orte. Did he have any condition that you noted?'

I shook my head.

'What was his age?'

'About sixty, perhaps older. It is hard to tell. He was so weathered by working outdoors all his life.'

'His mood?'

'He was curt.'

'Ill tempered?'

'A little . . .' I hesitated. I thought about how one acquires a reputation in life: one man for laziness, another for greed. Yet sometimes it is due to the ill will of others that a man has a particular mantle put across his shoulders. In truth I had seen no evidence of Elisabetta's uncle being bad tempered. His face had softened whenever he looked at her. Perhaps she reminded him of his dead sister, Elisabetta's mother. The man had a reputation for choler but now I tried to see him through the eyes of Elisabetta. He was lonely and old and worked hard and was impatient with those who did not.

'I see you are pondering my question, Matteo,' my master said. 'And it is right that you do. Every piece of information is relevant to the healing of the body.'

'You think perhaps his illness was progressing upon him and that might be the reason he was brusque? Could that not merely have been his humour?'

'Yes and no,' said my master. 'All things have causes. So even his humour might have its cause in some disease of the body. Cesare Borgia, a carnal and lascivious man, suffered grievously from what they call the French disease. This not only gives boils and can lead to death but has, I believe, a detrimental effect on the brain and thus upon how a man acts, even to the point of fits of madness.'

He looked at me intently. 'Bear that in mind, Matteo. You are of an age when you will begin to form romantic liaisons. Casual relationships are fraught with hazards of all kinds.'

I was embarrassed, but he did not notice. He had removed himself from the emotion of the moment and turned again to pore over his sketches. I realized that, even in extreme danger while working for Il Valentino, he had observed and noted Cesare Borgia's looks and behaviour. But now his mind was focused on the drawings before him. There was a difference here in how he and I viewed events. Whereas I too analysed the reason for her uncle's illness, I also saw Elisabetta running through the rain-soaked grass. The wind driving against her, the hem of her skirts soaked as, with Baldassare, she tried to drag the old man to shelter.

The Maestro left me, telling me to continue with my work and saying that we would deal with this matter later.

I found it difficult to concentrate. The passage from Petrarch I had found interesting no longer held my attention. My mind kept returning to Elisabetta's letter. If only my grandmother were alive. She would have known the best remedies for Elisabetta's uncle's condition. I had seen her attend old people similarly afflicted. I recalled her at the big gypsy camp at Bologna, where the leader of one of the major bands had lost the power of his limbs and the sight of one eye. As soon as his family knew that we were in the area they had sent for my grandmother to come to attend to him, and she had pored over her recipe book, seeking ways to relieve his symptoms. *My grandmother's recipe book!* It was still buried in the wooden box in the earth somewhere north of Bologna. I was sure I could find the place where it lay. But even if I could, it was too far for me to go now and dig it up to look for something to help Elisabetta. I was still wrestling with these thoughts and my studies when, an hour or so later, Felipe sought me out.

'Matteo, the Maestro has spoken to me and given me instructions regarding you.' Felipe handed me a parcel. 'There are medicines from the university hospital pharmacy contained herein, with instructions as to their use.'

I looked at him in surprise. I had not had time to seek out Marcantonio della Torre to ask his advice.

Felipe went on speaking. 'Your master has granted you leave from your studies to visit your friends, the dell'Orte family. I have spoken to the farrier in the town. He will provide you with directions so that you can find the road to their farm from here. Your master will pay the hire of a horse for you for several days, Matteo, so that you may take these medicines and visit Elisabetta and Paolo.'

I got to my feet at once. 'I would like to thank you,' I stammered.

'Don't thank me,' said Felipe. 'Thank your master on your return.'

I took the parcel from him.

'Go on. Go on.' Felipe flapped his hand at me. 'A horse awaits you at the farrier. Be mindful on the road and travel safely.'

Chapter Fifty-Three

To come to Kestra from Pavia I had to ride in a circle south of the city of Milan and take the road via the town of Lodi.

These roads were the ones less travelled by the military and therefore more pleasant. The land of Lombardy is somewhat different from that of Tuscany, but leaving Lodi and heading south into the valley of the river Po the scenery is no less beautiful. My route was via a deep groove in the land with escarpments of rocks and small cliffs. I rode past a gorge where the water tumbled and roared. It had been in such a place, under a waterfall, that I had been drawn into the life I led now. I turned away from there, following the instructions of the farrier in Pavia, and arrived at a roadway which ascended to Elisabetta's uncle's farm from the south.

I could see at once that the hand of the owner was not upon the place. The grass already grew too high in the field, while the chickens ran wild in the yard.

No one came to meet me.

Elisabetta was inside attending to her uncle. Baldassare, the neighbouring farmer, was also there. Two chairs had been placed beside the bed in the sick room. And here Baldassare and Elisabetta sat together, taking turns to nurse the patient by day and night. The old man was a shrivelled form of himself. He reminded me of one of the grotesques that the Maestro drew. His brow was down, his lips twisted to one side, his face horribly contorted.

And yet Elisabetta nursed him as if he did not repel her. As I entered she laid her hand on his head.

'Uncle,' she said in a loud clear voice, 'Matteo is here to see you.'

The old man did not stir on the bed.

Elisabetta propped a cushion behind him. 'Assist me here, Baldassare, please, to help my uncle sit up.'

Her uncle moaned and groaned as they did this. Baldassare spoke to him encouragingly and his eyes seemed to clear a little. He fixed the good one upon me and tried to speak and a dribble of spittle coursed down his chin.

'See?' Elisabetta declared brightly. 'He recognizes you, Matteo.'

'Uncle' – she leaned forward – 'Matteo has brought medicines from the best doctors. From the friends of Leonardo da Vinci himself! Rest now and I will prepare an infusion for you.'

'I have to tell you, Elisabetta,' I said, as we left Baldassare to keep watch in her uncle's room, 'that the best we can do is make your uncle comfortable. Using herbs will help him but he has an affliction of the body that may not leave him.'

We walked out into the stable yard. 'I suppose it was to be expected,' she said. 'He is old.'

I sensed that there was something else troubling her. 'Where is Paolo?' I asked.

'In the taverns of Lodi.'

'Ah.' I waited a moment.

'He spends too much time there with bad company. I am frightened for him.'

I began to reply, but we were interrupted by a visitor. A man of arrogant appearance had ridden into the yard and dismounted. He stared at the house and then made to enter the barn. I called on him to ask his business and his name.

'I am Rinaldo Salviati. I heard the owner here was ill,' he said, 'and came to look over the buildings with a view to buy.'

'There is nothing for sale here,' Elisabetta said angrily.

'But there may be soon, I hear.' He came closer to us. 'You must be the girl, the one known as Elisabetta.' He leered at her. 'I am unmarried. I could make an offer for you to be included in the purchase of the property.'

I clenched my fist and leaped at him.

I had never hit anyone before in a serious way. His nose exploded. There was a lot of blood and he howled, but I gained such a degree of satisfaction in seeing this that it frightened me. The seduction of power of one man over another.

He pulled himself onto his horse, jerked the rein and rode off down the road.

'Well, Matteo,' said Elisabetta. 'As far as making a match in this district now, you have quite ruined my chances.'

'If that was your best offer of marriage then they are well ruined.'

'It was my only offer, Matteo. You know that the story of my misfortune at Perela is common knowledge, therefore, for me, any offer of marriage is to be considered.'

Her words struck home. Of course the story of Perela would be known! This man whom I had punched was perhaps the only one prepared to overlook that fact. 'I am sorry—' I began.

Then I saw that she was laughing.

'I'd rather die in a dung heap than be wed to such as that,' she said. 'If I could have hit him myself I would have done so.'

I began to laugh with her. 'I am surprised that you did not,' I said.

'It's good to laugh,' she said. 'It's so long since I have laughed.' She grabbed my arm. 'Let's go berrying,' she said.

'At this time of year?'

'Come with me.'

'Your uncle,' I said; 'should we leave him?'

'Baldassare has been my faithful companion over these last weeks. I trust him absolutely.' She pushed me towards the side gate which led onto the meadowland. 'Now, Matteo. Now.'

She took my hand. 'Let's run,' she said.

We ran and ran and ran, until she could run no more.

'I have a stitch in my side,' she gasped.

I turned round. I wanted to kiss her then. Not because she was Elisabetta, but because she was a woman, and she was beautiful, and flushed, and my blood was hot, and it was summer and warm and—

I seized her by the wrist and made her keep running with me.

We arrived by the river. A large willow overhung the water's edge. We plunged inside, under the green tent of the branches to where it was cool, and there we fell upon the grass, out of breath.

We lay panting. For some reason that I could not fathom, tears started in my eyes. I put my hand across my face and steadied my breath for a few minutes. I rolled over on my side to look at her. She was asleep.

Like a baby she slept. And she looked as her little brother, baby Dario, had once looked when he slept, his arms raised above his head.

In Florence and Milan I have seen many, many paintings of women – ladies with eyes downcast, naked women, comely girls and courtesans: the depiction by the best artists of the day of womanhood, from goddesses to virgins. But there is nothing to rival the actuality of being close to a girl asleep – the breathing, living being of a woman; the shadow of her lashes, her cheeks blushed with the faintest hue of pink, her mouth curved with lips parted a little. I looked at Elisabetta for a long time, then I went and sat by the river edge and trailed my fingers in the water.

* * *

When we returned Baldassare was in the yard. He was helping Paolo from his horse. Paolo lurched and stumbled as he dismounted.

'My brother!' he shouted with a wild wave of his hands.

'Paolo.' I put my arm out to steady him.

He looked into my face. 'My brother, Matteo,' he said.

His eyes were like hot coals in his head. 'I had another brother once. But he died.'

'I know,' I replied softly.

'I killed him.'

'You did not.'

'Yes. I did. My cowardice killed them all.'

'No, no, Paolo,' Elisabetta chided him. 'There was no help for what happened at Perela.'

'Indeed there was.'

'No,' she insisted. 'There was nothing anyone could have done to save us.'

'But I was a coward,' he said. 'I should have at least tried.'

Elisabetta shook her head but she did not say any more. She only looked across to Baldassare. He stepped forward, and sliding his arm under Paolo's shoulder began to coax him towards the house to lie down. By their way of communicating with glances I saw that Baldassare had been here to help on previous occasions and I realized that Paolo was in the habit of returning home the worse for wear.

But Paolo broke free from Baldassare and came to me again before I mounted to depart on the long road back to Pavia. He thrust his face into mine and his eyes burned with a strange fire.

'Soon,' he said, and his words were clear and distinct. 'Soon will be my time for revenge.'

Chapter Fifty-Four

I returned to Pavia by the same route I had come.

There were troop movements on the main roads leading north: marching men with supply wagons rolling behind. When I spotted a column in the distance I pulled my horse off the road and cut away west to avoid them, then rejoined the road at a later point. As I got nearer to Pavia messengers, mainly in French colours, passed me, travelling swiftly on horseback. Just outside the town a group of mercenaries were sitting by the road-side, their horses grazing nearby. They stood up when they saw me, and their rough-looking condottieri captain eyed me and my horse as I approached. He raised his hand and beckoned me to join them.

'Ho! Over here!' he shouted. He held up a wine goblet studded with jewels to show me. 'Rich pickings if you ride with us. Gold! And women for the taking! A life of adventure for a fit young man like yourself with a fine steed. Come and join us!'

I returned his greeting briefly and shook my head. I was glad that I could already see the towers of the city and I urged on my horse.

Although it was supper time the streets of Pavia were crowded as I came in over the Ponte Coperto and along the riverside. I reached the university to find that many students had already given notice to quit their classes and were leaving, and that Felipe was packing up our things.

'It would seem that the Pope has turned on the French,' Felipe told me, 'and has allied himself to the Venetians.'

'The Venetians!' I exclaimed. 'I thought the Pope saw Venice as his enemy?'

'Only when they were gobbling up the Romagna,' said Felipe. 'Venice has now agreed to withdraw from the towns the Pope claims are his.'

'The French will feel betrayed,' I said. 'Do you think even Pope Julius would risk incurring the anger of King Louis?'

'It would seem so.' Felipe shrugged. 'At any rate Pavia is very vulnerable. It's on the main route north and south and, despite all its watchtowers, does not have enough fortifications to defend itself adequately. We are returning to Milan.'

'What will happen to the French in Milan castle?' I asked him.

Felipe spread his hands. 'I do not know.'

The atmosphere in Milan was one of tension.

In this the city reflected the mood of the country. The rulers of the Italian city states feared the papal armies and thought they must submit to the Pope's rule. Only Ferrara spoke up in defiance. Duke Alfonso declared that the d'Este family would not pay tithes to Rome, and he would brook no interference in how he governed. It was said that one of the reasons that Ferrara kept its nerve was because Lucrezia Borgia was seen by her people as their indomitable duchess who would not yield their state to any intruder. She had gone with her women to help build barricades against their walls.

But it was the French who were under most immediate threat. Pope Julius had declared that Italy needed to rid itself of all foreigners. He had referred to non-Italians as barbarians.

Barbarians! The French? I thought of the elegance and refinement of their court. Of the exquisite manners shown by the French captain, Charles d'Enville, to Elisabetta on first meeting her, kissing her hands roughened by farm work. The French would take it hard being called barbarians.

One day I met Charles walking just outside the castle by the Porta Tosa. It was becoming less usual for the French soldiers to be seen in the streets in their free time, and when they were some townspeople had taken to shunning them. But I liked Charles. He had kept his promise and wrote to Elisabetta occasionally and had sent her a little thank-you gift after dining at the farm. I had no hesitation in speaking to him.

'How can the Pope withstand against your army?' I asked him. 'It is the mightiest in Europe.'

'He will use the Swiss,' said Charles. 'They are the best mercenaries as it is their way of life. They survive the extreme winters by offering their men for hire. The Pope recognizes this, for it is from the men of Switzerland that he has formed his personal guard in the Vatican.'

I knew very little about military things but it seemed to me that France was much larger than Switzerland. Therefore there were more soldiers and money to pay them, and I said this to Charles.

'You forget about the kingdom of Naples,' he replied. 'It is full of Spanish troops. If Pope Julius asks them for help then the French and anyone else who resists him will be encircled.'

'Are you not afraid?'

'Certainly, yes. But I feel alive when I am soldiering, Matteo. It is the life for me, if not for you.' He paused. 'Though Paolo would have you be a soldier. You know this?'

I nodded.

'He came to see me at my barracks to speak to me and my commanding officer. He enquired if we would hire a band of men-at-arms.'

'He would not leave Elisabetta alone to take care of their uncle,' I said.

In the Maestro's studio at San Babila the discussion at meal times was mainly politics, but the arguments now were more fierce as to the merit of the actions of Pope Julius.

'He is making Italy safe,' Felipe declared.

'But his fire is dampened down,' said Graziano. 'He is getting old. The warrior is failing.'

'Which may make him more reckless,' observed my master.

The Sforza coat of arms began appearing daubed on the walls in Milan. There were those who supported the cause of Duke Ludovico's son, now in exile since the French had deposed his father. A French soldier was stabbed and three men executed for the crime. The French garrison was wary of being cut off from their supplies. Pope Julius had told the Swiss to plunder the north of Italy in an attempt to break the communication line between France and her troops.

I helped Francesco Melzi unpack our luggage from Pavia. He looked in wonderment at the illustrations of the anatomies. When he saw how many there were he gave a huge mock sigh and said, 'You went away with two boxes and return with fourteen.'

He spoke to Felipe. 'My father has a house at Vaprio on the banks of the Adda. It would be a safer place to store the Maestro's manuscripts. And if things become desperate here, I know he would offer the Maestro hospitality.'

As I listened to this conversation I wondered what would become of me if that happened.

That evening Felipe called me to speak to him. He was seated behind his desk and his words were very direct. 'Matteo. I know that you applied yourself well in your studies at Pavia. And our master says that you appear to find the anatomies interesting. Is this true?'

'Not so much the doing of them,' I replied honestly. 'More the information that can be gleaned from watching them being done and the insight this affords us about the human body.'

'So,' he went on, 'would you be inclined to study those subjects further if it were possible for you to be enrolled at the university there?'

My heart began to beat very fast. 'I do not see how that could be possible.'

Felipe clicked his teeth in annoyance. 'It is not for you, a boy, to say what is or is not possible.'

'Forgive me,' I said. 'I only meant—'

'Do me the goodness to answer my question.'

'If it were possible,' I said quickly, 'I would like very much to study at the University of Pavia.'

'Then, know this. Professor Marcantonio della Torre has agreed, as a favour to our master, to allow you to attend his lectures. When the new term begins he will be your sponsor and arrange for you to matriculate at Pavia.'

I wanted to run to the Maestro and fling myself on my knees to thank him and I told Felipe this.

'Indeed,' he replied, 'I expect that is why the Maestro asked me to be the one to tell you of your good fortune to forestall any such exhibition. You may repay him by working hard. Now, I believe the floor of the studio needs your attention.'

I picked up the broom as Felipe left the room. I had already swept the floor but could think of no better thing to do than to sweep it again.

A few days later Charles d'Enville came to see me. He had orders to ride out. The French had agreed to send forces to help Ferrara. 'Be careful when you are abroad in the street,' he said to me. 'The city is no longer safe.'

'You go to war again,' I said.

'I hope so,' he replied, his eyes lively. 'I loathe hanging about awaiting action. Better to be on the battlefield, doing what I do best.'

'The Pope has many divisions to bring with him,' I reminded him.

Charles laughed. 'The French troops are not downhearted. Let the Pope bring on whom he will, the Spanish from Naples, the Venetians, the Swiss, all his papal armies. We have the most brilliant leader, nephew to the king himself, Gaston de Foix.' He hugged me. 'I hope we will meet again,' he said.

* * *

Now a strange mood settled over Milan. A half-life of expectancy and dread. In some areas trade was already falling off. Even the courtesans who worked the streets no longer sought the soldiers' company. If the French withdrew completely there would be reprisals against those who had been friendly with them. Among the people still doing business were the apothecaries and, recalling my promise to Elisabetta to find an outlet for her produce, I went to the nearest apothecary shop.

I soon made an agreement with the old man who owned it. 'Trade may fall off but I will never go out of business,' he said. 'An army of some kind will return. Be it French or Italian, victorious or defeated, there will be wounded men. And of course armies always bring the pox. I will pay for any herbs sent to me.'

I was able to write to Elisabetta and tell her this.

Then, just before Easter, I received a letter from Elisabetta. She wrote to say that her uncle had died: *'Matteo, I would ask that you visit me at this time.'*

Her need must be urgent. She had never asked me for anything before.

The grooms at the stable were on edge. The French garrison scented betrayal, and the castle was preparing for attack. The commander had withdrawn himself and his officers to the more secure inner area of the Rocchetta. It was with difficulty and only on the basis of personal friendship that I procured the loan of the chestnut mare to ride out to the farm at Kestra.

The weather was bleak, with a chill wind blowing from the mountains. I knew that I must have the horse back by nightfall so I did not pause or look around me as I passed the place on the road where we had come across the Romany camp last summer.

My thoughts were of Elisabetta and the summons in her letter.

Thus I did not see the man who watched and waited among the thicket of trees.

Chapter Fifty-Five

At the farm signs of neglect were everywhere. Sheep had wandered among the crop fields, and precious farm equipment and tools were lying discarded carelessly on the ground. Inside the house Elisabetta and Paolo sat at opposite ends of the kitchen table. It looked as though they had been arguing.

Paolo leaped to his feet as I entered the room. 'At last!' he cried out. 'Someone who will talk some sense into my sister.'

I glanced from one to the other. Unlike many brothers and sisters they rarely fought with each other. They had suffered too much in their lives to allow trivial disagreements to come between them. It would have to be something serious to disturb their harmony.

Paolo led me to a seat. 'I have just told Elisabetta my plans for my uncle's money. We found a stack of it under his bed where he had hidden it, the old miser.'

'He wasn't a miser; he was a careful man,' Elisabetta contradicted her brother. 'If he had been a miser he would not have taken us in and fed and clothed us.'

'He would not give me money when I asked him,' Paolo said stubbornly.

'Because he thought you might squander it foolishly.' Elisabetta spoke calmly. 'And the money he hoarded is needed to pay taxes and dues on the land.'

'There is enough for me to have my own group of

men-at-arms,' Paolo went on excitedly. 'I can become a condottieri captain and we will join the French. They are going to fight the Pope. It was due to the papal expansion that I lost my family and now I have the chance to foil the plans of the Papacy.'

'The Pope is here on earth as the Vicar of Christ,' Elisabetta pointed out. 'You must not go against his wishes.'

'King Louis has declared that the Pope is a spiritual leader and cannot interfere in anything worldly,' said Paolo.

'It would suit King Louis to immobilize the only person who might unite Italians,' I said, quoting an observation made by Felipe.

But Paolo had found a focus for his anger and a way to expiate his grief.

'I have made my plans. I will buy arms and pay my men. I will be known as the Condottiere dell'Orte. We will wear black tunics with one sash of red slashed across the front, diagonally from shoulder to waist. By these red bands across our tunics we will be known and feared. *The Bande Rosse*. See, Matteo! I have already purchased the material and asked Elisabetta to make the sashes for us.'

I glanced to where Elisabetta sat. There were scissors and a bolt of crimson-coloured silk on the table before her. She made a helpless little gesture with her hands.

'Who will come to join you?' I asked Paolo.

He stretched across the table and grasped both my hands in his. 'You'll be the first of course, Matteo! It's what we've always wanted. What we swore to do together on the mountain above Perela. You remember? I still have my father's sword and I will strap it on. My band of men will fight against the papal armies. That is how I will take my revenge. And you will be my second in command, my faithful lieutenant.'

I looked at Elisabetta. She did not reply, only dropped her head to avoid my eyes. I noticed her hair, neatly braided and coiled at the nape of her neck.

'I must go and see to some things in the barn. When you've finished speaking to Elisabetta, come and see what I have prepared already.' Paolo got up and went off outside.

When he left there was silence in the room, then I said, 'You could refuse to help him.'

She raised her eyes to mine. 'How could I do that? He suffered such great humiliation at Perela. It almost killed him. Indeed there are times when I think it would have been better for him to have died at my father's side.'

'Your father ordered him to hide.'

'I think my father truly believed that those men would not violate his wife and children.'

'Those brigands were ruthless and without principle.'

'Yes. You and I know that, Matteo.'

My heart bumped hard at the shock of her words. What did she mean, '*You and I* know that'? I glanced at her but she had moved her gaze and was looking out of the window.

'From here I can see the distant tops of mountains,' she said, 'although I do not expect they are the same hills that we saw from our keep at Perela.'

In her fear of what lay ahead she was recalling her childhood, reaching back to fond memories for reassurance.

'I do not know what will become of me,' she said. 'Already Paolo has secured loans against the property. This is a good farm, but it needs good husbandry.'

'Men do live by hiring themselves out to armies and nobles,' I said cautiously.

'Yes, but it is not the life my parents would have wanted for Paolo. The farm is hard work but it is profitable enough . . .'

Her voice tailed off. She knew that Paolo would never be content to work and live as a farmer.

I tried again. 'Men can do both,' I said. 'In Florence under the advice of Niccolò Machiavelli they have their own citizen army, recruited, armed and paid for by the state. This would seem more sensible. It means that each person has an interest to keep rather than serving self-interest.'

'Ha!' said Elisabetta. 'We will see what happens if this fine citizen's army is put to the test. Against men with murder on their mind, what use are farmers, craft workers and guildsmen?'

'They are trained,' I persisted. 'They have their own uniform.'

'Yes,' Elisabetta agreed. 'Give a man a uniform' – she held up the red sash that she was stitching for her brother – 'put him in striking livery, with a fancy plume in his hat and a halberd in his hand, and he will march anywhere to the sound of a drum. But we know what happens then. The French captain Charles d'Enville spoke the truth when he told us there was little glory in battle. For many men in armies are mere criminals from the streets who are given free rein for rapine, murder, outrage, theft and killing. *That* will be my brother's future, to keep such company.' Tears started from her eyes and she rose up in distress. 'My brother has no life without his purpose and he will die if he does not become a condottieri captain. But if he does, I'll have surely lost him in a much worse way!' And she began to cry in earnest.

Her tears fell onto the red silk. Large watermarks spilled out across the material.

I got to my feet and went to where she stood. 'The fabric,' I said. 'It will spoil.'

I reached to move it, and suddenly her head was on my shoulder and her face was close below mine. I felt her tears then and they were warm as she pressed her face into the hollow of my neck. She seemed to sink against me and I had to hold her more tightly. Her hair uncoiled a little and the weight of the braid slid heavily onto my wrist and arm, and she rested there for some moments until we heard Paolo calling me from the courtyard.

I had to go to inspect his horses, and the arms and armour he had collected. There was a good arquebus, some swords and a few battered shields.

'Come and see! I have made a forge in the stable. The black-smith is already working.'

Paolo showed me his progress. The smith was working there, hammering out a sword blade. Several boys and a few ill-featured men hung around watching him and drinking ale.

'This is my friend.' Paolo hailed them as we approached. 'He will be the second in command.'

'Paolo . . .' I began.

But he went on without seeming to hear me. 'Matteo is a fine horseman and very handy with a dagger.'

'I cannot get away,' I ventured to say. 'Paolo, you know I am committed—'

He rounded on me then. 'Is that what you want to be all your life? A lowly servant?'

My face flushed. Was that how he viewed me? As a servant of the lowest type?

He flung his arm around my shoulder. 'I thought we had a bond,' he said. 'A bond of brotherhood, and more than that, an oath we took together as we left the convent at Melte.'

I shrugged him off and walked away.

At dinner we ate a meal together. The food was wholesome and well prepared. It was not like Paolo to hold a grudge and he was soon chatting. But Elisabetta was silent, watching me, and I had to force my replies and pretend to take his plans seriously.

When I took my leave of them she drew me aside.

'You do not need to fall in with Paolo's intentions.' She paused. 'There is no' – she sought the right phrase – 'obligation on your part. Despite the circumstances that brought our lives together.'

But I knew this was not so.

It was I who had caused the death of their parents, their baby brother and their sister.

My mind was as gloomy as the sky as I set off back to Milan. What was I to do? The Maestro in his generosity had opened up the prospects of my life in a way I had not imagined possible. Yet

Paolo spoke the truth when he said I had given my bond to him. No doubt a cleric would argue that a promise made under duress was not binding. Why then did I feel my soul shrivel at the thought of not keeping my word?

I made my way via the various farm tracks and on towards the junction to the main road into Milan. My thoughts occupied my mind and my mood, and thus I was not looking at my surroundings. As I came onto the road some distance after the main crossroads, my chin was half sunk upon my chest and so I gave the scene ahead no attention. In any case, at this point the thicket of trees would have obscured my vision as I approached the turn where the road was hidden from view.

Therefore I had no inkling of anything amiss, no suspicion of ambush. Before I was aware of them, my attackers were upon me.

Chapter Fifty-Six

The first man jumped up from the side of the road and seized my horse's rein.

I shouted out in shock.

He dragged my horse to a halt. I tried to wrest the rein from his hands but my enemy's grip was locked solid. Reacting in accordance with the inbred instinct of self-preservation, I kicked out at his face. But he'd anticipated some kind of retaliation and he kept his head down as he pulled furiously on the rein. I had no second chance with him, for by this time another ruffian had flung himself upon the horse behind me to drag me to the ground. A roiling scramble ensued. The horse whinnied and turned in a circle, thrashing her hooves to join in the resistance. With his free hand the man on the road grabbed at my leg, while the one behind me tore at my tunic and belt. Between them they began to overpower me.

But the chestnut mare was a spirited beast and did not take kindly to being set upon in such a manner. She snapped viciously at the man clinging to the rein and he screamed as she bit him. Then she bolted.

The rein was ripped from his grasp and he flung himself away from her flailing hooves. The other ruffian had his arms around my waist and managed to remain seated with me on the mare. His rough hands wrenched at my body. Half out of the saddle, I hung onto the horse's mane as she galloped full pelt.

The man behind me tore the dagger from my belt. I tensed for the blow but it did not come. Some part of my mind thought, He has my knife, why does he not use it? The horse was terrified, and, as the road straightened out, she increased her pace. Now the man grappled one arm around my neck. I could not fight him. My whole being was focused on staying astride my horse. Then he shifted his hand to my face, and I felt his fingers seek for my eyes.

I gave a great cry of fear and brought both my hands up to claw at his fingers. The next second I was thrown to the ground with such force that I was stunned for several seconds.

The horse thundered on, heading in the direction of Milan.

I got to my feet. My second attacker had managed to keep astride the chestnut mare. I guessed he must be endeavouring to gain mastery of her because, as I watched, her pace slackened. He would turn her when he could. But I had gained a little time. I must run to whatever shelter I could find. I looked back the way we'd come. In her panic the mare had covered a good distance from the wooded area at the road turn. At least I was far enough away from the first attacker to be safe from him.

Then from the trees a rider emerged.

My eyes darted about. The only shelter was some rocks a few hundred yards distant. I raced towards them. The little cover they might provide would have to do me. When I reached them I looked back at my pursuer. A man, mounted on a big horse, travelling fast. And further off behind him another man, running. What was this? There had been three of them waiting for me in the trees?

In the distance I could see my second attacker had turned the chestnut mare round and was galloping back the way she'd bolted. He was heading to pick up my first attacker, the one I had kicked in the face. Then they would follow the other rider in pursuing me. It would not take them long to cut me off.

I plunged among the rocks. The ground sloped away sharply. I was in a gully of some sort. A small stream flowed through the indent in the ground. Beyond it, further distant, I saw a spire and a tract of land that was vaguely familiar to me. On the way from Pavia to Kestra I had halted somewhere near here to eat at a place beside a river. The stream running below me must feed into this other river, some tributary of the river Po. If I could reach it then I might go where the horses could not follow.

I clambered over the rocks, leaped the stream and had gained the other side before I heard their shouts. I did not look back. I focused my energy on getting to the river. The man on the horse would have to take care of his animal so that it would not break a leg in this terrain. But the other two could abandon the chestnut mare and follow where I went. I was sure they would do this and move to close in on me from either side.

I scrambled along the gully as fast as I could, slipping and sliding as I followed the course of the stream. There was no hope of moving silently to evade them. They had seen me and were now shouting wild threats after me. But I was younger and fitter and I was keeping my distance from them when suddenly the stream ran underground and I was at the foot of a ragged bluff. There was nowhere to go. The watercourse was too narrow for me to follow, a mere burrow running through the earth, and the bluff too smooth to climb. I tilted my head back. But climb it I must. I could hear them gaining on me now, puffing and cursing with their efforts.

I stopped to pick up a flat, sharp- edged stone from the bed of the stream and then I flung myself at the rock face. There was a little indent about a foot above my head. I dug into the earth with my stone and hollowed out a handhold, then I reached up to it and, catching sight of a bush growing out of the scree, I stretched my fingers to grab it and pull myself up a little way. I needed to gain more height. Where I was now, although beyond arm's reach, would still be within their grasp if they stood one upon the other's shoulders. I chipped away another handhold above my head just as they arrived below me.

One of the men launched himself at the rock face. With a second to spare I swung myself up and just out of his reach. He fell back, striking his head on the ground. It was the one I had kicked in the face earlier. He was not faring very well today. His companion did not stop to tend to him but cast about at his feet. He selected a rock small enough to throw a distance but large enough to do me damage if it hit me. He positioned himself, legs spread, took aim at me and drew back his arm.

'No!'

The cry came from the third man on horseback. He waved his arms in the air. 'No!' he shouted again.

He was picking his way carefully along the stream bed. I did not wait to watch his approach but began cutting another indent to haul myself higher, away from them. I grew more confident as I went on. The two ruffians might be trained assassins but I was younger and more agile and had not forgotten the ways to scale a cliff. Only when I reached the top did I pause to look down.

The two ruffians had gone. The third man must have sent them off to find another way to pursue me while he waited, watching me. I studied him as I took a moment to recover my breath. He seemed a strange companion for the other two men. His horse was a thoroughbred, a black courser with rich trappings of purple velvet.

When he saw me looking in his direction he shouted something. But it was too distant to hear. He waved his fist to indicate that he wanted me to come to him.

Did he think I was mad? I stepped back from the cliff edge to consider which way to go now. There was a plain here at the top, sloping away to a densely wooded valley. I could see where the underground stream emerged and joined the river. I began to run. How much time did I have before they came round the long way and he followed on horseback? They did not have dogs so that meant I did not need to hold to the riverbank. And better not to follow that route, I decided when I got to the river. That was the way they would assume I would go. It led to a town, a place where I might lose myself in a crowd, the most obvious, the easiest escape. Therefore I would not go that way. I would choose another. Keeping to the cover of the trees, I found a forest track and struck out across country.

I ran through the trees without stopping. After about an hour I came upon a clearing with a few huts. These I avoided. If they had picked up my trail the people who lived here would say truthfully that they had not seen me. It might make my pursuers think I had taken a different route.

I had barely left that place and was about to return to the track when I heard the sound of horses' hooves, clopping slowly just behind me. By the path there was an oak tree in the full leaf of summer, and I swung myself up into its branches and lay still as the rider came into view.

It was the man who rode the black stallion.

How careless of me not to think of it! They had split up. He must have sent the two ruffians to follow the river while he himself explored this route.

He was not more than a yard or so from me. I could see his fine cloak trimmed with fur, his expensive gloves and his hat, the type that noblemen wore, with a long snood hanging from the brim.

He rode along the path. When he disappeared from view I dropped out of the tree and crept silently back the way I had come. I crossed and re-crossed my tracks. Then I climbed into another tree.

He was scarce four hundred yards away!

I saw what he was doing. Methodically going down each forest track, staring intently at the ground and looking from side to side, searching for broken twigs or any other indication of my presence. A man who hunted, and who had some experience of following a trail.

He knelt down, picked up some leaves and looked around.

I opened my mouth a little so that my breath would not be so laboured. Now he was close enough for me to touch. If he chose to look up I was finished.

A pheasant burst from cover along the path. Immediately he remounted his horse and went off in that direction.

I should have chosen to go towards the town. He was very clever to have tracked me this far, although he could not be certain that it was the fugitive he pursued who was abroad in these woods just now. There could easily be some other traveller around.

I retraced my steps, taking more care this time to move without disturbing the bushes. And then I saw a wall. It was a country villa or a large house and might perhaps have an outbuildings where I could hide. Beyond it lay cultivated land and open fields.

From the forest came the sound of a horse and rider.

I would have to take my chance inside the villa. He would not search the whole place. No one had seen me; no dog had barked. He could not be sure I'd gone this way.

Chapter Fifty-Seven

The wall was crumbling and easy to climb.

I was over it in a few seconds. In my haste not to be seen by my pursuer I jumped down, without looking, onto a garden path on the other side.

Sitting in the corner of the wall was a young girl sewing. She was dressed in the habit of a nun, but all in white. She looked up as I fell out of the sky at her feet.

I put my hand to my belt.

'Do not move or I will kill you!' I declared.

She stared at me.

'I have a knife,' I said.

'I am ready to die for Christ,' she informed me calmly.

That checked me, but I recovered quickly. 'You might not have to die,' I said. 'Only do as I say.'

'Do you intend to violate me?'

'What?'

'That is the part that I fear I would find the most difficult to bear.' She looked at me directly. Her eyes were tawny with flecks of green. 'At least I *think* it would be most difficult to bear. I have no knowledge of such an event so I cannot truly say. Although I've heard tell that it can be an enjoyable experience. But if I were to enjoy it, it would be a sin, would it not? Is it wrong to enjoy a forbidden thing when one didn't wish it upon oneself? Can one not take advantage of an unfortunate situation as it arises? After all, it's not my fault that it happened. You fell out of the sky. What am I supposed to do?'

Scream. That was the thought that came into my head. Any other girl would have screamed at once. But I was not going to suggest this to her.

She ran on without stopping: 'I will have to ask my confessor Father Bartolomeo about it. Yet he's so old I wouldn't want to trouble him with difficult questions. They say his heart is weak. It would be an injustice to cause him anxiety.'

'I—' I began.

She held up her hand. 'There is a new young priest who comes to confess us sometimes, when Father Bartolomeo is unwell. His name is Father Martin. Perhaps I will ask him. Our abbess does not often allow the younger nuns or novices like myself to be confessed by Father Martin. She reserves his visits for the elderly nuns. But Sister Mary of the Holy Redeemer, who is eighty-two years old, told me that after she had been confessed by Father Martin she then had to make a confession to Father Bartolomeo concerning the thoughts she had had about Father Martin. This seems to me wasteful of effort, and far from helping Father Bartolomeo when he's unwell it is in fact creating more work for him. What a conundrum! I'm quite at a loss to puzzle it out.'

The girl pulled her sewing work close to her face. She opened her mouth and, using perfect small white teeth, she snapped the thread. Then she stabbed her needle into a tiny pincushion and stood up.

'You look hungry. Wait here and I will get you some bread.'

'No,' I said and made to bar her way, but she was gone.

I stood open-mouthed. From the other side of the wall I heard a noise, the sound of a fist beating on the outside door! I was going to be captured. I cast around desperately and saw the girl hurrying back to me.

'When I was in the kitchen fetching your bread there was a commotion at the entrance and I risked a peep. Is there someone hunting you?'

I nodded.

'And will he kill you if he finds you?'

I thought of Sandino and his method of punishing those who crossed him. 'From this man,' I said, 'death would be a kindness.'

'If he is so ruthless then he will come through here. This being an enclosed order would not deter him.' She looked around.

I made to climb the wall to leave but she gripped my arm. Her hands were pale as lily petals but her fingers were strong.

'By staying here I am putting you in danger,' I said.

'If you leave now then you have no chance. Get under the bench,' she ordered me. 'I will spread my skirts about you. It is the best we can do.'

'If I am discovered he will kill you. The fact that you are a nun will not protect you.'

'Firstly,' she said briskly, 'I am not a nun . . . yet. In any case, I will say that you threatened me with your knife.'

'I do not have a knife,' I admitted.

'Then take mine.' From under the scapular of her habit she brought a carving knife. She raised her eyebrows at my expression. 'I thought it prudent to bring it with me when I fetched your bread from the kitchen.'

I took the knife from her and crawled quickly under the bench.

Loud voices sounded and I heard the march of feet on the path. Then an older woman cried out. 'By looking for a fugitive within these walls you are dishonouring the ancient laws of sanctuary!'

'Mother Abbess, the man I seek is very dangerous,' a man's voice said patiently.

Who was this person who could demand access to a convent with such authority? Not one of Sandino's usual henchmen. This man's tone was cultured.

'You and your sisters would be murdered in their beds, or worse, if I allowed this man his freedom.'

'Then search where you must.'

'Has this nun been in the garden all afternoon?' the man demanded.

'Yes,' the abbess replied. 'Sister, you heard what this gentleman has said. Has any ill-bred man disturbed your peace today?' she enquired gently.

'No ruffian has come this way, Reverend Mother,' said my little novice demurely. 'I've been sewing here for several hours in peace.'

'You are a good postulant who works so industriously. Go inside now. It is almost time for supper.'

Behind her skirts, under the bench, I tensed to run.

'Ah . . .' My little novice drew in her breath. 'If it pleases you to know, Mother Abbess, at my last confession I received a penance from Father Bartolomeo to abstain from a meal this week. So I will stay here and, using God's good light, continue sewing, if I may.' She bent her head.

'Of course, child.' I heard the abbess follow the man as he strode down the garden path towards the house.

'I think you should remain still for the moment.' The novice nun spoke to me very quietly as we heard the man stamping about inside the house. 'If he seeks you so avidly then he will watch our door. He'll send for help. And, as soon as he can, he will occupy the roads all around, then return tomorrow to search each place more thoroughly. So you must wait until nightfall before you leave.'

'I will go now.' I was beginning to be ashamed at how I had hidden away, using a nun to protect me. I pushed my head up from behind the bench.

'Shh!' she said sharply. 'We don't want to undo our good work. I have a plan. At sunset a man comes to water the gardens. He does this when the sisters are in the chapel saying Compline. He is called Marco and was a servant of my father's at one time and is very fond of me. I will contrive to speak to him and ask him to take you out of here.'

'How will he be able to hide me?'

'He brings us water in barrels in a handcart.'

'An empty barrel is the first place they would search for me.'

'I am not so stupid as to suggest that.' The little novice nun glared at me, her mouth tight, eyes snapping, and I saw what her temper might be like if roused. 'As part payment Marco is permitted to take some of the manure our donkeys produce. You will hide under it and he will take you to his own shack a few miles distant. Can you think of a better way to do this?'

I shook my head and crouched back under the bench.

'I am curious,' she said. 'You told me that the man who searched for you was murderous. And you are right, he is. But by your speech I took him to be a rough brigand, not a great nobleman.'

'Of what great nobleman do you speak?'

'The man who was in the garden searching for you. Don't you know him?'

'I do not. What is his name?'

'His name is Jacopo de' Medici.'

Later that evening I lay down under sacking in Marco's handcart and allowed myself to be covered in manure. The novice watched as he did this. She looked amused as she bent towards me to bid me farewell.

'God must be mindful of you,' she whispered.

'Your God must hardly think much of me if He places me in a cart full of dung,' I hissed back.

'Be grateful you are alive,' she retorted. 'He guided your steps to this nunnery. Think what might have happened if you had climbed the wall of an order whose habit had less commodious skirts. Bear that in mind if you ever have to seek refuge again in a convent.'

I heard her laugh, and she called out softly as we jolted away, 'Avoid the Carmelites at all costs!'

We were stopped almost immediately we left the precinct of the convent. There was no conversation. Marco was too lowly a worker to protest or question why his cart was being searched. I squeezed my eyes shut and made as small a bundle of myself as possible. But the novice had judged correctly. Each barrel was opened and examined but the manure was only prodded lightly. Then we were free to pass.

Marco took his time. Whether it was his way not to be flustered or whether he did it so as not to attract suspicion I do not know. But the hour and more it took us to reach his house gave me time to think. And the more I deliberated on the day's events the more unanswered questions there were for me to puzzle over.

My three pursuers were not common robbers waiting to ambush a lone unwary traveller. They had known who I was. Must have watched me travel that road in the morning and waited for my return. And how had they known that it was my custom to travel that particular road? As soon as I asked myself the question I knew the answer. The Romany. The small gypsy family who had camped there for the wife to give birth. Wherever he had gone he would have told that story – of the French officer who had forced him to move on with a new-born infant, and of the young man who rode with him yet understood the Romany customs and language. And Sandino, who had spies everywhere, would have nosed out my trail. Not enough to trace me through all the roads to the farmhouse at Kestra, but sufficient to get my scent and post a watch on that stretch of road to wait and see if I passed that way again.

They must have heard my approach. Yet they had not stretched a wire across the roadway that I would have blundered into it at speed. And the man who was their leader in this expedition had stopped them throwing rocks at me as I climbed the cliff. The priest in Ferrara had told me when I was a boy of nine, 'He who holds this seal holds the Medici in the palm of his hand.'

But now I saw that it was about more than the seal that I carried around my neck. They had tracked me so far and for so long, and killed the Sinistro Scribe. It could only mean one thing. This was vendetta.

My life spared for this reason. My blood chilled as I thought of it. Now that I knew the identity of the man as a Medici I realized why I must be captured whole. It was necessary to their honour to have personal vengeance upon me. And when they caught me, which torture would they choose? The rack? Red-hot pincers to squeeze the flesh? Or the one favoured by the Medici and the Florentines – the strappado? Tied by the wrists, hoisted high, and then let fall. Time after time until every bone in your body is loosed and jolted from its socket.

But although I had evaded capture this time, where now could I go? If I tried to return to Milan I would be found. Although it was still under the rule of the French, the Medici had power and money to pay spies to watch the city gates.

I saw then that there was only one course of action open to me.

I must send a message to Felipe and the Maestro telling them what I was about to do. Some day I might meet up with them again and be able to explain that I'd had no choice but to give up my place at the university. Circumstances had decided that I should pay the debt I owed for the wrong I'd done in my boyhood. I must accept Paolo dell'Orte as my condottieri captain and become second in command of his men-at-arms.

I would don the crimson sash and ride out with the Bande Rosse.

PART SIX
THE BANDE ROSSE

Ferrara, 1510

Chapter Fifty-Eight

As straight as an arrow flight, Via Emilia, the ancient Roman road, cuts across the great valley of the river Po.

And it was by this route, after an absence of seven years, that I entered the Romagna again. This time I rode boldly, with a body of mounted troops, towards the cities and the city states whose ownership was so bitterly disputed.

Beyond Bologna were the towns that Cesare Borgia had once efficiently and ruthlessly conquered. From his headquarters at Imola all the way to the Adriatic Sea, their names sounded out their bloodied history.

Faenza, where Astorre Manfredi, in order to save his town from being ransacked and his people killed, had agreed to join forces with Cesare and become one of the Borgia captains. Then, once lured from the safety of his own lands to Rome, he had been bound and thrown into the river Tiber.

On then to Forlì, where the bold Caterina Sforza had defied the Borgia to the last. When his men captured her children they shouted to her to come to the walls of her citadel. They held them up for her to see, and threatened to kill them before her eyes. She had lifted her skirts and called out in response, 'Do your worst. I have the means to make more!'

Senigallia, where I was when Cesare Borgia strangled his captains after pretending to forgive them.

It had been autumn that year too, I remembered. Terror and

341

foraging troops meant that country people feared for their safety and never knew which overlord they had to look to for protection. In all these years their land had been fought over and contested when it could have given bounty to the poor. My master was right when he lamented the cost of war. But as we went south fruit hung heavy on the trees, and no doubt in the quieter places people got on with their lives, gathering their stores for the oncoming winter. In the villages such as the one where the dell'Ortes had lived, they hoped to avoid the troubles and continue with their lives.

Similar thoughts must have been in Paolo's mind for he had his horse fall in beside me.

'We are coming near to Perela, Matteo,' he began.

'I know this,' I replied. And instinctively I knew also what his next words would be.

'I would like to make a detour and go there.'

I said nothing. Which I suppose was not kind. It meant that he had to ask me outright then.

'Will you come with me?'

'Once there, what do you intend to do?'

He looked at me in surprise. 'Why, nothing,' he said. Then after a moment he went on, 'Ah, I understand your hesitance. You think I might want to turn out whatever person has been installed in the keep to replace my father?'

I did not reply. I did not know what I thought about his plan to visit his childhood home. Only that I was unhappy at the idea of returning there.

We left our men at an inn not far from the main road. Paolo paid the landlord to provide a good meal and some wine, and gave his soldiers strict instructions not to annoy any of the serving women. We had no qualms at leaving them. For the most part they were a biddable bunch: young men like Stefano and Federico from the neighbourhood of Kestra, with hopes of glory and good fortune, glad to be away from the drudgery of farm work at this, the busiest time of the year.

Paolo and I then rode fast until we met the confluence of rivers that marked the place where we must cross the bridge to Perela. We went more slowly up the road to the keep. I saw him glance towards the gorge. Neither of us said anything. We both knew that there were wild animals in this area, and after so many years there would be no remains left of his mother and baby brother. I confess it was with a sense of relief that I saw that the keep was falling into ruin. The walls had tumbled down and the main door was no longer there, probably broken up for firewood. The locals must have quarried the available stone and no doubt carried off everything else of any value. The way in was open and un-protected. We rode through the archway and into the yard.

My heart stuttered in fear.

A raggedy tent was strung between two stakes and an old gypsy woman sat huddled next to a small bundle of burning twigs.

I turned my horse at once. 'I will not stay here,' I said.

To my surprise Paolo agreed with me. 'There is nothing here for me now.' He glanced around. The windows and doors were gone, as were most of the roof tiles. The house was open to the sky and the wind. 'Why disturb this poor woman if it gives her some shelter for the winter?'

Back on the main road we made good progress on our way to rendezvous with Charles d'Enville and the French light horse.

The French commander had arraigned his detachment of the army outside Bologna. He was hoping to have an easy run to retake it. The Pope was desperately ill and it was known that the Bolognese would welcome French help to restore their former overlord. They favoured the Bentivoglio family as their rulers rather than any legate installed by the Holy Father. But when we arrived the news was not good. The Pope had risen from his sick bed, quit Rome and arrived in Bologna to inspire his troops. Not only would he vigorously resist any attack on Bologna, he was intent on driving his campaign forward. Now that he had secured the help of Venice he saw no reason why Ferrara too could not be overcome and the d'Este family dislodged from their place.

The Pope's presence in Bologna put a different aspect on the situation. The weather had turned bitterly cold and the French troops wanted to be in a good billet for the winter, not waiting out in the field while the papal armies celebrated Christmas snug inside the city. Then messengers reported that the Venetians had sent an army to aid the Pope. The French were preparing to withdraw from their positions even as we arrived.

Paolo was heartbroken. He had been looking forward to some action, and had believed the stories that Bologna would be taken easily. He had promised our men that they would play a part in a major battle and that they would return home for the festival of the Epiphany laden with jewels and other booty.

Even Charles d'Enville was downcast. 'This is what happened with the Venetians at Agnadello,' he said. 'A firm command is needed else we will retire as they did and be forced to fight on the run.'

We attached ourselves to Charles's light horse unit and moved back north with the French troops. The papal armies mustered themselves and their allies and marched in pursuit.

The Pope's aim was clear. He intended to wipe out Ferrara. His wish was for the Papacy to rule supreme, from Rome to the borders of Venice. But little Ferrara defied his intent. When the Pope learned that the French were now aiding Duke Alfonso his famous high temper showed itself and he yelled that he would make Ferrara a wasteland – not a stone left upon a stone. He would see the city in ruins rather than let it fall into the hands of the French.

Charles told us that the Pope had sent envoys to Ferrara to relay his threat. But the duke and the duchess had laughed in their faces. They had taken the papal envoy to view their fortifications and artillery and the duke had patted one of his cannon and said, 'I will use this to send a message back to your Holy Father.'

The envoy had withdrawn in haste, fearing that the duke meant to fire him from his gun.

This story was one among the many told by the soldiers around the campfires at night. There were others, and, as may be expected, the ones concerning the fair Lucrezia were more outrageous. One wondered if there was any truth in them. It was said that she had bewitched Francesco Gonzaga, the Pope's gonfaloniere, so much that he had offered free passage and safety for herself and her children should she choose to leave Ferrara. Charles had it on good authority from his uncle, who was a cousin to the king, that their spies had intercepted letters to that effect. Yet Lucrezia had not deserted her duchy. Rather, she stayed in Ferrara lending encouragement to the people.

During that grievous winter, as the towns around Ferrara were conquered, she had ridden out in the city with her ladies. Dressed in her best finery so that the populace could see her, the Duchess Lucrezia gave alms to the needy and comfits to the children. The townsfolk had been reassured by her calmness and steadfastness.

Through November and December the Pope's divisions crept nearer. They took Sassuolo, then Concordia, towns allied to Ferrara. It seemed as though nothing could stop their advance. By Christmas they were encamped only thirty miles to the west of Ferrara and the Bande Rosse were sent to assist at the town they were besieging, a place called Mirandola.

In the early January of 1511 we encamped with Charles's cavalry and the next day looked down upon the opposing forces.

We spotted the papal tent amidst the others, the flag with the crossed keys fluttering above it, surrounded by the blue and yellow banners of his Swiss Guard.

'It is a ruse,' Charles told us. 'Our spies report that he sleeps in a rough hut so that the soldiers will see he suffers the privations of a winter campaign as they do.'

'He sets a good example,' I said. 'Men will die for such a leader.'

'He is not fit enough to mount his horse,' said Charles. 'Perhaps he will save us some trouble by dying first.'

'May he perish at the point of my sword,' declared Paolo.

'He has piles. Therefore any point will seriously discommode him,' Charles quipped, to much laughter.

But the indomitable old Pope recovered. Still unable to sit upon his horse, he insisted on being carried on a litter to watch the siege of Mirandola.

We waited. We were detailed to contain the flank. But we must only move against them if they launched an offensive.

Spies moved forwards and back among the enemy lines.

One morning in mid January we were told to prepare. Our target was massing in formation.

Then came a rider holding the message aloft and shouting, 'They attack! They attack!'

Chapter Fifty-Nine

Charles ran to Paolo and me. He grasped our hands.

'May your God go with you.'

His face was tense. He was thrilled at the prospect of the fight to come.

I too was excited. But my excitement was one of foreboding. I had an ill feeling in my bowels and a terror of running away. Was I a coward?

The alarums sounded in our camp, the drums rattled to call out our men.

The task of the Bande Rosse was to harry the foot soldiers here on this side of the siege. By attacking their flank we should draw their fire away from the town. If there was a breach, then it would give the defenders time to regroup and restore the damage. Our main target was a group of musketeers armed with heavy arquebus. The musketeers fired off deadly rounds of shot and were protected as they reloaded by ranks of pikemen. These pikes were six feet or more in length, and when massed into a schiltron almost impenetrable. It was hoped that the French light cavalry, led by Charles and supported by the Bande Rosse, unlike the heavily armoured knights on chargers, would be able to get in among them.

But this was our first battle. Charging with outthrust lances at sacks stuffed with straw and sword play with wooden blades had not truly prepared us for the noisy fearful thrill of a real engagement. Stefano and Federico moved their horses closer together, and almost without noticing Paolo and I did the same.

Mirandola lay before us. It looked small and vulnerable. The puffs of smoke from the artillery rose in the clear sky. The noise of the cannon carried to us on the frosty air. As we advanced forward we saw the extent of the massed army besieging the city. Rows of pikes glittered, their armour shone as they mustered and took formation, thousands of foot soldiers supported by light and heavy horse. I could identify Swiss, German and Venetian banners, with many other lords in their own livery.

Charles laughed. 'We are in for a merry day.' He drew his sword and kissed the blade.

'To victory!' he said.

At once Paolo followed suit.

'To victory!'

I felt compelled to draw my own sword and do the same. 'To victory,' I said.

Paolo swung round in his saddle. He shouted louder to his men.

'To victory!'

They drew their swords and a roar came from their throats. 'To victory!'

We proceeded apace, keeping in time with the marching men who would follow us in after we charged.

On a rise above the battlefield we halted.

The ranks of the foot soldiers in the d'Este livery raised their banners and shouted together.

'Ferrara! Ferrara!'

Charles moved his horse a little way in front of the line. In cavalry formation his light horsemen assembled behind their leader.

Paolo took his mark from Charles. He guided his own horse into position in front of our men.

I moved in beside him.

He turned and grinned at me.

My own throat was thick with fear.

Charles raised his sword high above his head. Before he brought it down to signal the charge he cried out.

'For King Louis, and for France!'

Paolo kicked his heels to urge on his own mount. As his horse leaped forward he too raised his sword and cried out.

'Dell'Orte!' he shouted. 'Dell'Orte!'

Our men took up the cry.

'Dell'Orte! Dell'Orte!'

And I found that I was shouting as loud as all the rest.

'Dell'Orte! Dell'Orte!'

Chapter Sixty

I heard the thunderous roar of horses' hooves, before me, behind me, around me.

The jangling harness, the sweating men. Some were crying, tears openly running on their cheeks as we charged. Some whooped in delight, in a madness of anger and excitement. The horses jostled for position, their hooves thudding on the hard ground. We descended upon our prey: ravenous wolves upon penned sheep.

We had the advantage of surprise. Their pikemen were still marching into place, bristling like hedgehogs, holding their long staffs.

Fifty yards . . . forty . . . thirty.

They turned with screams of terror, trying to rally into a defence formation.

We were upon them.

But their commander shouted an order and the rear line had time to obey.

Instead of rushing to aid their comrades, this back line drove their pikes into the earth. We could not stop our horses' charge. The pikes were tilted, pointed at the horses' bellies.

There was a shuddering shock as we collided with their ranks. The horses bellowed and howled as spears and pikes tore at their flanks and ripped into their stomachs. The animals' sounds were such as must be heard in Hell. Our beasts were not accustomed to this. They had been ridden in the cornfields around Ferrara, where we had groomed and combed and wormed them and they had grown to trust us. What foul betrayal we had committed to drive them into this carnage devised by man. Their terror and wild thrashing were hideous to behold.

Men clutched at their necks and faces as they fell under the downward curved slash of the cavalry sword. My arm jarred along its length as my sword connected with bone. A tall pikeman swiftly turned his staff and snagged my rein with the hook set there for that purpose. He pulled my horse's head down towards him.

The man had drawn a long dagger. His breath was in my face. Hot on the frosty air.

My sword was in my hand. But this is not the same as slashing out randomly at an unknown enemy. This is a man. A man who breathes and lives, and I see his eyes gleaming behind the slats of the helmet that covers his eyes.

This man had been in the fresco of the battle of Anghiari.

As I am.

The colours dazzle me. Before me is the standard bearer portrayed on the wall of the Council Chamber in Florence. His face twists with the effort to uphold the colours. All is writhing confusion.

And in that instant I understood why the Maestro painted as he did, with symbols and layers of meaning.

The Swiss soldier gripped me by the throat and raised his dagger.

There was a lurching crunch of horseflesh.

I was wrenched free.

Paolo had crashed his horse into mine, enough to loose the man's hold and give me respite. Now he brought his sword down.

The pikeman screamed, blood burbling in his throat.

Paolo slashed, and slashed at him again. His sword slicing

through the man's jerkin, his arm, his neck, a fountain of blood poured from my attacker.

'To me! Matteo! To me!' Paolo cried. 'Keep close, and I will protect you.'

He pushed his horse on through the heaving crowd. I gathered my reins and followed in his wake.

We had won through.

Then I heard Charles's trumpeter sound the rally and fought my way to where he was.

'Retreat!' He pointed his sword back up the hill.

'The retreat has sounded!' I yelled to Paolo.

'We should pursue!' Paolo shouted back to me.

'We must obey the command.'

'They are fleeing.'

'Come!' I seized his rein.

He tried to pull away. 'We will lose the advantage.'

'We cannot see what occurs elsewhere.'

His hands were slippery with blood. I looked down. As were my own.

'Now!' I screamed at him.

He blinked and jerked his rein free of my grasp. But he did follow me as I left the field.

Some of his men had dismounted to pull badges from tunics and rings from the fingers of the dead.

'Remount! Remount!' he shouted at them.

'Trophies. We are entitled to take trophies.'

One of our rougher fellows bawled at Paolo, 'I will not leave without my booty.'

Paolo kicked out at him. 'Remount!' he shouted. 'I, Paolo dell'Orte, have given you an order!'

The man picked up an abandoned pikestaff.

I rode round to his other side. 'Booty will be shared equally,' I shouted. 'But there will be none for any man who lingers here.'

I urged my horse away to give a lead. Behind me I heard the men who had survived follow us.

At the top of the hill we went to where Charles reined in his horse.

'To victory!' Paolo waved to him. 'To victory!'

But Charles was not smiling. Another French officer rode up to confer with him. Then a messenger came, and another.

'We are to fall back,' he said.

'What! I will not!' Paolo could not contain himself.

'Fall back at once.' The French officer gave his order in a voice that brooked no dispute.

'But we have won the day!' Paolo protested. 'We should press home our advantage.'

I heard Charles's officer speak to him sharply.

'Their artillery have broken through the walls on the far side,' said Charles. 'As we speak the papal armies are advancing on the city.'

We had been beaten.

'But we won!' Paolo insisted. 'Down there we killed their soldiers by the dozen. The few that were left ran away. That engagement was won by us!'

Charles shrugged. 'It may be that the gonfaloniere of the papal armies decided to sacrifice those men in order to achieve the greater victory elsewhere.'

'We cannot slink off like beaten curs!'

'Bring your men and follow me,' Charles retorted in a cold voice.

'What about our dead – our wounded?'

'They lie where they fell,' said Charles. He added abruptly, 'It is the way in war.'

He moved away but Paolo followed after him, protesting.

Charles reined in his horse. 'Listen to me,' he hissed at Paolo. 'This is war. Not a pretend battle, or some courtly joust where a few men are knocked from their horses for the entertainment of the ladies. This is war! As I told you at your dinner table in the farm at Kestra. It is a bloody and bad business.'

Paolo recoiled from his vehemence.

'Now, gather your men – the ones you have left – and follow me.'

Paolo stared after him miserably as Charles spurred his horse to a gallop. I ushered our band into some kind of order and we trailed after him.

It was reported later that before the rest of his troops surged through the great hole torn in the defence wall Pope Julius ordered a ladder to be propped against the breach. Then, supported by his retainers, he climbed through to personally claim victory.

On the nineteenth of January 1511 the siege was over. Mirandola had surrendered.

Chapter Sixty-One

We retired with the French army in good order to Ferrara. During the ride Paolo recovered his composure, and by the time we reached our billet he and Charles were on speaking terms once more.

'What happens to the wounded we have left behind?' I asked Charles.

'Let us hope they are cared for,' he replied. 'Important prisoners can be treated as honoured guests. Especially if they can be used as bargaining counters or will fetch a high ransom.'

I thought of our young men. If any survived their wounds, their lives were worth little to the opposing army and I said as much.

'Don't be too anxious,' said Charles. 'I doubt that they will be slaughtered out of hand.'

But we had heard that, although Mirandola had surrendered to save the populace, the Pope was now questioning the terms and wanted to execute some people as an example. And I knew that it was a simple matter to cut a man's throat as he lay upon the field of battle. It made it easier to plunder and, as they gathered the bodies up for burial, no one would question whether the act had been done before or after the engagement.

We had lost six men, one of whom was Federico. We had to restrain Stefano from going to look for him. They were boyhood friends from Kestra, and had hoped to return home as victorious warriors laden with treasure.

'A good fighting man is worth preserving,' Charles argued. 'And if your men have any sense they will do what any other survivor does and agree to fight for the Pope.'

'So it's common practice to change sides?' Paolo's voice was shocked.

'If you are a mercenary, then yes,' Charles replied. 'It's a business. And you hire yourself to the highest bidder, or the winning side.' He slapped Paolo on the back. 'Come, let us find some food,' he said. 'I could eat a sheep roasted whole.'

Unlike Mirandola, where the citizens had been starving, Ferrara had food aplenty. It was positioned near a broad part of the river Po close to the sea, and Duke Alfonso's firm control of the waterway meant that supply lines were intact. They were in a vulnerable position so they kept vast produce stores, for the city was a garrison overflowing with French troops. For months engineers had been barricading the city, knocking down houses and strengthening the fortifications. On the ramparts the walls were triple thickness with solid earthworks. The fires in Duke Alfonso's forges burned night and day making cannon, artillery and ordnance pieces – it was rumoured that even on his wedding day to the fair Lucrezia he had spent time in his foundries. But now this passion of his was proving invaluable to his people. Only weeks after the fall of Mirandola the duke took his cannon along the river Po to try to prop up fortifications at La Bastia. Paolo and I went with our detachment of men to help.

It was a skirmish that cheered Paolo enormously. The duke was a canny man and did not enter a confrontation in a foolhardy way so the papal troops sent to fight him were repelled. He returned to a hero's welcome in Ferrara. To have even a small victory after a winter of defeats and increasing despair was a signal for rejoicing. The people came into the streets and feted their brave duke who stood up for them against the might of Rome.

At La Bastia Paolo had sustained a wound from a musket ball, which had sunk halfway into his thigh. Attached to the armies were doctors, and barber surgeons to perform amputations, but their reputations were such that Paolo insisted that I dress his wound. Hot oil was the usual treatment for a musket ball embedded in the flesh. But at Pavia the medical students spoke of different types of remedies. I drew on this experience and my grandmother's healing knowledge and removed the metal ball, scrubbed the wound clean with salt and bound it with moss. He survived with no infection, although it left a scar.

Far from allowing the wound to disturb him Paolo took it as a sign of manhood. After two engagements he now looked upon himself as a veteran. Any hopes that Elisabetta had that her brother might be sickened by the experience of real battle were not going to bear fruit. Rather Paolo was enlivened by the men's camaraderie, which strengthened under duress. He polished his sword and sent word to Elisabetta to make more sashes as the ones we wore were now becoming stained and torn.

She had sent him a note of money to draw against some other surety he had taken out. But I noticed that he did not let me read her letter to him. I could only guess at what it contained. By the tone of her letter to me she was unhappy at the way he was dealing with their finances. She would not openly criticize him but I sensed her concern and that she was anxious.

The sureties Paolo has signed away will leave the farm vulnerable to our creditors.

She must have written to her brother in a similar way because when I asked him about this he declared, 'I have told Elisabetta that the French army is unbeatable. France is a much larger country than the paltry states that Pope Julius owns. They can replenish again and again. Who has the Pope called on to help him? The Spanish? Pah!'

We had enrolled more men and had no trouble finding volunteers when they saw that, despite our present inaction, Paolo had money to spend and they would be paid without fighting for the moment. I did not like these new recruits of ours. They were from a different part of the country and spoke a rough dialect and were less compliant than the men we had lost at Mirandola. We seemed less like the band of brothers that had set out so hopefully from Kestra. But Paolo was happy that he had more men to command and that there were indications of a battle to come.

Spies sent word from Bologna to the French. The Pope intended to return to Rome. As soon as he did so they would incite the townspeople to rise up against his representative. We should be ready to send reinforcements to help them.

Meanwhile in Ferrara it was as if they had already won the war.

Even through the season of Lent the Duchess Lucrezia organized lavish feasts and arranged entertainments to keep the soldiers amused. After Easter she declared a special time of rejoicing to celebrate the news that the Pope's hold on the Romagna was slackening. Charles d'Amboise, governor of Milan, had died, and she observed a suitable if short mourning period to mark his passing, but then, to welcome the young French commander Gaston de Foix, Duke of Nemours, she hosted a grand ball to which all army officers were invited.

I was included in this invitation.

And so once again I was in the presence of Lucrezia Borgia. The last time I had seen her was during her wedding celebrations, but my attention had been concentrated elsewhere, under instructions from Sandino to find the priest who had the seal that I still carried about my neck. I had been but a boy then, but found her allure bewitching, as it still was now.

Despite having borne children and endured difficult pregnancies, her figure was as slim as that of any young woman. She was very beautiful and wore clothes of high fashion. Gossip said that a team of dressmakers sewed every night to keep up with the latest style.

'She seeks to bedazzle the French,' I overheard a courtier say that evening at the ball.

'Let us be grateful that they respond to her artifice,' his companion replied. 'We are all the safer as long as they remain so as not to desert a lady in her hour of need.'

I watched her from a little distance away. She could converse fluently in French. Unlike Graziano I had no skill or knowledge in flirting, but I saw how the duchess leaned upon one officer's arm, then bent her head close to another and laughed merrily as they spoke to her. The effect upon these men was instant and visible. Their friends pressed forward to see this woman, daughter of a pope, sister of the infamous Cesare Borgia. They expected a monster. If not an actual demon breathing fire and smoke, then perhaps a dark lady, with black eyes, scarlet mouth and carmine on her cheeks. Instead they were confronted with a lovely woman, fair of face, whose hair shone with many highlights, from bronze to blonde and through to the sheen of white gold.

Her eyes sparkled. She smiled delicately. She quoted poetry, played musical instruments, and she could dance. She loved to dance. When she danced the floor cleared to allow her to dance alone, or with her ladies, or with a favoured gentleman.

This night she had chosen as her partner Gaston de Foix. This man, nephew of King Louis, was to take charge of the French army in Italy. He was tall and good looking, a charismatic and resourceful commander who deployed his own method of warfare of harry and retreat, moving his troops across country at speed. Now Gaston de Foix led Lucrezia Borgia onto the floor. And I, like every other person in the room, was watching them dance together when I saw Charles standing with a young girl whose back was to me.

He beckoned to me, and as I approached said, 'Here is a friend of mine whom you must meet.'

She turned.

And I looked directly into a pair of green eyes flecked with hazel.

Chapter Sixty-Two

'The Lady Eleanora d'Alciato da Travalle.'

Charles made an exaggerated obeisance as he presented the girl I had met previously in the garb of a nun.

She recovered first. Her gaze was steady, and she repeated my name as Charles said it.

'Lieutenant Matteo of the Bande Rosse.'

But Charles had noticed my reaction.

'You have met before?' He glanced from my face to hers.

'I hardly think so,' she said after a second's pause. 'For most of last year I was in a convent. After my father passed away I went into cloister to contemplate my future and to try my vocation.'

'On behalf of men everywhere may I say that we are grateful that you returned to the world,' Charles responded gallantly.

'And you, sir' – she addressed me – 'how have you been occupying your time recently?'

'I am attached to the French light horse,' I managed to reply.

'Matteo is too modest,' said Charles. 'He is lieutenant to the condottieri Captain Paolo dell'Orte, who commands the Bande Rosse. But before that he was a pupil and companion to the famed Leonardo da Vinci, and recently helped him with his anatomies at the medical school at Pavia.'

'Why, Messer Matteo, you will have expertise then in handling a knife, no?' she replied at once.

I am glad to say I responded as quickly. 'Only in so far as a situation might require me to do so.'

Charles sensed the tension and regarded us curiously. But I was hardly aware of his scrutiny. Eleanora's hair was caught back from her forehead in tiny plaits, with curls the colour of burnished copper framing her face. A gauze veil was pinned to the crown of her head. It was of the palest green and sewn round the rim with tiny seed pearls.

Then Charles said, 'Is it permitted to ask you to dance?'

'*Enchantée, monsieur.*' She turned and gave him the full benefit of her charm. '*Connaissez-vous La Poursuite?*'

'*Mais oui, mademoiselle,*' said Charles. '*Je la connais très bien.*'

'*Moi aussi,*' I interposed smoothly. Did she think to toy with me in this way? '*Si vous voulez danser, je serais enchanté de vous accompagner.*'

Her eyes opened wide. Within their depths there shone a darker green.

Charles withdrew at once.

She held out her hand to me.

I bowed.

Let you try me in Latin, I thought as I led her onto the floor, or even rudimentary Greek and you will find me your equal.

La Poursuite.

The dance of approach and retreat.

Her fingers brush mine.

I fix her with my gaze.

She lowers her eyelids.

I keep my face serious but inside I smile.

Graziano. How well you taught me!

She glances up. I look away.

Now she is following me.

'*If you seek to pursue a lady, on occasion you must affect to walk in the opposite direction.*'

Graziano's teasing, laughing voice is in my head.

I look at her with detachment and am rewarded by the flash of puzzlement in her eyes. Or was it anger? Perhaps annoyance?

'Take care that you do not overplay your hand, my friend.'

I started. It was Charles, whispering in my ear as I passed close to him in the dance. He was following my progress with an amused smile.

Afterwards Charles found me standing watching Eleanora attending to the duchess, arranging Lucrezia's gown as she sat down to take her rest on a gilded chair.

'If you want to woo that one,' said Charles, 'you will have to keep your wits alert. She is no fragile lady who indulges in courtly games.'

'You know her?'

'I know *of* her. Donna Eleanora is one of the Duchess Lucrezia's circle of ladies and, as such, is intelligent and more able than many others who attend at court.'

'She is a high-born lady and I am a condottieri lieutenant attached to a cavalry detail with the French army.' I spoke gloomily.

Charles laughed. 'You are independent and a man, and she is a woman. Go to, Matteo. Do not let her escape. Already there are other officers clustering round her.'

I went and stood near a pillar where I could be seen yet remain a little apart from the other guests. And waited.

Almost an hour passed until, with her arm linked to that of an older woman, she effected to walk past me. The older lady had played this game before and knew what was required of her.

'Why, there is one of our young condottieri captains!' she exclaimed. 'It's not right that he stands there alone when he risks his life in battle to defend us. Eleanora, we must speak to him. It would be rude to do otherwise.' She led Eleanora towards me, and after pleasantries were exchanged she stepped to one side, but remained close enough to hear and observe what passed between us.

Now that Eleanora was in front of me I could not speak. I had forgotten the little snippets of conversation that I had practised while waiting for her. Eventually I blurted out, 'Donna Eleanora, do you enjoy your life here in the court of Ferrara?'

She tilted her head as if deciding whether to take my question seriously. 'It has its amusements,' she replied slowly. 'But it is hard to enjoy life when so many are dying.' She paused and then said, 'But you must be more aware of this than I.'

I looked around the room. The bright silks and satins of the ladies' dresses mingled with the colours of the soldiers' uniforms – slashed sleeves and breeches, berettas with feathered plumes. How glorious it seemed.

'I was at Mirandola,' I said.

'The town that was lost?'

'Yes,' I said, 'and six of our men.'

Impulsively she stretched out her hand and her fingers touched my sleeve.

Her chaperone cleared her throat. Eleanora took her hand away.

'To see one's comrades perish must wound the soul.'

I glanced at her face. This was not mere platitude on her part. Her expression was one of intense sympathy. I thought of Federico, now dead, and how his friend Stefano no longer sang songs with the rest of us as we groomed our horses each morning.

'It is very perceptive of you to see that wounds are not only suffered by man's flesh.'

She blushed. And I saw that she took my remark as a compliment and I thought that this Eleanora was different from other women, who accepted praise for the style of their dress or the colour of their hair.

Suddenly there was a disturbance among the courtiers and

foreign envoys. Duke Alfonso appeared and spoke rapidly to the duchess. He wished to confer with his advisers. The Duchess Lucrezia gathered her ladies and they left.

Paolo came hurrying up with the news.

'The Pope is on his way back to Rome. We ride tomorrow to take Bologna!'

Chapter Sixty-Three

'Charles says Bologna is the prize above all others,' Paolo told me as we mustered our men the next day. 'It is the most prosperous city in the Romagna.'

From the wall of the *castello* an orator proclaimed to the people of Ferrara their duke's purpose on attacking Bologna. He put forward the unarguable right of our cause. Then he spoke of the valour of the armies, our unquestionable honour and the nobility of the deeds we would perform. A cannon fired from the battlements giving the signal for us to move out interrupted his speech. His efforts to continue were overwhelmed by the guffawing of the assembled soldiers and the cheering crowds.

The gun fired again, and we were off!

Towards the city gates in splendid formation the Bande Rosse rode together, with the clatter of our horses' hooves and the chinking of our armour and weapons giving a rhythm to our progress.

In contrast with the harshness of the winter campaign it was now mid May and the weather glorious. Paolo hummed a tune in time with the jingle of our harness and the *rat, tat* of the drums. This was an aspect of soldiering that any young man would enjoy. Resplendent in our crimson sashes, one hand on hip, the other gripping the reins of our horses, we passed below the balconies and rooftops where the women waved scarves and dropped handfuls of flower petals to cascade upon our heads.

I stood up in my stirrups and looked back at our file of condottieri. Even Stefano had brightened up this morning. His eyes were shining and he tipped the visor of his helmet to me. I raised my fist in reply and grinned at him. Then we were past the ramparts and on our way.

It was not long before we saw the red-brick towers of Bologna on the horizon and heard the roar and clash of a battle already begun. Our men spurred on their mounts, keen to reach a place of action. But Paolo and I were more experienced now, and were not prepared to allow a repeat of the mêlée at Mirandola. His voice, when he gave his orders, had an edge of authority that I had not heard before. I saw Charles d'Enville glance at him approvingly as our horsemen formed themselves into the required position alongside his.

The Papal Legate had already fled to Ravenna, a fortified coastal town thirty miles to the east. The defending garrison barricaded themselves inside the Castello di Galliera, and from there put up good resistance until Duke Alfonso's mobile cannon arrived and proceeded to blast away at the walls.

A breach soon appeared, widening rapidly as the other guns found their mark.

From inside the fortress we heard a series of explosions.

A message came to Charles. 'They are blowing up their own munitions,' he said. 'We have been asked to go in and persuade them to desist.' He unsheathed his sword and kissed the blade and his eyes shone as he gave the signal for us to charge forward through the gap in the walls.

This was a triumphant attack upon a weak defence and we galloped easily through their lines. We left it to the foot soldiers to mop up the last of the enemy and secure the fortress itself. And at last there was some plunder to satisfy our men.

As the news of the fall of the Galliera spread the citizens arrived in their hordes. Soon people were streaming away from the site laden with dishes and goblets and other furnishings. Some of the mercenaries sent to protect the fortress cast aside their weapons and joined the looters.

'We should find enough arms and clothing to keep us through the coming winter,' Paolo remarked to me. 'We might even capture as much as would give us supplies for the next few years.'

I glanced at him in alarm. We had signed with the French for one year. I still had hopes of attending the university in Pavia and had planned to finish with fighting when our contract was up. That time was approaching.

'But we have conquered Bologna,' I said. 'There is nothing else left to do.'

He did not answer me, and all I could do was follow him in the direction of the armoury.

A mob was in the building. They tore down the statues and silk hangings and ripped up the wooden floors, using axes to splinter the panelling on doors and walls. They cut pieces from tapestries too large to carry away. In one of the corridors I met Stefano, who hoped to be married when he returned to Kestra. He had a bundle of priests' vestments in his arms. 'I will take these home to my Beatrice. She will make herself a fine silk shift for our wedding night.'

Paolo and I chased off a group of marauding Bolognese and gathered up swords and lances and commandeered a cart to take them back to our billet. Paolo picked out pieces of armour for his own use. Over his thick quilted jerkin he buckled on a decorated Swiss breastplate and steel gorget. It suited him well, and he swaggered around with this ornamental collar like any young girl with a new necklace.

As night fell there was a recklessness about the city. The mood was wild and dangerous. I decided to stay indoors and sat down to play a hand of cards with the French officers. It was past midnight and we were engrossed in our game when Charles raised his head as one of his fellow officers Thierry de Villars entered the room. He had been to the university hospital to see a friend who had sustained a musket ball wound in his shoulder.

'How is Armand?' Charles asked.

'He is dying.' The man's voice broke.

Charles went to where a flagon stood on the windowsill and poured Thierry some wine.

'Such a simple wound.' Thierry punched his fist into his palm. 'One would think that they could heal it.'

'There are few doctors there,' said another man who was playing cards with us. 'The hospitaller monks do their best, but there are one hundred wounded for every friar.'

'Matteo' – Charles addressed me – 'I saw how you treated Paolo in Ferrara when he took a musket ball in his leg. You have some skill in medicine. Would you look at this man's wound?'

Chapter Sixty-Four

Thierry's friend Armand was gravely ill with a high fever. This was the result of infection, which was the usual outcome of a wound made by a musket ball. The torn flesh had been treated with hot oil and was now suppurating pus. I deduced that this poison was coursing through his body and perhaps travelling to his brain. He babbled, every now and then starting up and staring around wildly, as if he saw demons that we did not. His friend Thierry, who had brought me to him, stood by the bed with such a look of misery on his face that I could hardly bear to confirm to him what he already knew. I was too late.

But I made a salve of honey and alum and cleaned out the wound. I told them to stop using the oil, and gave different instructions for treating him.

To begin with Thierry demurred. 'Your words go against the directions that soldiers are given to deal with battle wounds like this.'

'This is the method that I advise,' I said and left him to it. To be honest I was a little put out at his manner, partly because I had been winning at the card game and held a good hand and was sorry to have been interrupted.

I went back the next morning and Armand was no better, but then he was no worse. The next morning he was the same. But in the afternoon Thierry sought me out and said that although the wound still had foul matter within it, his friend was now awake and able to converse with reason.

I returned to examine Armand's wound. Around the edges the skin was beginning to heal. I was very pleased with myself. While I was there a hospitaller monk came and asked if I would treat two other soldiers similarly afflicted. I had to admit that I found an immense gratification in my success, and a curiosity to see if my method would work again. And I thought that rather than losing money at cards and pining for the sight of Eleanora d'Alciato, the hospital was as good a place as any for me to spend my time while we waited for our next posting with the French cavalry.

A week or so later, when I went to the hospital, I was told that there was an important person there who wished to see me. This man was waiting in the office of the infirmarian monk, and introduced himself as Dr Claudio Ridolfi of the Medical School of Bologna University. He wanted details of my treatment of musket wounds.

'I did not seek to do this work,' I protested immediately. From my time at Pavia I knew that there were strict rules regarding doctoring. Barber surgeons were not allowed to give medicine, and even dispensing apothecaries must be inspected by the grocers' guilds. The clergy were forbidden to perform surgery, and anyone practising medicine who was not properly qualified could be cast into prison or worse.

'I took no payment,' I said, 'and only treated those persons as requested by the monks.'

'I have no wish to criticize,' said Dr Ridolfi, 'only to learn what it is you do, and how it is that you do it so well. For one so young you appear to have specific knowledge.'

'I was brought up in the countryside,' I said, now less anxious. 'From an early age I learned folk remedies. And I have some knowledge of the internal workings of the human body, having watched anatomies being performed by the Professor of Anatomy at the University of Pavia.'

'Would this have been Marcantonio della Torre?'

'That is his name,' I said.

'Then you have been greatly privileged. His work is renowned throughout Europe.'

I nodded. 'He is a very able and learned man.'

'*Was*.' Dr Ridolfi spoke slowly. 'If you were an acquaintance of his, then I am grieved to be the one to tell you. Messer della Torre is dead.'

'Dead!' I was stunned. He was not so old, only in his late twenties.

'I am sorry,' said the doctor.

'How did he die?'

'Of the Plague. He went to tend victims in Verona. He had family in that region and he succumbed himself to the disease.'

So like him, a true doctor, to go to help others at the expense of his own safety. This blow would leave my master bereft, I thought. Charles d'Amboise, the governor of Milan, who had welcomed the Maestro into the city, had died recently. And now Professor della Torre. Two of his friends, with whom he had shared his thoughts, gone.

Dr Ridolfi gave me a moment to recover myself and then said, 'I am interested to know why you did not first treat artillery wounds by the conventional method.'

'I do not know any conventional method.'

'I thought you said you studied at Pavia.'

'It was for a few months only, while my master worked there at his own anatomies and research,' I replied.

'Your master?'

'At that time I was with Leonardo da Vinci.'

'The great Leonardo! You have kept fine company in your youth, Matteo.'

'Yes,' I said. 'Now that I am older I appreciate this more. The Maestro was willing to support me to continue to study at Pavia, but—' I broke off.

Sandino pursuing his vendetta against me, and my duty to join Paolo's condottieri, had made me unable to take up the Maestro's offer last year. But always, somewhere I had thought these present trials of mine to be transitory. With the ignorance of youth I had hoped that some day I might return to Milan, and it would be arranged for me to go to Pavia to the university. But if Marcantonio della Torre was dead, cruelly taken by the Plague, the world had lost a good doctor, and I had lost my opportunity for advancement.

I sat down at the desk and took pen and ink. 'I will write out my recipe,' I told the doctor, 'so that you may have it and use it as you will.'

I had scarcely finished when Paolo and some of our men arrived at the hospital looking for me.

'Come!' Paolo shouted out. 'You must see this, Matteo. They are bringing down the Pope's statue.'

We went to the piazza, where a huge crowd had gathered, pushed our way through and gained entrance to a rooftop. They had tied ropes around Michelangelo's colossal bronze statue of Pope Julius. This statue was three times the size of a man and teams of men were dragging on the ropes as a fat Bolognese councillor struck a drum and shouted, 'Heave!' to co-ordinate their efforts.

'Heave! Heave!' The onlookers took up the chant.

Paolo clutched my arm as the statue began to rock backwards and forwards.

'Heave! Heave!' The crowd screamed encouragement.

Several of the city magistrates rushed out and ordered the soldiers to clear the square. These men tried to push the people into the side streets but, in peril of their lives, they would not move. There were a dozen urchins in every tree and people climbed onto the roofs of the surrounding buildings, vying with each other to have the best view.

'Heave! Heave!' The roar reverberated in the piazza.

Pope Julius's statue swayed terrifyingly, then the colossus smashed down upon the ground. Splinters of stone hurtled into the air as the cobbles burst asunder.

Citizens hoisted their children up to look at it, saying, 'See! Bologna brings the Pope to earth. We set an example to the rest of Europe.'

There was the sound of a trumpet and soldiers gathered in the square to chase away the people who were swarming all over the statue. The magistrates had to set a guard upon it. Then blacksmiths were called and they took off the head. This was dragged through the streets of the city, where people flung stones and lumps of dung at it, calling out, 'Here, Julius, take the tithes you demanded from us!'

The city of Bologna decided to offer the statue to Duke Alfonso. He sent word to have it delivered to him at once. He declared that he would melt it down and make it into a gun and name this gun after the Pope. This new cannon would be fiery and loud, and be known as Il Julio.

Chapter Sixty-Five

A special cart was constructed to bear the Pope's statue to Ferrara. Supported with wheels banded in steel and pulled by twelve bullocks, it rolled along the Via Montegrappa and out the San Felice gate towards Ferrara.

It seemed as if the entire population of Bologna had turned out to see the procession leave: guildsmen and washerwomen, market traders and merchants, artisans, courtesans, the middle gentry, clergy, professional craftsmen, nobles and beggars. The Bande Rosse had drawn forward escort detail and thus we rode slowly at the front of the cavalcade. Teams of road menders worked one day ahead of us to ensure the paving underfoot was secure enough to bear the weight of the cart. They were accompanied by a detachment of infantry soldiers to clear the road of other traffic.

Peasants stopped work to watch us ride past, and the inhabitants of villages along the way came out to greet the soldiers. They threw bunches of yellow buttercups, white daisies and other meadow flowers. These showered upon us and we laughed as we brushed them off our heads and shoulders. It had been a hard winter for these people but now, with the Bentivoglio family reinstated as their overlords, they hoped to have a summer of peace in this region. Paolo beamed with pleasure and the younger boys in our group whistled and yipped at the girls in the fields. It was our victory march, wearing the spoils of conquest, with compliments and applause from grateful admirers.

'We are part of history,' Paolo said proudly to me as we neared Ferrara and saw the throngs of citizens on the ramparts awaiting us.

An open-air feast was held that night. They lit a huge bonfire in front of the Palazzo dei Diamanti and the townspeople danced around the bronze body of the Pope.

There was a great mass of people in the inner city of Ferrara when Charles and I came from our billet in the early part of the evening. We struggled through the streets to the Piazza del Castello, where the celebrations were more organized. An area had been set aside for dancing, and musicians were playing folk tunes for the benefit of the townsfolk.

The duke and duchess had chosen to grace the event with their presence and sat on a raised dais watching proceedings. The duke soon tired of the revelry and slipped away, no doubt to build up the fires of his forges in readiness to roast the Pope, even if it was only his effigy. Donna Lucrezia had been crowned Queen of the May. She had flowers in her hair and was wearing a dress of filmy white lawn, and was attended by her ladies similarly attired.

Charles nudged me. But I had already seen the one whose form and figure I recognized.

Eleanora d'Alciato.

'I will take my leave of you.' Charles spoke in my ear. 'I have a different quarry to pursue tonight. There is a good gaming table in the inn over there. Happy hunting.'

Despite my coaching by Graziano and Felipe, I was unsure of the etiquette. I guessed that during Carnival, or on an occasion like this, the constraints were relaxed. Where was Charles when I needed his advice? And Paolo? He would be polishing his armour in readiness for the next battle. Could I approach a lady unannounced?

With a mask, anything is possible.

I paid a few coins and purchased a small eye mask from a street seller. I tied it on and went boldly forward.

'May I claim a dance with a beautiful lady?' I offered Eleanora my hand.

She drew back a little and pulled her cloak about her.

One of the courtiers in attendance placed his hand on his sword hilt. Having some experience of weaponry, I saw that it was a light blade with an ornate handle. The type carried for display rather than practical use. He was some poet or other, of which there were always a number hovering around the Duchess Lucrezia.

'I had hoped that the lady would recognize me,' I said softly. 'We have danced together before. But then of course it was the more sophisticated French dance *La Poursuite* and we were in a different ballroom.'

Eleanora gave a little gasp.

'The steps of this round are less complicated,' I continued, 'but very diverting none the less.' I paused. 'With my guidance I am sure that you would learn them easily.'

Her eyes flashed.

Aha! A hit!

Eleanora looked to the Donna Lucrezia. 'If I may?'

Lucrezia Borgia surveyed us with an amused look. 'You know this man?' she asked Eleanora.

'I do. We have met properly within your own palace, my lady.'

Donna Lucrezia nodded her permission. 'You may dance with Donna Eleanora,' she told me, 'but you must remain where I have sight of you, and I am restricting you to one dance only.'

I made an acceptance of her terms and extended my hand to Eleanora.

I led her down to the piazza.

The dance was a peasant round, traditionally performed in the vineyards during the time of grape crushing. We had to form ourselves in a circle and at once I felt a jar of jealousy as I saw that her companion on the other side was a man. I took her arm and escorted her to a different place in the ring so that she was between myself and another woman.

Did she smile to herself at my action? I did not have time to study her face for the dance began and was immediately lively.

In the first round we stamped our feet many times and she complained that her shoes were not sturdy enough for the rough cobblestones.

'Look!' she said. She raised her skirts a little and showed me dainty feet with rose-coloured satin shoes and rounded ankles encased in white stockings.

I offered her my boots.

She laughed. I saw her evenly spaced white teeth with her tongue between. Within my own hand hers was small and doeskin-soft. Her eyes had the flames of the bonfires in them, and we spun round in the circle and her hair came loose around her face in little curls, and her mouth was wet with moisture and I so, so, much wanted to kiss her.

Chapter Sixty-Six

When the dance was over one of the Duchess Lucrezia's attendants appeared to escort Eleanora back to her place on the dais. This man was not the fey poet but a more solidly built example of Ferrarese manhood and there was no time for any privacy.

He walked behind us as I returned her to the group of ladies.

We were almost there when she said in a low voice, 'I still have to discover, Messer Matteo, why it is you chose such an unorthodox way to visit my aunt's convent last year.'

Then the Duchess Lucrezia beckoned and Eleanora dipped her head and bade me farewell.

Over the next days the Ferrarese foundrymen worked to make the new cannon. Clad only in loincloths, their sweating bodies laboured under their duke's directions to transform Michelangelo's masterpiece into an implement of war. I went to watch part of the process and had a sudden image in my mind of the merry face of Zoroastro as he bent over the fire in his forge.

The molten bronze glowed red as the river of hot metal ran into the moulds set in the ground. With this intense heat and the power and majesty of the elements, I saw how easily men could believe in magical alchemy. We create form using other substances, transmuting the elements, bending them to our will. What being, other than a god, can do this?

When the new cannon was complete the duke sent a defiant envoy to Rome to inform the Pope that his holy person was now in another guise defending Ferrara. By poster and proclamation it was announced that Il Julio was ready. Then the huge gun was wheeled out for the populace to see, and we had a special day of games and jousting on the stretch of sward below the Castel Tedaldo.

Attended by their squires, the French knights paraded first. In surcoats of satin and gold, and seated on their warhorses, richly caparisoned in brocade and heavy velvet, they moved ponderously about the field. After these panoplied knights the stable grooms brought out the lighter animals to display their skills in horsemanship. They rode round and showed how their horses could be made to go at a gallop, and canter, then trot elegantly, or turn in a circle and shake their head. Everyone who watched marvelled at these things but I smiled quietly. These were easy tricks that any gypsy child could train a horse to do.

The men of the various condottieri made jousts at each other and broke wooden lances. And then it was the turn of the Bande Rosse. In the armoury in Bologna Paolo had found a Swiss army rule book and had been training our men in new formations. We cantered forward and, with a great shout, flung our hats in the air. Then we turned our horses away and galloped hard across the sward. Wheeling round suddenly, we raced back and leaned down from our saddles to scoop up our hats. I fancied myself as the best horseman there.

Was she watching me from the duke's platform?

To end the tournament the event known as the Ladies Prize took place. A long stake was driven into the earth in the centre of the field. It was studded with nails whose heads protruded enough for ribbons to be tied to each one. The men had to come riding past in a group and attempt to snatch these favours from the pole. The ladies taking part took some ribbons from their hair or dress and held these up so that all could see who they were and what colours they owned. A page made the appropriate declaration and the crowd repeated the name and colours as the lady tied her ribbons to the pole.

It required courage on the part of a lady to do this. Some refused, being too shy, or fearing that no man would choose to ride for their colours. Or yet again, a lady might shrink from pinning up her colours like this in public in case she suffered abuse from the wags in the crowd who were not averse to naming the current scandal associated with her name. A husband might find out his wife's infidelity in this way, having had no prior inkling of her impropriety.

I was watching for one person. My pulse quickened as I saw her among the rest of the ladies.

The Duchess Lucrezia had placed her own Borgia colours of mulberry and yellow at the highest point on the pole. As soon as the gallants lined up on their horses at the far end of the course saw her do this they began to jostle for prime position. Each wanted to be the one to seize Lucrezia's ribbons. But my eyes were on the lilac and pale-green bow that had been fastened a little lower down. Eleanora's dress was green brocade, slashed at the sleeve and neck to show lilac silk edged with white lace. When Eleanora had tied her ribbons on she had not held them up, nor waited for her name to be called. Rather she had fixed them on quickly and hurried away. And she had not glanced in my direction.

The field was crowded. Men dashed to their horses to win the favours of the Duchess of Ferrara. Most had changed into clean clothes for this last event of the day. I was dressed in a white linen shirt, ruffed at collar and wrist, but loosely laced across my chest to lie open for freedom of movement. I wore black suedeskin trousers with long boots which covered my knees. My gauntlets were of soft leather and I had a steel sleeve on my bridle arm, which meant that I had more control of my horse, for we had to ride bareback – no saddle or stirrups to help us. Gripping the horse with my knees, I felt the powerful flanks of the stallion between my legs.

The signal!

My horse leaped forward and I was in the rush.

Twenty men and only five favours to win.

I was close to the lead but I must not win the race: if I got there first, then I would be obliged to take the Duchess Lucrezia's ribbons. The others crammed in around me as I tried to hold them off, yet still allow the Ferrarese nobleman now out in front to reach the pole before me.

The animals' hooves threw up great clods of earth and the crowd roared as we thundered past.

We were at the pole! And the first man took the duchess's ribbons. Now the way was clear for me to take my prize.

I put my hand on the lilac ribbons.

But another man, older and heavier than I, aimed a blow with his fist at my face.

The onlookers screamed vile language at him.

I veered away.

He grabbed for the ribbons. They were tightly tied and he could not loosen them.

The crowd laughed at him and I came back into the fray. My horse breasted his and the animals struggled against each other. His mount bit out at mine.

But I had travelled with my stallion and groomed him every day and taken stones from his shoes and crept in by his side on the cold winter nights in the field outside Mirandola, and he did not fail me now.

So my horse reared against my opponent, hooves flailing. And the other horse neighed in fear and was driven out.

I stretched up.

I had the ribbons! I had the ribbons!

Now she must come to claim them from me.

The five victorious men lined up to return the favours. A fanfare called the ladies in turn to collect their ribbons.

The Duchess Lucrezia permitted her victor to kiss her fingertips.

To the hoots of the watchers the next lady slid her foot from her shoe and offered the tip of her toe.

The next two ladies proffered their hands.

The last trumpet note.

The page announced, 'The Lady Eleanora d'Alciato!'

She came down the steps and I nudged my horse. My stallion bent his foreleg and lowered his head down before her. The crowd laughed in delight and applauded.

I could tell she was pleased. Though she affected an air of calm superiority, this Eleanora d'Alciato, she could not hide her high colour and the dimples that went in and out when she smiled.

'I claim my kiss.'

My throat was dry. I could hardly croak the words.

She met my gaze. There was a current between us.

Her eyes fixed on mine. They darkened as she looked at me. Though the day was bright, the pupils of her eyes widened.

Then she turned her face.

And I put my lips to her cheek.

That night there was another great festivity in the square. I was there early to secure a position where I thought the duchess might appear with her ladies. But as the night wore on and she did not come I enquired from one of the royal courtiers if anything was amiss. The day's events had exhausted their good duchess, he told me. She had taken ill and had gone away to recover.

Chapter Sixty-Seven

Within a few days we learned that the Duchess Lucrezia had miscarried a child. She and her attendants would remain for an extended stay at the Convent of San Bernardino.

I was now bereft of Eleanora's presence and began to torment myself with thoughts that I had imagined she was attracted to me. Perhaps during this stay at San Bernardino she would think that the life of a nun suited her very well. She might decide to remain there and I would never see her again. I missed Eleanora, and my mood was mirrored by the court of Ferrara, who sorely missed their duchess.

Without Lucrezia there to woo the army commanders the French became restless. Charles told us that they would wait out another winter in Italy, but unless they won a decisive victory the French troops would be withdrawn. King Louis was becoming less interested in Italian conquests and more concerned for the safety of the heartland of France.

But even without his duchess by his side Duke Alfonso d'Este would not bend his neck to Julius. The capture of Bologna and his new cannon was a source of immense pride to him and annoyance to the Papacy.

'You would think the Holy Father would be flattered,' Charles joked with us, 'to have such a piece of powerful machinery named for him.'

But even though the Pope was once again very ill he could still pour out more fire than any cannon. He was beside himself that Ferrara would not yield to him. When he heard that the Bentivoglios were reinstated in Bologna he vowed vengeance on Ferrara for aiding his enemies. Duke Alfonso's envoys reported that Julius had dragged himself from his bed and raged through the corridors of the Vatican saying that he would have Ferrara if it was the last thing he did on the earth – that he would die like a dog before he gave it up.

Which served only to strengthen the resistance of the Ferrarese and their resolve to fight on. And Paolo wished to be part of that. But for myself, I did not know what course to take in my life.

When we had returned from Bologna letters awaited me from Milan. One from the Maestro and one from Felipe.

At last [the Maestro wrote], *we have news of the whereabouts of an errant boy! My pens are in disorder and my silverpoint pencil has been missing for days. Why is this? Because the person responsible for ensuring that these items are to hand has taken it into his head to run off without notice. How can I work efficiently?*

Yesterday I was walking by the canals on the outskirts of the city and considering how sluggishly the water moved. I thought upon the body of the old man we anatomized and how at that time we likened the constriction of the veins to silting. I turned to call your attention to this fact, and you were not there, Matteo.

I felt tears start in my eyes and I reached my hand out to touch the paper. It moved me that my absence was noted and I had not been forgotten.

Take care [his letter finished], *for to train another assistant would be a troublesome expense for me.*

A joke? I took it as such and smiled. And then thought later that there was sadness and regret in his words.

Felipe's letter was more brisk and practical.

You will have no doubt heard that the French troops in Milan are somewhat beleaguered at this time. Graziano sends his best regards and [I laughed at his next words] *asks that you recommend him warmly to the fair Lucrezia. He has been unwell of late else he would write himself. He hopes that you are upholding his teaching regarding your manners at her court.*

Then he added:

The master wishes you to know that, despite these difficulties, you would be most welcome, Matteo, should you ever return.

But I could not return at present. Paolo wanted to agree another contract with the French. Our men had to make their mark upon the document. The ones who had survived last winter and the battle at Mirandola were mostly prepared to do this. They were in better spirits after our success in Bologna and the feasting in Ferrara. Doctoring seemed more to my liking now than soldiering, but what choice did I have? Eleanora d'Alciato was a good enough reason to stay in Ferrara. The Maestro himself was finding it difficult to maintain his household. My place at the University of Pavia had been dependent on the good offices of Marcantonio della Torre. Now he was dead. Therefore I must also sign my name to the contract of my condottieri captain.

Our agreement with the French specified a certain number of men and horses so these needed to be brought up to the required amount. One or two of our men had deserted in Bologna. Another had fallen in love with a girl and had asked to be released from his bond. We needed to replace both men and horses. I sought out and bought the best horseflesh while Paolo recruited more men and armed and trained them.

These new men mainly had no provenance. They were the type who appear and attach themselves to whichever side is winning. Paolo had to work hard to contain their temperament, but he had become a good condottieri captain. He constantly sought new methods of soldiering from the French and put them into practice. He was beginning to prove himself a leader, and by dint of hard training he brought our new recruits to heel.

Paolo spent a great deal of money in kitting us out anew. He bought pistols and ammunition, gunpowder and shot. In order that we would be better protected in future battles he traded our thick leather helmets for ones made of steel, with side plates to guard the cheeks and a flap at the back to protect the vulnerable part of the neck. He purchased coats of buff leather and separate breast- and backplates to wear over these. To protect our hands we had leather gloves of the gauntlet type and also breeches with long riding boots.

As we prepared for a winter campaign France set up a rebel synod of bishops to defy the Pope. King Louis wanted them to clearly state that the Pope had no temporal authority in Italy. He demanded that Julius withdraw his forces from the Italian states that the French laid claim to.

To which, it was said, the Pope roared a reply: 'I am a Pope! And the Pope is not a chaplain to the King of France!'

But while King Louis conspired against him in one way, Pope Julius moved swiftly across the chessboard of Europe. He formed a new alliance called the Holy League, which included Switzerland, England and Spain. Now France was surrounded by hostile states. And Spain was sending soldiers from their kingdom in Naples to help the papal armies in Italy.

In Ferrara we prepared for the inevitable fight to come.

Then, in a letter dated just before Christmas 1511, Felipe

wrote to me. He said that it was becoming too dangerous to remain in Milan.

The Swiss have set fires outside the city. From the roof of the Duomo we can see farmhouses and vineyards burning. The Maestro intends to go to Vaprio on the river Adda. Francesco Melzi's father has offered him shelter at his villa there. We intend to move soon, as there is a fear that Milan may be surrounded.

Kestra was not so far outside the city.

Elisabetta was in danger.

Chapter Sixty-Eight

Paolo needed to remain in Ferrara to train our new recruits so I took with me Stefano and two others and set out for Kestra.

My aim in choosing Stefano was to do him a service. I wanted to give him the opportunity to withdraw from the Bande Rosse. He had been devastated at the loss of his friend Federico, and I thought that when he met up with his family again and saw his betrothed he would appreciate that life on a farm was preferable and safer than returning to Ferrara. But a strange thing happened as we made our way towards Kestra. Stefano, who had lamented so much after Mirandola and swore that if he ever saw his father's farm again he would leave it no more, had undergone a change of heart.

The taking of Bologna reversed his opinion. An easy victory and some plunder had made a different man of him. As we rode west he boasted of his exploits, and these became more grandiose and daring with every mile we covered. Gone now were his moans about the defeat at Mirandola, the hardship of the winter, the outbreak of dysentery. His tales were of the glory of conquering Bologna, of how we had sent the Papal Legate running to Ravenna and driven out the Pope's men. When he arrived at his farmstead, laden with bundles strapped to each side of his horse's rump and little packages for his girl tied to his saddle, he was given a hero's welcome. His family looked upon him with pride, and when they saw his booty they insisted that I collect him and his younger brother Silvio on my way back to Ferrara so that they could go off and bring them back more. I left him there, telling wild tales of his struggles with imaginary armies, and went on to Kestra.

At first I thought the farm at Kestra was deserted. There was no sign of life when my two companions and I dismounted. I gave the task of unpacking and stabling our horses to them and entered the house. Elisabetta was in the kitchen, stooped over, struggling to light a fire under the boiler.

I came up behind her and took the flint from her hands. 'Your kindling is too damp,' I said. 'A country girl like yourself should know that the flame will never catch unless the firewood is bone-dry.'

She gave a little scream of fright. Then, when she saw it was I, she burst into tears.

'What a welcome!' I exclaimed. 'And I a poor soldier returned from the wars.'

She wiped her tears away and we hugged each other.

'Oh Matteo,' she said. 'Matteo, Matteo, Matteo.'

'I can tell that you are not unhappy to see me,' I teased her. 'I hope you will be even more happy when I tell you that your brother Paolo is well and sends his love and many gifts to you.'

By this time my two soldiers were at the back of the house piling up the goods that I had brought from Ferrara. I told them to take some of the food we had brought with us and find a place in the barn to eat and rest, then I brought the parcels inside. I opened the one which was my own present to Elisabetta. It was a fine piece of Ferrarese cloth for which I had paid a large sum of money.

'What do you think of this?' I asked, holding it up for her to inspect.

She fingered the cloth in appreciation. 'It is heavy quality,' she said. 'I should be able to get a good price for it.'

'You would sell it!' I said. 'This brocade was bought specially to be made into a dress for you to wear at Christmas time.'

She folded the cloth and laid it upon the table. 'I can see that my brother has not kept you informed as to our true state of affairs,' she said. 'Let us eat first, then we will talk.'

She cut a piece from the salted ham I had brought and boiled it with some sweet white onions. As we ate she made me tell her of our adventures and I was pleased to recount the true story of how her brother saved my life at Mirandola. I have been told that I am a good storyteller and it may be that I embellished Paolo's actions a little as I described them to his sister that day.

'He charged on his horse to help me,' I said. 'It was like the times we played at Perela. Paolo was a noble knight for the crusade. He was a lion. He was a fierce Tartar warrior. He was a gladiator in the arena of the Coliseum. He was all these things. He saved my life.' And this was true. The core of the story was not false. Without Paolo, that day I would have died.

Afterwards Elisabetta told me how things were with her. There was a small income from her sale of herbs to the apothecary in Milan, but not nearly enough to run the farm. She led me through the house. The rooms were shut up. Most of the furniture was gone. We had eaten from plain crockery because she had pawned the plate months ago. She told me that over the year Paolo had sold off the fields one by one and then finally had mortgaged the house. The deeds were held by Rinaldo Salviati.

'The man who came here that day and insulted you?' I asked her.

'Yes,' she replied. 'The man whose nose you broke. And Paolo has not made the payments, so now we no longer own the house. In a month Rinaldo Salviati will foreclose and—' She broke off.

'And what?' I asked in alarm. 'Has he propositioned you in some way?'

'He has indicated that we might come to some arrangement.'

'You will tell him that no such thing will happen.'

'It is so simple for you to say this!' Elisabetta flared at me. It was the first time I had seen her angry. 'I know you have more empathy than other men, Matteo, but until you live as a woman you can have no idea of the constraints put upon us. I have no money, no land, no title, nothing. What am I to do? Where am I to go? How shall I eat? How shall I live?'

Chapter Sixty-Nine

The next morning I left Kestra promising to return as soon as I could.

We went into Milan, swinging south to do so, well away from the road where I had been set upon last autumn. Once in the city I left my men to wander in the area of the *duomo*. I gave them instructions to be on their guard and incur no ill, but to find out any information they could. These two were good men, inexperienced, but true of heart. Then I took myself to the Maestro's studio at San Babila.

There I found only Felipe walking about among the leavings of the workshops, sorting through the last of their things to take to the Melzi villa at Vaprio. He welcomed me warmly and I thought of the way I had been welcomed into this household from the beginning, and the manner in which Leonardo da Vinci had dealt with me in my extreme youth, with kindness yet firmness, as a true father would.

Felipe told me of the passing of Graziano, who had died a month previously. Of how our stout friend had joked to the end; telling our master that he must cut him open after he had expired, so that they could see that his stomach was swollen due to a cancer rather than his fondness for food and wine.

Then Felipe asked me if it was true that the Bolognese had toppled the great statue of the Pope. When I said that it was true, he left the room. I went to join him outside in the garden. I surmised that the thought of the felling of such a piece by a genius like Michelangelo was a physical pain to him. Felipe had worked with my master for many years. He knew the cost, the emotional investment and the physical and mental toll of creating something of that magnitude. And he empathized with the lowering of the spirit that an artist must feel on learning of its destruction. In his earlier days in Milan Leonardo da Vinci had made a plaster model for a massive statue of a horse, and it had been destroyed by soldiers using it for target practice.

We stood together in silence for a while.

It has been said often that there was rivalry between the two gifted men of these times, Leonardo da Vinci and Michelangelo. Their natures could not have been more opposite. Leonardo was supposed to have laughed at the other's favoured profession, stating that a sculpture could not portray the soul; that this could best be done via the medium of a painting, which showed the eyes of the sitter. Michelangelo, for his part, was supposed to have declared that only through the representations of the body in the three dimensions of a statue could true life be reflected and great Art created. Yet Leonardo sculpted and cast statues, and Michelangelo obeyed the Pope's command and painted a master-piece on the roof of the Sistine Chapel.

'We are the barbarians,' said Felipe. 'That we would allow such an outrage to take place.' He looked at me. 'Give me your own account, Matteo. Did anyone mourn its passing?'

'They rejoiced in the streets as it fell to earth,' I told him truth-fully. 'In Ferrara they made bonfires and burned the Pope's effigy to show what was to happen to the bronze likeness. And Duke Alfonso smelted it down in his furnaces and turned it into a huge cannon.'

Felipe sat down upon a bench. He put his hand upon his heart. 'Ah. I am become old,' he said. And then after a moment he added, 'As is your master.'

I sat down beside him. 'Has he truly forgiven me for not taking up the place at the university in Pavia?'

'You should go and speak to him yourself,' Felipe said. 'He is at Santa Maria delle Grazie. The Dominicans are complaining that the fresco he painted in their refectory years ago is beginning to peel from the wall.'

'How is he?' I asked Felipe.

'The deaths of his friends Marcantonio della Torre and Charles d'Amboise affected him deeply, and we still mourn the passing of the cheerful Graziano.'

Death. The cruel absolute that severs friends for ever.

Death. The Maestro's companion and mine on those nights in the mortuary at Averno.

'But Vaprio is peaceful,' Felipe continued, 'and he intends to sketch the geology of the region. It will be good for him to rest there a while.'

'What will he do if the French lose their grip on Milan?'

'He needs to see to his affairs and his income. As soon as the roads are safe I am to go to Florence to arrange finances. Then we must shift ourselves to find patronage and avoid the areas of war.'

'Where does one go nowadays to avoid war?' I asked.

There was a purpose to my asking Felipe this question, for my mind was concerned with Elisabetta's situation. I knew that Paolo had no intention of keeping the farm. I saw now that this was why he had asked me to go to Kestra while he remained in Ferrara – so that he did not need to argue his case with Elisabetta. Any money he had he was spending to equip the Bande Rosse. I was loath to take Elisabetta back to Ferrara with me because I did not think it a safe place.

'It may be difficult to follow the wider politics when you are engaged in the battlefield,' said Felipe, 'but you should know that the French will leave Italy. They cannot keep an army here while the Pope encourages young Henry of England to mass his troops against them on their northern frontier.'

'In Ferrara they believe the Pope to be a wicked scheming man.'

'The former Duke of Ferrara allied his state to the previous

Pope Alexander VI, Rodrigo Borgia, by marrying his son to Lucrezia Borgia. Thus at one time Ferrara sided with the Papacy for power and protection. Yet this Pope, Julius, appears to act for the good of the whole. He has begun monastic reform and brought out a dictate against simony. Unlike others in Church office he has not used his position to advance his family.' Felipe smiled. 'Of course, he favours the Arts, and it may be that I'm a little prejudiced in my opinion of him.'

Once again Felipe's objective thinking cleared my mind. 'So you think that Pope Julius's course is more benign to the state of Italy than any other way?'

'I think Julius seeks to place certain rulers in control of the city states,' said Felipe, 'and then he hopes to bring these together under the one authority of Rome. He has declared that Italian affairs must be in Italian hands. I find I cannot disagree with that. It may be that we are witnessing Italy struggling to be born.'

As we were speaking a thought entered my mind. I had told Felipe of my worry about Elisabetta and I now put a proposal to him.

'I could arrange your escort to Florence,' I said, 'if you would take Elisabetta with you. She would be in less danger in Florence than any place else at the moment.'

He considered for a minute. 'It would be useful for me to get there soon,' he said. 'We have some money in an account there that we have need of now. And,' he added, 'I have friends living on the outskirts of the city who might take her in. Theirs is a respectable house, and large enough to accommodate a lodger.'

I made an arrangement with Felipe and set off towards Santa Maria delle Grazie to find the Maestro. As I went past the shop of the apothecary who bought herbs from Elisabetta's garden another an idea came to me. On our return journey south I would make a detour and find the box that contained my grandmother's recipes. With those to help her Elisabetta might make some income to help sustain her independently.

Chapter Seventy

The Dominican monastery of Santa Maria delle Grazie was on the far side of the castle and I was conscious of the suspicious stares of the French sentries at my condottieri uniform as I strode past.

I found the Maestro sitting on a stool in the monk's refectory staring at his famous painting of the Last Supper of Jesus Christ with His Apostles.

I came into the room from the outside cloister and closed the door softly behind me. I stood for a moment looking at him, and felt such a surge of love and affection that I could not move.

He became aware of my presence and turned his head.

'Matteo!' He held out his hands. 'It is you!'

I crossed the room and went down on one knee before him.

'Come now, Matteo,' he said. 'I'm not a god, that you should genuflect in front of me.'

'I fear I may have vexed you by not returning to study at the university.'

'I am saddened that you may have missed the opportunity to explore the furthest reaches of that intelligent mind you possess.' He took me by the shoulders and raised me up. 'But you are still alive, that is what is most important. And I am very pleased to see you.'

He made me stand a distance from him so that he could admire my fine condottieri tunic and crimson sash.

'I am sorry if I have disappointed you in your hopes for me.' I spoke humbly.

'But the life of a condottieri captain is not without opportunity.' The Maestro waved his hand towards the other end of the refectory and Montorfano's fresco of the Crucifixion. 'If you look on either side of the Cross you will see the painting I made of Ludovico "Il Moro" Sforza and his family. The Sforzas were condottieri captains yet rose to rule the duchy of Milan – and if Pope Julius has his way will rule here again when the French are forced to leave.'

'It was not my true wish to be a condottiere. I rode out with Paolo dell'Orte because—' I broke off. I could not explain why, without revealing my fear and guilt.

'You had reason to do what you did,' the Maestro said thoughtfully. And then added, 'Since the beginning of your life.'

I did not know quite what he meant by that, but sensed it might lead me into territory I did not want to explore, so I turned my head to look at his magnificent fresco of the Last Supper. 'Is it true that the paint is coming away from the wall?'

'There is some damp which is causing distress. At least' – he smiled – 'it is causing the prior of the monastery distress. Whether the work is worth repairing, I do not know, considering that war is coming to the city and it might very well be destroyed in the conflict.'

He stood up, and I walked with him as he approached his masterpiece. It was as if we were entering the actual supper room and the living presence of the thirteen men gathered round the table. The immediate aftermath of the thunderbolt of the announcement of Jesus, *'One of you shall betray me,'* was apparent in the reaction of the Apostles to the words of their Master. The tension of the moment displayed by their various expressions of stunned disbelief and distress. The rictus of the outstretched fingers of the Christ's right hand mirrored by those of the Iscariot.

Judas.

The Betrayer.

I started as the Maestro laid his hand upon my shoulder. 'There is your namesake, Matteo.' He pointed to one of the Apostles on the left of Jesus. A man portrayed in profile, with a bright blue cloak and serious appearance. 'Saint Matthew,' he repeated, 'whose badge Felipe wears upon his cloak because he has a special devotion to this saint. Did you know that?'

My heart was beating very fast. I shook my head.

'Saint Matthew was a tax collector and he is said to protect those who deal with accounts. That is why Felipe feels an affinity with him.'

'I see,' I replied carefully.

The Maestro reached out and put a hand on each side of my head. 'You are an honourable boy, Matteo,' he said. 'When the time comes, I know that you will find your way to the truth.' He spread his fingers across my face, encircling my eyes with his thumb and forefinger.

'Matteo,' he repeated again – my name that was not my name.

Chapter Seventy-One

I brokered most of the gifts I had brought Elisabetta to obtain two horses for her and Felipe.

We made good speed on our journey back down the Via Emilia. Felipe was a competent rider and Elisabetta did not complain, though she tumbled exhausted from her horse when we stopped to rest on the first night.

I had set a hard pace for there was a reason I wanted to reach this particular place. In the early dawn I got up and roused Stefano. I told him that there was a matter I had to attend to and that he was in charge of the others until I returned.

We were in the countryside where my grandmother had died and I wanted to find the stream near where I had buried her box. Even after the passage of years I could do this for I had marked the spot with distinctive boulders.

I uncovered the rocks and scraped away the earth.

There it lay, made of oak wood, bound round and tied tightly with corded rope. Inside were her pestle and bowl and spoons and small sieves for preparing infusions. I heard them rattle as I lifted up the box. I knew that also wrapped up inside, in a waterproof covering, were her recipe book and other papers. The box was scarcely a foot and a half square and weighed not more than a ten pounds. What had seemed a large load for a nine-year-old boy I now lifted easily and slung across the pommel of my saddle.

As I gave the box to Elisabetta a terrible sadness came over me.

'Wait until you reach your new home before you open it,' I requested. I felt embarrassed at my obvious show of grief in front of her who had suffered so much in comparison to me. 'This is my grandmother's legacy and I gift it to you. Her tools to make herbal remedies and pills, and most importantly her recipe book. You might try to make these and sell them.'

'Ah, Matteo,' she replied. 'I see now the reason you bade me bring those cuttings and seeds from my herbarium.'

I gave Felipe all the money I had to cover the cost of Elisabetta's keep and promised to send more as soon as I could. Then I delegated Stefano and his brother Silvio, our latest recruit, to escort Felipe and Elisabetta through the hills to Florence. 'Do not worry about Elisabetta,' said Felipe. 'My friends have no living children of their own. They will not turn her out.'

It was time to say farewell.

Felipe took my hand. 'Stay out of the way of cannonballs if you can, Matteo.'

Elisabetta was inclined to cry but she set her chin and did not. 'I will write to you when I am settled,' she said. 'If I can earn any money I will find my own place and make it a home for you and Paolo. Bring him safe to me, if you can, Matteo.'

PART SEVEN
THE MEDICI SEAL

Ferrara and Florence, 1512

Chapter Seventy-Two

O n my return to Ferrara there was a banquet to celebrate the recent successes of the new French commander, Gaston de Foix.

Lucrezia Borgia, who had recovered her health after her miscarriage, was back in the *castello* organizing a meal of one hundred courses. It was to last from sunset to sunrise the next day, and was deemed an act of defiance against the new papal alliance, the so-called Holy League. And also, as Charles observed shrewdly, to show the French how important their presence was to the city and the duchy.

More than one room was set aside for this banquet, with trestle tables erected to cater for the large number of guests. These were covered with white and gold cloth and bedecked in greenery and red ribbon to celebrate the new year. Servants ran constantly between the kitchens and the tables, bringing food, and bowls of water and little towels to rinse one's fingers. Between each batch of courses the ladies rose from the table to attend to their toilet or stroll in the courtyards or along the terraces. The gentlemen escorted them, or assembled in groups to discuss the war and politics. It was still cold but musicians were placed in open tents in the garden to entertain those who chose to venture outside. During these breaks I went from room to room, and in and out of the apartments seeking to find one lady.

It was past midnight when eventually, from one of the

windows, I saw Eleanora d'Alciato walking in the company of two other ladies. I signalled to Charles and hustled him with me along a parallel way so that we would intercept them in their path.

We pretended great surprise when we met up. We exchanged courtesies, then Charles graciously took the two other ladies in charge, one on each arm, and walked them ahead of us.

Now I was alone with Eleanora.

I offered her my arm. She took it.

After my initial action to engineer our meeting I did not know what to do. Should I speak first? What should I say? I looked ahead to where Charles was chatting easily with his ladies. A comment on the weather perhaps? I cleared my throat.

'So now, Messer Matteo' – Eleanora spoke before I could begin – 'do tell me how you came to hide under the skirts of a nun in a convent garden?'

When I had first seen her in Ferrara I thought that at some time she might ask me this question so I had my story ready for her. 'I had been visiting some friends in the country,' I said, 'and was set upon by ruffians as I rode back to Milan.'

'How strange,' she said. 'Though he is known as a ruthless man, I wouldn't have thought that Jacopo de' Medici would wait to ambush an unwary traveller.'

'Nor do I,' I said smoothly. 'It is perhaps that he saw me fleeing and my attackers asked him for help in pursuing me by making up some lie to say that I had robbed them.'

'And had you?'

'Of course not!'

She regarded me thoughtfully.

'You saw that I carried no goods upon me,' I said. Then I added for mischief, 'Not even a weapon.'

She smiled at that, and said, 'That is true. Yet, I sense that you have not told me all of the story.'

'You have not told me all of yours,' I countered. 'How it is that you are at the court of Ferrara yet you know such a person as Jacopo de' Medici?'

'He visited my father's house in Florence once. I was much smaller, only a child, which is why he would not recognize me.'

We had come to a fork in the path. Charles had turned towards the *castello*. I hesitated and then gently pressed her arm to guide her in the opposite direction.

She glanced back but allowed herself to be led away. 'I must not be gone too long, else my absence will be noticed.'

We walked a little more. We came to a fountain. The water supply had been turned off for the winter, and the puddle of water left in the bottom of the bowl was frozen. She sat down on the ledge and touched the ice with her fingers and shivered. I had the urge to put my arms around her, to warm her by holding her close to me.

She asked me about Leonardo da Vinci. 'My father took me to the Church of the Annunciation in Florence when the Leonardo cartoon of the Virgin and Saint Anne was displayed there.' She put her head to one side. 'You have known him. Is it true that he made the symbols of the Three in One in this painting?'

'He does not say what is in his paintings,' I replied. 'We can but guess.'

'His circle of love between the figures was unique,' said Eleanora. 'Many artists came to look at it and learn. He is a genius.'

'Yes,' I said. 'He is.'

'Do you wish to become an artist?'

'Oh no. I had thought at one time I might be a doctor.'

'They say that Leonardo da Vinci dissected bodies in the darkness of the night to seek the source of the soul?'

'He dissected corpses in order to discover how it is that the human body functions.'

'You were there!'

She was quick. I saw that with her one would have to keep one's mind alert.

'And is that why you wish to become a doctor, Matteo?' she went on. 'Because you gained insight into the workings of the body?'

As I considered my reply it occurred to me that by this conversation I was gaining insight into her mind. An illumination as to who Eleanora d'Alciato was, and how she thought.

'When the Maestro, da Vinci, investigated the internal organs he would always discuss with me their function, and how they could be impaired by accident or disease. And then we would discourse on how they might be repaired. For a time I studied under the direction of a friend of his, who has since died. Professor Marcantonio della Torre, who lectured at the medical school in the university at Pavia.'

'There is a famous library at Pavia,' she said. 'Is it as wondrous as its reputation?'

'It is. I read some of the books there.'

'I would love to see it!' Her eyes were bright. 'My father educated me himself and he had an extensive library. I studied Aristotle and Petrarch, and have read Dante too. But my father's books were sold to pay his debts when he passed away.' She sighed. 'A double loss to bear: I loved him and his books so well.'

'How is it that you are now at the court of Ferrara?' I asked her.

'When my father died penniless my uncle took me in. It was very generous of him for he already has four daughters of his own. They are young, but soon it will be time for him to marry them off, so he wants me settled quickly. After my father's funeral he arranged for me to marry a respectable Florentine merchant. This man had half a dozen children by his three previous wives who died. My uncle believed I would be grateful. The man, although older, had some money and my uncle thought that caring for the children would take my mind off the loss of my father. I was unsure and upset and said I could not undertake such a thing at that time. I went to the convent where my aunt is the abbess and she gave me shelter. But I was not suited to the monastic life so the abbess wrote to Duke Alfonso, who is a relative of hers, and he granted me leave to come here for a while.' She stood up. 'And now I must go back to the house. The next course will have begun and I am seated within sight of the duchess. She will wonder where I am.'

She moved to pass me but I stepped to block her way and she was against me and I could not resist touching her face with my hand.

Her skin was soft and she put her hand over mine and placed it along her cheek.

'Eleanora,' I whispered.

The sound of the serving bell came to us across the night air.

'I must go in,' she said.

Chapter Seventy-Three

While I had been in Milan the French army had begun a series of successful campaigns to recapture the smaller towns around Ferrara.

Gaston de Foix reminded me of another commander that I had watched operate in the Romagna years ago. The townspeople had no time to prepare for his attacks. His method of swift travel to arrive at a place and fall upon his unsuspecting enemy was similar to Cesare Borgia's way of operating. For this type of campaign the Bande Rosse was in demand to support the main force. Our men were known to be well equipped and properly trained in the arms we bore.

But the sacking of the towns troubled me. This was not the chasing out of armed soldiers as it had been in Bologna. It was the abuse of citizens. Paolo had a way of ignoring facts, of blinding himself to things he did not wish to deal with. As he had done by selling the farm and not foreseeing the consequences for his sister, so he was set on continuing with his goal of seeking revenge against the armies of the Pope, not seeing that it would be for always, battle after battle, never ending.

When we got back to Ferrara after the latest brief campaign there were letters awaiting us from Felipe and Elisabetta.

Elisabetta wrote to say that the house in Prato, where she was now staying, had a garden. Felipe's friends were an old couple, quite frail, glad of her company and help in the house. They had allowed her the freedom to plant any herbs she chose. Already she had secured an agreement with an apothecary in Florence. When the plants began to flower in the spring she intended to open my grandmother's books and prepare recipes of her own.

Felipe had successfully completed his business in Florence and had managed to secure a safe conduct back to Milan and was now at Vaprio with the Maestro.

In the spring the French held a war council. They proposed to attack Ravenna. It was the last big fortified city in the Romagna under Vatican rule, and an apostolic seat.

'The Pope will not allow Ravenna to fall,' said Paolo. 'If Ravenna is taken then it wipes him out in the Romagna.'

'Therefore by attacking Ravenna,' said Charles, 'Gaston de Foix will force the papal armies to engage. And that way we could have an end to this taking of towns, losing them and retaking them again.'

So it was decided. The French and the Ferrarese would muster every man and weapon to bring an end to this conflict.

Before we left to undertake the siege of Ravenna the Duchess Lucrezia commissioned a fanciful pageant to show the successes of the French led by the splendid de Foix. It involved moving structures, with players dressed as soldiers posturing about a huge stage set up in the main piazza.

Donna Lucrezia sat at the front to watch the spectacle. The evening was long, and she and her ladies came and went during scene changes. At one of these breaks I contrived to speak to Eleanora in the courtyard of the church that was being used as a rest room for the women.

'I came to say goodbye,' I called softly as she walked with another woman through the doorway.

Eleanora stopped and looked round. Her companion saw me first. She was a young girl with a mischievous face. She put her finger to her lips and pushed Eleanora towards me. I drew her into the shadows of the cloister.

'Tomorrow the Bande Rosse leave for Ravenna,' I said. 'I wanted to speak with you before I left.'

'Why?' she demanded.

'Because—' I stopped and looked at her more closely. She seemed angry. 'Have I offended you in some way?' I asked her.

'Answer the question I asked you first, sir,' she snapped.

'I have a deep feeling for you and I wished to see you and hear your voice again before I left Ferrara.'

'And have you no consideration for my feelings?'

'It is my consideration for you that brings me here to this cloister tonight.'

'If that were true then you would not go to war again. Why do you remain with the Bande Rosse?' she asked. 'If you recall, we had a conversation to the effect that you were not suited to being a soldier.'

'I have an obligation to the Captain Paolo dell'Orte,' I replied. 'He believes that the Papacy brought about the ruin of his family and I am contracted by honour to help him fight to avenge this wrong.'

'Did you not discharge this duty when you took Bologna? The Pope's Legate has been driven out of the most important city in the Romagna. This is enough surely? Do you not think that you might conduct your own life as you wish?'

I had thought of this. The doctor at Bologna, Claudio Ridolfi, had indicated to me that if I shared more of my remedies with him he might gain me a place in his medical school. And now that Elisabetta would transcribe my grandmother's recipes this might be possible. But Paolo had signed us on for another term of duty, and Elisabetta had charged me with bringing him safe home to her.

'It is complicated,' I said to Eleanora. I could not explain the debt I felt I owed the dell'Orte family. I could not tell her of my shameful part in their downfall.

'The Pope will not give up Ravenna easily. He is sending every soldier he can spare to help them. If you go to Ravenna, Matteo, you will die.'

'I have told you of my obligations,' I said. 'What else can I do?'

'Take responsibility for your own destiny,' she replied with spirit. 'A man can do this while a woman cannot.'

I cupped my hands around her throat and drew her to me. She stood very still. I could see a tiny freckle at the side of her eyebrow, the downy hair on her temple, each silken strand separately. Her top lip quivered.

I put my mouth on hers, top lip to top lip, bottom lip on bottom lip. But I did not press my lips against hers. I waited. I let her breathing mingle with mine, until I felt her quicken, and her breath begin to come in little pants.

Then I kissed her. And she allowed me to do this.

As we separated I said, 'I will come back for you.'

Her eyes cleared and then focused.

'And I may or may not be here,' she replied.

Chapter Seventy-Four

I thought that she might not come to watch us ride away.

But when I looked up to the battlements as we passed through the gates of the city the next day, I saw Eleanora standing there with the rest of the ladies. I raised my gloved hand to my helmet in a salute and was rewarded with a flutter of lilac and pale green ribbons.

Charles also saw this movement and rode beside me as we left the city gate and headed south to cross the river.

'Lilac and green ribbons,' he said. 'Would that be the colours of Eleanora d'Alciato?'

I felt my colour heighten.

'Be careful, Matteo.'

'How so?'

'I know you, my friend. You do not dally and make sport of love. With you it is all or nothing. I would not see you hurt.'

'Why are you saying that?' I said in annoyance. 'She is not like other court ladies who play with men's affections.'

'Of course she is not,' Charles soothed me. 'But whereas a woman can give her love to whomsoever she chooses, the matter of a marriage contract is not hers to decide.'

'A marriage contract! There is no marriage contract prepared for Eleanora.'

'Not yet,' said Charles. 'But she has rejected the nunnery and she is almost seventeen, so her guardian must have plans for her future.'

So it had not been a casual conversation when Eleanora had spoken to me about the lack of freedom a woman had. Perhaps she thought I was aware that her uncle planned a match for her. I now saw more meaning in her last words to me.

When I had told her I would come back for her, she had said, '*I may or may not be here.*'

We arrived outside Ravenna just before Easter.

Charles reported to us that the allies of the Holy League had come up and taken position where they believed they were safe, on the south side of the river Ronco. The French engineers swiftly constructed a pontoon bridge. On Easter Sunday morning Gaston de Foix led his troops across the river and arranged them in a crescent facing the Spanish earthworks. At the same time Duke Alfonso moved his cannon to where he saw a weak point on their flank.

Our infantry went forward. From the enemy ramparts murderous fire poured from their cannon and war wagons. Great swathes of our men fell, never to rise again.

But the Ferrarese artillery was not idle and when they began their barrage the cunning of Duke Alfonso showed. His guns had been set to enfilade the enemy trenches and the Spaniards were caught and could not escape being killed.

It was evident that the casualty toll would be vast. Charles, who usually thrilled at the sight of battle action, was tense and his face became grim.

It was a relief when it was time for the French light cavalry, the Bande Rosse among them, to charge the enemy position. We were no longer the inexperienced lads of Mirandola, but fighting men who yelled with blood lust and rage as they galloped into battle. But if we were not callow youths, neither were the men we faced. And they also had a gifted and expert commander, the Spaniard, Ramón de Cardona. He now signalled his own light horse to come up. And then it was hand to hand, horse against horse. In the dense thickness of the struggle there was not time to look around, to note whether one's comrade had fallen or to rescue any other who was being overcome.

Suddenly a shout went up. The Spanish infantry were leaving the field. We had won!

But then, disaster. Better that we had lost the day than what befell now.

In pursuit of the Spanish division, whom he rightly guessed were experienced troops being withdrawn to fight another day, Gaston de Foix turned his horse and rode out onto the causeway. Urging on his men, he chased the fleeing infantry, intending to destroy them. But de Cardona and his men escaped, and in the mêlée Gaston de Foix was brought down and killed.

Ravenna was ours. The victory was to us. Pope Julius defeated, but at what cost?

The Spanish commander had eluded capture and taken his best men with him. France and King Louis had lost, utterly lost, one of the best and most brilliant soldiers. And it was only when they began to pile the bodies in bundles that the complete extent of the massacre was realized. Thousands and thousands of men on both sides had died. Court poets and scribes and historians always exaggerate the figures of the fallen, so that when they tell their tales of war at banquets and feasts the victory of the winner seems more and the defeat of the enemy greater. At Ravenna there was no need for hyperbole. The dead bodies of the men defied any counting.

More than ten thousand men. Among them Stefano and his young brother Silvio.

And Charles d'Enville.

The cannonball that struck Charles showed less mercy than the halberd that tore him apart at Agnadello. The shot blew his arm and half his face away. The day after the battle Charles died of his wounds and I could not save him.

Our troops entered Ravenna. A week later the Plague struck.

Chapter Seventy-Five

'I cannot leave.'

Paolo looked at me. He had come to tell me that the remnants of our army were preparing to return to Ferrara and we should go with them.

'These people are suffering,' I said. 'I have the means to help them. I cannot leave.'

He nodded slowly in a beginning of understanding. 'You are a doctor,' he said. 'As I am a soldier.'

The plight of the citizens was becoming more awful than that of the survivors of the two armies. The Plague was rampant in the poorer quarters. In those areas the city council had decided to shut up houses, nailing the windows and doors shut with wooden bars so that the people lying ill inside could not escape. Their calls and shouts for succour were heart-rending, as were the piteous cries of their children.

I recalled that the nun at Melte long ago believed it to be carried in clothing, and under her care I had survived contact with the Plague. I ordered all clothing worn by victims and their families to be burned. Then I sent our men to seize the clothes that had been taken as booty from the homes of the nobility and I distributed these to the naked. Our men were very frightened. I did not blame them. Marcantonio della Torre, who must have had more knowledge and skill than I, had succumbed to this disease. It was a more deadly and insidious enemy than we had faced on any battlefield, but it was battlefield none the less and I had to find a way to fight it with as much skill as any army general. And in this endeavour I discovered Paolo had great strength.

'We must unlock these houses,' I said.

'No,' he said. 'We must not.'

'We cannot leave the people who have been shut in to starve to death. They might not even have the Plague.'

'If we ask the men to unlock the houses they will mutiny,' reasoned Paolo. 'They might even massacre those inside to keep them from coming out.'

'I cannot stand by and witness people starve to death when there is food freely available.'

'There is another way,' said Paolo.

He explained to me that he would instruct his soldiers to knock a slat from the wooden shutter of each house and call out to the inmates to say that food and water would be pushed through each day. But the soldiers would also warn them that if they tried to leave the building they would be executed.

'They need more than food,' I said. 'They need medical attention.'

'They cannot have it, Matteo.' Paolo regarded me seriously. 'You yourself must appreciate this. You must help our doctors treat the French wounded, else the army quartermaster will not give us to access the food stores. Also, if you attend to those citizens where they lie sick, stricken with the Plague, then you would go from house to house, unceasing, and you would die of exhaustion, or someone will kill you, or indeed you will catch the disease.

'You will retire to a safe clean place,' Paolo went on, 'and there you can treat people.'

'But I—'

'Matteo, this is how it must be,' Paolo said firmly.

In this I let myself to be guided by him. And I found that many people did not have the Plague, but only dysentery, or boils, or scabies, or some other eczema that had flung the city officials into a panic to declare them unclean.

One day a French army officer of high rank came and spoke to me. 'You have attended Spanish soldiers here while there are Frenchmen waiting to be seen. I order you not to do this.'

'I am not a doctor,' I replied, 'I only help those who come to me in desperation. When a man is brought to me naked I do not know his race or allegiance. I will treat the sick, and if you do not allow me to do so, then I will treat no one.'

He went away.

Victory in the battle of Ravenna was claimed by the French.

When King Louis heard of the death of his nephew, Gaston de Foix, he wept. He said that he wept not only for his own loss, but also for that of France. He declared a day of mourning for his court. Then he let it be known to his ministers of war that no more French royal blood was to be spilled on Italian soil.

Paolo wrote to tell the parents of Stefano and Silvio that their sons were dead. I thought of the day at their farm only a few months ago, when Stefano's girl had held the white silk he had brought her against her body and teased him to imagine how she would look when she wore it at their wedding.

It fell to me to write to Elisabetta and tell her that Charles had perished. I knew that she would grieve for him, for although they had only spoken once, they had corresponded with each other. I made of him a hero, crediting him with a daring exploit, and inventing a quick painless end for him. I did not feel any guilt in doing this. He had been a brave and kind captain and his memory deserved no less.

I did not join in the main march back to Ferrara but remained for a while in Ravenna. This was in order to ensure that those remaining citizens still succumbing to the Plague had their last suffering eased. It was also that I had no stomach for any triumphal procession. Therefore it was only weeks later, when I returned to Ferrara, that I learned a most important prisoner had been captured at Ravenna. A powerful ally of Pope Julius who was using the Papacy to help him reinstate his family to what he considered their rightful place as rulers of Florence. This man was Cardinal Giovanni de' Medici.

Chapter Seventy-Six

In keeping with his status as a son of Lorenzo the Magnificent, the most influential one-time ruler of Florence, Cardinal Giovanni de' Medici was lodged in the royal apartments and allowed freedom of movement.

Immediately I arrived in Ferrara I was summoned to the *castello*. The cardinal had been hawking in the Barco and had injured himself when dismounting from his horse after the hunt. He was very fat and I was more inclined to think that he would have injured the horse.

The duke's chamberlain, who had greeted me, said, 'I have heard that you are more than a mere condottieri lieutenant, Messer Matteo. You are required to assist in the treatment of the Cardinal Giovanni de' Medici. The skin of his leg was torn open and it has now become infected. It is known that you have some medical ability so you will look at his injury and see what might be done to heal it.'

I could have said I was unable to help. But it would have been foolish to incur the annoyance of the duke and duchess. Being near a Medici gave me cause for disquiet and I was nervous as the chamberlain led me to the cardinal's rooms, where he lay upon his bed being visited by the duchess and one of her cousins.

I need not have worried. The cardinal had no interest in me as an individual. He was short sighted, and in any case did not want to watch as I examined his leg. He turned his head away while one of Donna Lucrezia's ladies held his hand.

If I had been a servant I would have been completely ignored as I went about my work, but my reputation for healing meant I had some status. The duchess watched me as I bent to look more closely at the wound, then she made a comment. She was well educated, slipping easily from one language to another, but for this remark, in order to be private and as she was speaking to one of her own kinfolk, she spoke Catalan.

Which I could understand.

'The young doctor, Dorotea' – Donna Lucrezia's voice was languid and sensual – 'he shows a shapely leg beneath his tunic, don't you think?'

I tried to keep my face still, but I could not hide my discomfort.

The duchess looked at me curiously. She had surmised that I understood her.

Her cousin Dorotea saved the situation. 'He blushes!' she cried out gaily. 'By your gesture, madonna, he guesses at your meaning.'

They laughed together at my embarrassment.

This lady sidled over to me. 'They say you have healing hands, Messer Matteo. Would you like to place them upon me? I have such an ache.'

'Hush, Dorotea,' Donna Lucrezia scolded her. 'You are too forward in your manner.'

As I wrote out a recipe and made to take my leave Donna Lucrezia rose from her seat and handed me a gold coin. 'For your trouble.'

'It is no trouble for a great lady such as yourself,' I said.

'Ah, I recognize you now!' she exclaimed.

I could not speak. It was not possible. It had been so many years ago, only a glimpse in the crowd. But she was an intelligent woman.

'You are the gallant that seized Eleanora's ribbon in the joust!'

I breathed again. 'I – I am,' I managed to say.

'And' – she laughed – 'claimed your reward so eloquently.'

I bent my head to acknowledge her compliment.

'Making your horse bow down like that. It is a trick that gypsies teach their horses, is it not?'

I was grateful that my head was bent and I raised it slowly.

'I remember when I was a girl in Rome,' she went on, 'there was a horse fair held every year and we watched from the windows of the Vatican as they performed for us. They were the best of horsemen, running up and down with the horses to show them off to us.' Lucrezia Borgia looked at me not unkindly. 'I am very sympathetic to the affairs of the heart, but you should know that Eleanora d'Alciato de Travalle will be soon contracted in marriage. She is warded by her uncle, both her parents being dead. She has little dowry, so, there it is, the convent or marriage.' She paused. 'Of course, a man can happily accept a woman with no fortune, although he himself would need to have some money of his own. If such a one appeared, who could make an offer . . .' She paused again. 'It might be possible . . .'

Chapter Seventy-Seven

The wisdom of the Spanish commander Ramón de Cardona soon became evident. At the siege of Ravenna, having seen that the city was lost, he had retired, husbanding his best troops to enable them to fight another day. His infantry were a formidable and well-armed force. They now met up with the rest of the papal army and began to gobble up the disputed places of the Romagna.

Our exhausted troops were sent in batches to help garrison some towns around Ferrara. It would be a defensive action only. Decimated by our losses at Ravenna, we could not regroup in sufficient force to engage in any battle, far less mount a campaign. The Venetians and the Swiss, despite their mistrust of each other, were coming together. Under the direction of the Pope, they would control the northern part of Italy. The time had come. The French would have to leave Ferrara and get to Milan while the roads were still open to them.

This information came to Paolo and me by gossip and hearsay. Since the death of Charles and many of the French officers we'd had little contact with what was happening within the French army and the councils of war.

But I received a note from Eleanora asking to meet me privately by the fountain in the garden of the castello after dark.

I went there alone and waited. It was close to midnight before she appeared.

'I could not slip away earlier,' she whispered.

I made to take her in my arms but she withdrew. 'I came to inform you that Duke Alfonso is on his way to Rome.'

'To Rome!'

'Hush!' She glanced about her. 'It will become common knowledge eventually, but I thought it would be to your advantage to know this now. He has gone to make peace with the Pope.'

'I am grateful to you for telling me this,' I said. I touched her arm and she shivered.

'I came also to tell you that I am leaving Ferrara.'

I stepped back. 'When? Why?'

'My uncle' – she looked away – 'wishes me to marry. There is yet another older man whose wife has died and he has made an offer. I am to travel to my uncle's house at Travalle near Florence and meet him there.'

'Eleanora!'

She would not meet my gaze.

'Eleanora.' I grasped her hand and made her look at me. There were tears unshed in her eyes.

'Has a marriage contract been signed?'

'No.' She frowned and shook her head. 'I am first to be inspected by his family to see if I am worthy. That is the way of it.'

'It does not need to be the way of it,' I said. 'If I had money or patronage then I might approach your uncle—'

'Shush.' She put her finger to my lips. 'There is no point in useless speculation, Matteo. We are not able to live our lives as we would wish.'

I thought of what both she and Elisabetta had said to me regarding the difference between the wishes of a man and a woman.

'What would you be, Eleanora, if you could do anything you wanted?'

'If I were a man?'

'I am a man, yet I cannot do what I want.'

'Then you tell me. What profession or trade would you follow if free to do so?'

'I think now I would become a doctor,' I said. 'And you? What would you do if free to occupy yourself as you wished?'

'I would like to study the texts of humanity. As women we are taught to read, yet unless you enter the convent there is little opportunity to further your knowledge. And' – she managed a smile – 'I do not want to be a nun.'

'Several women attended the dissections at Bologna,' I told her.

'I do not know if I could endure that, but I would like to attend a class given by one of the philosophers.'

'And' – I moved nearer to her – 'if you were free to choose whom you wished to marry?'

'How could I, a mere woman, make that decision?'

I brought my face close to hers. With the end of my tongue I traced the outline of her mouth: I drew it along the outside edge of her top lip, and then along her lower lip. I stood back and looked into her eyes. She returned my gaze. Her eyes were wide and green as emeralds. I leaned forward, not touching her, and inserted the tip of my tongue between her parted lips.

She made a tiny moan.

There was the noise of someone approaching, the footsteps of the guard marching along the walkway.

She shrank back. 'I must go,' she whispered.

'No, wait,' I called, 'please—'

'Who is there?' The soldier had his pike at the ready as he approached.

I stepped to where he could see me and identified myself. By the time I had assured him I was not a papal spy Eleanora had gone.

Paolo was as alarmed as I when I told him that Duke Alfonso was on his way to Rome to try to agree terms with Pope Julius.

'There is no future for us here, Matteo,' he said.

'I do not want to go to France,' I told him firmly.

'Nor I,' he agreed. 'But I do like soldiering. In some way it makes me feel close to my father.'

'Then listen to me.' I had already thought out what I might say to Paolo. 'The republic of Florence has its own citizen army,' I told him, 'as conceived by Niccolò Machiavelli. You might offer your services to them. It would suit you well and Elisabetta lives there. I will come with you,' I added. And I told Paolo that I hoped I might attend the house of Eleanora's uncle and offer a marriage settlement.

But I had no money to do this. Nor the means of obtaining any. Save the one thing of value that I owned.

Chapter Seventy-Eight

A lone in the small barraca where Paolo and I slept at night, I unwrapped the seal. The shape of it fitted neatly within my palm and the gold shone dully in the lamplight. The balls of the Medici coat of arms sat proud of the surface, with the shield contained by the wording inside the rim.

MEDICI . . .

How much was it worth?

If a man had some money, it might be possible . . .

Lucrezia Borgia herself had said it.

Eleanora's uncle saw her as a piece of business to be taken care of. The money I would get from selling the seal would give me enough wealth to convince him of my good intentions.

Eleanora left Ferrara for her uncle's house the next day.

So I began to investigate the traders in Ferrara with a view to choosing one who might be interested in buying such an object as the Medici Seal. It took me several days of careful research before I finally selected a suitable goldsmith. Early one morning I went into a shop near the Ponte d'Oro, took the Medici Seal from the bag around my neck and placed it on the counter.

The shopkeeper's eyes stretched wide as he examined it. First he weighed it, then he took a tiny goldsmith's tool and scratched the outer edge.

'This looks genuine.'

'It is,' I said. 'And I warn you. Do not trifle with me for I have no time to haggle. Make me a decent offer, or I leave and go elsewhere.'

He raised an eyebrow, pursed his lips and then mentioned a sizeable sum of money.

'Double that,' I said, 'and give me it in gold and you can have the seal now.'

He spread his hands. 'I don't keep that amount in my shop. Come back tomorrow.'

'This evening,' I told him. I drew my dagger and placed the blade along his neck. 'And if you speak of this to anyone I will cut your throat.'

Paolo and I used the rest of the day to prepare for our departure. We packed a few things on our two best horses and rode them to a spot outside the city walls. I told Paolo that I had a debt to collect, and that I would go and do this while he waited there with both animals. Then we would set out for Florence.

I went to the shop an hour before the appointed time. I waited in an alleyway and watched the door, but the business of the street was as normal. As there was nothing untoward happening, at the appointed time I stepped out from my cover, crossed the street and slipped into the shop.

As soon as he saw me the goldsmith drew aside the curtain that screened his workshop at the back. 'Come through here,' he said.

I put my hand to my sword.

He clicked his tongue. 'There is no one waiting to rob you,' he said. He pulled the curtain wider and I saw that his little cubicle was indeed empty. 'It's only that I want us to be private from anyone looking in from the street.'

We both went inside and he let the curtain fall behind us.

At that moment we heard the outside door opening.

My dagger was in my hand even before the goldsmith whispered, 'I have not betrayed you. I am as keen to acquire the seal as you are to sell it. Let me go and get rid of whoever this is.'

He pushed my arm away and went out through the curtain, greeting his new customer effusively.

A man's voice spoke. 'The Great Seal of the Medici family has been brought to this shop. I want it.'

'The Great Seal of the Medici?' The shopkeeper expressed astonishment. 'I have never even heard of such a thing.'

'Don't hinder me in this.' The man's tone was impatient and menacing. 'I have searched a long time for the Medici Seal. My spies reported that you borrowed money today, naming it as surety for your loan. Therefore you have knowledge of its whereabouts. I rode many miles to get here, and I am prepared to pay well for that information.'

There was a noise, as if a bag of coins had been thrown onto the table.

'Here is what I will give you.'

'It is a goodly sum,' the shopkeeper said slowly. 'For that amount of gold I will try very hard to obtain the seal for you.'

'Where is the young man who brought it to you?'

'If I give you the seal, why do you want him?'

'I have my reasons.'

'Why punish him?' The shopkeeper's voice was strained almost pleading. He was anxious to avoid bloodshed in his shop. 'Why take revenge upon this youth if you recover what you want?'

'That is my business,' the man said stubbornly. 'Look, you may keep that bag of gold and I will bring you another the same weight if you lead me to the boy.'

There was a second of silence. The time it took for the goldsmith to fix the price on my head.

He would only need to roll his eyes in the direction of the curtain and my enemy could run me through without even seeing my face.

I heard the intake of the man's breath, and at that instant I knew the goldsmith had betrayed me.

Chapter Seventy-Nine

I ran.

Lowering my head, I propelled myself out from behind the curtain and through the shop. Hands grabbed at me, my tunic tore, but I wrenched away from them in a frenzy.

'Stop!' the stranger's voice shouted after me. 'Stop!'

Then I was in the street, with them pursuing.

'Thief!' The goldsmith's cry got more attention. 'Thief!'

People hurried to their windows and shop doors.

'Thief!' They took up the cry. 'Thief! Thief!'

There were those who skipped out of my way and urged me on – urchin lads and young men, glad of any opportunity to flout authority. Others flung rubbish or pieces of vegetables and fruit. A variety of objects hailed after me as I charged down towards the river.

I was on the bridge. If I could gain the other side I might lose them among the vennels in the wharves.

'A reward!' I heard the stranger shout. 'Ten gold pieces to the one who catches him!'

A man ran from a shop on the other side of the bridge. A burly butcher with a cleaver in his hand.

'Don't harm him!' The stranger was now closer behind me. 'I want him whole. Anyone who hurts him will be flayed alive!'

The butcher threw down his cleaver and spread his arms to prevent me passing.

I glanced back.

The stranger, who had left the goldsmith behind in the chase, was advancing towards me. He stopped as I faced him. It was the man from the woods near Kestra, the one who had tracked me to Eleanora's convent.

Jacopo de' Medici.

He saw I recognized him, and he smiled. It was a smile without pity. He was studying me, his eyes flickering over my body, then back to my face. He could see the dagger at my belt and the sword at my side. But he had his sword in his hand.

I looked at his weapon in fear.

'I—' he began.

There was a sound behind me. I whipped round. The butcher had taken advantage to creep closer. But in so doing he had moved to the central, wider part of the bridge. Still, I doubted I would get past him. He was a broad man. Yet as he was so broad, he would be slow on his feet. And I knew that I was nimble. If I could not gain the far side of the bridge, there was still another way I could go.

'No!' Jacopo de' Medici flung down his sword and leaped to catch me.

But I had jumped onto the parapet, vaulted over and plummeted down into the river.

I tried to dive deep.

But although it was summer the water was cold. The shock of my fall and the cold hit me together and blunted my dive. And once in the water I could not recover myself, for more than the cold, the current claimed me. Thick and fast it broiled around my legs and body and drew me down. I could not breathe. My lungs were straining for air, my head bursting, and my limbs would not obey my will. I was under the waterfall again but this time there was no rescue. I would not survive this.

I felt my body go limp. The light above me was grey, the water around me also grey. As grey as the paint on the Maestro's ruined fresco, as grey as Rossana's face as she lay dying. The grey of the tomb. And I thought of her, Rossana, and wondered if I would see her again after death. And I thought of her sister Elisabetta, and then of Eleanora. And as I thought of Eleanora I tried so desperately hard to kick out, to flail my arms to the surface.

The current that had almost killed me served to save me. For it brought me so far and so fast downstream that my pursuers could not follow, and at the first bend where the force of the water slackened, I caught hold of an overhanging tree branch. There were men with torches searching both sides of the bank. I could see the fire from their flares and hear them calling to each other. But I crawled away from them as fast as I could and went to the place where I had arranged to join Paolo with the horses.

It was hours past our meeting time but he was there, waiting faithfully for me. When he saw that I was dishevelled and soaking wet he laughed and said, 'I think perhaps you did not collect the money that was owed to you, Matteo?'

'I did not,' I said. 'Not only that, I am pursued. We would do well to be long gone from Ferrara before daylight arrives.'

Chapter Eighty

We mounted and rode.

My clothes dried, for it was a warm summer night and our pace was fast. We were going by side ways and tracks that we both knew from having ridden out in the countryside so frequently when training our men. A few miles beyond Bologna, when it was time to turn towards the mountains and Florence, Paolo said, 'There is a shorter way. When you were in Kestra and Milan helping Elisabetta, I went riding with Charles all around this area. There is path through the hills here past the Castel Barta.

Castel Barta.

Why did my mind stir at the sound of that name?

Castel Barta. I repeated the words. It was as if the wind had moved and then the world held still, in the way it does prior to a storm.

We rested in the darkest part of the night.

Paolo fell asleep as soon as he lay down. But no sooner did I start to drowse than I had a nightmare. I had fallen into a great lake. The water was bubbling into my mouth, and I began to choke. There were flashing lights before my eyes, but then these changed into the torches of men hunting me, and then into candlelight, and there was the sound of music in the background. And the water was gone and I was on a hard floor made with

Moorish patterned tiles and these were cool to my touch. But then I could no longer hear the music and suddenly I was under water struggling, and I could see myself from a great height and I knew that I was dying. And, very close to my ear, someone spoke a name.

I awoke with a shout.

'Who is there?'

Paolo muttered, 'Go to sleep, Matteo. Rest a little while more.'

But the name I'd heard was not my own. It was the name of a place. The place my grandmother had been anxious to reach before she had died. Castel Barta.

When Paolo woke up I said to him, 'I must go to this place, Castel Barta.'

'It's not far from the road,' he said, 'but it is a ruin.'

'Nevertheless,' I said, 'I must see it for myself and perhaps find out what caused its ruin.'

I claimed it to be a kind of pilgrimage in memory of my grandmother, and Paolo agreed to wait on the road while I went to look at it. So that I would make better speed I unbuckled my sword and left my horse behind.

'Don't delay,' Paolo called after me. 'We should try to reach Florence before nightfall.'

I made my way up a mountain track to the small hunting lodge set on the cliff top. It was in ruins as Paolo had said. This place had suffered the same fate as Perela. As I climbed a rock was displaced from the cliff above me. I looked up and saw a small opening. I waited, expecting a rabbit to run out, or a to bird fly up. But nothing moved. I had long cast aside the belief that disturbances of the earth were made by creatures known as Cyclops, who made the fires for the god named Vulcan. The Maestro had told me that the earth heaves and trembles sometimes, according to the forces of Nature.

I entered the courtyard and looked around. There were few walls left intact. As for Paolo at Perela there was nothing for me here. Yet I had to see for myself. I walked over and went inside what would have been the main hall. The heels of my boots sounded out on the tiled floor. I glanced down.

The tiles below my feet had a pattern of the Moorish fashion.

I stood still.

The early sunlight showed the pattern clearly. I crouched down and stretched out my hand to touch them.

And then in front of me a shadow moved.

I looked up.

Sandino stood before me.

Chapter Eighty-One

'S andino!'

'Yes,' he said softly. 'It is I.'

Neither of us moved. I was unable to, my blood and bowels turned to water. He was poised, watching me. His arms hung loose by his side. I saw his fingers with their yellowed thumbnails, long and curved and hideous.

'When I picked up your trail and found out that you were back in this area I knew that finally you would come this way, boy. I only had to wait long enough.'

I put my hand on the corded pouch at my neck. 'Here, take this cursed Medici Seal.'

'I have no interest in the seal now,' Sandino replied. '*You* are my prize and I have waited a long time to claim it.'

He made a move, just a slight easing of his body forward, but enough to let me see that he had a long knife concealed in one hand.

'You seek vendetta on me.' I stood up carefully, keeping my gaze fixed on his knife. 'But you will not find me easy to kill.'

'Why would I want you dead?' He shifted himself so that he was between me and the door. 'You are worth more to me alive.'

'You are working for the Medici?'

'I work for whoever pays the most. At present it's the Medici. They have offered a reward to anyone who brings you to them.'

I snatched my own dagger from my belt but in the second that it took me to do so he was upon me. For a stocky man he was agile,

435

and as he pounced he slashed at my weapon arm with his long knife.

I spun away from him and smashed my fist into his face.

Sandino reeled back. He had not been expecting that. It was a parry I'd learned from the Ferrarese: according to them a man, when armed, thinks only of his enemy's weapon and forgets he has another hand to use.

But Sandino was a brigand and had not lived so long by being careless or weak. He launched himself forwards again. I flung myself at his feet and tripped him and then rolled away along the floor. He had fallen heavily over me and his knife dropped from his grasp and slid away across the tiles. We both scrambled to get to it. I reached it first, but before I grasped it he had pinioned me, his arms clutching at my legs and dragging me back. We struggled together. He loosened his hold on my legs and I kicked out. I heard the clatter as his knife was booted to the other side of the room.

But now he had his arms around my chest, locked like a vice. I stabbed at him with my own dagger but he was gripping me from behind and I could not reach any vital point. He gasped as I kicked at him but he was much stronger than I, and did not let go. I felt my ribcage bend under the pressure. He was squeezing the life from me. As I weakened he inched his arms up my body. His grip was across my throat. I could not breathe.

I slumped down on the floor.

Now his fingers seized my skull with such force that I thought he would crush it. He pressed his fingertips hard onto my eyelids. Then he manoeuvred round so that he was in front of me.

'He said he wanted you captured whole,' Sandino grunted. He hooked his thumbnails into my eye sockets. 'He did not say he needed you with eyes.'

I let out a wail of terror.

I heard him grunt again.

A great fountain of warm liquid spouted onto my face.

It was blood. I could smell it.

He had gouged out my eyes!

Chapter Eighty-Two

Blood was pouring down my face, over my nose, into my mouth.

I was drowning in my own blood.

My eyes! I could see nothing. I put my hands to my face. I could feel the deep scratches his nails had made on my skin. I was sobbing with fear. My eyes were open yet I could see nothing. My face was wet. It was blood. I knew it yet I could not see it.

I was blinded. He had taken away my eyes.

There was a scuttling sound on the tiles beside me. He was coming at me again. But there was no need. With that amount of blood loss I was dead or soon would be.

I fell down upon my knees, crying and beating my fists upon the tiled floor. I was blinded. Eleanora would not love me now. How could I bear to live?

I raised my fingers to my face. I felt my eyeballs, the orbs in their sockets. What had happened? And why had he stopped attacking me? I could hear him still grunting and groaning.

A hand was on my back.

'Rise up, Matteo,' a voice said.

It was Paolo.

I began to cry even more wildly and shout out, 'I am done for! There is a brigand here who set about me! Take care, Paolo! Save yourself!'

'I have done for him,' Paolo said.

He came close and spoke to me in a calm voice.

'When you did not return I came to look for you. I saw this man attacking you and drew my dagger and stabbed him in the neck.'

'He is dead?'

'He is dead.'

'You are sure?'

'Most certainly. He lies in a great welter of his own blood and does not breathe. I killed him. He is dead.'

I moaned quietly. The thing I had wished for all my life had come to pass and I could not rejoice. Sandino was dead but I was blind.

'Wait here,' said Paolo. 'I will use my helmet and get some water from the stream.'

He came back in a few moments. 'Here, drink, and I will bathe your eyes.'

'Paolo,' I whispered, 'I cannot see.'

'This doesn't surprise me,' he said. 'He has pressed your eyes so viciously that they are scored and scarred with blood. But given time you may regain some of your sight.'

As the cool liquid splashed about my face a rainbow shot across my vision, dazzling and burning like fire.

'Can you see nothing?' Paolo asked.

I rolled my eyes. The coloured lights had gone. I shook my head. Then I felt for Paolo's hand.

'We should go,' he said. 'I will put rocks upon this man's body so that buzzards will not come and attract others to the place. It may be he is one of a band and they'll look for him.'

But Sandino had been alone. However he was paid and however he acted, it was for his own gain.

I made a bandage for my own eyes to protect them against the sun. Paolo took me to our horses and helped me into the saddle. We went slowly now, with him leading my horse by the rein, but we did not stop at any point in the day during that ride. At sunset he bathed my eyes again, and we lay down for the few hours of darkness of a summer night.

The next morning Paolo shook me awake. I sat up and his face blurred before me. I reached out my hands and touched his mouth and eyes. 'It is you,' I said. His features were grainy and unclear but I could recognize him as Paolo. I burst into tears.

We hugged each other.

'Once again you have saved my life, Paolo dell'Orte.'

'We are brothers,' he replied. 'What else should I do?'

Chapter Eighty-Three

B y the time we reached the outskirts of Florence I had good
sight in one eye and partial in the other. But my face was so
torn and bruised that I was in no fit state to present myself
at the house of Eleanora's uncle.

'Better not to enter by the front door anyway,' Paolo
counselled me. 'Even though Eleanora was at the court of Ferrara
you can't be sure where her uncle's sympathies lie. If he is for Pope
Julius and realizes that you have fought with the French he might
have you arrested. In any case' – he laughed – 'at the moment
you have the appearance of a robber, so his porter will not let you
through the gate.'

We had made the steep and difficult ascent to the area where
Eleanora's uncle lived in the hills to the north of the city, and had
now halted our horses some way off and were looking at the
d'Alciato villa.

'I must see Eleanora,' I said. I was anxious lest she agree to the
signing of a marriage contract before I had at least a chance to
speak to her. 'I will watch the house and seek some way to gain
entry.'

'Then I'll leave you and go on to Prato,' said Paolo. 'The closer
I am to meeting Elisabetta the more I realize how much I have
missed my sister over this last year or so.'

'I will find you after I have spoken to Eleanora,' I promised
him.

We embraced and he ruffled my hair, the way an older brother might do to a younger sibling.

'Have a care, Matteo,' he said.

I left my horse tethered among some trees and went forward between the vines and olive groves to where the house stood behind a high wall.

The d'Alciato estate was simpler to enter than the convent where I had first met Eleanora. It had been constructed neither to keep people in nor out in any serious way. I found a small door that led through the side wall of the property. Although it was locked I easily gained entry. Once inside I looked around. There was a kitchen garden laid out near the back of the main building but much of the rest was quite wild and overgrown in parts: clumps of flowers, plants, trees and bushes with paths leading in and out. On a patch of grass was a large tree in full leaf. From its height I should be able to see the back door and the windows of the house which gave onto the garden. I picked up some small stones from the ground and put them inside my shirt. Then I climbed up and concealed myself among the branches to await any opportunity that might present itself to me. As I waited I thought of the Medici who sought me. He had told the butcher in Ferrara not to kill me, and Sandino also had those instructions. It was August, but I shivered. Jacopo de' Medici did not just want me dead, he wanted to torture me. Eleanora had said that, by reputation, he was the cruellest of the Medici. He must need to make an example of anyone who stole from him, to show to others what would befall those that flout his power.

In the afternoon a woman came from the house, a nurse by her dress. She shepherded a clutch of little girls in front of her. There were four of them – Eleanora's cousins.

Then I saw her. Eleanora. She was walking behind them, a book held in one hand. Her hair was unbound and hung around her shoulders, dark, as her face was fair. Her dress was plain burgundy with white lace at her throat, the sleeves wide at the shoulder and closed tight at the cuff.

'Anna' – I heard Eleanora address the nurse – 'you may go and rest. I will mind the children for a while.' She laid her book down on a stone bench that stood on the grass not far from the tree in which I hid, and devoted herself to amusing the children.

For an hour or more they played as girls do, making believe they were at a great ball and dancing with imaginary lords and ladies. Using the flowers from the garden, they made garlands for their hair, Eleanora helping the littlest one. They strung the bells of the foxglove around their necks and used the little slippers from the fuchsia bush to place upon their fingernails to make them appear painted purple. I felt an ache as I watched them, and I knew the pain I felt was for the times at Perela, when Rossana and Elisabetta had enjoyed their girlhood with such innocent games.

The sun was lower in the sky when the nurse came back and called to the girls.

'It's time to wash and change. Are you coming in now, Eleanora?'

I held my breath.

'I will wait and read for a little while,' she replied.

The girls skipped after the nurse into the house. Eleanora sat down on the bench. She looked around her and sighed. Then she opened her book.

I took one of my pebbles and threw it down to land at her feet.

She stood up.

'Who is there?' she said.

I dropped from the tree onto the grass.

'Ah!' She put her hand to her breast.

I made a bow to her.

'Once again you fall out of the sky, Messer Matteo.'

She attempted to say this calmly but her voice was not steady.

I backed into the overgrown bushes and beckoned her to me.

She walked slowly. Then she was in my arms and we clung to each other.

'I thought I might never see you again,' she whispered.

'I followed you as soon as I could,' I said. 'I would follow you to the ends of the earth.'

I buried my face in her hair and I hugged her tightly and I felt the softness of her against me. We kissed. And kissed again. There was a wildness in our embrace, a thrilling, frightening passion. Her heartbeat resonated with mine in an unsteady rhythm. She drew away a little, but returned to put her mouth on mine. She took the fleshy part of my bottom lip between her teeth and bit it softly.

I took her in my arms again, and this time I was master of the kiss and she submitted to me.

When we broke apart she put her hands to my face and touched my scars. 'What ill times have befallen you?'

'My journey here has not been uneventful,' I said. 'But a long-time enemy of mine is dead and I am much easier in my person' – I covered her hands with my own – 'although a little battered by the experience.'

She told me how she had fared since we had last seen each other. Next year her uncle's eldest girl would be of marriageable age. He wanted to have Eleanora married before then. If this did not happen, her chances of a good match would be lost once the rest of his girls came of age.

'My uncle summoned me and, although the Duchess Lucrezia was sympathetic, the duke declared that I must go. My uncle is only trying to do what he thinks is best for me,' she explained.

'Has he contracted you in a marriage?' I asked.

'It was about to be done, but with things now in such a state here the papers are not signed.'

'What state do you mean?'

'Don't you know?' She looked at me in surprise. 'Florence is in turmoil. The French are in full retreat through the Alps. There has been a conference at Mantua, a meeting of the members of the Holy League to share out Italy among the victors. It has been decided. The Sforza family are to rule in Milan, and Florence will have the Medici.'

'But how can this be achieved?' I asked her. 'Cardinal Giovanni de' Medici is in the hands of the French. They captured him at Ravenna and brought him to Ferrara. I saw him there myself. He was well treated but he is still their prisoner. And the French intended to take him with them when they left Ferrara on their way north.'

'They did, but he was rescued during the journey and managed to escape to Mantua,' said Eleanora. 'The Pope has promised him an army to help him regain Florence.'

I wondered how Pier Soderini and the City Council would greet this news. Did they believe that Niccolò Machiavelli's militiamen would be able to defend them? The Pope had the Spanish on his side, with their skilled soldiers and many pieces of ordnance. I remembered Ravenna, and their wily commander, Ramón de Cardona. He had cannon that was almost equal to that of Duke Alfonso. And I had seen what happened to a city that was taken after siege – Bologna and Ravenna, the casual killing, the wanton destruction of beautiful things. What would these troops do to Florence, the jewel of Tuscany?

I tried to put myself in their heads. Which way would they approach? I imagined the terrain around Florence, the hills that surrounded her seat in the valley of the Arno. I'd had sight of the city from the mountains when I came from Melte, from the hill at Fiesole when I was there with the Maestro, from the pass by Castel Barta through the hills, and now from Eleanora's uncle's villa. Which way was open to an army approaching with soldiers and cannon to capture the city? I remembered pacing the streets of Imola with Leonardo da Vinci as he measured out each footstep and drew the houses and streets: the angle of every turn, the alignment of the corners. The outcome of his map as if he were a bird looking down upon the land below. If I were to view the terrain in such a way, which route would I choose?

And then I saw something else quite clearly. The Medici believed they owned Florence. They would not see it ruined by siege or sword. They would capture some other place close by and destroy it, and thus make an example to show the Florentines what fate awaited them and their city, should they continue to resist.

'I know what they will do.' I spoke aloud. 'They will attack Prato.'

I turned to Eleanora. I kissed her face, her neck, eyelids.

'I have friends in Prato. I must go and warn them.'

'No!' she cried. 'Matteo, don't put yourself in danger again.'

She put her arms around my neck and I felt my sense of duty weakening. But then I spoke to her, and although she was beginning to cry she listened to me. 'I am bound to go to Prato,' I said. 'If our positions were reversed, Paolo would come and rescue me. It is due to his quick thinking and bravery that I am here in this garden with you now, not lying dead on a mountain pass.'

'I will lose you.' She was crying now in earnest. 'You will be killed. And then I too will die.'

'Hush, hush.' I tried to dry her tears. 'I will come back, but there is something you must think on about our situation. I have no income.'

'Why do you tell me this?'

'It affects how things can be between us,' I said.

'What makes you think I would be concerned with the amount of money a man can lay claim to?' she asked.

'It is useful to have it.' I smiled. 'The obtaining of bread to eat is facilitated by its ownership.'

'Don't mock me!' Her eyes blazed.

'I did not mean to mock you. I intended only to relieve the situation with humour.'

'Humour! Being a man and having the means to control your way in life means that you may jest about such matters. But women cannot.'

'I am sorry for having offended you.' I tried to draw her to me, but she resisted. I let her go then and spoke seriously. 'Eleanora, I must go to Prato immediately and help my bond-brother Paolo and his sister Elisabetta. Forgive me for having offended you and let us not part here with a quarrel.' I went to her and kissed her lightly on the mouth. 'As soon as Paolo and Elisabetta are safe, I will return here and I will speak to you and your uncle. You may wish to consider if you would accept an offer of marriage from a penniless condottieri lieutenant.'

I went out through the garden door quickly lest I should falter in my resolve. But at the foot of the hill I could not resist turning one more time to look at her.

It is a memory I have of her, standing there, quietly weeping. Then I went on to find my horse, more slowly now, for my own eyes were filled with tears.

Chapter Eighty-Five

Cardinal Giovanni de' Medici and the papal commanders sent a messenger to parley.

The city magistrates treated him with disdain. They had confidence in the militiamen now assembling in the main square, lining up in neat ranks with shining helmets and gleaming breastplates. From the top of the basilica bell tower Paolo and I watched the emissary ride away, back to the enemy forces gathering outside the walls.

'What do you think?' Paolo asked me, indicating the mass of infantry and horsemen ranged against us.

'There are rather less of them than I thought there would be,' I said.

Paolo pointed to the far road that wound its way along the river. 'There is a baggage train approaching, moving very slowly.'

My eyesight was not yet completely restored, and at first I could not make out the bulk of movement he spoke of. But then after some minutes I saw it. I drew in my breath.

'Cannon?' I asked him.

He nodded. 'Spanish cannon. One of the sentries I spoke to said he'd heard that they might bring it up from the south.'

We had found out that the Spaniards, who would readily take the field for the Pope, were reluctant to fight for the Medici. But Cardinal Giovanni de' Medici had melted down his gold and sold his jewels and bribed them to continue. He now led them himself

451

and encouraged them with stories of the wealth awaiting them once they entered Florence. He had paid for their best arms and men. If the arrival of this good cannon was the result, then it would go hard for Prato.

Paolo turned to me. 'I think we should put the women in the church.'

In this matter Elisabetta did not argue with us. Paolo and I lifted the mattress with the old lady upon it. Elisabetta followed with the medicines and as much food and water as she could carry. A few women and children had already made their way there and the monks were ushering them inside. We found Elisabetta a good place at a side door near the steps leading down to the undercroft. If she had to flee, she was close to the door. If she needed more secure shelter, there was the crypt. We told her that one of us would come to the door every night to ensure she had enough food. Then we left her. It was all we could do.

They did not parley again.

Instead they brought the cannon to a spot that was outwith the range of our guns. I stood with a group of militiamen who had been detailed a section of the wall to defend. We made a trial shot at them from the guns at our post. Our ball fell short and one of the militiamen laughed and said, 'If we cannot reach them, then they cannot reach us.'

They took their time in setting their cannon. For an hour or so their bombardiers moved the pieces about, forward and back, jacking them up and down, until they settled on the best aim. Then they brought the metal balls and put them in a pile beside each piece. They had about nine for each cannon. Six cannon. Nine balls each. Fifty-four balls. And how many other pieces of artillery did they hold in the rear?

I walked along behind the wall we were defending. We had some breastworks built up but they were not deep. I thought of the defences of Mirandola and of Ravenna and how they had been breached. On my way I met Paolo. He was of the same mind. We went to speak to the commander. He would not listen.

'From where they are now they cannot strike us,' he declared. 'All their effort is for nothing. They will have to reassemble their cannon and move forward. Then our shot will destroy them.'

It was not this man's fault. He had never been in war, never experienced a campaign. His last taste of action was when the French had come to Florence and left behind the artillery he now used: short-range falconets and old-fashioned demi-culverins. He did not know that the Spanish were now the most professional soldiers in Europe.

They waited until the next day. Through the night we watched their campfires. We could hear them laughing and singing. Paolo and I went to see Elisabetta. In addition to food, Paolo gave her a dagger and I brought her a sword that I had found lying beside a slumbering militiaman. That one of them could sleep with his sword unbuckled while under siege gave an indication of their understanding of war.

Elisabetta slipped the dagger under the pillow of the old lady, Donna Cosma.

'You will know what to do with that?' Paolo asked her.

Elisabetta nodded.

We embraced and hugged each other and she cried a little.

'I will pray,' said Elisabetta. 'I will pray all night for you both. Know that, and take comfort from it.'

One of the priests came to bless us. The last time a priest had blessed me it had been Father Albieri laying his hand upon my head as a boy. I had been close to death then but did not know it. But now I was very aware of how much danger we were all in. I told Elisabetta to drag a bench against the door when we left. And at dawn we bade her farewell.

* * *

I went back to my position on the wall. My scornful militia soldier of yesterday was on duty there. He was trembling with excitement.

'They are preparing to fire!' he said. 'We have been spying on them from first light, and they are preparing to fire now.'

I edged my head over the wall just in time to see the gunner for their first gun in line go forward with his taper to light the fuse.

'Take cover!' I shouted.

There was a muffled roar and a few seconds later a great splat. The ball was on the sward in front of us. It had fallen short.

'I told you! I told you!' The militia soldier was almost dancing in delight. 'They cannot reach us! It is as I said. They cannot reach us!'

But I knew the cannon beside it would have been set for a much longer range.

'Get down,' I shouted at him. 'Get down, you fool.'

The roar of the next gun sounded and the ball came flying over our heads. It socked into the wall behind us, tearing off a huge chunk of masonry.

Seconds later the third piece fired. It crashed directly into our parapet, blasting a huge hole in our defences and completely obliterating my dancing militiaman.

They had found the mark.

Chapter Eighty-Six

We had about twenty minutes' grace as they adjusted the other cannon to match their third shot.

Paolo and I bawled orders and the Florentine militiamen, slack-jawed with shock, responded as best they could. They ran scurrying as we commanded them to collect furniture from houses and shops and build it up against the walls.

'It is not enough,' said Paolo in agitation. 'It is not nearly enough.'

But it was all we had time for. By mid morning their cannonade had begun in earnest. Heavy smoke hung in the air as each explosion rocked the parapet. They were concentrating fire on one part of the wall. They meant to make the breach and enter there. As we rushed to defend the place I saw a flood of citizens – the old, and women carrying children – hurrying to the church.

Then their guns stopped. I had been counting each blast. They had not used all their ammunition. What had happened? I risked a look. Their infantry were advancing to the breach. Crossbowmen with large palliasses made an impenetrable shield. Behind them a schiltron of pikemen protected their musketeers. They wheeled into strict formations of diamond shapes and waited. But none of the Florentine militiamen from Prato rushed out to challenge them.

'Fire our cannon!' Paolo roared. 'It is time to fire our cannon!'

No one answered him.

He sent a messenger to the battery. The man came back and said the commander there was dead. There were only three gunners left and they were doing what they could. They managed to shoot off a ball, which brought down a swathe of infantry but did not halt the advance. The enemy moved forward more briskly. Now they were under the arc of our cannonshot. It was too late for us to return fire.

They took aim with their crossbows. Their target was our bombardiers. Through the deadly rustle of the arrows we heard the dying shrieks of the men defending the abutments on our walls. Then the arquebuses came forward from the ranks.

They loosed a volley of shot. Then another, and another.

Beside me Paolo staggered back. I looked to him. There was a great smear of blood across his chest. How could that be? He had on his breastplate and his collar.

He was still upright, a stupefied expression on his face.

Then I saw the reason for the blood. There was a hole in the centre of the metal.

'You are wounded.' My voice trembled as I spoke. 'Paolo, you are wounded in the chest.'

He looked down.

'Ah,' he said. 'That is why I cannot stand.'

And upon saying that, he fell at my feet.

My heart gave a great leap of fear, and I bent and unbuckled his armour, both front and back.

'Inferior metal,' he gabbled as I was doing this. 'I should have purchased a breastplate from the Milanese. They have the reputation for the best quality armour.'

I thought, He is delirious.

I had to stop the bleeding. I took my dagger and tore off my shirt sleeve, wadding the material against his wound to staunch the flow.

Behind us there was uproar. Then hordes of militiamen charged past us, pushing and shoving and flinging down their weapons as they went.

'They are running away,' Paolo gasped. 'Save yourself, Matteo. Save yourself.'

His blood was seeping through the rough bandage I had made. Paolo needed help and medication and I thought of Elisabetta. I lifted him up.

Behind me I heard the sound of the invaders pouring through the breach.

I half carried, half dragged Paolo to the church. I thumped on the side door.

From inside they screamed out, 'Sanctuary! Sanctuary! You must honour the sanctuary of a holy place!'

'I have a wounded man here!' I shouted. 'One of your own defenders. Let us in!'

'Go away!' they shouted back. 'Go away!'

I raised my fist and I battered on the door.

'Dell'Orte!' I yelled. 'Dell'Orte!'

Elisabetta pulled the door open. People within tore at her, clawed at her hair and skirts, trying to stop her. But she pushed the door wide enough ajar for me to carry Paolo through the gap before it was slammed shut again.

The women inside threw the bench back against the door. From the nave came the sound of breaking glass. A flaming brand was thrust through the broken window and a dozen children began howling at the same time.

We stretched Paolo out on the floor. I examined the place in his chest where the gunshot had gone in. It was close to his heart. He was dying.

Elisabetta looked at me. I shook my head.

She poured water on a cloth and dripped it onto his lips.

He opened his eyes and looked at me and said quite clearly, 'My brother. You are my brother.'

'Yes,' I said. 'But do not speak, save your strength.'

'I had another brother once. But he died.'

'I know this,' I said.

'I killed him.'

'You did not.'

'Yes, I did. My cowardice killed them all.'

'No, no, Paolo. That is not true.'

'Yes it is.'

He gripped the front of my tunic and pulled me to him. 'I have never told you this, Matteo, but I heard them.'

'What?'

'I heard them,' he repeated.

'Who? Who are you speaking of?'

'My sisters. My sisters screaming.' He put his hands over his face. 'I hear them still.'

'What happened was not your fault.'

'Don't you hear what I say?' He spoke with sudden strength. 'I heard my sisters begging for mercy. My mother, as she leaped from the window, clutching Dario, cried out as they were dashed on the rocks below. I heard all of this and I did nothing.'

I took his hands in mine. 'It was not your fault,' I repeated.

'But I was a coward. I should have come out of the hiding place and fought.'

'If you had come out from your hiding place you and your sisters would have been murdered,' I said. 'You would have fought, but you would have fought and died.'

'I am dying now, am I not, Matteo?'

I could not answer him, nor could I take my eyes from his face. Therefore he read the truth in mine.

'Better I had died then,' he said, 'than do what I did, and live the life of a coward.'

'Then you would have disobeyed your father's ordinance,' I said.

His eyes searched my face.

'A son cannot disobey the law his father sets down.'

'My father did not know that his family would be so cruelly treated.'

'Your father was a soldier,' I insisted. 'A soldier in the employ of the Borgia. He must have seen what soldiers do, what some men take as their right when conquering.'

Paolo seemed to consider this.

'Who would have rescued Elisabetta and Rossana?' I pressed on. 'They would not have managed their escape without you. They would have been slaughtered on the mountainside. And it was you, and you alone, who gave Elisabetta reason to go on. You took her to live with your uncle and she made another life for herself. Therefore your father knew that you must be saved. And if you had disobeyed his rule, how could you raise your face to his in Heaven?'

Paolo nodded. His eyes were filmed. He was slipping from us. I placed my lips to his ear.

'You will meet him, your father, in Heaven, and you will be able to say, "My father, I did as you commanded me. It has troubled my mind ever since and cost me grievously, but I did the thing you asked." And he will say to you, "Welcome, my son," and he will call you by your name, "Paolo". And you will see them all. Rossana, and your mother. They will kiss you. And little Dario will run to meet you, and you will swing him on your shoulders as you used to.'

My voice faltered. I glanced at Paolo's face. His eyes were staring, sightless. I put my fingers to the side of his neck. No pulse beat there.

Had he heard me? I sat back on my heels.

'Matteo!'

I turned.

Tears were running from Elisabetta's face.

'Matteo!' she sobbed. 'What wondrous things to say to him.'

I put out my hand and shut down his eyes. There would be no time for a proper funeral, no opportunity to hire a good orator to make a speech for the passing of this young man. No one would fashion a death mask for Paolo dell'Orte. But I would not forget his face. Paolo was a true brother to me. He saved my life at Mirandola and again when he killed the brigand Sandino on my behalf. In his life he had little to be ashamed of. It was I, Janek the gypsy, also known as Matteo, who carried true guilt.

I am the traitor, the knave, the coward. I am the one to be despised. No mother or father will run to meet me in the land of the saints. The dell'Orte family will not greet me kindly or let me walk with them among the clouds.

I rubbed my face with my hands as sobs racked me.

Elisabetta had knelt down beside me to say a prayer beside the body of her brother. She put her arm around my shoulder.

I leaned against her. 'There is something I must tell you,' I said.

Chapter Eighty-Seven

So I told Elisabetta the true story of the boy she knew as Matteo.

I told her first of all that my name was not Matteo, but Janek.

Janek, the gypsy.

I had no fine father who had died leaving me in the care of a wicked uncle. I had only a grandmother. She had loved me, it is true, but she was a gypsy. A Romany woman with great skill in healing. She had died and I had been left destitute and had resorted to thieving, an occupation in which, I found, I had great skill, especially in picking locks. Then I had fallen in with Sandino and his gang of brigands, who promised me good food and my own pirate ship if I did this one task for them. Sandino instructed me to steal a most precious thing, the Great Seal of the Medici family, which he told me had been looted from the Medici Palace on the Via Larga in Florence when the Medici were forced to leave the city many years ago.

We had to wait until after Lucrezia's Borgia's wedding to Duke Alfonso in Ferrara, and then I found a certain priest, a Father Albieri, who took me to a room in a house with a locked cupboard where the seal was kept. When I had stolen this seal, the priest and I returned with it to our rendezvous point with Sandino. There the priest told Sandino that he had brought him the true treasure. And when the priest had said this Sandino had spoken to one of his men saying, 'The Borgia will pay us well for the Medici Seal.'

And Father Albieri had been shocked, for he had thought Sandino was working for the Medici. And the priest saw that he had been betrayed in this. But it was too late for him to escape. Sandino killed the priest by hitting him with his cudgel. So I tried to run away.

But Sandino came after me and I fell in the river and the companions of Leonardo da Vinci rescued me. They wrapped me up in the cloak of Felipe, the master of the household. As I revived after almost drowning they asked me my name and, next to my cheek, I saw the pilgrim badge that Felipe wore on his cloak, and I recognized it as the badge of St Matthew. Felipe, who was trained and employed to do accounts, had a devotion to the disciple of Christ called Matthew, who had been a tax collector. So, not wishing to tell my real name, I took that one for my own.

Thus, as the boy Matteo, I came to Perela. I was happy to be with the dell'Orte family, and I loved them and was fearful to tell the truth in case they cast me out. And when we left I believed I was safe and did not know that Sandino would track me there. But when I was at Senigallia I heard Sandino's men speak of the planned attack on Perela, so I had ridden as fast as I could to warn them. But I was too late. Thus it was my fault that they had suffered in such a way. I did not deserve to have Paolo and her call me brother. I did not merit their good grace.

'It was not Paolo the brigands sought when they ransacked your father's keep,' I told her. 'I was the boy they searched for.'

'I know some of this already, Matteo,' said Elisabetta.

I stared at her. 'How can you know any of this?'

'I have had years to ponder on what befell my family,' she replied. 'There was always a mystery there. I was unable to think properly as Paolo and I journeyed to Milan, but after we settled on my uncle's farm I began to go over in my mind the things that had taken place. I thought about what the monk in the hospital in Averno had asked us, and then, when he wrote to me with more information, I pieced it together. For the men who attacked our keep did not ask for Paolo by name, they asked about a boy. And I came to believe the boy they sought was you, Matteo.

'Also' – she paused – 'I read through your grandmother's papers that were in the box you gave me alongside her recipe book.'

'Her papers?'

'Yes,' said Elisabetta. 'She—'

A hellish hammering began at the main door of the church.

'Open up! Open up in there!'

'Sanctuary!' the people around us wailed together. 'Sanctuary!'

There came the thud of a battering ram and the sound of splintering wood.

An older woman hoisted herself up to one of the windows and called to those outside.

'This is a church where women and children are sheltering. Go and take what you want in the town and leave us in peace.'

'There are soldiers in there!' a voice shouted. 'We saw them go in.'

The woman looked at me, then she called back, 'The soldiers were wounded and have since died. There are only women and children here now.'

Beside Eleanora an old man got up from his seat.

'You!' He pointed at me. 'Get out there and fight. By remaining here you jeopardize us all.'

The thudding on the door started up again.

'I will go,' I said.

'No,' said Elisabetta. 'It's a trick to get us to open the door. Then they will rampage through.'

'I will go out via the bell tower,' I said, and as she began to protest I went on, 'It sounds more like a mob out there than proper troops. Perhaps I can draw them away from here.'

'If you go out, Matteo, you will die.'

'Yes,' I said. 'But then, perhaps you will not.'

'Do not go out for that reason.'

'Not only for that reason,' I said. 'Look at them.' I indicated the children huddled in against the sides of their mothers and the old people. They were mainly peasants or workers, those too poor to afford to have arms to defend themselves, the weak, those who could not escape in time, or buy their ransom. 'For all of them,' I said.

We went into the bell tower and climbed the wooden ladders to the top. I pulled up the rope of one of the bells. 'I am going to throw this outside and climb down. Cut the rope, or draw it up quickly when I reach the ground,' I instructed Elisabetta, 'else they may gain access this way.'

She took my face into her hands and kissed me. 'Know this,' she said. 'You are my brother and nothing you ever were, or said or did, will ever make me think ill of you.'

I turned away quickly to save us both from tears. Then I flung the rope from the top of the tower and, grasping it hand over hand, I lowered myself down.

When I was ten feet or more from the ground I spun round to look below me. The buildings around the piazza were on fire and groups of soldiers were rushing about carrying their spoils of war. The mob in front of the church had temporarily stopped their assault on the door. They could not have spotted me or they would have rushed to attack me. I slid down the rest of the way as fast as I could, then I yanked on the rope end to signal to Elisabetta to cut it at the top or pull it up quickly.

Drawing my sword, I ran to the front door of the church. Immediately I saw the reason the battering on the church door had stopped. On the front steps, facing a mob of mercenaries and camp followers, stood two figures. One, dressed in red, was the Cardinal de' Medici. The other, holding a sword, was Jacopo de' Medici.

Upon seeing me Jacopo de' Medici pulled a pistol from his belt.

Chapter Eighty-Eight

I stood still. At this range a sword was no defence against shot.

'Here,' he said to me. 'Take this and stand with us.'

I stared at him stupidly.

'To me, Matteo! Or whatever you call yourself. Now!'

I jumped to beside him and took the pistol.

Just in time, for the mob, seeing their attention diverted, surged towards us.

Cardinal Giovanni de' Medici was fat, and in his robes he made a huge red splash against the door of the church. 'Stop!' he bellowed. 'In the name of the Lord God. In the name of the Vatican, and of the Pope in Rome, I command you to turn away from this house of God!'

But a dragon unleashed cannot be re-chained. These men were mad with battle lust, ravenous with the need to satisfy themselves with gold, loot, women and killing. It was a lost cause. You cannot plead or reason with a mob.

'Listen to me,' he thundered. 'Anyone who steps across this threshold will suffer the wrath of the Medici!'

That checked them, but it was plain that it would only last a moment. Then they would be upon us and tear us apart.

Instead of moving back Jacopo de' Medici stepped forward to meet them. He addressed the two or three at the forefront of the main group.

'What is your name?' He pointed to the man in the centre.

The man would not reply, but someone in the crowd shouted, 'Luca! His name is Luca!'

'Matteo!' Jacopo commanded me in a loud voice. 'Strike your flint and aim your pistol. If anyone in the crown moves, anyone at all, shoot first this man named Luca.'

I raised my pistol and took aim, placing the weapon along my arm to try to keep my hand from shaking.

The man Luca stepped back quickly.

'The cardinal and I will kill the men on either side of him,' Jacopo added with a malicious sneer.

Luca's two companions looked at each other in confusion. Then they too moved back a pace or two.

'Shoot them in the belly,' Jacopo added loudly. 'That way you have less chance of missing. And they will die in agony.'

'Let us aim lower,' advised the cardinal. 'That way, even if they survive, they will be fit for nothing.'

One of Luca's companions slid into the crowd behind him and disappeared. Luca and the one who was left exchanged desperate glances.

'We'll find another place,' said Luca's friend. 'There are plenty of other buildings in this town for looting.'

'Yes.' Luca turned to the crowd behind him. He raised his hands high above his head. 'To the town hall!' he shouted. 'To the town hall!'

The crowd shuffled and turned about.

But Cardinal Giovanni de' Medici was not finished with him. 'Know this, Luca,' he shouted after him in a loud voice. 'If this church is violated I will seek you out. The retribution of Heaven and Earth will descend upon you.'

My legs weakened and I leaned against the door.

Jacopo de' Medici grabbed me roughly and turned me

round, pushing my face against the door of the church. With his fingers he gripped me by my neck. Then he took the pistol from my hand.

'I have no skill in marksmanship,' I told him. 'I doubt if I could have made true aim at him.'

'It would have made no difference had you done so,' said Jacopo. 'The weapon is not loaded.'

Chapter Eighty-Nine

s Cardinal Giovanni de' Medici organized soldiers to guard the church, I made a plea to Jacopo de' Medici for the safety of Elisabetta and the old lady Donna Cosma, and a decent burial for Paolo dell'Orte.

Jacopo de' Medici agreed to my requests on condition that I gave my word that I would not try to escape him again. He detailed armed men to escort me until he would summon me to his presence.

A priest was called and he conducted a funeral service for Paolo, and my bond brother was laid to rest in the crypt of the basilica. Then the Medici men-at-arms carried Donna Cosma in a litter to her house and I helped Elisabetta settle her there.

'I must leave you now,' I said to her, 'and go and discover what fate the Medici have planned for me.'

'Before you do,' she replied, 'there is something you should know.'

She unwrapped the bundle in which she had carried the medicines and food to the church. 'With your grandmother's recipe book were these documents, Matteo. You have never read them, have you?'

'No,' I said. 'As I young child I did not know how to read.'

'To compile these books your grandmother must have been able to read and write. Didn't you think it strange that she never taught you these skills?'

'I didn't think about it.'

'I believe I know why she wanted you to remain illiterate,' said Elisabetta. 'These documents pertain to you. She would not have wanted you to read them. If you had understood the information they contained when you were a child, you might have spoken about them, and put yourself in danger.'

'In what kind of danger?'

'All kinds of danger. Most particularly abduction or murder.'

'I do not understand. Let me see.'

'There are several things here, letters and other documents, but the most important is this.' Elisabetta handed me a piece of parchment. It was a baptismal notice with the date, 1492, and the child's name written upon it: *Jacomo*.

'What has this to do with me?' I asked her.

'That is your baptismal certificate, Matteo.'

'That cannot be,' I said. 'I am Janek. It is the name my grandmother always called me.'

'She would do that to protect you.'

I looked again at the certificate. The priest had signed it along the bottom: *Albieri d'Interdo*. Albieri d'Interdo. The same priest who had led me to the Medici Seal in Ferrara.

'The rest of these papers leave no doubt, Matteo,' Elisabetta went on. 'You *are* that boy child.'

I looked again at the baptismal certificate, and this time I read it more carefully: *On this day at the twelfth hour I baptized a boy child, newly born to the woman Melissa and the man, Jacopo de' Medici.*

I saw the name written there.

My father.

Jacopo de' Medici.

Chapter Ninety

M EDICI.
    I am Medici.
    The Medici.
Selfish, arrogant, proud, greedy, disdainful, brutal.
Wise, artistic, noble, generous, stately, compassionate.

For two days the conquering troops raged through Prato. Men
gone mad – slashed and pillaged and set fires and destroyed the
town, killing more than two thousand people.

Florence surrendered. Cardinal Giovanni de' Medici, his
brother and his cousins entered the city. Pier Soderini had fled and
Niccolò Machiavelli was banished.

Florence was returned to the descendants of Cosimo and
Lorenzo the Magnificent.

Jacopo de' Medici summoned me to his presence. He was
ensconced in a house near their former palace on the Via Larga
and my guards took me to where he sat in an upper room behind
a huge desk.

'I have had great difficulty in finding you these last years,' he
said. 'You were expert in eluding those I sent to track you down.'

'I thought you meant to have me killed,' I said. 'I have only just
now discovered that we have kinship.'

'I would term it more than mere kinship!' he snapped. 'I am
your father.'

470

I met his angry look with one of equal force. 'While you pursued your own life, others fulfilled that role.'

He glared at me. Then his look softened. 'I will relate to you the circumstances of your birth and then you may judge me.'

He told me he had been my age when I was conceived. The Medici used Castel Barta as a hunting lodge and my mother was the daughter of the housekeeper who lived there to look after the building. The housekeeper was an intelligent and honest woman, part Romany and very skilled in folklore, with great knowledge of natural things. Melissa, her daughter, my mother, was only fifteen when she and Jacopo de' Medici fell in love.

'I did love your mother most passionately,' Jacopo said. 'You were the result. But I was contracted in marriage to another family and I could not legitimize your birth. So you stayed there with your mother and grandmother and I visited as often as I could. Your mother died in the summer of 1494, when you were about two years old. Those were troubled times. A few months later there were riots and unrest and the Medici were driven from Florence. Our enemies would have killed you. The safest thing I could do was to make you disappear. We obtained a gypsy wagon and your grandmother took you away. It was at this point that the Great Seal of the Medici was given into the safekeeping of a kinsman of the Medici, the one priest that I trusted, Father Albieri, of the parish of Castel Barta.

'The Medici were dispossessed, and had to wander round the courts of Europe seeking help where we could. I was a hunted man myself and could not even send your grandmother money for fear it would be found out. And then I lost track of where you were. Your grandmother had travelled as far north as Venice so that you would be safe, but the Plague was rampant in the last place I knew you had been. I came to believe that you and your grandmother had perished.

'To begin with, the brigand Sandino was an agent of the family of the woman I had married. She was not wicked but she was very jealous, and a woman knows when she is not loved. The years passed and there was no child. She would fly into rages, accusing me of being unable to give her children, and I, in anger, one day declared that I knew my seed could bring forth a son as it had already done so.'

'She said nothing.'

'One should fear rage that is silent. Anger that boils and rants is a perceivable danger and can be dealt with, but quiet malice is a deadly foe.'

'My wife found out that you had been born at Castel Barta and she engaged Sandino to hunt you down and kill you. But to begin with he could find no trace of you.'

'Then Cesare Borgia entered the Romagna to try to secure the papal territories by any means, and he also used Sandino as one of his many spies. By this time Sandino had picked up your trail by means of information from an assassin he knew. This man had bought poison from an old gypsy woman he said was keeping a young boy concealed in her wagon.'

'Why, I remember that man!' I exclaimed. 'He forced my grandmother to make some poppy juice for him. She was very frightened, and as soon as he left we moved on through the mountains during the night.'

'She was wise to do so,' said Jacopo, 'for now Sandino was very close to you. But he needed to be sure that you were the boy he sought. He knew where you had been born so he went to the parish priest of Castel Barta, Father Albieri, and pretended he was working for me and that I wanted to find you to bestow money and title upon you. Father Albieri said he did not know where you were but that he would be able to recognize you if he did meet you again.'

'But how could he?' I asked. 'He had not seen me since I was a young child. My grandmother did not take me anywhere near Castel Barta until she knew she was dying.'

Jacopo de' Medici got up and came from behind his desk. He

turned my head round in the same manner as he had done when pushing my face into the church door at Prato. 'Just below your hairline there is a mark on each side of your neck.'

The mark of the midwife's fingers. I recalled the quip made by Giulio, Wardrobe Master of the castle in Averno, when advising me to have my hair cut.

'Father Albieri was a good man, but naive,' Jacopo went on. 'He told Sandino that if you were indeed Jacomo de' Medici then you were the true owner of the Medici Seal, which he had been given to keep in trust.

'Sandino saw the opportunity to make a great deal of money. The seal could be used to forge many kinds of documents, bank orders, letters of conspiracy, enough even to bring down the Council of Florence. He knew that Cesare Borgia would pay him well if he could bring it to him. Therefore Sandino devised a plan whereby he would have both you and the Medici Seal.

'For safety Father Albieri had hidden the seal in the garden of his cousin in Ferrara. He did not tell Sandino the location of the seal but said that he was travelling to Ferrara to attend the wedding of Lucrezia Borgia and Duke Alfonso. He told Sandino to arrange for you to come to him on some pretext, and if you were truly Jacomo he would bring both you and the Medici Seal to an agreed rendezvous point. He did this in the belief that Sandino was intent on taking you safely back to your true family.'

'Yet when we met he did not tell me my true identity,' I said.

'You were a very young boy. He probably thought it wiser to keep the secret and allow me, your father, to be the one to tell you.'

'The priest did insist I carry the seal,' I said. 'And I think that was how he had arranged with Sandino to tell him that I was indeed a Medici. For when we arrived at our rendezvous point Father Albieri kept his hand on my shoulder and spoke distinctly to Sandino, saying, "I've brought you that which you sought."'

'And as soon as he had uttered those words his life was forfeit,' said Jacopo dryly. 'Sandino had no further use for him.'

'I should have guessed there was some subterfuge being played out,' I said, 'for the lock I had to open was very simple. And although I did not think anything of it at the time, the priest, Father Albieri, asked me to kneel for a blessing. When I did so, he put his hands on my neck and parted my hair at the back. I believed he was giving me absolution for my sin of theft, but he was confirming that I was your son.'

'He commented on these marks when he baptized you at Castel Barta,' said Jacopo. 'Though anyone with close familiarity with the Medici would see that your bloodline is apparent by the set of your eyes.'

I put my hand to my face.

Jacopo noticed and said, 'It is very obvious to me that you are Jacomo, my son.'

The set of my eyes.

There was one man who had looked most intently at my eyes. Leonardo da Vinci. In the monk's refectory in Milan he had used his fingers to encircle them. At that time he had said, 'You will find your own truth, Matteo.' Now I had found the truth – or rather it had found me. And it was confusing, exhilarating, and profoundly disturbing.

'Because of me Father Albieri lost his life,' I said.

'He sent word to me that he was meeting my agent Sandino and would escort you and the seal into my presence. I knew at once that Father Albieri's life was in peril for I had not employed any agent called Sandino to look for you, as I believed you to be dead.'

'Sandino murdered the priest,' I said. 'He battered his head until his brains spilled out of his skull.'

Jacopo nodded. 'Yes,' he said. 'I can see why. Sandino would need to kill Father Albieri to prevent him from coming to tell me that my son was found and that Cesare Borgia had the Medici Seal.'

'I saw Sandino do it. It's why I ran from him.'

'You did well to escape. Sandino would have murdered you for his own gain without a moment's thought. When Father Albieri disappeared, I realized that I must meet cunning with cunning. I made it known that I wished to employ Sandino, and that I would pay double what any other person offered if he brought you to me alive.'

'I think that saved my life,' I said.

'I am glad that I have been of some value to you.'

I acknowledged his point with an inclination of my head.

'My instructions to Sandino were that he must keep me informed at all times as to his progress,' said Jacopo. 'And I also let your description be known throughout the gypsy community, and asked them to contact me if they had any news of you.'

'So that was how you came to be pursuing me in the forest near Lodi!'

'You must tell me how you eluded capture on that occasion.'

'It is to do with the length of cloth required for the habits of monastic orders of the Church.' I thought of myself hiding under Eleanora's skirts. And then I thought of what I had been doing earlier that day at the farm with Elisabetta and Paolo, and all the events that had entangled my life with those of the Dell'Orte family came rushing into my head.

'I see that I have given you much to think about.' Jacopo de' Medici had been watching my face.

'In avoiding capture over the years I have brought trouble and mishap to those who helped me,' I told him. 'There are people to whom I am obliged.'

'Then it is your duty to honour the debts you owe in the best way you can,' he replied, 'and as your father I will help you to do this.'

So I raised my hands and, for the last time, lifted the corded pouch from round my neck. I placed the worn leather bag on the desk and opened it up. From inside I took the Great Seal of the Medici and I gave it into the hand of my father.

He held it up so that the sunlight slanting through the window shutters shone on its surface. 'You have done well to keep it safe for so long.'

In truth I did not know whether I was pleased with this praise or not.

Jacopo de' Medici then rubbed his fingers across the raised matrix of his family's coat of arms. 'My cousin, the cardinal, will be especially glad this is back in safekeeping. He may wish to use it to authenticate his first Papal Proclamation.'

'He is only a cardinal,' I said in astonishment. 'I do not think our present Pope would let anyone to make a Papal Bull on his behalf.'

'Pope Julius is dying,' said Jacopo. 'In the Vatican, before long, there will be a Medici.'

Jacopo returned the seal to its pouch and placed it around his own neck. Then he took me by the shoulders and stared into my face.

'My son,' he said softly. 'Before you leave to go about your business, I would like you at least once to call me father.'

'Father.' I tried the word. It did not sit easily on my tongue.

Chapter Ninety-One

There was one man whom I regarded as a more true father.

And as I went to find Elisabetta I began to think how I might contrive a way to repay the support Leonardo da Vinci had given me during the most troubled part of my life. To him I owed a debt above all others. Without the intervention of the Maestro and his two companions I would have drowned under the waterfall. His own breath brought me back from the dead. And throughout the life that I had lived, from rough boy to manhood, I had been nourished by his guidance, his intellect and his generosity of spirit.

Elisabetta was back in the house in Prato. In part recompense for the damage to the town the Medici had agreed to replace the roofs of the buildings still standing. Donna Cosma lay on her mattress in the room on the ground floor. It was clear that she did not have long to live. I went with Elisabetta to sit in the garden and I placed a bag of coins Jacopo de' Medici had given me on the table.

'This money is yours by right,' I said, 'for the losses you have suffered. It will help you to establish an apothecary shop of your own and you may live here independently.'

'Matteo,' she said, 'I am going back to Kestra.'

'Kestra? There is nothing for you there.'

'Baldassare is there.'

'Baldassare?' I said in surprise. Then I recalled the man from the neighbouring farm who was always there helping whenever I visited Paolo and Elisabetta. 'The farmer, your uncle's neighbour?'

'Yes,' said Elisabetta. 'That is the man.'

'He is much older than you.'

'I know, and it is one of the reasons that I have accepted his marriage offer. He is dependable and will give me stability.'

'Do you love him?'

'I have a deep affection and respect for him, as he has for me.' Her face had the appearance of contentment.

'I believe that will be sufficient for both of us,' she said. 'He has asked me often over these last years to marry him. I put him off because, when my uncle's farm was lost, I felt that I had nothing to donate to the marriage. He did not care about that. It was me that he wanted. But now I have learned the recipes from your grandmother's books and am able to make her healing medicines, I can bring this skill and income to Baldassare as my dowry.'

'This also can be your dowry.' I pointed at the bag that lay between us on the table. 'I gift it to you as your kin brother. On the condition,' I added, 'that you ask me as a guest to your wedding ceremony.'

I wrote Eleanora a long letter.

I let her know my real identity, and also the things that had happened to me before we met. I asked her if she might understand the constraints I was under and be sympathetic to the actions I had taken.

I also told her my plans for the future. That I wanted to attend the medical school in Bologna, where in time I might become a doctor.

I stated that I would be happy if she would share this new life with me. That I recalled she had expressed an interest in the works of the influential thinkers and writers. That with my father's patrimony she might pursue her interests as I continued my studies.

I told her that I loved her.

Chapter Ninety-Two

I n time I received a letter inviting me to call at the Villa d'Alciato to discuss a marriage contract between myself and Eleanora d'Alciato.

Jacopo de' Medici had appointed a secretary to accompany me in order to agree appropriate terms. Eleanora's uncle was a stout merchant with a florid face, and we sat in his office while he fussed over each detail, adding and deleting clauses here and there. Songbirds were chirruping to each other near the windows. The last time I had spoken to Eleanora we were in the garden, and I remembered how we had kissed on that occasion. Today was very hot, with the shutters drawn against the sun. I doubted if she would be outside, and I wondered whereabouts in the house she might be.

A memory came to me of us dancing together in the piazza in Ferrara, her face upturned to mine.

I stood up.

'Please excuse me,' I said.

Eleanora's uncle glanced up, nodded and returned to his scrutiny of the document in front of him.

I opened the door into the hallway.

A flurry of skirts.

I ran after her and gripped her wrist.

'You listen outside doors!' I laughed.

She struggled to free herself and I saw that she was not amused.

'Of course I am listening!' she said. 'Do you think I would allow myself to be haggled over like meat in a market and be content to know nothing about it?'

I raised an eyebrow. 'I thought it was by your good grace that I had been invited here to come to an agreement for our wedding?'

'Well then you were wrong, sir,' Eleanora retorted. 'My opinion was not sought in the matter. My uncle read the letter you sent me and he decided that your offer must not be refused. He told me that he would take care of everything. He said the Medici had money to spare and we would have some of it.'

'Money!' I exclaimed. 'This is not about money, Eleanora.'

'Indeed it is,' she said. 'That, and fear.'

'Fear?' I repeated in bewilderment.

'How could my uncle refuse a request from a Medici? He would be too frightened not to comply.'

'Are you frightened of me now?' I asked her, and as I did so it occurred to me that it might be no bad thing if this crackling, spitting Eleanora were to be a little bit frightened of me.

In answer her eyes flashed emerald fire. 'I do not give myself to anyone for fear, or for gold.'

I dropped her wrist. 'I thought you loved me, Eleanora,' I said stiffly. 'I am sorry if I was mistaken. I will go now and instruct the secretary to break off negotiations.'

'Yes, you do that,' she said. And as I turned away she called after me scornfully, '*Jacomo de' Medici*.'

'What?' I turned back and faced her, feeling my own temper rise. 'Why do you call out my name in such a manner?'

'Is that not who you are?' She pulled my letter from her sleeve. 'It is how you signed yourself when you wrote to me.' She stabbed her finger angrily at the paper.

'What of it? Am I to deny my rightful birth name?'

'I do not know any Jacomo de' Medici!' she cried. 'The man I love is called Matteo!'

The Medici Seal

I stretched out and plucked the letter from her grasp and tossed
it away. Then I took hold of her wrists with both my hands and
pulled her to me. And we kissed until we had to stop in order to
breathe. Then I held her close to me and I said, 'For you, then, I
will always be Matteo.'

Chapter Ninety-Three

'I will call you Matteo.'

The Maestro cupped my face with his hands and he kissed me and embraced me warmly.

He had come to Florence on his way to Rome. Jacopo de' Medici's words had come true. Pope Julius had died and Cardinal Giovanni de' Medici was now installed in the Vatican as Leo X. And at my behest the Medici had offered artistic commissions for Leonardo da Vinci to undertake in Rome.

'Matteo,' the Maestro said again, and he put his arm around me and led me to sit beside him on a bench.

I was reassured by his greeting. For although I had written to him and told him all of my true life history and asked his forgiveness, I was apprehensive as to how he would welcome into his presence a person who had deceived him.

'When I first met you, I lied—' I began.

'Of course!' he interrupted me, laughing. 'You took a name to use that was not yours.'

'You knew from the very beginning!'

'I surmised it afterwards. I noticed you glancing at Saint Matthew's badge on Felipe's cloak as you awoke.'

Truly it should not have surprised me. I had seen his sketches. The Maestro's eye could record, by pen on paper, the motion of a bird in flight.

'It intrigued me that you should do that,' he went on. 'And as the days passed, many things about you fascinated me: your speech, your wide knowledge, your directness, your general manner.'

'It was much later that I wondered if you had some inkling,' I said. 'When we stood together before your fresco of the Last Supper in Milan.'

'Ah yes,' he replied. 'On that occasion you were anxious lest I should be disappointed with you for losing your place at Pavia University. And you were brooding on my image of the Iscariot.'

I recalled how he had drawn my attention away from the face of Judas to that of Matthew, the Apostle, and reached out with his mind to try to ease my troubled thoughts.

'There was always something about your eyes that was familiar to me, and seeing you there in the refectory made me think of Lorenzo de' Medici, whom I knew as a young man.'

'He would be my natural grandfather. By all accounts an honourable man.'

'You have tried to be honourable, Matteo, and discharge your duty as you saw it. There is an innate truthfulness in your conduct, Matteo, despite the lies you told.'

I bent my head. 'I apologize for any trouble I may have caused you and your household.'

He smiled. 'You more than made up for it in interest and humour. You may wish to know that, as he lay dying, Graziano spoke of you. He fancied that Lucrezia Borgia might comment on your dancing skill at some ball in Ferrara, and that you would mention his name to her as your dancing instructor. Therefore he could boast that the most notorious woman in Europe had his name upon her lips.'

I smiled at these words.

'So you see, Matteo, even when you were absent, you were always in our thoughts. Graziano talked about you often, and Felipe occupied himself in trying to arrange some way that you might pursue your studies. And I—' He broke off.

I looked into his face. His eyes were on a level with my own.
'We all do love you, Matteo.'

Ignoring his protests this time as we said farewell, I did kneel
before him.

'I forgive you any transgression most readily,' he told me. 'A
boy must find his own self in order to become a man, and you are
a man now, Matteo.'

The Maestro reached out and drew me to my feet and we
embraced.

'It is a difficult challenge for a person to find his own identity,'
he said. 'And though you may have avoided the truth, Matteo, it
followed you and found you, and now you must live it, as a good
man does.'

This is how it was with him, the Maestro da Vinci. His
expectations made those who knew him aspire to meet his trust.

Thus I became resolved to be a good doctor and a good man.

Acknowledgements

Mairi Aitken, artist
Margot Aked
Professor Susan Black
Rosey Boyle
British Institute, Florence
Laura Cecil
Sue Cook
Annie Eaton
Dr Lucio Fregonese, University of Pavia
Joe Kearney, artist
Sophie Nelson
Hugh Rae
Lucy Walker
Random House staff
Pupils of The King's School, Worcester
The Family
And, always, and for ever, Tom